FAMILY SNAPSHOT

JESSIE HARKER

First Published in Great Britain in 2023
by Mostyn March Publishing

www.mostynmarch.com

www.jessieharker.com

1

THAT ONE NIGHT

APRIL 1981

Sixteenth birthday party. Parents on holiday. It could not have been more obvious if a billboard had been erected in the front garden. The voices, the smoke, the alcohol; the industrial volume Two-Tone spilling out from behind the drawn, shadowed curtains.

Sadie hung at the gate. Now that she had negotiated the subterfuge to get her out from beneath her guardians' watchful eyes, she'd much rather be down the park, swigging from the bottle on the swings. On her own or with the normal crowd, she didn't care. Tonight, she wasn't in the mood for a party.

Too late. Lizzie was impatiently beckoning through a crack in the curtains.

Sadie pushed open the unlocked front door, edging between the teenage couples lining the hallway, lapping and fumbling. Her lip curled.

'Come on, what kept you?' Lizzie pulled her through the dark slurping hallway. 'There's hardly any buff left.'

Sadie swept the bottle of Cinzano she had nicked from the off-licence away from her school friend's eager grasp.

'Oh, fair enough, I've got my hands full anyway.' Lizzie tripped back into the lounge, obviously not in desperate need of any more alcohol. And there she left her, to go back to her own (fairly arguable) 'buff'. Sadie had never noticed any interest in Justin before. But this was a night of opportunity, evidently.

She fell over somebody's legs and crawled to an empty corner, lighting a cigarette and looking out over the room with little hope or anticipation. Clearly, the pairing of Justin and Lizzie was going to be the norm for the night. *Was it in the rules or something?*

But left to herself, for once, in this dark anonymous corner, she settled. Loud music, the forbidden fags and alcohol and a growing pleasant haziness; nothing to complain about that. And none of the clock-watching or shouting-match-anticipation that usually defined her evenings out. She was, *of course*, at the circus on Sarratt Green with Lizzie and her family, and then christening their new video machine. That latest piece of fiction seemed to satisfy John and Barbara, and they said she could stay out until midnight. She had been quite well behaved that week and deserved the trust, they said. *As if.* Maybe she would take the bottle down to the swings in the park anyway? Immerse herself in her fantasy world in the dark hours, free from the expectation of having to be home too soon for a change.

Until *any* expectation, and the edges of everything, blurred into unreality. She didn't even like Cinzano...

A roar of motorbikes cut through the haze. The front door slammed, and a mass of new, strident voices powered through the hallway. With forced awareness, Sadie looked out into the room. It seemed quieter now, highlighting the disturbance beyond, which waved in and out of her ears. The door crashed against the wall and a group of leather-clad, long-haired, heavily bearded young men stepped in. Nobody interfered.

The newcomers snatched up the remaining alcohol. Objective Two. Sadie found herself wedged into the corner by one either side of her.

'Alright?' the voice from the left drawled in an exaggerated cockney accent. Such was the norm for those in Rickmansworth who wanted to look hard. 'What you doing all on your own, then?' It spluttered over a rapidly emptying can of Harp. Sadie didn't answer. She wasn't even sure her mouth was functioning, let alone her legs to take her out of here to her solitary park-life.

The man nodded to the other one, threw him the remainder of his four-pack, got up and left. Her new companion picked up the empty bottle of Cinzano.

'You haven't drunk all that, have you?'

Sadie giggled.

'That's my girl.' He pulled a can from the four-pack and offered it to her. 'How old are you?'

'16.'

'Excellent.'

It seemed peculiarly important to him.

The next half an hour passed through a haze. It wasn't quite that she didn't know what she was doing, just that what she was doing seemed devoid of importance, questions or consequences. As if she was watching it, with curiosity and openness, happen to someone else.

Except for the pain. Suddenly, that was very real to her. Now she was somewhere else, not being pawed in the corner by this stranger. *Where*? She vaguely remembered the stairs.

Consciousness briefly returned at this stark reminder that she had not been here before, and she really oughtn't to be here now. From somewhere, she found her voice. She backed away. And then she was struggling. The mist clearing to nothing but the fact that this wasn't where she was supposed to be at all.

'No!'

And she saw herself then, from her clouded awareness, afraid, as this thoughtless experiment became something else.

'No! Please!'

He stopped, for a moment. At least she thought he did. There were voices at the door, raised and laughing. He looked down at her, for once meeting her eye. A strange expression, almost frightened too...? But the voices, cheering, chanting. And he closed his eyes, put his hand over hers, and carried on. The both of them in darkness...

There was some discussion at the door as he crawled off her. *Jesus no, not them too*! But they were leaving. And through the haze and nausea of alcohol and shock, Sadie just made out the outline of his face through the dim light of the doorway as he glanced back at her. Then the others clapped their arms around him, laughing, and took him from the room.

2

IDENTITY

'Well, thanks for keeping the gatecrashers busy last night. Nothing got smashed.' Lizzie appeared at the bottom of the bed that Sadie had been taken to. Forced into consciousness, in bits and floods, the previous evening came back to her, the alarm rising in her throat with the nausea. Now, so suddenly, she was not alone. Far too late.

She turned her head into the pillow. 'Go away.'

Lizzie ignored her, dropping down onto the bed . 'How're you feeling, then? Chucked up yet?'

Sadie squinted up at her. 'Who was he?'

'I don't know,' Lizzie replied, still inappropriately cheery. 'One of the Ricky Randoms. There were seven or eight of them. At least he doesn't come from round here. It'll be alright, only a couple of us know, we won't spread it.'

'I ought to go home now. My brother'll be mad,' she said, as if the panic had passed. John was already apoplectic that last week she'd hacked off her long blonde hair and dyed it jet black. It had been bright red a few weeks before, until John had physically dragged her into the hairdressers to have it removed. She knew her knee jerk insurrection was driving them both up the wall. And staying out all night would be a very sore point indeed...

Sadie trudged the mile and a half to her home, the cool air doing nothing for her thick head and other-wordly consciousness. Her head pounding, her body aching, she pulled her sleeves down over the bruises around her wrists. She cried all the way home. She never cried.

She pushed open the gate to the 1950s pebbledash semi belonging to her brother John and sister-in-law Barbara, persuading herself that she'd lived enough to cope with this. Existing in this closet world with these two, since her father died when she was eight and her mother drunk herself into the coffin to join him shortly afterwards. That was training enough in the ways of the world, surely. Yet still, in the privacy of her room, she cried again.

She put it off for as long as possible, but had to emerge eventually to face the apocalyptic rage of her guardians. *Staying out all night? Was that all? For fuck's sake. Don't they know anything?* These adults; these irrelevancies. Her hurt and confusion turned to defiance as she threw it all back at them. The vented anger bringing a new, but untrue, venom to her words.

And she lay down on her bedroom floor with U2 now. This wasn't how it was supposed to happen with Bono. He loved her. She would have enchanted him, unknowingly, until he was unstoppably drawn to her in loving embrace. Taking them both to a place of ecstasy. Where she knew and he knew, and they would be together forever from that moment on. That was her reality. Not this.

But she had this now. And she would cope. Because she was world-hardy and knowing and strong...

. . .

'Hey Sadie, what was it like...? Was he big...? Was he good...?'

'Slag...'

Back in the classroom, her activities on Saturday night were clearly common knowledge, despite Lizzie's assurances. And just like the usual contradictions in a room full of teenagers, some were sniffy and condescending, others were gleeful and inquisitive. They all knew Sadie as a bit of a rebel, with a budding sexuality highlighted by her couldn't-give-a-shit posture and fulsome adolescent breasts. She'd been the first to a bra all those years ago, and the kudos had steadily grown. But she was smart and academically astute without trying too hard, and popular enough without the need to flaunt tales of adventure and conquest. Despite her irreverent, curious nature, she wasn't the type for a drunken shag at a party. She was saving herself for her Bono, who would eventually come, in some guise or other. And this contradiction only added to the buzz of enquiry and excitement.

Sadie tried desperately to steer through it with her usual wit and nonchalance. But all she wanted was a name. Why, she didn't know. It would not be the right one. But the best she got was a collective picture of the Ricky Randoms, taken by the brother of one of her classmates when he was trying to ingratiate himself into their notorious midst. It was not much help to her. Most of the young men in the photo had their backs to the camera, and even if they hadn't, she wasn't sure she would place him. There was one on the end, though, turning his head and laughing. His face obscured by the ubiquitous long hair and heavy beard. Was that him? Not sure. They all looked like that. They all looked *wrong*. She didn't want to see any of them.

She stuffed the photo in a lockbox at the back of her bedside drawer and turned the key. As she similarly forced the experience to the back of her mind. Where it belonged, submerged once again by fantasy. A fantasy that obliterated it. Because it wasn't supposed to be that way.

And day by day it was getting easier, because she had that talent, to conjure another reality. Especially as the nightly terrors and the lurid curiosity of her classmates subsided with her unwillingness, or inability, to elaborate any details at all. Because there were no details. It had never happened.

But if it had never happened, how come she was so scared three weeks later? How come she was so panic-stricken six weeks later? How come her life had ended nine weeks later in the school toilets with that coloured bit of paper...?

She had to sit her O'levels. Once, with so many dreams and plans, they had no significance to her anymore. She told no-one, and she did nothing.

'For goodness' sake, Sarah, that was tomorrow's lunch! What is the matter with you...? Look at the state of you! You'll need a whole new wardrobe soon. Do you think we are made of money...?'

For over two months after her exams, Barbara merely equated Sadie's extra weight with the extraordinary amount she seemed to be eating. Her baggy clothes hid it well, and they hardly spoke anyway, except to shout. Especially after a slip of paper confirmed that Sadie had achieved nine O'levels but had no intention of going back to school. How could she?

'Oh, that's right, just waste your life away with your tapes and your fridge raids... Don't you know how lucky you are...?'

Barbara was just so tired of her permanent lodger's moods and tears. Sick of her husband's baggage by now. His little sister used to be such a charming girl. Now look at her. The focus of their lives. Trying every day to lay the tracks and keep her firmly on them. But now more than ever, she was a runaway train, with a destination entirely her own. It just would not do. It would not do at all.

Not in Bushey Heath.

3

JOE

'You dirty little bitch!'

It had to come. The outsized clothes, the late night fridge incursions, the permanent residence in her bedroom, could no longer hide her. But the response was worse than even Sadie had feared. Her upright brother just slapped her; Barbara bursting into uncontrollable tears. By the end of the week, she had her marching orders.

'Your name is Joe...'

This tiny, alien thing blinked back the drops of tap water from his pink, round brow. Held clumsily above the sink in the shared bathroom of this ramshackle block of bedsits, Sadie christened him herself. Just like she did everything herself now.

Alone through the remnants of winter, passing into spring. Like the passing of the clouded indifference into something else. Something that he smiled at now. Something that she saw in him. Now she no longer saw that other person. This was a new life, unblemished by his origins.

If only she could say the same.

'Your name is Joe. And you are mine...'

This time, for the first time, on this bright summer's day, she felt it. There had not been a moment in the last six months that had not been suicidally hard. But it was summer now. At least it was warm.

As she prepared to go out, to take Joe past the twitching curtains once again, Barbara stepped in through the unlockable door. The two stared at each other. It was almost funny. Sadie stood, having shared Joe's bath, three days after an especially profitable jumble sale, looking at her worn and dishevelled sister-in-law, her face drawn by sleeplessness and sadness.

Barbara nervously scanned the modest room.

'Why don't you sit down,' Sadie offered, her surprise mutating into stiff politeness.

Barbara nodded, her eyes heavy. 'Is that—?'

'Joe,' Sadie replied. She could say his name now. She knew his name. She knew *him*. Her life now. 'A boy.'

'Joe,' Barbara repeated, looking deeply into the baby's sparkling blue eyes. He didn't get those from his mother. Or anyone in the family. But they pierced her.

'Can I hold him?' The tone was so pitiful that Sadie did not hesitate. But as soon as Joe snuggled into her arms, Barbara held him away, her tears wrenching gulps of air from her chest. Sadie took the baby from her, laying him down to instinctively see to her distraught sister-in-law.

And so it turned out that this troublesome, wayward teenager now had what this other woman wanted. *All* she wanted. Because she could never hold a child of her own.

'I'm sorry.' Sadie's first instinct at this revelation was to feel the distress and comfort her.

'God, how can you be so nice?' Barbara sounded almost contemptuous. 'You've grown so much older.'

Sadie shrugged. She'd been told it before. She'd lost much of the post-pregnancy weight, but seemed to have grown somehow in stature. Despite her youth, her body had rounded, her face had defined, and she emanated a more mature attractiveness and bearing.

'Here...' Barbara fumbled in her bag. 'We missed both your birthdays.'

Sadie unwrapped a sweatshirt for herself and two sleepsuits for Joe. One pink, one blue.

'We didn't know, of course,' Barbara mumbled. 'I can take the pink one back.'

'No, of course not. It's fine. Joe's a little too young to have his personality defined by his sleepsuits.'

Barbara's brow furrowed. She'd never had any imagination, or even inclination, to break 'the rules'. Sadie suspected it was one reason she married such a pompous arsehole as John.

'Really, thank you! It's very kind of you.'

The enthusiasm bewildered Barbara even more. But gifts, of any colour, were rare in this new household.

'I didn't expect you to be like this.'

'It's a good day today,' Sadie smiled. 'We were just going out, actually. Would you like to come with us...?'

Throughout the summer, Barbara visited regularly. They went for walks or shopping, adults together now. Sadie found it OK. Someone at least to talk to and watch her plans develop. And Barbara seemed to loosen as she encouraged her in her ambitions. Yes, she should take those A'level evening classes in September; why not make the most of her good brain? They'd mind Joe... Of course, take a job in the daytime too, drop him off at the house on the way. That would be no problem...

And so it started. The transference. Sadie working all day,

studying all night, and Barbara and John gradually moving in. A night here, a night there, a weekend in the country...

'No, don't wake him. Why don't you just go on back to your flat? We'll keep him here tonight...'

Joe was speaking now. He still said, 'Mummy.' And nine months left on her course, even a little in the bank, a place with two rooms paid for by her student benefits, Sadie knew that was exactly the way it was going to stay.

'But you're so young,' they said.

'You've got a whole life ahead of you,' they said.

'It's good that you want to make something of it now. You shouldn't have to be burdened with a child,' they said.

'He's got everything he needs here. We can give him a good life. You should go and take yours...' they said.

A burden?

And the rows that followed were strangely familiar.

It was time for them to be alone again.

Sadie gave up her job and managed on the dole. Offered a place at West Sussex University in September; glimpses of optimism pushing through the clouds of reality on a budget holiday in Margate that summer. Her life felt like it was just beginning.

And perhaps it was...

4

TWO NEW FRESHERS

SEPTEMBER 1986

'There Mummy, my garage there! Yes. Beanbag there. Where's my Anglia? It's got no telly...!'

Their new home. A ground floor room in the four-storey campus block of Ellis House, West Sussex University. Inside the room, boxes and bags were piled high. Her whole life stacked before her. It wasn't much.

But that which belonged to Joe was being mapped out quite conclusively. He had been so excited by this new adventure. Sprinting from wall to wall, directing the relocation. His spirit, his energy, his volume in direct inverse to Sadie's own. The mountain to get here had wiped her out.

By eight-thirty, Joe finally at rest on his beanbag bed, she crawled onto the mattress at the other side of the room. Closing her eyes and willing the continuing uphill climb tomorrow to have more foot holes.

'The Bot... an...ic...al... So...'
    'Society.'

'Yeah, yeah, the Botanical Society. Oh, please Mum, can I join that? Can I? *Can I...?*'

Freshers Week, and Sadie was attempting to enrol Joe in as much as she could. But, she feared, even with his advanced skills at nature spotting, this might be a step too far. She settled for the nursery and swimming lessons. And he would have to, as well. The bespectacled young woman on the stand smiled engagingly at them anyway. Being on campus with a small child was certainly earning her some recognition. And at four-and-a-half now, Joe was growing into a rather endearing little boy. With his wide open face and mop of golden hair, accepting of his somewhat minimal lot, and meeting everything with a typically cheerful giggle, open curiosity and relatively intelligent chatter, people could not help but be approachable, accommodating and kind.

They were an interesting pair. She with her fresh, casual look, unconventional in her motherhood as she played and held and entertained him. He bound to her always. A unit. And a unit that, despite his natural ebullience, Joe seemed to have no desperate desire to expand. Except in the direction of the Botanical Society, evidently.

But within a month, she had made some friends, and so had he.

'Thank you, I'd love to... This is my son, Joe. Would it be OK if he came too...? Yes, it is just us. My husband's away on business. Long term. Thought it would be nice to do something for myself while he's away...'

Every time she had to repeat it, she turned cold. It felt necessary, but it never felt right. And she hated deceit, which is why that is where the stories ended. No more was ever forthcoming.

And pretty soon people learned just not to ask.

5

JAY

'This is sensational, Jay! They'll love it.'

'Well, it wasn't all my doing. We just thought we should have something original for the panto this year. Kev wrote half of it. And Jeremy invented the Chief Gnome.'

'Yeah, but I love the comedy love story vibe. And in the most ridiculous setting. I'm definitely going to be directing this. Where are we going to get a six-year-old boy, though...?'

As if that was the only problem, Jay laughed to himself as he tramped the campus grounds, pulling his jacket around him in the cooling October air. Typical Paul, he always wanted to direct. Well, OK, let him... Shit! Late for practical again. He broke into a run; and then slowed to a more customary dawdle. Maybe they wouldn't miss him. Again. He'd have to think of a better excuse than yesterday, though. Or last week's lame defence...

Joe ran across the green, giggling at the adventure, firing an imaginary catapult at a statue and disappearing round a corner. But a minute later, he was feeling quite different. Finger in mouth, he kicked the grass, the abstract statues and angular buildings frightening him now. They all looked the same, offering no clue which direction was where he should be.

'Hey there,' a student approached and dropped to his level. 'Are you lost?'

Joe's tearful blue eyes locked pitifully on the student's own. He nodded cautiously and miserably.

'Where's mummy then?'

'I don't know...'

It was the most distressing of prospects; those three little words. Joe always knew where she was. With him. Or else he was safe somewhere, knowing that she would be soon.

'I ran away from nursery.'

'Well, that wasn't very clever, was it?' the student laughed.

'It was nearly finished!' Joe protested, and the student giggled again. So Joe did too.

'Shall we go back there, then?' He stood up and held out his hand.

Joe did not take it. 'No.' His lip quivered again. 'I want my mummy.'

'Alright then. What does mummy study?'

'Humanities!' Joe proudly announced, the prospect of help, as well as his eagerness to show that he knew how to say it, making him less wary by the second.

'OK, shall we try to find her instead?'

Joe squinted up at the hand held out for him, still not sure about that idea. But, seeing something indefinable that he liked, and deciding he wanted to maintain eye contact with this cheerful person, he held out his arms to be carried instead.

'Cheeky little bugger, ain't ya?'

'Yes!'

The student laughed again and picked him up. 'So what's your name, then?'

'Joe Emmett,' he declared confidently.

'Well then, Joe Emmett, my name's Jay. What is it?'

'Jay!'

'Spot on. Right then, let's try the Humanities building, shall we? See if we can find mummy...'

Enjoying the ride and Jay's cheerful banter, they traded lives in the few minutes' journey. 'Jay and Joe, Joe and Jay, lots and lots for us to say,' the boy sang, giggling heartily.

The lecture rooms were empty. Classes finished for the morning, Jay tried the next door cafeteria. 'Can you see her, Joe?'

Joe turned in his arms, eyes roaming the room, then he gleefully shot out his arm. 'There she is!'

He was safe. He was home.

'Hi, I think this might be yours.' Jay stood right beside her. She was clearly somewhere else; head down, a clouded vulnerability in her expression, searching, but still lost. Then she looked up, and a sharp intensity immediately wiped it away.

'What are you doing with my son?' She sprung up and pulled Joe from his arms, whipping the cigarette from her mouth and swinging Joe into the seat beside her. Jay turned the chair opposite and sat astride it, leaning over the back of the seat to face her with a similarly direct expression.

'I found him wandering about lost. Out on the green.'

'Why weren't you in nursery?' She turned to Joe, leaving no doubt of her annoyance.

'I left early.'

'You don't leave early, Joe! You leave at twelve-thirty when I come to collect you. You know that.' Joe bowed his head in silence. 'Thank you,' she muttered, barely glancing at Jay.

'S'alright,' he shrugged. 'Got on famously, didn't we, Joe?'

'Yeah!' Joe enthused. 'Jay plays the drums!' he giggled, joyfully banging the table.

'Does he? Well, thankfully you do not, so you can stop making that racket right now!'

'I'll give you a go sometime.' Jay winked at the boy.

'Oh, yeah!'

She glared at him. 'Do you mind? He's noisy enough as it is, thank you very much!'

'Oh, Mum...' Joe whined, which was met with a silencing stare. 'Can I have a drink, please?' he said instead, much more subdued, as his mother irritably stubbed out her cigarette.

'You can wait until we get back.' She picked up her books and rose abruptly.

'I'll get it,' Jay offered. 'Do you want another coffee?'

'No, thank you.' She pulled Joe from his chair.

'OK,' Jay held up his hands in surrender. 'See you around, Joe.'

'Bye, Jay...' The little boy waved over his mother's shoulder, chewing his lip.

Jay turned his chair and leaned back, realising he was doing exactly the same.

6

DESTRUCTION BETWEEN FRIENDS

Every morning before she got out of bed, Sadie took three deep breaths and told herself that today would be fine. This week, however, the batteries appeared to have run out on the mantra.

She'd been rude. She knew that, and it lowered her spirits even more. The friends she had made were used to the times she became indifferent and brusque, and seemed to make allowances, but it made her feel no better. And it was not the thing to introduce to strangers. She knew that too.

But it did not help that Joe had taken an annoying interest in rhythmically banging tables, chairs, and anything in his path for the last two days. This was not particularly welcome at the nursery. And Sadie was not particularly in the mood to be told so, especially by the formidable Mrs Turnbull.

And this headache. Four spoonfuls of crap instant coffee in a chipped mug of tepid water in the Union canteen was doing nothing to shift it. As if she could still hear Joe's symphonic percussion over breakfast this morning.

'Hello again,' a cheerful voice interrupted the plummet.

'Oh... hello.'

'How's Joe, alright?' Jay seemed unfazed by her cool greeting as he flopped into the chair opposite.

'As a matter of fact, he's rapidly driving me round the bend. Banging furniture, pots, children's heads, anything. Perhaps next time you want to inspire the next Phil Collins, you'll pick on someone a little less impressionable.' Sadie lit a cigarette, sighed and stubbed it out immediately. And when she looked up, he was gone.

It didn't seem to be preventable sometimes. The tightness in her limbs, the constant whirl of anxiety in her stomach, and the heaviness banding her brow, which just translated into this cool, sparky abruptness. She so wished people could see it. See how it really was. But that would involve a level of honesty in which she no longer had any skill. She was a closed book. She'd slammed it shut. It was no use wishing it open all of a sudden. Which only left telepathy. And then perhaps she would not be forced into these apologetic lies and retractions all the time...

Spotting Jay in the corner of the Union canteen again the next day, an unread book and half-eaten sandwich in front of him, Sadie was at least glad of the opportunity for another one. 'Sometimes I forget what kindness is.' It sounded contrived, but it was not. She was always sincere in her many retractions. 'I just wanted to apologise. I won't disturb you.'

'Ah, it's boring anyway.' Jay turned the book and pushed it aside. 'I accept your apology. Though I don't know why you bothered.'

'Many people don't want to know. There are those that are very kind to me. I forget to be grateful sometimes, and I know how dangerous that is. People can only take so much rudeness.'

'True.'

'Jay! You're late for rehearsal,' a voice bellowed across the room. 'Come on!'

'Always late for bloody something,' he grinned, raising his

hand to the presence at the door and cramming the last of his sandwich into his mouth. 'Tara...'

'Oh, but your book—!'

Too late. The hefty tome remained on the table. *Evolutionary Trends in Plant Biology*, she read; J Barratt, 9 Sutherland House scrawled on the inside cover. She put it in her bag. She'd take it back this evening...

Joe was having one of those afternoons. It couldn't fairly be described as naughty, just boisterous. He had that gift. To wear you out in two or three short hours. To pound away incessantly whilst not quite overstepping the boundary to prompt a really cautionary response. Every little thing seemed worthy of his curiosity and comment. The questions, the running commentary, the sprinting, the slaloms, the touching. Like a constantly firing tank, bulldozing the landscape of their life. And Sadie following like a minesweeper behind. Clearing, replacing, responding...

And she stood with her hands in the sink now, no more than fingering the dinner washing up. Staring into the bubbles, circling them around her fingers. As if their quiet softness could somehow touch her. In some strange way, it seemed to be working.

Until an unusually orchestral ripping sound cut through the trance. She turned; all progress into calm instantly obliterated by the sight of Joe standing with a handful of pages of textbook in his hand, whilst the rest of it hurtled across the room and crashed into the sideboard.

'Joe!' Back to the mother minesweeper. But now the exclamation was entirely without this afternoon's accepting patience. 'What do you think you are doing?' She snatched the pages from his hand. 'Oh, Joe...'

'I'm sorry,' he whimpered.

'That's not much good after the event, is it? It isn't my book, Joe! What the hell am I going to do now?'

'Whose is it then?'

'Never mind that! Oh, sometimes, Joe...'

'I'm sorry,' he repeated. 'Whose is it?'

'It's your friend Jay's,' she sighed.

'Jay?' Joe's eyes popped. 'What are you doing with his book?'

'Never mind that either!' This was beginning to return her pounding headache. 'But I can tell you, young man, you'll be taking it back to him to apologise. And if we have to buy another one, it can damn well come out of your sweet money, do you hear me?'

Joe looked so pitifully concerned, it was almost enough to divert her. Although she knew it was probably the potential loss of the sweet money than anything else.

'Where is he?' he quietly asked. Well, perhaps not...?

'Oh, I suppose we could go there now,' she muttered. 'Come on then, here you are.' And she thrust the battered book into his arms.

Joe seemed far less moved by the time they had crossed the grounds to Sutherland House. A row of bright orange marigolds were still in flower lining the path, and he was merrily listing their medicinal and herbal properties. Sadie, on the other hand, could feel the anxiety pulsating again. Wasn't it her responsibility, really? Of course it was. Every single thing he ever did was hers. Sometimes it felt like they were some kind of Janus, and she had to hold the two faces together. Because they were both her. It was all *her*...

Jay opened the door, cigarette in mouth, looking slightly worn. Clearly surprised to see them, he removed the cigarette and smiled anyway. 'Hi!'

'Sorry to bother you,' Sadie shuffled Joe forward. 'But you left your book in the Union.'

'Oh Jesus, is that where it was? I've practically ransacked this place.' His smile broadened.

'Only Joe's got something to say to you, haven't you, Joe?'

Joe held out the book in his two little hands.

'I'm sorry, I ripped it. I was playing. I didn't mean to, but it just did... I'm sorry, Jay...' He glanced up at his mother and back again. 'I'll pay for it out of my sweet money.'

Jay looked as if he had inexplicably been offered a bunch of flowers and a box of chocolates, not a ruined botany textbook. He crouched down to Joe's level and took it from him. 'Well,' he smiled, tousling the boy's golden mop of hair. 'What's a little destruction between friends, eh?'

'Honestly, we'll buy you a new one.' Sadie was quite clear about that. The thing was in pieces. Although she was considerably less clear about the funding source.

'Rubbish,' he scorned. 'I'm glad to have it back, that's all. Don't worry about it. Nice of you to bother.'

'Can I play on your drums now?' The weight instantly off his conscience, Joe was eagerly back on the launch pad.

'Joe...' Sadie hissed. 'Sorry.'

'S'alright,' Jay laughed. 'I'll show you, if you like.' He pulled the door behind him. 'That OK?' he checked her hesitance.

'Well, if you're sure you don't mind?'

'Na,' he cheerfully dismissed. 'Come on then, they're down here...'

They followed him downstairs to a basement full of musical equipment.

'Here you are...'

Joe immediately took Jay's outstretched hand. Sadie stared at him in surprise. But Jay had already pulled two drumsticks from a container by the side and handed them to him.

'Come on then, come and have a go.' He lifted Joe onto his lap and plonked them both down on the drum stool. Sadie watched as he helped Joe hold the sticks, her son giggling furiously as Jay held his wrists, curling his fingers round the boy's little hands and directing them onto the drums, in a fairly rhythmic manner, while his bouncing legs provided the bass and hi-hat accompaniment. A ride Joe was enjoying as much as the mindless hitting things, obviously.

'Hey!' he screamed, gleefully bouncing up and down on Jay's knee. It was such a picture, Sadie had to laugh. That was a bit of a surprise, too. She hadn't had one of those scheduled for that day...

Jay eventually stopped. 'Whoa, quite a little package, ain't ya?'

'Sorry,' Sadie began defensively, the laughter instantly lost. She knew Joe would happily thrash around forever, wearing anybody out, as well as several holes in their equipment.

'Hey, who's bothered?' He swung Joe into the air, over the hi-hats and back down to the floor. Another excessively welcome ride, as Joe shrieked in delight.

Jay took back the sticks. Then he changed his mind.

'Na, there you go, you keep them.'

'Can I?!'

Jay thought he might have mistaken a pair of battered old drumsticks for a week at Disneyland. But Joe cut through the bemusement once again, waving the sticks around his head and demanding, 'I wanna play some more!'

'Joe,' Sadie cautioned. 'It's past your bedtime, anyway.'

Joe moaned heartily at this, of course.

'Hey there, you gotta get loads of sleep if you want to be a drummer, you know,' Jay said with mock sincerity. Joe looked up at him and nodded solemnly, which only made him laugh even more. 'He's lovely.'

Sadie raised her eyebrows and shook her head, but couldn't help the smile.

At the top of the stairs, she nudged Joe. He knew what that meant. 'Thank you,' he said.

'Anytime. You come and see me again, won't you?'

'Oh, yeah! Tomorrow. I'll come tomorrow!'

'Joe...' Sadie shook her head apologetically, but Jay just giggled again.

'Thank you for the book. And I mean it. Anytime...'

Sadie lay awake that night. Joe had always been a little wary of men, often treating them with slight suspicion, and certainly more at home with women. But as the picture of him happily bouncing around on Jay's knee circled her mind, she wondered... At least maybe he was growing. It must be a good thing. She carried a deep gnawing anxiety about his fatherless life every day of hers. That was the very fastest button on the cement mixer of her worries. Which is why she always invested the utmost effort in ignoring it. God forbid she didn't want anyone close enough to her to be a father to him. But maybe it was a good sign if he was beginning to ease in the company of other men.

He couldn't avoid it like she did.

7

SMART KID

If Joe had seemed in his four and a half years as happy as his mother to steer clear, there was evidently one man now who he was not seeking to avoid, and he did indeed expect to go and see Jay the next day. Sadie, of course, would not allow it. She knew the things people said out of politeness. Joe recovered reasonably quickly, as he usually did, but his indiscriminate banging of any solid object just intensified that week.

The only thing that competed with his newfound joy for percussion was his long-held fascination with the natural world. The nursery children's Thursday morning ramble was Joe's favourite of the week. Traipsing around the university grounds in search of winter flowers, plants and animals was exactly the sort of activity Joe loved, and he threw himself into it eagerly. It was an interest he had picked up at a very early age. Since Sadie had no money to take him anywhere else, they went to parks and gardens, where Joe quickly developed a passion for all that he could see, hear and touch there. Sadie borrowed library books so she could answer his questions, and now he knew the names of most things and was way ahead of the other children, and some of the teachers too. They had to frequently restrain him from wandering off on his own.

A necessity they obviously missed today...

It was the biggest greenhouse Joe had ever seen. And, double delight, the door was open. He happily strolled in. Strange men and women in white coats and goggles stood over benches of plants and equipment. One of them looked up, and he rapidly changed his mind, reaching his hand back for the door handle.

'Hello there,' she smiled, putting down her instruments and lifting her protective eyewear. 'Hey look everyone, it's a little kid.'

'I... I came in to see the flowers,' Joe mumbled apologetically, his hand on the door.

'It's alright, you can see them.'

Joe hesitated. He didn't really want to stay in this weird place anymore.

'Come on, I'll show you if you like.' She held out her hand. 'The experiment can wait.'

The bewilderment was scaling up into a hint of fright now. All these strange faces. But he tentatively put his hand in hers and she led him between the benches. Joe had had plenty of opportunity to learn that most of these relaxed, carefree students were perfectly harmless, and often quite exciting. Nevertheless, new ones were usually met with a touch of trepidation and hesitance. And there were a good deal of new ones here. And they all looked very odd, in their funny clothes and big glasses, with their alarming array of alien instrumentation. This clearly was *not* a greenhouse.

The door from the adjoining building opened and more white coats walked in. Minus the goggles. Joe spotted Jay immediately.

'Joe,' he smiled, dropping his papers to his side and stepping forward. But Joe had already pulled his hand from the girl and was eagerly running to him. His delight at the familiar face undisguised, he threw himself at Jay as he knelt down to his height. Jay was a little overwhelmed, and more than a little moved. It seemed a somewhat exaggerated display of affection. Hugely welcome, thank you very much!

He plucked the boy off the ground. 'What you doing here, then?'

'I didn't know anyone was in here,' Joe whispered, wide-eyed, but now without the slightest trace of discomfort. 'I came to see the flowers.'

'Friend of yours, Jay?' A voice called.

'Yeah,' he turned Joe to the lined benches. 'Everyone, this is Joe.'

'Hi, Joe!' rang casually back from them all. Joe beamed and waved. They were alright now. They were Jay's friends...

'Why are you wearing that?' Joe giggled, poking him in the chest. 'You look like a doctor.'

Jay had to join the giggling, taking in the boy's endearingly conspiratorial expression. 'Well, we have to wear these so we don't get anything on our clothes. We do experiments, you know? Cut things up and stuff.' Jay pulled a B-movie horror face which erupted Joe's giggles again.

'But why are you in the greenhouse?' he stealthily demanded, still as if they were sharing secrets; and still as if he couldn't quite describe this bewildering place in any other way.

'Well, we've got to do experiments on these plants, see?'

And now Joe lost his smile. 'You mean you cut up the flowers?'

'Yeah, that's right.'

'But they'll die! You can't kill them!'

Jay hesitated. Clearly having landed himself in unknown child territory, he opted to bend the truth a little. 'No, we don't kill them. Look, we could take one leaf off, right? The plant still grows, but we can do things with the leaf to find out stuff, yeah? And then we'll know how to grow more flowers and make bigger ones! Get it?' He hoped that would do.

Evidently it did. An enlightened smile spread across Joe's face. 'Oh, yeah! Bigger ones? Cool!'

Three years Plant Sciences analysis, that pretty much summed it up. Jay wished his tutors would make do with so little.

'Can I see?'

'Yeah OK, come on then...'

Jay carried him around the shelves of plants. Joe named as many as he could, much to Jay's surprise.

'Say, you're pretty clever, aren't you?' he laughed. 'Smart kid.'

Joe was, of course, delighted. He adored any kind of praise and always looked for it hungrily. A few minutes later, though, probably a few more than it should have been, reality began to bite.

'Hey Joe, how come you're on your own then?'

Joe's enthused face fell and his mouth dropped open. 'Oh, I was with the nursery, we were out and...' he faded away, biting his lip.

'Oh dear,' Jay said lightly, trying to avert the boy's tears. 'Never mind, we'll go and find them, yeah?'

'I'll get into trouble,' Joe whined.

'Nonsense! You're with me, ain't ya?'

And that, together with Jay's ubiquitous grin, seemed to console him instantly.

Jay tramped the grounds nearby, but there was no-one in sight so, with Joe's (largely nonsensical) direction, he headed towards the nursery. He'd never even noticed it was there before, really. The place looked deserted. He pushed open a classroom door. Sadie was sitting on a table and one of the teachers had an arm around her shoulders. Jay was quite moved again. This child thing was all a bit of a mystery.

'This what you're missing?'

Sadie jumped off the table and sprung towards them.

'Where the hell have you been with him?'

'Bringing him back here, actually,' Jay sighed, as she roughly pulled Joe from his arms. 'He wandered into the botany lab. Good job I was there really,' he added pointedly.

'I'm sorry,' Sadie conceded. 'Forgive me. I was upset. Thank you so much.' She smiled weakly, her breathing steadying, and her enveloping grip on Joe loosening. 'As for you, young man, just wait until we get home, that's all...'

Joe looked over her shoulder as they walked out, anticipatory tears in his big blue eyes, his lower lip beginning to quiver. Jay smiled at him, but to no avail this time.

'Hey, listen...' He caught them up. 'I...er... just thought maybe I could look after Joe sometime, you know, if you wanna go out, or something?'

The air stiffened with Sadie's painful hesitation.

'Well, that's...' she seemed to have to remember how to construct a sentence. '...very *kind* of you, really, but I don't think so. Thanks.'

Jay paused as she turned away. Should he pursue this? *Why* was he pursuing this? But, strangely, it only took one more look at the boy, his eyes raised to him over her shoulder.

'Look, I know you don't know me very well, but I'm not a bad sort of guy, you know? And we get on famously, don't we, Joe?'

'Yeah!' Joe enthused with his normal mirroring of any natural ebullience.

'He's a smart kid. I've got loads of flower books he can look at.'

'Yey!' Joe continued, as if he'd been offered another week at Disneyland.

'And we can play on the drums, can't we, Joe?'

'Oh, yeah!' Joe clapped his hands together.

'Look, do you mind?' Sadie stopped in her tracks, teeth gritted.

'Mummy!' Joe protested as she strode away again. 'I want to—'

'Be quiet, Joe! I've had enough of what you want. What do you think you're doing running off like that? It's getting a very bad habit, Joe, and I won't have it. Do you hear me?'

'Yes,' he replied meekly. 'But Jay—'

'And I don't want to hear another word about Jay, alright? Not another word!'

Jay wandered back to the lab, deflated. He could hardly not be from her demeanour, even if he hadn't heard her final words to her son. He didn't really know what he was doing; he had just found himself liking the idea of being with the little boy sometimes. He didn't really know why. Or perhaps he did, he just didn't want to admit it. Joe had shown him open affection; something Jay had been starved for years, despite his natural inclination to give it out. The total rejection of his efforts hurt him more than a little.

He was irritatingly inclined to that as well.

8

CENTRE STAGE

The university Christmas Pantomime was getting dangerously late for rehearsal. The drama club had all voted to give *Bottom* a go, Jay and Kevin's offbeat comedy love story set in the bottom of the garden world. But there was one remaining point of contention – the role of the six-year-old boy.

'Look, it's a comedy, right? It's easy. We don't need a kid, just put the shoes on the knees, you know the thing.' Kevin was leading the move to keep the play child-free. Several others agreed.

'Maybe, but I do think it would be better with a real one.'

That was probably it then. Paul was indeed directing. Self-appointed. And people usually did what he told them.

'I know a little boy that'd be great for it...'

Walking home that night, Jay regretted his impulsive suggestion. It didn't take the Brain of Britain to work out that Joe's mother would take some persuading to let him do anything like this. By the look of it, she was reluctant to so much as speak to him. Did he even want to try? Would Joe even want to do this? Or have the ability? Somehow, he felt that he would...

Jay woke up the next morning with the resolution that he'd give it a go anyway, and hung around the nursery until they emerged. He pushed himself away from the wall and caught them up.

'Hi there,' he smiled, although not as broadly as usual.

'Jay!' Joe beamed, regardless.

'Hello.'

Good grief! Her greeting was almost pleasant. Jay's smile blossomed. 'Listen, sorry, don't want to be making meself a nuisance, but I've got something a bit important to ask you. Would you mind?'

She looked a little bewildered, but seemed to be reasonably acquiescent. So far. 'No, of course not. Uh, why don't you come and have a coffee with us?'

And Jay just beamed too. Clearly, he and Joe had a lot in common in response to the slightest hint of encouragement. This one being the unexpected normality of the invitation, unaccompanied as it was by any suggestion to 'fuck off...'

'Would you mind if I asked your name?'

'Sadie.'

'Jason,' he smiled, holding out his hand. 'Jay to my friends...'

Jay noticed their room was much bigger than his own, and said so.

'Yeah, it's because of Joe. They were very good.'

'Even so, it must be very difficult for you.'

'We manage.'

'You on your own, then...?' Big mistake. OK, he was learning... 'Nice car park!' he instantly changed tack in response to her arctic glare, nodding towards the play mat in the corner. And her expression changed again. Jay wasn't quite sure what the new look directed at him meant, but suddenly she was laughing.

'Nice car park? OK...'

And he seemed forgiven.

He sat down at the table, surveying the room. There was a mattress against one wall, with a large beanbag on the far side. The rest of the room was surprisingly clean and tidy, with only a few toys scattered around, apart from the car park, which was piled high with toy vehicles of every description. There were cupboards around the wall and a wardrobe exactly like his own, but she had her own kitchenette, with a small cooker, fridge and sink.

Joe crawled onto his knee. 'This is a Ford Anglia. They stopped making them in 1970. The boot opens, look! I keep a bean in there...'

Sadie brought over a mug of coffee and a beaker of juice for Joe. She looked at her son and then apologetically at Jay. But Joe's careless imposition and his free nonsensical gibbering didn't seem to be in the least bit bothersome to this man. He was evidently trying not to laugh, his arm encircling the boy as he was so enthusiastically introduced to the bean. It touched and bewildered her both at once.

She returned with a packet of biscuits. Joe dived straight in. She tapped his hand, and he withdrew immediately, picking up the packet and offering it to Jay and then to her. Jay smiled, reflecting that he really was an amazing balance between childish exuberance and adult good manners.

And model cars, botanical Latin and dried beans.

He instinctively wanted to know more then, about *both* of them, about their situation. But clearly, you go there at your peril, however innocent the enquiry...

'So?' she prompted, with a giggle reminiscent of Joe. 'What is this important thing? It sounds very exciting!'

For a moment, Jay just looked at her, glimpsing the girl beneath. She could be no more than 25, surely, near his own age, with a youthful playfulness behind all that guarded responsibility.

'Ah, well, not altogether sure you're gonna like this. But I can only ask, can't I?'

Sadie lost her humour then. He went on immediately.

'Well, I belong to the university dramatics society and we've got this Christmas panto that we've written and are going to perform—'

'Oops, dropped it.' Joe wriggled towards the floor. Jay draped him over his arm and dangled him to the carpet. A manoeuvre Joe found even more exciting than the retrieval of the bereft bean, and he shrieked with laughter as Jay swung him back onto his lap. His little arms held firmly around Jay's, he returned to valeting the Ford Anglia.

Why was she staring at him like that? Lose the smirk, Jay... He took a mouthful of coffee and went on.

'Thing is, there's been a lot of argument over one of the parts, because it's supposed to be a six-year-old boy. Some wanted one of us to do it, on the floor, you know, daft shoes on your knees. But the rest of us wanted a real life kid.' He took another mouthful of coffee, giving Sadie a moment to antici-pate what was inevitably coming. 'Well, I co-wrote this thing and I know what I want. And... so, I wanted to ask what you thought about Joe taking the part.'

'Yeah, yeah, I'll do it!' Joe was circumventing any need for a response from his mother. Nevertheless, he got one.

'Shut up, Joe.'

A heavy pause followed until Sadie attempted to voice her reservations. 'I don't know…'

'Well, I didn't expect you to jump at it immediately,' Jay smiled kindly.

'He's not six. He's not even five.'

'Nearly!' Joe protested. Jay winked at him.

'I know,' he replied. 'But he's a smart kid, and that's all we want. Look, it is a liberty I know, but I immediately thought of Joe because we need a smart kid who'll do as he's told. That sounds very authoritarian, but what I mean is we couldn't handle a kid who's going to run around shouting and screaming all the time.'

'He's quite capable of it, you know.'

'Yes, I'm sure, but I think he would do as he's told, wouldn't he? I mean, you know, he seems to…'

Jay didn't quite know how to express this. Being 'authoritarian' and 'doing what you're told' were not acceptable behaviours in his world. And he wasn't at all sure if it was any different in hers. With this kid thing… But he seemed to have got away with it, as she conceded, 'Yeah, I guess so, most of the time.'

But still, this new venture seemed to be prompting an uncomfortable level of anxious consideration. 'I mean, what would it involve? I wouldn't want him out late or anything.'

'I know, I understand that,' Jay nodded. That much seemed obvious, even for a childcare novice. 'We'd always rehearse his parts first, never after 7pm. As for the actual thing, that would be a late night I know, but… well, no, it's up to you. I don't want to put any pressure on you. I understand your reservations.'

'Thank you,' Sadie concluded, which moved him. She looked down at Joe, munching a biscuit and watching this like a tennis match. 'And you'd like to be in Jay's panto, would you?'

'Oh yeah, please!'

She sighed, but her lips twitched into an experimental smile. 'And you'll behave yourself and try very hard?'

'Yeah,' Joe nodded eagerly. 'I will,' he added solemnly to Jay.

'Alright then. If he can do it. If it proves too much for him, I'm afraid we'll have to pull out, but OK, we'll give it a go.'

'Great! Thanks.' Jay gave Joe a gentle squeeze. 'You'll be wonderful, won't you?'

'Sure,' was his bold reply, and they all laughed more freely then.

'So, would it be alright if I took him along tonight, to get the official approval and all that?'

'OK. Not too late though, please.'

'I could call for him about six. Would that be OK?'

'Alright...'

Joe was very excited that afternoon which, as usual, translated into the most enthusiastic boisterousness and unfocused babbling. But by six o'clock, he was also rather nervous. Never vocalised, that too was quite usual. But he'd been hanging onto Sadie's trouser leg for the last half an hour, and the conversation was like an episode of Junior Mastermind – with her imposed specialist subject of *theatre*.

Sadie tried to convey this to Jay when he arrived to collect him, without exposing her son to a full-scale disclosure that he did not *entirely* have the confidence of Laurence Olivier. Joe hated such admissions.

'And... this is difficult, I'm sorry...' she hesitated. 'But I know what it's like. Can you just keep the joints and alcohol out of his way, please? And some of the words? It's a job and a half in this place, I know, but I would appreciate it.'

'Yeah, sure, of course.' That much also seemed obvious. And Jay guessed that it, too, would be his responsibility. Now that he really had put himself in this position of temporary guardianship. OK, he'd give it a go...

Sadie prized Joe away from her jeans and deposited him in Jay's waiting arms. He reached back for her though, putting his hands round her cheeks to kiss her, before he settled, reasonably contentedly, around Jay's neck. And once again, Jay felt a little strange amidst all these interactions. This kind of affection, dependence, open display... it was all rather alien to him. But it never failed to move him.

As they trotted across the campus grounds, Jay told Joe that acting was easy. It was just about pretending. And he bet Joe would be so good at it he could probably even pretend he was six! This proved the most ingenious distraction from any remaining hesitance; a game Joe absolutely delighted in playing from that moment on. That would be OK, he declared, because he knew the Latin name for daffodils, could write his own labels for the nature table, and Mrs Turnbull had only last week given him an infants' school Janet and John book. Nobody else got one.

Jay was not entirely sure that these would be the evidence that the WSU Dramatics Society would be seeking. Except perhaps for the Janet and John. Obviously, it would be helpful if he could actually read the lines. But they would, more obviously, be looking at him first...

Well, they were just a bunch of clueless students; what did they know about the appearance of a six-year-old? As Jay had first anticipated, the rest of the players fell for him immediately, and agreed to have him in the production the moment his elevation to Janet and John had been proven. Following Jay's finger across the script, reading aloud his opening lines with a somewhat dramatic delivery, Joe was delighted that this elicited such a level of encouraging grinning from so many new faces. And he spent the rest of the hour entirely engaged with the banter and planning constantly thrown around him. Even if he didn't have a clue what most of it was about. Jay's own trousers, however, were also apparently adhesive that evening, as Joe never left his side. Always looking up to him for security and guidance. And always met with a wink or a smile of encouragement...

Joe clutched a batch of stapled paper as Jay carried him back to Sadie's room.

'He was just great.'

'Look Mum, I've got my *lines*!' Joe repeated the word he had heard so many times that evening with the glee he always displayed at the acquisition of new vocabulary.

'His are underlined in red. I expect he'll need some help.'

'Yeah, of course.' Sadie let herself enjoy the prospect. 'We'll sock it to 'em, won't we, Joe?'

'Yeah!'

'Well, if you need any help, you know where I am,' Jay concluded, rocking on his heels and slapping his thighs. 'The next rehearsal's Friday afternoon. Is that convenient?'

'I've got lectures then. Joe goes to a friend's on Friday afternoons. It's Room 14, just down the hall. Could you pick him up from there?'

'Sure. 14, OK... And thanks again. Now I better get back and see what they've decided for me...'

.   .   .

Joe babbled for ages about his new adventure, even when tucked up in his beanbag bed, and Sadie struggling with the competing demands of a four-year-old verbal artillery and the philosophy of Nietzsche. But it was infectious, and she even sensed a tiny hint of excitement within herself. She hadn't been around this kind of activity for years.

Just as long as she didn't think too much about that.

9

JOE AND JAY

'Always late, busy doing nothing, and running going nowhere...'

Jay heard his father's voice as clearly as if he were sprinting across the campus beside him. And yes, he was late (again); and yes, he was busy (as usual). But, he hoped, trying to do *something*. And to go *somewhere*.

In his second of his three-year course, six years out of school when he started on this new path, he was still struggling to catch up with his younger classmates. And maybe he shouldn't be quite so occupied elsewhere – with the band and the drama club – especially as it would be very hectic now, with extra rehearsals and line-learning. But he liked it this way; he wanted to be busy. It shut out that bloody voice, for one thing. And all the others, including his own...

By the time Jay got back to the rehearsal, the full cast for the panto had been decided. He had mixed feelings that those in power had dumped him in the leading role of the love-struck pixie. Flattered, of course, he always took compliments with the utmost surprise and gratitude. But the responsibility weighed heavy. At least most of Joe's scenes would be played with him, so he could keep an eye on him and help him. Another responsibility that hung on him now. And one that he was not in the least bit accustomed to. But, as he had had ample opportunity to learn earlier that evening, with the obvious magnetism of his trousers, his cuddles and his smiles, it was one that didn't seem to be all that unpleasant.

Regrettably, it quickly became apparent that he didn't have the same effect on everybody in the room. Anna, playing the lead garden fairy, the object of his affections, was making no secret of her indignance at having to play opposite him. And not the suave, rugby-playing Jeremy who had also been in the running. As always, one insult lay heavier on Jay than thirty compliments. OK, he knew he was no six-foot beefcake but, as the Director said, at least he bore a passing resemblance to a pixie. Anna, model willowy with swept back hair and Adams Family nails, was not at all his idea of a garden fairy. And not at all what he'd pick for an object of his affections, either, for that matter. And he wouldn't say that, so why did she feel she had to?

The eternal paradox: wouldn't want to spend more than five minutes with a person, but still punctured by the hurt and insecurity. And for a curious moment, it was a hurt and insecurity that suggested having a child glued to you, grinning and giggling and poking you in the face, was a bit of a loss.

As usual, Jay danced these things out of his mind, providing the usual sideshow of his cheerful humour.

Anna didn't seem to like that much either.

By the end of the second full rehearsal on Friday, with Joe back on the stage and trying his first scenes with Jay, the rest of the cast and crew were more than convinced they had made the right choice in the pair of them. Joe had difficulty with a few of the words, inevitably, but Jay was sure he had quite an advanced reading and acting talent; a relief to him and a delight to Joe to be told so.

'We've got to go to Janet's, remember?' Joe said, as Jay turned the wrong way into Ellis House. He'd been absent-mindedly looking forward to telling Sadie, too.

'Ah, yeah. Good job you're here, innit?' he winked, retracing his steps towards Room 14.

'He's a really great kid, isn't he?' he said at Janet's door, as Joe went to hang up his anorak.

'Well, yeah, I guess,' Janet replied. 'Bit of a handful at times.'

'Suppose. It must be very difficult for Sadie, really...?'

'Yes, it is. I know it gets to her. She's got a lot on her plate. It took a lot of guts to get here. Even so, it's a bit difficult to remember that all the time, especially when she's in a mood. She don't half get them,' Janet smiled wearily.

'Um... do you know anything about Joe's father?' Jay continued to fish.

'The story is he works abroad.'

'You don't think so?' Jay whispered. Her scepticism was written all over her face.

'Well, sounds a bit like he's in the nick, doesn't it? He's away for a couple of years, you know.'

'Oh, poor Sadie. I don't suppose she gets any support from him, then?'

'No, I don't think so, but she really doesn't like to talk about it.'

That was no surprise to Jay at all, in the short time he had known her. But as Joe ambled back to them, the fishing expedition had to be aborted.

'Well, I'll see you Monday then, Joe,' he smiled and left them to it.

But he was unbearably curious as he walked back home. Not unusual. Always one to reach out to people, much less at home with small talk, it often got him into trouble. And he'd seen already that he could get himself into a great deal of trouble with that kind of curiosity here. None of his business, he knew. Although that rarely stopped him...

Over the next couple of weeks, Sadie wondered how many steps away from madness she was approaching. Apart from the heavy schedule of looking after a pre-schooler and keeping up with her studies, she had to rehearse Joe every day. She was impressed by his ability and commitment, too. But it was so difficult when he couldn't do anything on his own. She was also none too pleased when he returned from a rehearsal and asked her what 'fuck' meant. It was incredibly difficult keeping that side of life away from him in this place. He was being forced to grow up long before normal.

So her mood was dark as she sat in the Union, having a quick break before picking Joe up from nursery, when Jay walked in.

'Hiya!' He squeezed down opposite in the small corner booth. 'Want another?'

Wordlessly, she shook her head. He got up and returned with his own, just as she lit a cigarette and stubbed it out immediately. She sighed, pushing her fingers through her hair, opening the packet again and tossing it, empty, aside.

'Here, have one of mine.'

'I'm trying to give up,' she muttered, as he lit one himself.

'Why?' he laughed, dragging deeply and leaning back in his chair.

'It's nearly Christmas, that's why, and I haven't got a penny for Joe!'

Jay took the cigarette from his mouth and stubbed it out. 'I'm sorry.'

Sadie screwed up her face. 'Not your problem, is it?'

It certainly wasn't a good enough reason to vicariously waste a cigarette. She eyed the crumpled remnants in the ashtray, the pull of it highlighting only too clearly that this was going to be just another uphill battle.

Jay was rather less moved by the wastage. 'Filthy habit anyway,' he grinned. 'Bloody hard though, innit? To kick it, I mean. I've cut down, used to smoke about thirty a day, now it's only seven or eight. And I haven't touched anything stronger for eighteen months.'

'Well done.' It sounded sarcastic.

'Sorry, we were talking about you.'

'No, we weren't.'

'Well, let's...' Evidently, he couldn't stop himself.

'I've got to fetch Joe.' Sadie scraped back the chair, swinging her heavy bag over her shoulder.

'You've got plenty—'

'Goodbye,' she cut him dead. 'And another thing. You wouldn't believe the words Joe comes out with after your rehearsals. So will you and your *oh-so-sophisticated-mates* please try to remember that he is a four-year-old child!'

Jay looked sadly after her as she marched from the room. He'd had enough rejection that morning. He'd hoped for some pleasant conversation, not more.

The play was not going as he would like. He wasn't too worried about his performance – everyone said it was hilarious – but Anna seemed increasingly antagonistic towards him; her distaste fully elevated by an entourage of bitchy followers, who turned up at every rehearsal to make a nuisance of themselves from the front row. And anything Anna didn't like, they didn't like. And anything they didn't like, bloody well knew it...

Finally escaping at the end of another rehearsal that evening, at which Jay had been treated to a full-scale education on his inadequacies, he retired to his room via the off-licence and got thoroughly and hopelessly trollied. Something he had not done to that extent for years. He remembered the days when it was a frequent occurrence. Days that he had left far behind. Now his insecurity took many other forms. This one helped nobody. He knew that.

By the next rehearsal the following afternoon, Joe was supposed to know all his words. Sadie was confident that he did. Jay arrived to collect him, looking rather worn and dishevelled.

'Look, I'm sorry about yesterday,' she said. 'Really. I know you've probably had too many apologies from me already, but I am sorry.'

'That's OK,' he sighed.

'Are you alright?'

Jay vaguely raised his head and nodded.

'You look a bit pale, are you sure?'

'And you care, right? I'm sorry, sorry, sorry... We'll be back about five, alright...?'

Alone now, in the silence she still struggled to get used to, Sadie twirled her coffee mug on the table. Sometimes she was in danger of forgetting that others had their problems, too. It worried her. She had grown up the willing receptacle for other people's troubles. It was a role she had once played well. Now she had so much to cope with on her own, it was a skill she seemed to have lost.

So many things lost now...

With that in mind, she offered Jay tea when he returned with Joe. He didn't look as if he really wanted to, but accepted anyway. A friend from the block had loaned Sadie his portable TV while he was away for the week, so Joe happily ate in front of that, leaving them a little peace at the table.

'Are you sure you're alright?'

Even if it had only been a few occasions of meeting, Sadie couldn't fail to know that this edgy, heavy silence was not like this man.

Jay looked up from his plate to see a genuine concern in her open face. It moved him. 'Yeah,' he conceded to it. 'Just a couple of things I felt like forgetting, so I got very drunk and very silly yesterday. So haven't been feeling too brilliant today,' he laughed weakly. 'But I'm fine, really, thanks. What about you? How are the fags?'

The blanket was lifting.

'None since yesterday!'

'Well done!'

'I hope I can keep it up. It'll save a good few quid a week.'

'Yeah, it's a big consideration, innit? Can't be easy for you, especially.'

Sadie shrugged, and Jay sensed that door was closed as well.

Not that he seemed able to stop himself from trying.

'He looks happy,' he nodded towards Joe. Despite her own closure, a key had been turned in his reluctant door, and it was now firmly open for verbal business.

'David Bellamy,' Sadie smiled. 'Joe's hero. He does puzzle me sometimes.'

'Yeah, he's very up on nature and stuff, isn't he? How did that come about then...?'

The words disappeared into an edgy silence; her mouth

cautiously opening and closing, as if she were testing, and rejecting, thoughts and words.

But then, some of them tentatively formed sound. 'Well, I used to take him to the park a lot. I couldn't afford a lot else. I used to read nature books from the library and we'd go plant spotting to try and interest him. Thankfully, he picked it up.'

Jay paused, but then decided to have a go. 'Look, I don't want to tread where I'm not wanted, but I know you're in your first year and Joe's nearly five. How did you manage... well, to get here?'

Sadie got up to clear the table. 'I don't really want to talk about that.'

'I'm sorry, I understand,' he lied. 'But it is a fairly innocent question. I'm sure you get asked worse.' Still, the door was open and his tone was light.

'Yes, I do,' she snapped. 'And they usually come straight after the innocent ones, OK?'

'Sure, I'm sorry, of course...'

Tea things cleared and Joe whining because there was no more David Bellamy *and* no ice cream, Sadie was at a loss for what to do next. She glanced at Jay, having silenced Joe's moaning with a chocolate biscuit.

'Oh, sorry,' he smiled weakly. 'Miles away. Expect you want to get shot of me now.'

Sadie was not at all sure that she did, and this only bewildered her into more mixed messages. 'Well, you're quite welcome to stay. I expect you've got plenty of other things to do, that's all.'

Inevitably, Jay did not know how to take that. But since he seemed to have lost his earlier desire to be alone, he decided to be honest. 'Well, I promised myself a night off,' he shrugged. 'Fancy some company, actually. Do you mind?'

Sadie smiled, which rather surprised him. 'No, of course not. Joe, get up out of that and let Jay sit down, please.'

Joe looked up from the TV and tumbled off his beanbag immediately.

'Hey no, don't worry,' Jay protested.

Joe looked between them.

'Honestly, it's the only decent thing we've got,' she said.

'I'll tell you what, then. We'll both sit on it.' And much to Joe's delight, he swung him high off the floor, sinking into the beanbag and depositing him back on his lap.

Joe immediately settled himself. He'd punched the buttons to BBC 2 and was now engrossed in an old Lassie film. He gave Jay a bewildering summary of the plot so far, before leaning back, thumb in mouth. And Jay smiled to himself; the little boy had a habit of relaxing him.

Sadie dropped down onto the mattress behind them. Jay glanced back with a slight, warm smile, which she returned. And again, it surprised him. As well as catching his breath a little. It was the kind of smile that lit candles and quasars...

By the end of the film, Joe's eyelids were dropping, sprawled against Jay's stomach, playing with the wool of his jumper as an accompaniment to his thumb. He came alive briefly to ask if he could stay up to watch New Faces. Sadie conceded, but by the first advert break, he was fast asleep.

As soon as he noticed, Jay's attention never returned to the TV. There was a strange calm in his being now. A warmth; a connection. Something completely alien to him.

'Oh blimey, I'm sorry.' Sadie shuffled off the mattress. Joe was wedged into Jay's armpit, his thumb not entirely preventing a stream of dribble from his open mouth. She crawled to the TV and turned it down.

Jay registered the embarrassment, but he didn't understand it.

'Don't be...'

She did not speak, standing chewing her lip. Jay did not understand the confusion on her face either, but decided to speak his thoughts anyway.

'Nobody's ever... I can't think of the word... *responded* to me like this before, I guess,' he shrugged, feeling foolish immediately. 'He's such an affectionate little boy, isn't he?'

'No. He isn't.'

Full hat-trick. Jay couldn't comprehend this one either. What was this, then? Was the little boy Laurence Olivier, after all? If this wasn't real, the constant performance was worthy of an Oscar, at the very least.

'Oh, he is with me. Sometimes he'll let Janet or Karen hold his hand...' Sadie paused, feeling a little hot suddenly at the territory shifting into truth. 'But,' she ventured anyway. 'I'll be honest with you. If you're a bloke, you haven't got a chance. Well, that is what I *would* have said...'

'Yeah, I guess I have noticed. He's not comfortable with men, is he? At the rehearsals, I mean.'

'It does worry me,' she mumbled, and Jay felt a fresh surge of sympathy and warmth.

Before he went and ruined it. 'Does he get on OK with his dad?'

The change was as swift as lightning. 'That's none of your business!'

Jay opened his mouth to counter the force of the retort, but settled on an apology instead. Sadie ignored it, abruptly lifting Joe from him. She strode to the door. 'Well, I have to get him to bed now, if you don't mind.'

He could probably have heard the door slamming behind him if he'd been at home in Sutherland House...

. . .

A rock thrown into her pool again, Sadie did not like the ripples still coursing through her some two hours later. Those who knew her better knew not to even mention Joe's father, and she had become accustomed to it never arising. Because he didn't exist. No longer obliterated by teenage fantasy, but by adult reality. The reality of her life now. A life so very different from cider in the park, world-weary fantasy, and Bono. A life now of solitary focus and hard work.

And bitterness and hate.

And love for her boy.

10

DRAMA CHAMELEON

December was growing into itself, and with it Sadie's confidence to do without cigarettes. She even exaggerated her old habit to save a little more for Christmas. Joe was counting down the days, had settled into nursery, and loved all the newfound attention from the student actors at the panto rehearsals. All of which settled Sadie a little more, too.

And when she returned from lectures one morning to find a note pinned to her door to say that Jay was tied up with 'a problem', and could shew drop Joe at that afternoon's rehearsal, she willingly accepted. A chance to see for herself what all the fuss was about...

Doors banging and voices raised, Joe led Sadie through the foyer into the auditorium, his mouth twitching with unease at the disturbance. This is not what he had been so excited to show her. They edged between the seats towards the stage, the fierce arguments from all directions becoming more distinct. Joe bit his lip and clung to Sadie's leg.

'Bollocks!' Jay threw at someone across the stage, which was immediately lobbed back with further argument and several worse words. Sadie winced.

She put her hand over Joe's ear and stroked his hair. 'I don't think they need you today. Let's go to the park, shall we?'

'OK,' he sniffed.

'Hey!' Paul bellowed from the stage. 'Where the fuck do you think you're taking him?'

Sadie turned slowly and retraced a few steps, breathing steadily. 'Joe wants to do your play very much,' she replied coolly. 'But he is not staying around to listen to language like that.'

'Oh, for fuck's sake, come back!'

She swung round again. There would be no further doubt about this. 'God knows it is hard enough in this place! Listen, he is not some oh-so-worldly-wise student, he is a four-year-old child! So you better just watch your mouth or get on your knees and understudy. Do you get that?'

The room fell silent, broken only by a titter from the wings. Paul had, as usual, made himself less than popular with some of the cast and crew.

'Look, we need the kid this afternoon. So if we're good?' he patronised. 'You said he was six!'

'Oh, fu—' Jay stopped. 'Get stuffed.'

'What's the use?' another voice called from the stage. 'We haven't got a show now anyway...'

Silence fell at last. They'd exhausted all the responses to that already, with a full child-unfriendly vocabulary.

Jay threw down his pointed pixie hat and stormed off the stage. 'I'm going.'

'Oh, don't be so childish, Jason. Come back here!'

'What for, eh?'

'We'll get someone else.'

'Yeah? Like who? Like fu— who? Oh, I don't care, you can count me out.'

Jeremy stopped him in the aisle, his hand on his arm. 'Don't be ridiculous—'

Jay shook it off. 'Look, you put on the bloody pixie hat! Advertise that. Get a list as long as your arm of volunteers. Just try getting it all together in two weeks. Just try!'

Paul jumped off the stage and shoved him into one of the front row seats. 'Look, you know we're not blaming you for this. How many times? You're damn good and you know it. What's the use of us all giving up, eh?'

'I told you we should have had understudies, Paul,' said a kelpie in a red hat.

'Oh, don't be stupid Gail, we don't even have enough players. You should know, you're playing three parts!'

Joe started to cry. 'I don't like him,' he sobbed. 'We're not going to do the show!'

'Of course you are.' Sadie stroked his hair. 'They'll find someone else. Don't you worry.'

She was beginning to realise something of what was going on. Anna, the garden fairy, had thrown in the towel, seemingly putting the whole production up the spout. She'd been less than enthusiastic for weeks, but a particularly heated argument with Jay the day before had been the final catalyst. And nobody seemed to know what to do about it, as the silent stalemate pulsed on. The hopelessness only highlighted by Joe's poignant tears, which nearly moved Sadie to the same fate. He had worked so hard. They both had.

Paul's shoulders slumped, and he blew out a surrendering stream of air. 'Bugger you, Anna. OK, everyone, I'm sorry. Maybe next year, eh?'

Joe wailed. Everyone looked in his direction. And Sadie

knew then what she had to do. For him. She took a deep breath, blinked back her own tears, and opened her mouth.

'I'll do it.'

The words were squeezed through concrete. And they didn't seem to have got very far either, as everyone just stared at her.

'I said I'll do it. I know the part.'

Despite the continued bemusement from the stage, like a magic spanner on a leaky tap, Joe shrieked and threw his arms around her.

'Uh, well, have you done any acting before?' Paul eventually spoke, as the silence seemed to be getting out of hand.

'Well, yes, quite a bit. It was sometime ago though.' She bit her lip. If she appeared confident, the turbulence beneath was making her nauseous. What on earth was she doing this for? Well, she knew that: Joe. But the very thought of it was doing somersaults in her stomach. She'd been a virtual recluse since those days, full of school plays, assemblies and shows. A lifetime ago. How could she possibly reconcile those two worlds now?

Thankfully, she didn't notice Jay's disturbing gaze.

'It's a big part, you know, and you've got eight days.' Paul was still playing cautious.

'For two pins I'll change my mind, so don't say anything, OK?' But she did have one advantage. 'Like I said, I know some of it by heart, anyway... Joe is my son, you know,' she added as Paul continued to look as if she'd landed from Mars.

'No, I didn't, actually. You know what the part is, then?'

'Yes.'

'And you'll do it?'

'I said so, didn't I?'

A smile inched up Paul's face. A few others starting clapping. Jay just continued to stare.

'Great!' Paul concluded, looking her up and down in a way

that would normally provoke a chair being thrown at his head. 'Yes, you'll be great.'

But although she might not have looked like it, Sadie needed the reassurance. This was all just igniting yet another whirlwind of anxiety.

Joe, however, was busy planting wet kisses all over her face.

She was not given the chance to acknowledge any further trepidation anyway. Paul threw her straight in with the first scene. Everyone else knew most of their lines, so she looked a little odd reading hers, but considering this handicap, she seemed to fit in pretty well. They were all hugely relieved and impressed. And she felt something then, with the smiles and laughter and praise, that she had forgotten existed.

The only person on the stage who did not join in was Jay, who, when he came to the fore in the second scene, muttered his lines in virtual monotone.

'What's the matter with you?' Paul demanded, a bite of edgy sarcasm remaining. 'Are you still feeling *rejected*?'

Jay glared at him and marched off the stage.

'For fudge sake,' Paul sighed. 'What the heck is wrong with this cast? We have a more mature four-year-old...'

Nineteenth century philosophers had to take a very back seat that week. But by the following Monday, Sadie had learned all her words, and they had rehearsed the first two Acts adequately. Much of her anxiety had subsided with the acceptance and acclaim of the group. But she could never totally banish the unease. It was a very foreign feeling to her now, doing group work, as this very much was. But then there was something else; some other unfamiliar emotion surfacing... *She missed it.* The realisation was clear enough to bother her greatly. She wasn't allowed to miss things. Ordinary things.

She wasn't an ordinary carefree student, she mustn't forget that.

Not much chance of it, anyway, with Joe always on hand to remind her. And as if to emphasise the point, he was given a gold star for his model of a triffid the next morning at nursery. Well, it looked like a triffid and Sadie suggested he claim that as deliberate. But Joe's undisguised excitement at the accolade sent him into the most enthusiastic of vocal and physical performances. Until, parading it around the room above his head like a model aeroplane, he connected with a stray piece of Scalextric, dropped the thing, landing himself squarely on top of it, and squashed it flat. He was, of course, inconsolable. But the proverbial plaster on the mental wound was as natural to Sadie by now as the steady stream of praise and acknowledgement he constantly demanded. And so she switched gear with barely a flinch. And Joe was pretty soon drowning his sorrows in cuddles and ice cream.

She was so tired...

11

IN THE CLUB

Three days to go and the drama club launched into Act Three. Jay, who had snapped out of his mood to play his part, but slipped back into it offstage, failed to even turn up this time. Paul was furious. Sadie, conciliatory as she was with four and a half years' soothing practice, suggested trying through without him. This, of course, was quite impossible, but at least they could do the lines.

But they were perilously short of time, and Paul had no hesitation in ensuring Jay turned up the next day by appearing at the biology lab at three-thirty and frogmarching him across the campus. At least he was there now, if only in body.

'Look, you're not helping her much, are you? You know she's great. What's the matter? Can't you stand to split the applause? We all know Anna was very much the co-star, Jay, but please don't let us down.'

Jay glared at him. 'You know I don't care about that!'

'Just knuckle down to it then, will you?'

Jay raised his eyes skyward. 'It's just that I seem to

remember we got this far before!' And he marched off stage again.

But he didn't leave this time; he couldn't, he knew it wasn't fair. Still, he sat miserably in the dressing room.

Joe followed him in, taking his arm in his little hands. 'You don't talk to me anymore, Jay.'

'Joe,' he sighed, picking him up and hugging him on his lap. 'If only you could understand...'

Joe eagerly hugged him back. He had so missed his cheerful warmth, the jokes and giggles, and some indefinable quality about his nearness. 'Are you worried about the show?'

'Yes, I suppose you'd say that.'

'Just like mummy. I'm not. I'm looking forward to it! Mummy's got a bigger part than me, though. So have you. That's why you're worried.' Joe always had an explanation for everything. 'But she says she hasn't done Act Three yet, and she's worried because you didn't turn up yesterday. She says Act Three's difficult. But I don't think so, because I'm not in it much!'

Jay raised a small, sad smile. 'It is difficult, Joe. That's why Anna left. Do you remember?' Well, that wasn't entirely true, but it didn't help.

'I'm glad she left.' It was the only response open to Joe. His mummy was here now, all the time, and nobody was being nasty to his new friend.

And Jay knew it was no use. There was only so much therapy he could expect from a four-year-old. 'I suppose we better get back then...'

He carried Joe back to the stage, just in time to hear Paul say that any potentially show-stopping intimacies would be left until the dress rehearsal. His tone was teasing, but Jay deliberately busied himself with Joe. *Christ, this was ridiculous! It's only a pantomime, for God's sake...* But he just seemed to have lost all enthusiasm for the project now.

He understood it more than anyone else. After all, they had only seen some of the antagonism between him and Anna. They hadn't been followed home by a bunch of drunken baying girls last week; or had to keep the beat whilst being sarcastically pelted with condoms on stage in the Union function room the previous Friday night. Clearly you don't cross this gang. The Pink Ladies had nothing on them. Thankfully, his bandmates had thought it was all rather funny. Naturally, he didn't admit there may have been a touch of irony in the stage-aimed gifts. And the bass player's ex-girlfriend had even offered to help him use one. That, of course, reinstated his pride a little. But after seven pints of Bishops Finger, he had circumvented any need of a response by falling off the bar stool...

The huge collaboration by the bottom-of-the-garden world, after which Pixie Jay was to express his undying love for Fairy Sadie, was going rather well. Packed to the gills with parody of all the worst chat-up routines known to man, the backstage crew was in fits of laughter, which invariably had the effect of elevating Jay's mood quite substantially. It was always so. And by the time he actually had to do the thing, you were looking at a man who appeared entirely without the word 'insecurity' in his vocabulary...

The dress rehearsal, and the costumes were fabulous. Although they all felt very silly in them. And Jay couldn't help overhear Jeremy commenting appreciatively about Sadie's low cut, fairy-whore dress. Just as well Anna's merry band of witches were no longer here to catch such inappropriately approving comments from the object of her desires, or Sadie would be on the receiving end of their foul tongues and uninvited gifts too... But her costume was rather endearing. And being slightly more endowed than Anna, it certainly left a lot less to the imagination. A fact that Jay couldn't fail to have noticed either.

'Alright, we'll conclude it tomorrow,' Paul announced. 'You don't mind kissing him, do you?'

Jay pretended not to be listening.

'What?' Sadie laughed.

'Well, we don't want another Anna disappearance, not just before performance night.'

'Oh, don't be ridiculous,' she scorned, but could see he wasn't entirely joking. 'You're not trying to tell me that was it!'

'Let's just say it didn't help. She wanted Jeremy to get the part. Been trying to get into his trousers for months.'

'Oh, leave off,' Jeremy called from the wings.

'For goodness' sake!' Sadie laughed even harder. 'In that case, she's an even bigger twat than I thought. And you haven't got a very professional attitude, have you? It's acting, haven't you noticed?' She turned to Jay. 'I don't if you don't, OK?'

He shrugged and nodded. It was another BAFTA winning performance in its nonchalance.

But it was under fire. 'Of course he doesn't,' Kevin sniggered. 'Who wouldn't?'

Jay glared at him, but Kevin just wiggled his eyebrows and mouthed back, 'Right? Who wouldn't?'

Jay glanced at Sadie, but averted his eyes immediately. He'd have to renew his subscription to The Stage. He really wasn't any good at hiding his emotions. For the most part they were indelibly printed on his sleeve.

But she didn't seem to have noticed either exchange, as Joe yawned at her side. She lifted him and announced they were leaving.

The conversation turned on her as soon as she was out of

earshot. 'Well, I reckon we need to get her into the Club as soon as this is over,' said Paul.

'Think someone got there first, don't you think?' Jeremy sniggered.

'Oh, *what*? That's outrageous! Wanker!'

'Mmm...' Paul ignored Jay's indignant retort and attempted to return to the other 'club' – this one. 'I think we better try.'

'She won't,' Jay concluded irritably. 'She only did this for Joe. I'll bet you any money you like you won't get her to join.' And he jumped off the table and left himself.

But he felt OK as he walked back to his room. Just OK. Maybe she had relieved him of some of the insecurity. Because, yes, it was in his vocabulary. In big bloody red capitals. And yes, he was pretty good at hiding it, and a lot else. It just didn't seem like that to most people, judging by the volume and enthusiasm of his recitation of most things. He was known as an open book.

Well, that was just fine. And in the end, this was going to be a very good night. Because he was good at this. So was she. And so was her adorable boy. And with any luck, he was going to get a pretty hefty dollop of two of his favourite things on Saturday night. Laughter and applause.

That couldn't be bad...

12

CURTAIN UP

The dressing rooms were buzzing with the inevitable excitable nerves. Sadie had no room to acknowledge her own. She barely had time to change. Joe was having a hard time. He'd seen the audience taking their seats and was suddenly convinced he couldn't remember his lines. It threw Sadie into a bit of a panic herself, trying to calm him whilst attending to her own dress and make-up. In the end, she had to pack him off to Jay, hoping he was more ready than she was.

Joe trotted back to the men's dressing room, where Jay sat dressed and made-up. He lifted him onto his lap, cracking jokes and tickling him, casting a veil of distraction and silliness to reassure them both. It seemed to work.

'Beginners to the stage, please...'

Jay carried Joe back to Sadie in the wings. The curtain opened. She kissed his hair, turned him to the light and gave him a little push. Joe looked back at them, the fear returning to his eyes.

'Go on, Joe. You'll be great,' she whispered. Jay winked and blew him a kiss. And, together, this was all that was needed to propel him forward. He skipped onto the stage.

All those faces. Joe hesitated at the full auditorium, the lights and the hush. He skipped around a little more than scripted. Sadie stood in the wings, chewing her lip. Jay squeezed her hand, just as Joe came forward to the front of the stage. 'I'm all on my own today. My friends are not here,' he sighed dramatically. 'I wish I had someone to play with.'

There was a collective 'Aaaah...' from the audience. And Sadie breathed again. Her face immediately softened, and Jay dropped her hand.

The first Act, in which Joe discovers the fairy garden world and a web of plots is woven, went very well. The audience seemed to be enjoying themselves and there was plenty of laughter. Sadie hugged Joe in the wings in the short interval that followed. 'You're doing fantastic!'

'You too!' he beamed...

Over an hour later and Fairy Sadie was finally conceding that Pixie Jay was quite lovable. Throwing himself around after her in the preceding minutes had not caused Jay too much damage, but he bumped his head when he pretended to faint at her declaration, and now felt a little dizzy.

Or was that the climax of this show...?

The Finale, and Sadie grinds her cigarette into the ground, Olivia Newton John style, ordering him off the floor for the celebrated kiss. It was nearly ruined when they found their noses in the way, twice, and Sadie almost collapsed in giggles because of it. But the audience, completely engaged with the production by now, took it to be intentional and cheered raucously when they finally got it right.

Both held to their instructions. They had to remain with the kiss while sinking to their knees and reclining on the floor. Joe runs in, turns aghast to the audience and scuttles away to close the curtain. They then conclude the show out of view of the audience, banging and squeaking floorboards with their hands and feet, and making exaggeratedly passionate noises. Trying not to laugh at each other as they gasped and moaned behind the curtain.

'You're a natural,' Jay mouthed cheekily, the light mood seducing him. She poked her tongue at him with a suppressed giggle, similarly transformed by the conclusion of this effort.

'Alright, see you tomorrow then,' Pixie Jay concludes.

'Fine, OK,' Fairy Sadie replies, and they could be heard exiting from opposite sides of the stage.

The applause was loud and warm.

'I knew I should have told you which way to go,' Paul laughed in the wings. 'Thank God they thought it was scripted!'

Nothing could spoil Jay's mood now, though. He loved applause, a great surge of energy rising within him as the cast assembled to take their bow. The curtain raised and everyone trooped out together, except Jay, Sadie and Joe, who came up the middle seconds later, to roars of approval. They all held hands, Joe in the middle, giggling furiously, wide-eyed at such an enthusiastic response.

And Sadie had not felt like this in years; the noise, the laughter, the cheering. The climactic exhilaration at the conclusion of all their hard work. And although she knew the dangerous implications of that, she let herself enjoy it for the moment. Her chest heaving much needed oxygen and her face bathed in the broadest light and smiles.

Jay had a job taking his eyes off it...

The Lambrusco flowed freely in the dressing rooms. But Sadie changed quickly. How she would love to stay with this group of happy players. But she had a very tired little boy to remove from the increasingly raucous environment and put to bed.

Jay caught her eye over the neck of the bottle he was enthusiastically swigging without the aid of a glass. She smiled and shrugged over Joe's shoulder, as he hung silently around her neck, thumb in mouth and eyes closing. Jay's sympathetic smile masking a distressing level of disappointment that they could not stay and share his inevitable high...

Walking back in the cold, quiet darkness, Sadie still felt that high. But tucked up in bed not long after, the curtain finally closed with crushing anti-climax. Suddenly aware of how much she'd missed that kind of atmosphere and camaraderie over the past five years, the realisation was stark.

She turned over to watch Joe sleeping, knowing that her own sadness must not turn her from her responsibility.

He was enough.

13

CHRISTMAS

'Can I go and say bye-bye to Jay?'

Neither had seen him since the end of the show, and Joe was excessively keen to rectify that now. Sadie was trying to pack. With the show over, she had been forced to confront the reality that they could not stay here for the holidays, and they had nowhere else to go. So she had had to swallow all her unease and phone John and Barbara to ask if they could spend Christmas with them. She was apologetic about the lateness of the request, but needn't have been. They were delighted. Perhaps it should be no surprise. Although Sadie's expedited departure that summer had not been pleasant, it had prompted them into an immediate application for adoption – of another child. Sadie had been relieved about that. But as nothing real had emerged so far, they clearly relished the prospect of pretending with Joe again.

It was the last thing Sadie wanted. She'd even toyed with the idea of taking Joe to a hostel for Christmas. But she knew she couldn't. He would have some luxury.

Joe had expected that all the students spent Christmas

together and was very surprised they were all going their separate ways. Although he adjusted reasonably quickly to going 'home', he clearly viewed this small room and the delightful band of colourful characters around him as his home now. Sadie often felt guilty at his blind acceptance, but it certainly made life easier for her. In the way that he did in so many ways. Easier. Harder. Impossible sometimes...

'Can I give him one of the posters I made in nursery?'

'Have you got enough for Uncle John, Aunty Barbara and the Turners next door?'

Joe pulled a face and shook his head. 'I can make another one.'

Sadie frowned. Paintboxes on the dining room table would not be acceptable at Byron Avenue.

'Please. I want to give it to Jay.'

The university was emptying fast and the facilities closing down, and Joe was going to miss his friends. But it was clear there was one friend he was going to miss very much. He'd spent weeks of rehearsal glued to this man, until Sadie had arrived on the stage, and even then the cement was set. It confused and bewildered her still. But moved by his insistence, she conceded.

'Come on then,' she smiled, and Joe sprung up to fetch his artwork. It was a painting of a Christmas tree, deep in blue snow, with 'Happy Christmas' written across the top. Joe was very proud of that. He had been the only one allowed to write his own message. It was just about legible. Which was more than could be said for the 'Jay' he attempted to squeeze on the end now in bright green marker pen. Most of which ended up on the table...

. . .

'I was hoping I would catch you!' Jay's smile was immediate and broad.

'Joe wanted to say goodbye, didn't you, Joe?'

Joe held the picture behind his back and stood on tiptoes to prompt him down to eye level. Jay smiled and crouched down, but before he could speak, Joe produced his masterpiece, immediately wrapping his arms around his neck. 'I hope you have a nice Christmas, Jay.' Then he kissed him. A wet, chocolatey, child kiss, which just about landed on his lips. Sadie watched this fresh layer of affection with some astonishment.

Jay, meanwhile, could not stop his eyes moistening as he looked down at Joe's present. 'Thank you, Joe,' he choked a little. 'It's lovely. I'll put it straight on my wall.' He knew he would. In fact, it would have gone there right now if he didn't already know that he was taking it home with him. To light the darkness...

Joe beamed at the accolade, regardless of which wall.

'Here you are, then. You have a great Christmas too, eh?' Jay reached for a wrapped square parcel on the table.

'Oh, wow!' Once again, Joe looked as if he'd never received a present before. 'Do I have to leave it until Christmas Day?' he begged his mother. But Jay saved her the uncertainty of working out which was politest.

'Yeah, you open it with all your other presents, eh?'

'Thank you,' Sadie said. 'That's really very kind of you. He doesn't get a lot.'

'Don't mention it.'

'I'm going to my Uncle John and Aunty Barbara's in Bushey.' Joe took the spotlight back. 'Do you know where that is? It's in Watford.' As if that would help.

But it seemed to register with Jay. 'Are you now?' he replied, catching the distaste on Sadie's face. 'Well, do you know where Chorleywood is?'

'Yeah, that's where the nature reserve is!'

They knew it well, seeing as it had free entry and only a 20p bus ride with a benefit card.

'Well, that's where I live. Or that is, where my parents live,' Jay added with a twitch of disdain that matched her own.

'Yeah?' Joe clearly found this just as exciting. 'I can come and see you! I think you can walk there, can't you?'

'No, I don't think you'd walk it,' Jay laughed. 'Anyway,' he glanced at Sadie, realising the difficulties that expectation might present to her, however much he loved the idea. He'd never received a present with so much apparent affection behind it, and it moved him deeply. 'I'll see you next term, eh?'

'OK,' Joe nodded, but he turned at the door. 'I'll miss you, Jay.'

'Oh, and I'll miss you too...'

Barbara and John were very pleased to see them, and Sadie had to fight her unease and distaste from the outset. Two days in, and they were already suggesting shopping trips on their own with Joe, buying him clothes and parading him round their festive dinner party like a trophy. And *their* fucking trophy at that! She did not want to be here. She did not want this to be her base. And she did not want Joe to be here, either. Being told not to drive his cars over the cushion covers; being told to be quiet when he was explaining the relative merits of an Aston Martin over a Mercedes; being forced to eat sprouts and corrected in his eating habits; being educated that spending time on a stage with a group of wayward students was not the right thing to do. And he had been so eager to tell them about it as well.

However much she forced herself day by day to keep a lid on her temper, Sadie vowed to make alternative arrangements by Easter. She knew what they wanted, and it made her uneasy still. And worse, it was making her boy uneasy. Joe was confused by these new rules. Things were different at the university. That was his life now.

Yet there was a strange security in knowing that John and Barbara were there, if anything were ever to happen to her. Even if she wanted them 'there' *elsewhere*. Away from her. And away from her son.

Joe settled into it a little better than her and still managed to stamp his personality on the new structure, despite the baffling new rules. Barbara took him out to buy something for Sadie for Christmas. She was bewildered by his attitude and a little irritated by his persistent babbling, as she picked up a nondescript bottle of bubble bath from a shelf in Boots. But his mum didn't want that, Joe insisted. Corky and Eric from the second floor brewed beer in the baths, and most people opted for the showers. Instead, he dragged Barbara into Woolworths and bought a bumper pack of pens, a large pad of paper and a Snoopy pencil case. It wiped him out of his saved pocket money, but he clutched his haul, smiling contentedly all the way home...

Christmas Day, and it was really Joe's day. He was delighted with his new clothes, games and toys, and was liberal with his hugs and smiles, saving a special cuddle for his mum. As if he knew how much she had scrimped and saved, investing the nicotine withdrawal, to buy the little bike with stabilisers, on which he tore around the garden the minute John and Barbara allowed his escape.

When it was too cold and wet, he would march around the house with his second favourite present – the small drum with shoulder straps that Jay had given him. Although Sadie limited its use as well, as she sensed he was rapidly driving John and Barbara to meltdown.

She had been very touched by his present. He had painted her a picture to go with it. She was told it was a reindeer. It had 'Happy Christmas Mummy, Love Joe' written on it. And he openly boasted that he had chosen the present and wouldn't let Barbara make him buy bubble bath. Barbara and John looked sternly on that, especially as Sadie seemed to encourage the rudeness, hugging him tightly as they giggled over it together.

'When can we go and see Jay?'

How many times had she heard that in the days that followed? Days when it was cold and quiet and the distraction of the new bike and drum were unavailable to him. Sadie thought Joe had accepted this was not going to happen. Eventually forced to send him to his room as the demands grew, her stomach twisted with a new seam of unease.

Unbearably restless by the New Year, she tried not to let it show, but there was still over a week before they could return to the university. And Joe was clearly getting fidgety, too. He didn't really understand why they were still here and just wanted to go 'home' now...

Bundling him out of John's car on January 10th – Escape Day – bike, bags and cases stacking on the pavement, Sadie breathed deep the cold winter air, as if her lungs had not had the exercise for the last three weeks. John did not turn from the wheel as they politely waved him off – too dangerous, no doubt – and a spontaneous smile inched up her face, swinging her laden arms along with Joe, across the station forecourt. With his little rucksack full of toy cars and flapjacks, banging a marching tune on the drum hanging from his neck, they paraded onto the platform, and simultaneously burst into giggles.

They *were* going home now...

Joe was delighted to be back in his beanbag, eagerly looking forward to what lay ahead. Including the full reign of the floor as a highway, engagement with his nonsensical chatter, and the constant presence of 'wayward students'.

The first thing he wanted to do, though, was show Jay his new bike. Sadie was flustered. She'd had plenty of time to think about this, but he hadn't mentioned Jay in nearly a week, so perhaps he had slipped down the radar. She said no. Just a reflex. They were back now, the two of them, their safe, shared haven. She said no again. Joe pouted with dissatisfaction. She told him that Jay would not be coming back for a few days because some courses started later than others. 'Oh,' Joe said, and that was all. She was a hopeless liar, but Joe was too young and trusting to know. They went to the park and no more was said about it.

Sometimes she wished she could lie so convincingly to everyone...

14

BACK TO SCHOOL

Joe returned to nursery and Sadie to her lectures. He rode his new bike everywhere and, when she had her hands full, Sadie allowed him out on his own, with the promise that he would stay around the building. He did, more or less, until he heard a familiar voice.

'Hey, Joe!'

As soon as he saw Jay, he raced towards him, peddling furiously, jumped off the bike and threw himself at him.

'Hey!' Jay swung him high into the air. 'Who's got a lovely new bike, then?'

'Meeee!' It could probably be heard in Chichester. 'Mummy gave it me for Christmas.'

'Well, it's a powerful little thing, isn't it?'

'Yeah! I wanted to show it you, and thank you for my drum. I'm only allowed to play with it sometimes, but it's great!'

How much Jay had missed the volume and enthusiasm of the boy's affection.

'But Mummy said you weren't back yet because your course

starts later, or something.' Joe squinted in confusion. Jay was standing right in front of him. And Mummy was never wrong.

'Yeah, well, I got back yesterday,' he lied, having been here all week.

Sadie called from an open window.

'It's my lunchtime now. You come.'

'Oh, well, maybe I don't think I ought to...' Sadie's lie had reminded him of her unease with him, despite the more relaxed times they had shared during the panto. He missed that. 'But I'll carry you back, shall I?'

'Yeah!'

'Here you are,' he said, just inside the open door. 'One hungry little boy.'

'I thought I told you to stay around the building.' Sadie virtually ignored him.

'I did!'

'Joe...' The tone silenced him as it always did

'Uh, see you around then, Joe.' Jay sensed he wasn't exactly being welcomed.

'Can't he stay, Mummy?' Joe persisted, climbing onto the chair behind his lunch. 'I haven't told him about our Christmas yet.'

Sadie didn't know what this feeling was, only that her growing unease with all this was somehow intensifying. There was a deep nervous churning in her stomach, she could feel her heart beat and a rush of heat to her head. But instead of attempting to rationalise it, she sighed irritably, and inexplicably turned it on its head.

'Oh yeah, sure, he can stay as long as he likes! He can look after you. I'm going out.' She grabbed her coat and bag, pushed past Jay and slammed the door behind her.

It was unreasonable. He had classes all afternoon. But if he thought about it, he'd much rather play with Joe. In fact, he didn't even have to think about it...

Sadie returned early, guilt inevitably overcoming her knee-jerk fight and flight, only to find them gone. She'd been into town to look for something for Joe's birthday next week. The expense never seemed to end. She had not found anything meaningful that she could afford, and on top of everything else, she sank onto the mattress and cried. It happened like that sometimes. So normally controlled, it was as if the tension had to be released somehow. Her limbs unwrapped from their box of rigidity, the internal waves finally crashing to the shore...

A knock on the door dragged her up, attempting to disguise the evidence of her emotion. But it wasn't Joe and Jay, it was Paul. He'd come to get her to join the dramatics society and offer her a part in the next production. But Jay had been right; no amount of persuading would succeed. Although Sadie was sorely tempted, the same feeling that had prevented her from truly enjoying the Christmas show stopped her. The red lights of danger at the perimeter of her carefully constructed cocoon...

A spirited noise in the corridor cut through Paul's persuasions. Evidently sharing some secret joke at the door, Joe would not get down from Jay's arms for a moment, and Jay caught a look in Paul's eyes as he glanced between them that he did not understand.

'I thought you had classes Thursday afternoon,' Paul said.

'I do.'

'I'm sorry,' Sadie muttered, barely meeting his eye.

'Sometimes there are more important things, eh Joe?' Jay smiled down at the boy, as if he had not heard the apology.

'Yeah!' Joe readily agreed, although he didn't know what he was talking about.

'Well, you were right, Jay. I can't get her to join the Club.'

Jay shrugged in an unspoken 'told-you-so'. Sadie looked at him, her irritation resurfacing.

'Well, I suppose there's no point in staying any longer,' Paul concluded. 'Thanks anyway.'

'I'll come with you.' Jay lowered Joe to the floor and abruptly followed him out.

Sadie could see the bewilderment in her son's eyes, his thumb instantly to his mouth. She quickly tried to divert him. 'I've got ice cream. Chocolate! Did you have a nice afternoon?'

Joe's smile returned immediately. Ice cream *and* conversation revolving around him? That'd do nicely.

'Yeah, we played drums. Jay says I'm real good!'

'I'm sure you are, then.'

Joe climbed up to the table. 'I didn't know you were going out. Jay ate your lunch.'

'Well, some little people have birthdays next week, don't they?' she continued to mask the guilt with an attempt at matching his jollity.

'Oh, yeah!'

Tears averted, Joe babbled away about drums, cars and birthday presents, as she tried to make the pre-ice cream dinner and forget about the whole damn thing.

'Oh,' he threw in. 'I couldn't find our photos. Jay wants to see them.'

'They're in the shoebox, in the drawer, there.'

'OK, next time I see him, I'll show him.'

And, finally, no more was said about Jay...

Janet was distinctly peeved. If he didn't shut up this minute, she'd shove that bloody Ford Anglia down his throat. It was her turn on the Joe-rota for one of the afternoons Sadie couldn't get out of a lecture. Normally she didn't mind too much, especially as the burden had lightened considerably since the end of the profanity-ridden panto rehearsals. But today she had work to do, and Joe did not want to play on his own.

Joe squinted up at yet another gritted teeth sigh. He was a bit bored with his cars today and Janet wasn't playing. He knew he always had to work on her a bit, but that didn't seem to be having much effect today. She wasn't half so much fun as Mummy, anyway. Or...

'Can we go and see Jay?'

This was by far the best option Janet had right now. Increasingly irritated by his persistent sighs and noises, she agreed to the walk.

Jay opened his door, illicit cigarette in mouth and coffee in hand, looking as if it was taking a tremendous effort to concentrate on his studies. 'Hello!' he beamed, reprieved from the battlefront. 'Come in! Coffee...?'

'Oh, I may as well,' Janet sighed. Clearly, this was not going to be a very productive day for either of them.

'Have a good Christmas?' Jay broke the silence that followed. It was not exactly relaxed.

'Yeah OK, you?'

Jay nodded noncommittally.

'I did!' Joe announced with flourish.

'Yeah, we know *you* did,' Jay winked, tousling his hair.

'Bet no-one else in the house did with you around.'

A short, stunned silence followed as Janet registered Jay's surprise at that last remark. Although it didn't seem to make any difference. 'What did you get from your daddy, then?'

Jay's mouth dropped. He glanced at Joe, whose eyes lowered, his fingers picking at the carpet.

'He doesn't send me things,' he mumbled. 'I think it's a long way... I don't know...'

If Janet regretted what she had said, she wasn't showing it. She put down her coffee and announced it was time to go.

Joe did not move.

'Can't I stay with Jay?

'Well, I don't—' Janet hesitated, glancing at Jay.

'It's OK.'

'Yeah, but I don't know if I ought to leave him.'

But Joe wasn't having that. 'I want to!' he demanded. 'I love Jay.'

Just one of those things... But it knocked Jay sideways. And all he wanted at that moment was to hold the boy to him.

Janet scanned them both, a bit like Paul had the other day, as Joe shuffled to the security of his side. 'Well, OK, I suppose...'

As the door closed behind her, Jay looked down at Joe, pulling up more carpet with his fingers.

'Right then, little man, what we gonna do today then?'

Joe shrugged.

'The sun's shining!'

Joe remained unmoved.

'It's my birthday tomorrow,' he eventually said, unusually quietly.

'Is it?' Jay smiled again. 'Are you going to do anything special?'

'I don't know. Don't think so.'

'Well, we'll see about that,' Jay muttered. 'Now then, what about this afternoon? What are we gonna do now?'

'I don't know...'

'Come here,' Jay sighed, lifting him onto his lap. Joe put his hands around Jay's arm and leant back against his chest.

'I love you too, you know,' Jay whispered, kissing his hair.

Joe raised his head and, finally, smiled. Leaning back again, thumb in mouth, no more plans, jokes and diversions needed in this moment...

. . .

Sadie was not there when they returned to Ellis House. Janet let them in with her spare key, quite content to be relieved of duty for a while longer. It didn't feel right to Jay to be here uninvited, but it didn't bother Joe in the slightest.

'Do you want to see my photos now? They're in that drawer, you get them.'

Jay felt even less relaxed about rifling through her drawers, but did as he was told. Inside was a shoebox of photos and documents, including a small pile of papers labelled 'Joe'. A thin wooden lock box lay beneath, almost hidden at the bottom of the drawer. Jay's hand hovered over it all, with his usual curiosity. But he closed his fingers around a slim photo packet labelled Christmas 1986, and decisively closed the drawer...

Joe was clearly as at home in front of a camera as on a stage.

'Can I have one?'

'I 'spect so. We got lots.'

'Perhaps we better ask Mummy.'

'She won't mind. Which one do you want?'

'That one.' He pointed to two near identical snaps of Joe sitting on the carpet playing, but looking up at the camera and laughing. It captured his spirit completely.

Joe wrinkled his nose. 'Why d'you want it?'

It was not all that common for Jay to be stumped for words, but he couldn't form a response to this one.

Because I want you with me all the time now...?

'Because it's nice,' he settled for, cuffing Joe with the packet. 'I'll put them back.'

Now, however, his curiosity got the better of him. He pushed aside the pile labelled 'Joe'. Medical and vaccination cards, nursery letters, premium bonds... And there, on the bottom, was his birth certificate. Jay's heart beat a little faster, his fingers twitched...

He took a better look anyway.

Name: Joe Emmett
Mother's Name: Sarah Jayne Emmett
Father's Name:

'What you doing?' Joe piped up from the floor cushions.

'Nothing.' Jay flipped the drawer closed and returned immediately.

'Can you read me a story?'

'OK. What d'ya want? You go and get something.'

Joe scrambled to the wardrobe and pulled a book out of a brimming box.

'Noddy's New Car,' Jay read, and smiled approvingly. 'Is it a Ford Anglia?'

'No, stupid. It's a Noddy Car!' Joe looked completely bewildered at Jay's density as he climbed onto his lap. But he loved the way Jay had voices for all the different characters. Noddy had clearly been castrated somewhere off the Old Kent Road, and Big Ears was a cross between Father Christmas and Geoff Boycott. Joe was completely absorbed, thumb jammed in mouth, playing with a stray bit of wool in Jay's jumper as an accompaniment.

And Jay had never felt like this before. Relaxed, yes, but he was not sure he had really known the meaning of the word before. Warm, close, affirmed...

Before it was all ruined.

Joe raised sleepy eyes and his smile was automatic as Sadie came in. Jay's was more experimental, watching her turn unnecessarily to shut the door, and stay there for a moment.

'What are you doing here?'

It was a tone that Jay had come to expect by now. He sighed. God knows, he was insecure enough about this already.

'Just leaving,' he replied, lifting Joe from his lap and getting to his feet.

'You haven't finished the story! Jay, come back!'

Joe's voice followed him out of the door and pulled his heart. But he kept on walking.

Joe stared at his mother.

'Why did he have to go, Mummy?'

Sadie ignored the question, silently unpacking her shopping bag. But that was never enough for Joe, she should know that by now. He got up and tugged on her trousers.

'Mummy, why don't you like Jay?'

Usually so skilled with Joe's constant questions, and often rather amused, Christ, how she hated them at times...

'Sometimes you're nice to him and sometimes you're not.'

Sadie turned and knelt by her son. 'My only concern is you Joe, I don't care about him,' she said, much more gently than she felt.

Naturally, Joe did not understand. 'Why don't you like him?' he simply repeated.

'You like him, do you Joe?'

'Yeah, I like him lots!'

Sadie forced a weak smile and managed to get away without answering the question with the promise of fish fingers. She was pretty good at that, too.

Over tea, she gently made enquiries of her own about why he wasn't with Janet. Learning that he had insisted on going to see Jay only intensified her anxiety. *Anxiety?* Or was it? She wasn't sure what it was. She just didn't like it. She had a boy to nurture, a degree to achieve, a pile of presents to wrap, and a room to decorate. And a fucking great thumping headache.

She didn't need this unsettlement.

15

BIRTHDAY BOY

Joe's birthday, and Sadie was determined to make the great fuss that he loved. She crept out of bed before he stirred and pinned balloons around the room. All his breakfast things had candles and decorations around them, and a banner across the door proclaimed, 'Happy Birthday Joe!'

There was a package from John and Barbara, a present from Janet, and a couple more from others on the block. Sadie let him open them after breakfast in bed. She was skipping classes today, and she watched him, happy only that he was happy.

Joe was delighted with all the small toys and books he received, beaming with joy at being the centre of '*so much*' attention from '*so many*' people. He looked up at her, banging a clumsy paradiddle on the table in anticipation of more. Sadie smiled and produced a heavy square package, with a couple of smaller gifts on a trailer being pulled by a toy dump truck. Joe tore at the paper of his biggest present. It was not in a box; Sadie had found it for a tenner in the back of the free local paper.

'Hey, I can watch in here all the time now!' Joe's eyes

popped as he uncovered an old portable TV, immediately jabbing at the buttons. 'It doesn't work!'

'You have to plug it in, silly. You know that. Like the kettle, yeah?' Sadie laughed. 'We'll try it later, when Mr Bellamy comes on, OK?'

'Yey!' Joe punched the air, eagerly turning to the dump truck. From the trailer he unwrapped another Noddy book, the Cortina he had been after since his friend George brought one to nursery after Christmas (yellow, good, that was apparently better than George's green one) and a tube of Smarties. And tied to the bumper was a kite. After some explaining, Joe was very enthusiastic about the kite, and threw himself at Sadie. George didn't have a kite *at all*...

A knock on the door broke through their giggles.

'Will you give this to Joe, please?' Jay stood, shifting from foot to foot, eyes lowered. Sadie sighed, suddenly hating the unease, and knowing she had put it there.

'You give it to him. He'd love to see you,' she added with the lightest tone she could manage.

'Jay!' Joe shrieked. 'Look what I got! A telly of my own. And a kite thing. You fly it in the air on a string. And look! A Cortina. It's yellow!'

'Lovely,' Jay laughed, his discomfort dissolving in the boy's affection and enthusiasm. 'Yellow, excellent. Just as it should be.'

'Is it?' Sadie whispered with a bemused grin.

'No fuckin' idea,' Jay whispered back... 'Who's a lucky boy, then?'

'I am! Aren't I, Mum?'

Sadie nodded, though she rarely felt it.

'And what's all this, then?' Jay pointed to the scattered array of other presents.

'I got three more cars, I got that one already, and a game and two books. I don't know what that is.' Joe poked the slide rule and box of SMP Maths Cards from John and Barbara. 'But look, Noddy... Goes... to...?'

'Toyland.'

'Toyland, yeah. You can read it when you've finished the last one.'

'Oh, thanks! Beats functional genomics, that's for sure. Well, you have done well, haven't you?'

'Yeah, lots of people give me things!'

'Here you are, then. Cop another one.'

'Thanks!' Joe beamed again, tearing the paper off the heavy package Jay plonked on the table. His mouth dropped. There were two big hardback books that he could hardly hold as he pushed them apart; one about plants, the other about birds. They were very colourful, lots of pictures, and very expensive looking. Joe was thumbing through them already, and silence fell at last.

'Would you like some coffee?' Sadie offered.

'Uh... thanks,' Jay stuttered in surprise. He followed her to the sink, while Joe remained unusually silenced by the chapter on river waders. 'Look, I didn't want to ask in front of Joe because I respect your decision, but I wondered if you'd let me take you both out, for a pizza or something, for Joe's birthday?'

The silence pulsed with renewed unease.

'Haven't you spent enough already?'

'Tell you the truth, only one of them's new. I already had the other one. Grown out of it a bit, though. I'm nearly 12 now, you know?'

Sadie was inclined to join his instinctive giggle; a giggle that rather hinted that he could be no more than 11-years-old. But she couldn't.

'Even so...'

'Look, just say yes and don't worry about it.'

'No. It's very kind of you, thank you, but I don't think so.'

'Why not?'

'I thought you respected my decision.'

'Yeah, yeah,' Jay sighed. 'I just don't understand you. I really don't.'

'Well, you don't have to, do you?'

Hands up in silent submission, he turned away...

'What you gonna do this afternoon then, Joe?' he asked, as Joe closed the book. Diving into a bowl of sweets, Joe looked to his mother.

'I thought we'd take your new kite to the park.'

'Yeah!'

'Well, why don't you do that on Saturday when I've got the drama club minibus? We could all go up to the South Downs. And meanwhile this afternoon there's always—'

'You've got a bloody cheek, haven't you?' Sadie finally exploded. Joe froze mid-chew. 'Get out of here! Why don't you just fucking leave us alone?'

Jay got up from the table. What else could he do, in the face of that? If the tone had not been enough, Sadie's constant efforts to keep those kinds of words from her son could not fail to hammer the point. He left the room in silence.

'Mummy! Why did he have to go?' Joe demanded the moment the door closed.

Sadie sank down into a chair. 'Did you want him to stay?' she sighed.

'I like him!'

'I know you do...Look, why don't you run after him? See if he'll come back.' She rubbed her forehead, weary of the whole business now. She had been driven to a level of outburst she rarely allowed, however frequently it clattered about in her mind, and it left her with a mixture of churning emotions. One of them was regret...

Joe hared out of the building and ran all the way to Jay's side. 'Will you come back?' he panted.

Jay stopped and tried to smile. 'I'll see you another day, Joe. You better hurry back now, or your mum'll be cross.'

'She won't. She told me to run after you and see if you'll come back.'

'Oh, I see...' He did not. 'Even so, I don't think I will.'

'Why not?' Joe whined.

Jay sighed and knelt by his side. 'It's not her fault, Joe, but Mummy doesn't like me very much. So it's best if I see you another day, eh? When you're on your own.'

Joe's eyebrows knitted. 'Sometimes she's nice to you. You laughed a lot when we did the show.'

Jay smiled weakly at the memory. It seemed so long ago. 'Yeah, well, I dunno,' he shrugged.

'I dunno,' Joe copied. 'You should like each other. I want you to like each other.'

'Sometimes it's difficult for different people to get along, Joe.' Jay tried to find an appropriate explanation. Unlike Joe, he did not always have one. 'Now I've got a lot of work to do, so I'll see you, eh? You have a nice afternoon flying your kite.'

'OK,' Joe replied and skipped off, his voice disappearing behind him. 'See you...'

Jay was not sure if he preferred it this way, or if he would have liked to hear some more protest. But it was for the best. He had no wish to cast any further disruption on his birthday...

Sadie was still sitting staring at the table when Joe returned, on his own; the weight of her regret made all the heavier by the new carriage of guilt, as he explained that Jay was 'busy'. But Joe was onto the next thing and wanted to be gone. And she welcomed it, like a rising tide that lifts a boat run aground.

Breathing the cool air of an afternoon in the park; a boisterous, joyful boy in love with a bit of plastic on a piece of string; fat chips and chocolate ice cream; and sharing a beanbag in front of a new TV.

Normal things. Uncomplicated things. Beautiful things.

16

SOUTH DOWNS SUNSET

Joe was bored. The nursery children had donned their hats and coats to play outside with bats and balls. Joe was no longer interested in hitting things for no reason, so he decided the nursery bin lid would make a good snare drum instead. Then he pinched George's plastic rounders bat, so now he had two bats to practise his paradiddles.

Jay heard it from the path on his way to lectures before he even saw Joe. Followed by George's wailing and the teacher shouting Joe's name. He watched as Joe stomped off to stand facing the nursery door, bowing his head and kicking the gravel.

'Hey,' he whispered from the shrubbery.

'Jay!'

'In trouble?'

'Yeah,' Joe pouted.

'Hmm,' Jay sniggered. 'No drums in school, them's the rules.'

Joe frowned.

'Good work, though,' he winked, and Joe lit up. 'Anyway, I

gotta go, and you better stop talking to a rhododendron or they'll think you've gone mad.'

'OK,' Joe giggled, forgetting his brief detention. 'See you tomorrow!'

'Eh?'

'You are taking us to the Downs, aren't you? In the bus?'

'Uh, I don't know, Joe.'

'But you said!'

'It was just a suggestion, Joe.'

'But you said!'

'You'll have to ask your mummy, Joe. It's up to her...'

Sadie was annoyed. She hadn't realised Joe was expecting the trip. But insistence was approaching tantrum, so she conceded and took him round to Jay's room. He was somewhat cool as he let them in.

'OK, we'll come tomorrow,' she said unwisely.

'Oh, will you?' he replied. 'How very kind of you. Well, isn't it a pity that I've got better things to do, so I won't be able to let you do me this huge favour?'

'I didn't mean it to sound like that,' she mumbled.

'What do you mean, then?' he demanded profoundly, wanting to make her ask for it. For a change.

'I meant...' she began, with difficulty, 'that if you were still willing, Joe would very much like to go to the South Downs tomorrow, please.'

'You mean you're going to let him stay around me for a whole day on his own?'

'I...I thought your invitation stretched to both of us?' Sadie squirmed.

'Oh, you'd like to come too?'

'Well, you did say...'

'Yeah, but you didn't, did you? No, sorry, better things to do.'

Sadie looked down at Joe's silent bewilderment.

'You wouldn't let him down like this.'

'Why wouldn't I? Because I care for him? Well, that's out of the question, isn't it?'

They both now looked as if they were about to cry any minute. It inevitably moved Jay out of his indignation. 'Just let up, will you?' he sighed. 'I do care for him. Very much. And I hate it when you obviously think I'm going to hurt him.'

Sadie turned her head away.

'I'm not taking you in that kind of atmosphere,' he concluded. 'You either lighten up, or forget it.'

She nodded silently. Whether she wanted to or not, she had to accept his terms, for Joe's sake.

'OK,' he sighed. 'I'll see you about eleven, Union car park, alright...?'

Saturday dawned bright and crisp. Sadie made a conscious effort to banish her reservations, smiled and said hello, making unaccustomed small talk as they climbed into the front of the minibus. And within half an hour, it was getting considerably easier. Jay was not exactly reckless in his driving, but he liked the speed and agility he seemed to manage, dodging in and out of cars on the A286. And Sadie was conscious that she was enjoying it. As she was enjoying his incessant chatter.

Joe was laughing most of the time, too. Whether anything was funny or not didn't really matter, only that the atmosphere was good. Joe had a radar-sharp antenna for atmospheres. And this one was more than a little blip on the detection screen.

They plumped for a quiet country car park near Midhurst,

Jay having them both squealing with laughter, reversing at terrific speed up a hill.

'Jay!' Sadie shrieked, holding onto the dashboard as well as Joe, as he swerved past a wooden post and into a parking space. He turned to her, eyes alive, to find her laughing breathlessly.

And he, too, felt good as they tramped the gravel path up the hill. Truth be told, he liked her. When she was like this, she was good to be around. Like during the Christmas show. And he had Joe as well, just now. What more could he ask?

Sadie watched from a bench as he raced Joe around the top of the hill, pretending to be running as fast as he could, puffing and panting, constantly lagging behind her perpetually giggling son. It was nice to watch... *Except*... There was always a *but*. This nagging reservation she had about him playing with Joe like this. So like a... *father*. And a damn good one at that. But she knew she had to remain light that day. That was the deal. So she tried to block out the thought, because it distressed her deeply...

For a while, she remained the spectator as Jay helped Joe get his kite into the air, pretending to be entangled in the string, and then pretending that the kite was pulling him around out of control. Sadie could not help but join Joe's laughter from the sidelines as Jay yelped, running around and rolling on the grass. Joe absolutely loved these antics. She tended to play with him in this kind of way. Perhaps a little less conventional than his nursery friends' older mums. But Jay was much more exaggerated. Running around the top of the hill, disappearing down it, screaming at Joe to save him. And Joe just ran around after him, laughing helplessly.

'Ergh!' He finally landed flat on his face on the hilltop. 'It's stopped! Joe! Joe! Quickly, grab hold of it!'

Joe ran up and wrestled the kite from his outstretched arm.

'Careful now, it's a maniac.'

'It's alright, *I* can control it,' Joe proudly announced, running away from the obediently flying kite. Jay smiled, dusting himself down and strolling back to the bench. He flopped down, dropping over his knees, regaining his breath, and turned his head to her with a broad grin. To his continued surprise, she laughed again. She had a very infectious laugh, he noticed, not for the first time. Very warm, very inclusive. It transformed her.

Then, to both their surprises, she blurted, 'You're so good with him, you know? He loves it.'

Jay smiled more meaningfully then...

They enjoyed a chilly picnic before walking on. A brief chance to quietly enjoy the South Downs beauty at sunset, as Joe ran ahead with his kite, visiting all the dogs on the way.

'He loves dogs,' Sadie smiled as they watched him pat another one. 'I do hope people don't mind. He goes up to every dog he sees.'

'Who could mind?'

'Still, I have to watch him. It hasn't happened yet, but some dog might decide he doesn't want to be patted.'

'Yeah. It must be so difficult sometimes. People don't realise, do they? At least us without kids. You have to watch him every minute.'

'Yeah, that's right. I think it's second nature now. I've learned to do two things at once. Like write an essay and keep an eye on him at the same time.'

'I don't know how you do it... What made you decide to come here?'

'I seem to remember you asking a similar question before.'

'Oh, OK,' Jay sighed.

Sadie glanced at him in the silence that followed, and was suddenly weary of the whole locked away, silent, lonely thing. 'I just wanted to get away and do something for myself,' she said.

'I felt very stifled in that place. Where people knew me. Knew what I was.'

Jay looked at her hopefully. What did she mean? Was she confessing to the lies she'd told?

'What you were?' he prompted.

Sadie's calm waters were disturbed again. She'd let that slip, now she had to explain. 'I was very young when I got married, and then he... Oh bollocks,' she sighed. 'What's the bloody use? I'm just so tired of it...'

Jay could see her distress, gathering like storm clouds, which he well imagined could erupt into a drenching any minute. He really had no interest in upsetting her further. He'd broken in this far. There was no need to prolong her discomfort, if he could. 'Let's just forget it then, eh? It isn't important.'

She briefly met his eye. And there was that look again. As if the world was a slightly scary and baffling place and she was a helpless victim of its merciless vicissitudes. It didn't come that often. More commonly, there was a much firmer steel in her clear green eyes, and the abrasion that so often followed. But it was alarmingly moving when it did arrive, seemingly unbidden, but equally content to set up home in those youthful, exposed features. And it always had the same effect. As if you just wanted to pick her up right there and then, wrap her in duck feathers and insist that the world just bugger off and leave her alone.

'You're very kind, really,' she mumbled.

And the feeling doubled...

Jay was only too glad for the day to continue, but the invitation back to their room still surprised him.

'Sleepy?' Sadie smiled down at Joe as she carried him in the door. He nodded, his eyes heavy. 'Fetch your stuff then, and I'll get you ready for bed...'

She'd barely filled the kettle before Joe had found his pyjamas and was wandering around with them, protesting that he wanted to go to the toilet.

'Hang on a minute then—'

'Jay'll take me.' Joe tugged his hand instead. 'Toothbrush!' He added, grabbing it from the cupboard. Jay followed blindly, but not before catching the shock on her face on his way out...

This was getting beyond understanding for her. There were more and more areas in Joe's life that he was inviting Jay into. But before she could pick through her feelings on that, they were back. Joe, still sleepily chatting, thrust his pyjamas into Jay's arms.

'Sorry, don't worry about that,' she fluffed.

'It's alright,' he replied, but it was more like a question; which Joe answered for her by holding his arms up for the removal of his jumper.

'OK... one, two, three, up!' Jay ripped it over his head, making Joe giggle again. It was his favourite jumper, he explained. Mummy had knitted it, with 'Joe' written in large letters on the front, and '90' on the back. He then proceeded to explain who Joe 90 was, as Sadie had explained to him, while Jay helped him into his pyjamas.

Joe gabbled and danced through his usual nighttime routine, showing Jay how he folded his clothes and placed his shoes under the chest of drawers, before lazily stretching out his arms to be carried to his beanbag. Finally, he reached for his drumsticks and tucked them under the duvet with him. And a wave of emotion crashed over Jay. He did the very same thing as a child, every night.

'Goodnight, Mummy.' Joe reached to pull Sadie's cheek to his little wet mouth.

'Goodnight, Joe,' she whispered back, turning off the light in his corner of the room.

That was normally the conclusion of the nightly ritual, at which Joe would turn over to sleep. But tonight he stretched his arms out again to whisper, 'Goodnight, Jay.'

Jay, standing mesmerised a few feet from him, just about managed to shake himself to return the 'Goodnight'. Joe's eyebrows knitted and his face clouded with a mixture of expressions that Jay did not understand.

Joe widened his arms. And Jay could barely accept that the boy was just demanding to show him even more affection. He knelt by the beanbag, Joe's little arms encircling his neck as he planted a similar kiss on him. 'I've had a lovely day,' he smiled, turned over, and closed his eyes...

Jay joined Sadie at the table at the lighter side of the room. They sipped their coffee in silence.

'Sorry, I'm not much company, am I?' Jay laughed.

'What are you thinking?' she asked unexpectedly. She didn't know why. Not now. Why should she care? 'Is it Joe?' She didn't know why she was pursuing this either. But at that moment, it just felt like putting on an old pair of slippers that you thought you'd thrown out, only to be reminded that they were the most comfortable item in your wardrobe.

Jay glanced at her gently concerned expression, but hesitated. What kind of woman *was* this, really? Who in a turn of a breath could bite your head off *and* look at you as if she could read your mind?

'Look, I'll be straight with you,' she said, looking directly into his eyes. She did that from time to time. It was a little unnerving. 'I am confused. I've treated you badly because of that sometimes, but I'd like us to be straight with each other now...' She sighed, the direction lost. 'Oh God, I don't even know what I'm talking about...'

The talking, rather than the listening part of the old communication duo, seemed much harder for her to recover. It was one reason she rarely attempted it nowadays.

'It's my fault,' Jay responded, and Sadie was both puzzled and moved by that. *What* was his fault? He glanced towards Joe in the dark corner. 'He means a lot to me. I don't know what that makes you feel. I know you've got a right to be concerned... It's so difficult. I—' He sank back in his chair. 'Oh hell, you don't want to hear it.'

Sadie looked at him with the continuing warmth of those old slippers. A warmth she hadn't felt since the classroom days when she used to cry with the girls who recounted their problems to her. She felt privileged then; she did now. Yet for the last five years, she'd thought of little else but herself and her son.

'I do want to hear it,' she said, wondering how she could ever forget that others had their troubles too.

Jay raised his head, and within milliseconds, it was quite apparent that talking was not his problem at all. The dam had been broken with those six short words, and his story came pouring out. The mother who spent all her time drinking gin and playing Canasta with her card club. The father he never saw, except when he started to come to him at night to show him things he did not want to see. The drugs, the drink, the gang he joined, the lonely years that followed... Sadie barely had to offer a word of enticement. The floodgate was open.

And all this meant, as Jay now concluded, that Joe was the only person who had ever openly shown him love. Or indeed that he had ever loved, except his mother, who rejected it anyway, until it gradually faded away.

And he was so full of it. That, too, was quite clear.

'I'm sorry. I'm sorry...' he pulled back instantly, seeing the tears in her eyes and kicking himself that he might have reminded her too closely of her own troubles.

'No, *I'm* sorry,' she whispered. 'I'm so sorry. It must have been awful for you.'

Jay's jaw dropped. She was crying for him. For *him*, for Christ's sake!

'I... I don't want you to be upset for *me*... I'm sorry, I shouldn't have bothered you. You've got quite enough problems of your own. Sometimes I can be so incredibly selfish.'

'Well, you've been incredibly *un*selfish today.'

'Oh, have I?' he snapped unexpectedly. 'So you've missed the point, then? You're not the incredibly observant being I just mistook you for.'

Jay immediately caught the sensitive bewilderment in her eyes, but before he could instantly retract, she had changed.

'Well, that's your problem, isn't it?' She scraped her chair back and took the cups to the sink. 'I'm tired now. It's getting late.'

No more cue needed. He stopped at the door. No, another apology would be futile. And he closed it silently behind him.

He kicked through the grass on his short, dark journey back to his room, as he wanted to kick himself. What was the matter with him? They'd had such a good day. And this last half hour? It was like he had jumped into a place of safety. A place to put his darker thoughts and emotions. The tears of the clown. Accepted as much as the red nose and the painted smile... Why did he insist on bulldozing everyone with his mercurial moods? Either he leapt on them with excitable enthusiasm or he was dragging them down a ditch with his inhibitions.

And why did he have to snap at her like that?

Just at the point when she was showing him something else.

17

AN UNEXPECTED EVENING

A lie in. It was becoming a bit of a fantasy. In a normal student dictionary, that's what Saturday spelt. Come to think of it, that's what most of the days of the week spelt. Sadie was trying it this morning. Joe was pretending he had allowed it. In his version of the dictionary, it meant that Mummy answers questions, provides guidance, listens to the history of the Ford Cortina (again) and locates his socks, from a horizontal rather than a vertical position.

She gave up by eight-thirty and they went out for a walk with Joe's kite and bike...

'Just wondered if you wanted to go to the big gig tonight?'

Joe was asleep in bed and Sadie was seriously contemplating following him, when Janet appeared at the door that evening with this ridiculous question. And she wondered why Janet was pretending she was an ordinary student, as well.

'Well, I can't, can I?' she whispered, cocking her head to Joe in the corner.

'That's what I mean. I thought I'd offer to mind him. I've got a bit of work to catch up on, so I wasn't going to go. Jay's band's headlining, aren't they?'

'Yeah...' Sadie was, in fact, unusually alert. She just couldn't face the prospect of either Saturday night TV or another bloody essay on Erasmus. Bedtime just seemed the best option. Until now. 'Well, it would make a change.'

'Off you go then.'

Sadie grabbed her bag. 'Thanks ever so much, Jan!'

'Are you going like that?'

'Yeah,' she said, barely glancing at her mud-splatted jeans and sweatshirt.

It was alright for her, Janet thought, as the door closed behind her. Sadie didn't have to worry about the way she looked. She was never on the pull. Besides, she had the kind of face that needed very little embellishment. For herself, it was a never-ending struggle of trying to impress. She wished she didn't feel obliged to throw a cement mixer of make-up on her face every waking moment. Even on a trip to the common room. There was always the chance that Bradley, the electronics engineer from upstairs, would be there. Hmm, that was not a pleasant connection to make in Janet's mind at that moment. Since last Thursday, actually, when Bradley had taken her aside to ask whether Sadie really did have a husband, and did she like Chinese food...?

It had been so long since Sadie had been out in the evening, she didn't think twice about being alone. And the band was very good, she thought. The vocalist was a bit weak, but they certainly got the crowd going, and it was all thoroughly under-pinned by the most energetic drumming Sadie had ever seen or heard. Jay looked as if he'd been born on that stool. Move over Larry Mullen. But then, Larry Mullen had moved over quite a while ago now. Joining Bono on her swift slippery slope into reality. And she realised then, it had been a very long time since she had a clue what she was talking about. Despite her and Joe's avid appointment with Top of the Pops every Thursday night, the days of her encyclopaedic knowledge of musical fashion were long gone. She better shut up if asked for any further opinion.

But she also recognised, in that small moment, that she missed it. And she missed the engagement of her feet. Well, they were moving now. Bloody hell if she wasn't actually enjoying herself! Especially when some of her course mates spotted her and seemed eager to join in.

A memory came to her mind then of Mrs Harris, her games teacher, who had sent her and Lizzie out of the room during a dance lesson for eschewing the Scottish Reel in favour of John Travolta. Lizzie had executed the moves like a carthorse, but Mrs Harris later remarked that Sadie might consider nurturing her obvious gift for rhythm and movement when she next visited the careers room after her mock O'levels. *Where the hell had that gone now, too?* Well, there was a lot of teacherly advice that had to be forgone in the rather different place she had landed after her mock O'levels.

But the gift, if that was what it was, was evidently still there...

'Hey, they were good,' Adam, a new student on her course, commented, standing very close to her ear as the crowd called for more.

'That drummer's awesome,' Steve added. And for a second, Sadie felt a little proud.

'Yes, he is,' she agreed. And he was Joe's friend.

'Did you see that thing he did juggling those drumsticks?'

Sadie had indeed seen it. She'd be surprised if it had passed anyone by, even the indifferent posers skulking about at the back by the bar. Jay had briefly taken the spotlight during an extended instrumental break, storming round the kit, twirling and throwing the drumsticks up and down between beats. All in perfect time. And at the end he just chucked them over his head, stood up, arms thrown wide, his hands beckoning to the audience, demanding their total and undisguised accolade. Sadie could not prevent a completely engaged and somewhat stunned grin spreading over her face throughout it. And it was coming back right now at the memory...

'Pity about the singer, though,' she added.

'What's wrong with him?' Julie snapped unexpectedly.

'Oh, uh...' Sadie stuttered, the spontaneous grin fading as she realised, without knowing why, that a spot of diplomacy might be in order. 'Not that much, just thought he was a bit... weak... in places... some of the time...' she continued to dilute.

'Well, I'd like to see you do better!'

Adam could see Sadie's bemusement. 'Julie's new boyfriend,' he said, moving even closer.

Sadie's cheeks burned. 'Oh, I'm sorry,' she muttered. But, thankfully, the band was returning for an encore, saving her any further embarrassment. For the moment...

Jay was happy. It had all gone rather well on the whole, although he had some reservations, mostly around the vocals, which he thought he could do better himself. But as they were a relatively newly formed outfit, he was pretty satisfied. He always felt a little shut away behind his kit in a place like this where the back of the stage was so dark. Only getting any real connection with the audience during his somewhat exaggerated demands for adoration after the instrumental. But there was a moment when he had spotted Sadie in the middle of the crowd, dancing away with a bottle of Orangeboom pressed to her stomach. As if it wasn't enough of a surprise to see her there at all. So, in his present light mood, he skipped off stage and pushed his way through the crowd.

'Hi,' he said cheerily. Sadie smiled, glad to be rescued again from Julie's continuing argument. 'You came then.'

'Janet's minding Joe.'

'Look, I'm sorry I snapped at you last night.' He shuffled on his heels, pushing his fingers through his hair.

'It's forgotten. I'm sorry too.'

Jay could see the edginess returning. That clearly wasn't in her plan for this evening, judging by her rather looser than normal performance on the dancefloor earlier. And he knew which one he'd prefer. So he just smiled.

'You were very good!' she said.

'Thank you!'

'What the hell was that thing in the middle?'

'Oh, did you like that?' He lit up. 'Just a little wake up call, you know. In case anybody's getting bored.'

'Really? Well, I guess it would have that effect. I've never seen so many body parts move so fast!'

'Oh, keep talking. I like this! Hey, would you like to come backstage and tell that to Dave, the singer? He thinks it's bollocks.'

'Well, he would, wouldn't he?' she grinned knowingly.

'Reckon we'll have to get a new one, anyway. He's the one that's bollocks. What d'you reckon?'

'Oh, I see!' Julie swung round.

'Ah, hello Julie,' Jay grinned. Unlike Sadie, he clearly didn't feel the need to be compromised.

Julie glanced at Sadie, standing close to him. 'Oh, I see very clearly now—'

'Oh, belt up Julie, for fuck's sake.' Jay cut in. She opened her mouth to retaliate. 'Shut up. We're all thoroughly sick of your whingeing. And no, we didn't put your little *suggestions* into the format.' Julie looked as if she was about to scream at him. 'Look, he ain't no good, and you're a bloody pain in the arse, so leave it out, will ya?'

Julie stormed off, and Jay just laughed. Sadie had never seen him like this before. But she was not overly fond of Julie, so she joined him.

'Have you—?' Jay began again, but Adam started at the same time.

'Oh, it's the drummer. You were awesome, man.'

'Uh, thanks,' Jay replied, looking up at him, at least six inches.

Adam touched her arm. 'Back for coffee in my room, Sadie?'

'Do you want to come?' she said.

Jay hesitated. 'Can't really. Got to put me kit away.' Besides, he was hardly invited.

'Oh OK, I'd better go, see you...'

And she left him to his inevitable anti-climax.

Performance was like that...

Sadie was surprised to find herself the only one at Adam's. It ruffled her for a moment, but she scorned her discomfort as they sat at opposite sides of the room, talking about Erasmus, Nietzsche and the Victorian Poor Laws.

A pleasant enough end to an unexpected evening, despite its relative normality. But normality was unusual for this particular student. And she was beginning to think she'd like a bit more of it...

18

ADAM

Jay couldn't believe the way he was chucked out of the band the following week. How could the others be so two-faced? Just because Dave owned most of the equipment. Where was their artistic ambition? Well, it was their loss, he *tried* to persuade himself.

But he'd let himself go too far. Created a scene. A lot of unnecessary things were said, on both sides. Now he was without two of his best friends, who refused to speak to him, and without the occupation of rehearsing. Everyone on his course seemed to be working much harder than he was, and for a while, he considered jacking it all in, even though he'd come this far. *Against the odds*, as some might say. Wouldn't that be typical of him to throw his security out of the window yet again? On top of everything else, he couldn't stand the chorus of 'I told you so' echoing venomously around Chorleywood... And what would he do? Where would he go? He couldn't bear the prospect of returning to the parental home, tail between his legs. No, he'd stick it out, and do his best to hold on.

He had been round twice to see Joe, his compensatory light

in all of this. But there'd been no answer on both occasions, and then again, he'd found Joe out on a nursery trip and Sadie at home with Adam. He left sharply. Where was that little boy? He began to resent his absence, and his own apparent dependence on him. He hadn't seen him for over a week, though he'd spotted Sadie a few times, and she always seemed to be with Adam.

And he wondered... Wondered if there was anything between them. It was none of his business, he concluded. But still, he couldn't seem to shake it. He stared at the book, open unread on his lap, alone in his room that night. Yes, he missed her, too. Bugger. Why did he always have to be so intense? It always ended up hurting him in the end...

For Sadie, it was more a matter of events than planning that she found herself spending so much time with the new student. Adam had a lot of catching up to do, having missed the first term entirely, and he seemed to want to do it with her. Anyway, he'd helped her understand a few points of philosophy himself; he was pleasant, intelligent and witty, never involved Joe, and it seemed unheavy enough...

'You have to go, Sadie.' Adam had just returned from two days of open lectures at Birmingham University. They were virtually compulsory for the first-year Humanities students and were being repeated next week. But Sadie couldn't see how that would be possible; there were obviously no creche facilities.

'I could have Joe for the night,' Adam offered breezily. He'd not seen much of the boy, but he seemed alright. It would be easy enough, wouldn't it?

Sadie hesitated. For days. But Adam was so encouraging. And *very* persuasive. Every day...

Adam was taking it slow. Quite clear of his intentions, but he knew she would not be an easy chalk up. Just gentle progress; she wouldn't have noticed yet. Yes, she had a kid. That was way out of his instinctive arena. But he always went for her type. And Sadie also had this incredibly appealing girl/woman face. What he described to his mates in the bar as a 'buy-me-a-lolly-and-fuck-me-face.' But it was obvious he would have to accommodate the kid as well, if he was going to get anywhere near to doing either. So he would. Bare minimum, mind. But this scale of favour must be worth a few rungs up the bedroom ladder, surely...

Oblivious to any agenda, and with time running out, Sadie finally decided it would be alright to leave Joe with Adam. It would only be one night. And Adam seemed *so* keen.

Joe, however, was not. He wanted to come with her. She bribed him on the promise that Adam had a 25-inch screen TV *and* a video recorder! And she'd bring him a present from Birmingham.

Joe was tired, anyway. He'd had a very busy week with one thing and another, and he'd burst his armbands thrashing around in his swimming lesson that afternoon. It was not only his pool tutor who had been exhausted by his usual energetic display. But Sadie knew he would be less trouble for Adam this way; less boisterous.

She was wrong.

19

CHOOSE ME YOU

Joe rolled another car over Adam's table. This was boring. The 'huge' TV sat silent on its stand; the row of video tapes all with incomprehensible names and dark, scary pictures.

He added some sound effects and a bit of chair acrobatics.

'Sit down!' Adam responded, barely looking up from his course notes.

Joe sat on his hands and sulked. That wasn't interesting, either, so he launched a car into the air. Then another; and another.

Adam sighed loudly and slammed his book shut. Clearly, he had even less patience than Janet. He ushered Joe out of the room and took him to the Union cafe for tea.

This, on the other hand, was excessively exciting! Joe was not usually allowed in here. He ordered lots of things and ate hardly any of them. Instead, he ran around the room, looking at everything and talking to everyone, finally sending a tray of crockery crashing to the floor. Adam was asked to leave and billed for the damage.

For a while, Joe was apologetically subdued, allowing

Adam's anger to cool a little, back in the unwelcome quiet of his room. But it was *really* boring now. And something else that Joe could not define. His stomach fizzed, and he felt like crying. No Mr Bellamy, no playmates, no car park, no verbal combat. No Mummy...

He'd just have another little run around the room then.

'Sit down!' Adam ordered, for the umpteenth time.

'I don't want to!'

'You'll do as you're told.'

'I want to go home,' Joe whined.

'Well, that makes two of us.'

'I want my mummy!'

'Sit down!' Adam bellowed as Joe tore round the room again.

'I don't like you!'

'Well, I sure as hell don't like you either!'

Joe began to cry, pushing a pile of papers onto the floor in unfocused defiance and frustration.

'Look what you've done! They were all in order!'

Joe ran to the door and thumped on it. 'I want to go home! I don't like it here. I want to go home!'

'Sit down and shut up!' Adam rifled through his dishevelled papers, but Joe only repeated his screams, the pitch rising higher and higher. 'Look, if you don't shut up...' Adam took a step towards him, but Joe just screamed all the more. 'I said...' he stepped closer.

'Let me out of here! I want to go home!'

Adam grabbed his arms and shook him. 'Shut the fuck up!'

Joe stopped, eyes wide. Then just screamed all the louder, thrashing his arms around in an attempt at release.

'Be quiet!' Adam shouted back, holding his arms so tightly now that Joe cried in pain as much as frustration.

'Let me go. I hate you! I hate you!'

'I won't tell you again!'

Joe surged forward and bit his arm. Adam drew back in surprise, and then in reflex, his hand crashed into Joe's cheek. Joe staggered off balance, but Adam pushed him out of the way and stormed out of the door.

Joe lay on the floor, wailing. Nobody came. He tried to get up. He felt dizzy, so he cried even more. Still nobody came. He pulled open the door and ran out into the night.

He ran one way and then the other, heading for the lights of the Union. There were a few people in the foyer. He ran towards a girl.

'I want my mummy!'

Her boyfriend stepped forward to comfort him. Joe stared at him, backing away. Then he ran again. They went after him, but lost him. Joe ran into the bar. As if hypnotised, he stopped, staring at all the students gathered there.

'Hello little fella,' another man said. Joe stared at him in horror. 'Are you lost?' The man stretched out his hand towards him. And Joe screamed the place down. There were people at the door now. He ran. There was nowhere to go. They were everywhere.

He was everywhere...

Jay strolled into the bar, oblivious, but stopped before the crowd of students gathered around a howling child. Joe was like a caged animal. Hysterical screams merged into nonsensical, uncoordinated words. 'I hate you. I hate you!' Then, 'Daddy, daddy. I hate you. I hate you!'

Jay rushed forward, as everyone looked on helplessly at the screaming boy.

'Joe...'

Joe swung round, and Jay was profoundly disturbed by the

terror in his eyes; a deep bruise forming on his left cheek, his eyes red and puffy from crying. For a moment, he just stared. The boy was a stranger.

'Joe...'

Joe's expression twitched, but remained branded by fear and confusion. Jay stepped forward and knelt by him. He backed away.

'Joe?' Jay was getting more and more disturbed by this. 'It's me...' He edged forward, but Joe ran again. Jay was on his feet instantly. He caught him and swept him off the floor.

'No! No!' Joe thrashed in his arms.

'Joe,' Jay whispered, his mouth to the boy's ear, containing him as best he could without hurting him. But with a particularly violent wriggle, Joe slipped out of his arms. He ran again. Jay was after him immediately, but two men caught him at the door. He screamed even louder. The pleading was pitiful. Jay could feel his own tears welling.

He approached again, gently. 'Joe...'

Once again, the boy turned. He stopped thrashing the two men and stared. He tugged at the arms that held him. They would not let him go. The screaming started up again, but it was not the same. Jay came closer. Joe pulled and pulled, but still they would not let him go.

'Jaaay...!'

'It's OK.' Jay touched one of the men's arms and they released him. And Joe just hurled himself at him. Jay scooped him up, and he sunk around his neck. Holding his head to his shoulder, he rocked him. 'Hey now, it's OK. Everything's alright. You're safe now...' He carried him from the room at once, rocking him slowly, rubbing his back, and gently whispering calm and security.

Joe cried quietly on his shoulder as he walked across the campus to Sadie's room. It was the obvious place to start, but of course there was no answer to his knocks. He was not surprised.

'Where's Mummy?' he gently whispered as they crossed the grass to Sutherland House.

Joe wailed again. 'She's gone. She's left me!'

Jay very much doubted that, but the questioning seemed only to refuel Joe's sobs, so he dropped it to calm him again. In the kitchen, he warmed milk on the stove and wet a tea towel with cold water. Still holding Joe securely to him, he remained silent until they were back in his room. Joe had not moved, clinging to him, his head into his neck.

Jay sat him down on his lap, gently held the cold towel to his bruised cheek, and helped him drink a little of the warm milk.

'No more tears?'

Joe shook his head. Still traces of fear, but his face now clouded with confusion more than anything else. He held on tightly to Jay's encircling arm.

'Where has Mummy gone then?' The calmer silence prompted Jay to gently open enquiries again. And Joe was a little more rational in his reply this time.

'Birmingham.'

'Oh? What for?'

'A course.'

'I see.' He did not.

'She's left me,' Joe whimpered. And then, as if realising what he had just said, the tears sprang again. 'She's gone! She doesn't want me either!'

Jay pulled him closer. 'Sssh now, you know that's nonsense.' But he pondered on that word, 'either'. Joe had been screaming 'daddy' in the bar. Surely not. Surely it could not have been his father who did this to him? All sorts of possibilities flooded Jay's mind. Perhaps he's returned unexpectedly?

But he's 'unknown', isn't he? Although he knew that blank space on the birth certificate could mean a hundred things. None of them good.

'Who did Mummy leave you with?' Despite the gentleness of the enquiry, Joe's just started crying again. He could get no sense out of him. 'Was it your daddy?' he ventured, so tentatively.

'No. He hates me. They all hate me!'

This was clearly getting nowhere. Jay tried another approach. 'Who then? They'll be wondering where you are.'

Joe stiffened. 'Don't take me back there. Please. Please let me stay with you. I want to stay with you. You won't hurt me, will you? You won't go away,' tumbled out of his mouth.

Jay blinked back his own tears. 'No, you'll stay with me now. You'll be alright with me.'

Joe's clenched fists uncurled, and his head dropped back to Jay's chest.

But there was one more question that had to be asked.

'Where did you get that bruise, Joe?'

'He hit me,' Joe replied, fists tightening again.

'*Who* hit you?'

'Adam,' Joe concluded simply, as if he should have known.

So it fitted together a little better now. Sadie had to go on a course and she'd left him with Adam. Not quite as sordid as it might have seemed. Even so, he'd driven him into this state and thumped him one too. Jay could feel the rage boiling. But for now, he could also feel Joe's exhaustion, and he had to work out what he could do.

'I think you should be in bed,' he smiled, handing him the rest of his warm milk. Joe drank it obediently, and Jay lifted him up.

Joe momentarily panicked. 'Don't take me back there!'

'I won't,' he whispered softly. 'You stay here with me tonight, OK?'

Joe nodded and, for the first time, there was a hint of a smile. 'Where will I sleep? You haven't got a beanbag.'

'Well, just 'cos I love ya, you can have the bed, alright?'

Joe giggled. 'Where will you sleep?'

'I'll sleep on the floor.'

Joe's eyebrows knitted. 'There's room!' He pointed to the mattress that lay untidily on the floor.

'Yeah, I suppose there is.'

'Sometimes I sleep with Mummy.' Joe lost his smile then. 'Will she come back?'

'Of course she will!'

And Joe's smile, finally, secured. Mummy's coming back. Jay said so. And he was here now...

Tucked up in bed in one of Jay's T-shirts, Joe sleepily drawled, 'Are you coming to bed now?'

Jay glanced at his watch. Half past ten. 'Well, I might as well...' There would be no *plant cellular process responses to environmental stressors* tonight. Only his own...

Joe immediately snuggled up to him as he turned off the bedside lamp. Curled into his chest, heavy eyes closing, he muttered, 'I love you, Jay. Don't go away.'

Jay's eyes pricked with the tears he had been holding since he'd walked into the Union bar. 'I won't,' he whispered. 'I love you, too.' He kissed the boy's hair and closed his eyes to sleep.

Only he knew he would not manage much peace. He hated Adam with a passion that almost matched the warmth he felt for this little kid who had just barged into his life one day. He only hoped he could avoid coming into contact with him again. It would be difficult to contain himself...

. . .

Joe was much chirpier the next morning, and he held onto Jay's hand with utter trust as they tramped the campus grounds to the nursery. Promising to pick him up at twelve-thirty, Jay left for his class – after he had run back to his room and stripped the bed. Joe had weed all over it. A fact Jay had instinctively not drawn to the boy's attention that morning. *Wasn't he a bit old for that?* Jay was still learning. He could only guess that, despite the return of Joe's natural smile, bladder control was an unconscious casualty of his continuing distress. Jay was making this up as he went along, of course. He had no textbook for this one, and absolutely no experience.

Well, he was getting it now...

He was late for practical, and then had to stay behind for a few minutes to finish an assessed experiment. And when he arrived at the nursery, breathless and running, there was no sign of Joe. Mrs Turnbull told him they'd had a note from Sadie that he was in the care of a friend today, Adam Burrell.

'Fuck!' Jay turned and sprinted out the door again.

He ran all the way to the Humanities block and scoured the place for class lists to find Adam's details. No luck. He ran across campus to the Senate House, bursting into the Admissions Office and begging and blathering until he'd come away with Adam's room number. Then he hared back across the campus, up the stairs three at a time at Sinclair House.

As soon as he reached Adam's corridor, he could hear Joe.

'I don't want to! Let me out. I hate you...! Jay! I want Jay...'

And with that last desperate call of his name ringing in his ears, Jay hammered on the door.

'Who the—?'

He had already pushed past Adam into the room. Joe scrambled from the floor and jumped into his arms.

'And you so much as even speak to him, *ever* again, and I'll smash your fucking face in!' Jay could barely restrain himself from doing so now. But holding Joe to him, he swept out of the room.

'Where were you? Where *were* you?' Joe sobbed.

'I'm sorry Joe, I got held up.'

'He just came storming in and took me away. He was very cross. He didn't know where I was. He says Mummy will be very angry with me. But I don't want to go there! I want to stay with you!'

'And you will. Everything'll be alright now. And Mummy won't be angry with you. Not at all. You can stay with me until she gets back.'

'She'll be back this evening,' Joe said, instantly cheered by all these things.

'Are you sure?'

'Yes. Adam said.'

'OK.' Jay pushed open the door to his room. 'Well, now,' he smiled at last. 'How would my special little boy like to go into town for lunch?'

'Oh, yeah!' The immediate enthusiasm was as much for the accolade as the treat. Joe loved to be Jay's special little boy. 'Can we go to Wimpy?'

'Course we can.' Jay put him down and hunted for some money. 'You'll need a coat.'

Joe fished in his pocket. 'I stole our key off Adam!'

'Top work!' Jay winked. 'Right then, let's go and get it, shall we...?'

It was a cheering afternoon in Chichester, in its simplicity and ease. Joe devoured his Wimpy, and they went round a few shops, hand in hand, chatting randomly. Jay bought a couple of cheap little toys, which Joe was delighted with. But while he searched the racks of the record shop, he temporarily forgot his responsibilities, until the manager dragged Joe up behind him with the words, 'Would you kindly control your son or take him out of this shop?'

Jay did so instantly, forgetting his search. Joe was meekly apologetic, but it hadn't even entered his mind to be cross. It just reminded him, once again, that Joe needed constant supervision. That's what real guardianship was about.

And now... he was ready for it.

The shop manager's exact words didn't really occur to Jay until the man at the ice cream van blatantly mistook the boy for his own as well.

Joe was quiet as he sat on the bus stop bench with his ice cream, his eyes fixed ahead of him. 'Everyone thinks you're my daddy,' he said, beneath a face full of Mr Whippy. His tone put Jay at an immediate loss for any kind of response at all. He glanced down at the boy, Joe looking searchingly back at him. His wide, open face, eyes the deepest blue, just like his own; he could see why, a bit. But that wasn't the point. People's mistake only brought to Joe's mind his father's absence in his life.

And all Jay could think of to say was, 'I'm sorry,' which he knew was lost on him.

'Why haven't I got a daddy?'

Jay looked down at him again. Joe's eyes were moist. He put his arm around him. 'You have,' he whispered.

'That's what Mummy says,' Joe replied, eyebrows knitted. He never really understood this. 'She says that he's far away and I might never see him, but I've got one...'

He was so openly searching for answers that Jay nodded.

Joe's nose wrinkled in confused indignation. 'But what's the point of having one if I never see him?'

Jay sighed. 'There isn't any point, Joe. It's just the way it is for some little boys and girls. You just love your mummy. She'll take good care of you.' He hoped that would do, as he gave the boy a gentle squeeze. Really, he didn't have a clue what to say.

Joe nodded distantly. But it clearly wasn't the end of the matter.

'Does Mummy choose my daddy?' he piped up again a moment later. Jay was equally stumped for an appropriate answer for a five-year-old. And the questions were getting harder and harder.

So he just decided to be honest. 'That's usually how it happens, Joe.' But Joe still looked so pitifully sad, he added, 'And maybe someday she'll choose you another daddy. One that you can see.'

Joe instantly brightened. 'Yeah?'

'Yeah,' Jay patted his hand.

'Can I choose him?'

'No, Joe. It doesn't work like that. Mummy has to do it.'

'Oh...'

The bus arrived. Jay paid, and they took their seats.

Joe looked up.

'Do you think if I asked her really nicely, she'd choose me you...?'

20

TRUST?

Jay wondered how he had ever made that bus journey home. He felt his responses to Joe's questions were completely inadequate, but he knew nothing. He had to be so cautious. However much it filled his heart to hear Joe's wish, he knew the ground he was treading was quicksand.

But they got on so well, Joe mirroring everything he did. Making tea, Jay put on a sparkly party bowler hat, a remnant from Joe's birthday, adding a pair of sunglasses and having Joe in fits of giggles as he boogied across the kitchen floor holding a wooden spoon as a microphone, singing Blues Brothers classics. Taking his hand in an exaggerated dance, Joe copied his every move. Not even a knock on the door could still them. Jay shimmied across the room, jiving with Joe as he kicked it open. 'Enter the madhouse!'

Janet stepped in and stared at them. Jay hadn't stopped and when he did, he just grinned at her, wooden spoon microphone in hand.

'Uh, I heard some noise and just thought I'd check that everything's OK...?'

'Oh yeah, we're fine! Bit crazy, eh Joe? But they haven't come to take us away just yet.'

Despite Joe's giggling, Janet surveyed him closely. 'Sadie didn't say anything about—' Her eyes widened at the bruise on his cheek. 'Sure you're OK, Joe?'

Jay stopped his larking instantly. 'That was not me.' But not wanting to return Joe's consciousness to any of that, he grinned again. '*This* is me!' And he swept Joe off the floor, swinging him round and into his arms. 'Really, everything's cool, eh Joe?' he wiggled his sunglasses, Eric Morecambe style.

'Yeah, everything's cool!' Joe copied, bouncing in the crook of his arm.

Janet glanced between them, both flushed and brimming with fun. And there was that look again...

But there were more pressing matters now. 'Shit, the beans!' Jay darted to the cooker to peal the glutinous mess off the bottom of the pan. 'Oh well, can't have everything...' He chucked the pan in the sink and reached for another can.

'Shit, the beans!' Joe gleefully repeated.

Jay looked mock guiltily at Janet. 'Oops.'

She raised her eyebrows at him. 'Well then, if you're sure...'

'Absolutely. Nothing to worry about. Just a slight change of plan. I'll stay with Joe until Sadie gets back.'

And Janet finally conceded and left them to their horseplay...

Tucking Joe into his beanbag later that evening, with a temporary replacement pair of drumsticks, Jay stroked his hair. 'OK?'

Joe nodded. 'When's Mummy coming?'

'Soon.'

'Where are you going to sleep?'

'I'll wait until Mummy comes home, then I'll go back to my room.'

'Oh,' Joe whined. 'Can't you stay? There's room in there for two,' he gestured to the mattress. 'I've tried it.'

Ooh, nice thought... An unbidden and rather vivid image flashed across Jay's mind then. It was quite stunning in its technicolour entanglement, and Jay found himself distressingly aroused. Where did *that* come from? And when the hell did it become a nice thought...?

'I don't think Mummy would like that very much,' Jay coughed.

'Yes, she would. She gets cold, you know.'

'You just get to sleep, you,' he poked him playfully. Joe giggled and reached for his usual goodnight kiss. And within minutes he was fast asleep, as Jay settled himself, and his trousers, at the table on the other side of the room.

Opening the door, her coat already half off, Sadie stopped. Her eyes roamed between Joe, asleep in the dark, and Jay sitting in the dim light, staring over a Noddy book on the table.

Jay could not read her reaction, but he had a fair idea of potential based on past performances. *How to play this?* He hadn't really arrived at a suitable conclusion in his couple of hours of quiet solitude.

'Hello...?'

'Hi,' he whispered, getting up. 'Look, I know you'll be wondering what I'm doing here,' he hurried, before she had a chance to speak. Or hit the roof. 'Let me make you a coffee, there's some explaining to be done...' However this should be, he wanted it told in a slow logical sequence. Yet he fully expected to be read the riot act at that moment.

Nothing came.

'Is anything wrong?' Sadie dropped her bag and went to Joe. 'Is he alright?'

'Yeah, yeah, he's fine. Just this minute got him off actually,' Jay lied, but it did the trick as she withdrew without disturbing him. She joined him at the kettle. He could see the concern in her eyes.

'Look, I'm sorry if you didn't want to see me here. It was a bit unavoidable. Come and sit down.' He handed her a mug of coffee. 'Course go alright?'

'Yeah, yeah fine,' she waved away such trivia.

'OK,' Jay sighed. 'I know. Well, I guess I'll just tell it like I found it... Last night I went into the bar and found Joe there—'

'*What?*'

Jay hurried on. 'He was on his own, screaming and crying and rushing about. It... well, it was a bit disturbing, actually. He wouldn't let anyone near him. He eventually ran to me, but— well, he needed some calming down...' He paused; her face was disassembling, in utter devastation. He breathed in and pushed on, hoping he could get to the bit where he might help piece it together again. 'He told me, when he'd calmed a bit, that you were away and you'd left him with that Adam bloke. But he pleaded with me not to take him back there. Not that I would have, not after the state he was left in—'

'Where was he? What happened?'

Jay put his hand over hers. They both glanced at Joe; she quietened, and he withdrew.

'I don't really know what happened. But something did, that's for sure. Joe was hysterical and—' he stopped. Was there really any point ladling it on? The look on her face now was enough indication of what this was doing to her. 'Well, he stayed with me last night. I took him to nursery this morning, but I was late getting back and Adam had already picked him up. Anyway, I went to his room and Joe was screaming and crying again, so I'm afraid I just carried him out of there. We let ourselves in. We've been out most of the day.'

'Oh, God,' Sadie's head dropped into her hands. 'How could I have done that?'

'It's not your fault—'

'I'll kill him. What did he do to him? I'll bloody kill him!'

'I don't know what happened,' Jay repeated. 'But... well, you ought to know. He's been talking about his dad rather a lot. I mean, I've never heard him bring it up before.'

Sadie glared at him. 'He hardly ever does.'

'I'm sorry...'

'Jesus!' She finally broke, thumping the table and getting to her feet. For a moment she was unsteady, then she went straight to Joe. Jay sighed in anticipation.

'Sadie, uh—'

'Christ almighty! What is this?' She stared across the room at him. He slowly shook his head. It wasn't necessary; she knew instinctively that the deep colouring on Joe's cheek had not come from him.

'Joe. Oh, God... Joe,' she cried, pulling him into her arms, and trying, but failing, to kerb her emotion.

'Mummy?' he drawled. 'I'm glad you woke me up.'

'Oh, Joe,' she cried, rocking him securely. 'I'm sorry, Joe. I'm so sorry...' She pushed him away to take a better look. Sniffing back her tears, she touched his face. 'Does that hurt?'

'A bit...' And then, as if reminded of the whole episode, he grabbed her arm. 'Don't send me there again. Please don't send me there. I thought you'd left me. I thought you'd gone!'

'Oh, Joe,' she whispered, pulling him back into her arms. 'I'll never leave you. *Never*. And I'll never send you there again. I'm so sorry.'

'Jay'll have me. Jay loves me,' Joe continued, with barely any letup in the vice tightening around her heart. She had to stifle her sobs.

'Yes,' she said, looking to the other side of the room. 'He does.'

'And I love him, too!'

'I know you do.'

'We've had lots of fun. I'll tell you about it in the morning. And you can tell me about your course.'

Sadie smiled, a small, broken smile, at her adult-child; forced into this 'grown-up' world of betrayal, and abuse, and abandonment... 'Yes, we'll think of a treat tomorrow, shall we?'

'Yey!' Joe clapped his hands and Sadie lowered him back into his beanbag. 'I'm glad you're home, Mummy,' he concluded and closed his eyes to sleep again.

Sadie sat staring at him for a moment, until her crying became too audible and she moved away.

Jay was disturbed by this. What could he do with it? It tore at him to see her stumble in the middle of the room, covering her face with her hands and muttering, 'Oh God, I don't...' then trailing away. He could not bear to sit and watch it a moment longer... He got up and tentatively put his hands on her arms.

'Don't blame yourself. It's not your fault.'

'You can see the damage it's done!' she cried. It was true; Adam had left his mark far more than a bruise on Joe's cheek.

'Oh, I can't... I don't know what...'

'Don't upset yourself,' Jay continued softly.

'How much more can he take?' she pleaded.

'How much more can *you* take?'

And as her tears flowed freely now, he could do no other but pull her to him and close his arms around her. As he had done with Joe. Willing her calm, securing her. He felt so deeply for what she was putting herself through. Even so, showing his support in this way was not without its anxiety, considering her past responses. Yet she turned her head on his shoulder and clung to him; his grip tightening, attempting to contain this despair.

But as soon as she regained a hint of calm, she pulled away from him, tossing her head back. 'I've got to go and get Joe's things.'

Jay sighed. There it goes again... But he would remain with this, and continue to do what he could. 'Let me go. You're upset. You'll only upset yourself more.'

'I can look after myself, thank you!'

'Oh, OK, OK...' Jay held his hands up and stepped back. There really wasn't anything more he could do, in the face of this repeated rejection.

Sadie caught his raised hand. 'I'm sorry. I'm sorry... I... I'm grateful to you, I really am. I don't know what would have happened without you...'

Jay was intrigued by her. He could see so clearly that any length of rope she was giving him was so terribly hard for her. To express any kind of need, or dependence, wrapped the rope around her neck and left her choking. Yet she could freely take his hand like this. One so obviously subconscious; the other a frightened, observant conscious, building the barricades, firing the defence. Occasionally one would overstep the other, like when she had begun to open up to him the other day. And just now, when she let him hold her. Then the tables would instantly turn; like when she backed away from his hold on her just now. And at this moment, perhaps realising the gentle movement of her thumb over his fingers, she dropped his hand as suddenly as she had taken it...

'Would you go for me?' she ventured. 'I don't think I even want to speak to him ever again.'

Jay nodded. 'Of course...'

When he returned a few minutes later, Sadie was sitting at the table, staring across the room at Joe.

'One pair of pyjamas, one toothbrush, two drumsticks, some clothes, four cars, Cortina - yellow - and various bits of literature.' Jay dropped the stuff on the table.

'Great, thanks,' she replied, scanning the pile and trying to remember if it was all there.

'Well, I suppose I better be going,' he concluded, pushing his hands into his pockets and rocking on his heels. 'I've got some packing to do meself.'

'Where're you going?' Sadie looked up immediately and kicked herself for being bothered.

'Just to my brother's in Chesham for the weekend. It's his birthday. He's 40 tomorrow, so they're having a bit of a do.'

'Oh,' Sadie smiled faintly. 'That'll be fun.'

'I doubt it,' Jay muttered.

'Oh? Why not?'

'It's a long story. I'll bore you with it one day.' He shrugged and made for the door.

'Look, Jay...' she stopped him. 'You know... Thanks.'

'Anytime,' he smiled more securely then, and left.

The warmth Sadie felt towards him, as the door quietly closed, was just another alien feeling to her. Deeply upset by the happenings of the last couple of days, trials like this had always made her withdraw a little more – herself and Joe and the unit that they were; cementing another brick in her defensive wall. She'd never had anyone who shared any of the burden with her. There'd never been anyone she really wanted to, either. But Jay *had* shared it that day. He had been there. He had rescued and cared for her son. And not out of mere obligation, but out of... *love...*?

She did not know why it had come to be like this. This stranger that Joe had latched onto so readily, who he said he loved, and who had returned that love. The cold finger of anxiety threatened to chill her again. Above all, she had to protect her son, and such an attachment carried with it great risk. But today, yesterday, she had failed to protect him. The fact that Jay so evidently had, must surely suggest that risk was worth taking...?

21

OBNOXIOUS UNCONTROLLABLE

If Sadie found herself more optimistic than she might have from this trial, she still maintained a heavy responsibility and realism. She could hardly not do. Especially when Joe woke up crying in the middle of the night. He'd wet the bed; and he knew it this time. Although Sadie could not know that Jay had been forced into a similar trip to the launderette the day before.

But she didn't need the textbook; she quickly sorted him out and took him into bed with her, where he calmed enough to resume his sleep. But that she could do the same. The guilt was crushing...

For the next few nights, Joe crawled into her bed in the middle of the night. He was disturbed at nursery, too, being unusually obstructive and sulky. He was better when he was with her, although he had taken to following her everywhere, clinging to her and getting upset when she wasn't near. And when her voice raised on the sixth or seventh repeated request to tidy the table for tea, he swung round and screamed, 'Shut the fuck up!' But it was his response to her angry look that followed, as she marched over to deposit him in the Calm

Down Corner, that distressed her far more. He flinched. And she couldn't leave him there. She just enclosed him in her arms and sat down with him quietly for a while. She never heard that phrase again. As if she didn't know where it came from. And that flinch? It sickened her.

Joe's clinginess over the next week inevitably made practical tasks more difficult. But she knew where it came from, and if she had put him there, then she would give him whatever he needed. So she skipped a few lectures, cancelled any babysitting, and stayed with him whenever he was not in nursery. For that time, he would have her undiluted attention.

When she finally shared a class with Adam on Thursday, the confrontation was unavoidable. He defended himself by saying that Joe was an uncontrollable, obnoxious brat who needed teaching a good lesson. That was a very raw nerve with Sadie. In her heart, she knew it was not true, yet any criticism of Joe was a wound to herself. Unfortunately for Adam, he got the worst of a very sharp tongue that morning; Sadie's usual weapon of defence... But she ended the morning in tears in the solitude of her room.

She forced composure to keep her distress from Joe that afternoon, but he did anyway seem to be recovering balance. They were in the middle of their tea when Jay appeared at the door. 'Hello,' he said, with noticeable reserve.

'Hi! Come in!' She stepped aside immediately.

Jay was momentarily stumped into immobility.

'Here,' he said, proffering a small bunch of wildflowers.

'Jaaay!' Joe powered over and jumped on him.

'And you, young sir...'

'Thanks!' Joe ripped off the bag to find a self-destructing car. It was out on the floor within seconds.

'Oh, Jay...' Sadie knew how expensive they were. He put his hand over her mouth with a knowing grin.

'Thank you, these are lovely,' she conceded, depositing the flowers in a coffee mug and putting them on the table, where they brightened the room. 'We were just having tea. Have you eaten?'

'Sorry, bad timing. No, actually. I've only just got back. Been in a field for the last couple of days.'

'Oh?'

'Field trip. Only this time, they were literal. I ask you, in February!'

'March,' she grinned.

'Oh, yeah, it is now,' he laughed.

'I haven't got much, but you're welcome to what's left of the spag bol.'

There was an unfamiliar looseness about her, which Jay had only glimpsed before.

'Don't go to any trouble.'

'It's no trouble,' she replied, lighting the hob and replacing the saucepan. 'Finish your tea, Joe, then you can play, alright?'

'Oh, but—'

'After tea, Joe.'

Joe dragged himself up to the table, leaving the open box on the floor. He powered through his meal with a higher purpose in mind now, crashing the fork down and looking up at his mother expectantly. 'Go on then,' she smiled. Jay laughed. Their interaction never ceased to amuse him. And once again, he admired her for Joe's combination of childish exuberance and adult good manners.

'Where was this field, then?' Now they had been relieved of Joe's noisy chatter and plate-scraping, Sadie appeared quite open to a little adult conversation.

'Little place just north of Llanelli,' Jay smiled. 'Fu— sorry, *very* cold.'

Sadie grinned at his efforts with the language, but Joe cut

short any further exchange. She might have known. But, for once, it was not her that was at the receiving end of his demands.

'Hey, Jay,' he squealed. 'I can't see where the pieces go!'

Jay shrugged, shovelling the last forkful of food into his mouth. 'Duty calls. That was great, thanks.' And he was on his knees instructing Joe on the workings of his new toy.

Sadie looked at them both, deep in consultation. And she had to shake herself back to the business of clearing away...

Pretty soon, the toy car was hurtling across the room, exploding into every piece of furniture, with Joe giggling in delight at the destruction. And when she'd finished the washing up, they all had a go.

'Come on, Joe, bedtime.' Despite his enthusiasm for his new toy, Sadie could see him struggling to keep his eyes open.

'But it's Thursday!'

Sadie sighed with an accepting smile. 'Alright then. Put it on.'

Joe scrambled away to the TV.

'Top of the Pops,' she explained to Jay.

He laughed. 'Isn't he a little young for the charts?'

'My fault, I fear. Now he loves it. I usually let him stay up a bit longer on Thursdays to watch it...'

So with the fire on close to them, they lined up on the mattress in front of the TV. Joe climbed onto Jay's lap, glued to the action, wiggling about to anything that particularly took his fancy, attempting to keep time with his drumsticks. And this week, he had Jay's direction, holding his hands and slapping them onto his legs in slightly more timely accompaniment. With a little flourish here and there. Joe was enthralled.

Nevertheless, he was barely awake by the end of the programme. Jay watched as Sadie moved the beanbag to his sleeping corner, put him to bed, turned the TV down and brought more coffee. There had been no question about his staying. There was some gear changed here. And he loved it.

'Thanks,' he said, accepting a mug. 'Thanks for letting me stay.'

'I suppose you expected me not to even let you in.'

'I didn't mean it like that...' Sadie looked sideways at him. 'Yeah, I did, didn't I?'

She shook her head, reflecting his wry smile, and found herself without her usual pricked defences, for once.

'How's it been this week, then?' he asked, now that he could.

Sadie sighed. 'He's been upset. Sleeping badly, very clingy, not behaving in nursery, that sort of thing.'

'Oh...' Jay hadn't really considered that. This child business was still rather new. But now that she had said it, it seemed entirely obvious. Just like the laundered sheets.

'He's getting better. I think he's coming out of it.'

'Yeah, he seems alright to me.'

'He's pleased to see you,' Sadie replied and was seen to regret it. Jay lost her for a moment. But then, as if a current had shocked her, she sparked back into life.

'I saw Adam today, for the first time.'

'Oh, yeah? How was it, bad?'

She nodded. 'He said a lot of things about Joe. And me. Apparently, I am a "prick-teasing little tart" and he only feigned interest in my son to get into my knickers.'

'He *what*...? That... that...' Jay spluttered.

'It doesn't matter,' she lied. 'Wanker.'

'Too fucking right!' But Jay could see her agitation. He misunderstood it. 'Please, don't let that upset you... I could kill him, really...'

'Oh, I don't care about that.' Still, that was not entirely

true, but she had far greater concerns. As usual, though, she needed the prompt.

'What then?'

'Oh, it... it was all about Joe, mostly,' she muttered, pulling at her fingers.

'Yeah? And what gems of wisdom did he have about Joe an' all?'

'He said he was uncontrollable and obnoxious and... well, a whole lot of things...'

'Oh, yeah?'

'I don't know. I get so paranoid about it sometimes.'

'About what? What people think of Joe?'

'Yeah, I guess,' she sighed. 'It's my responsibility. It rests on me. Far more than anything I would care to do. Particularly in this place. In this place, anybody can be a prick-teasing little tart. Not everybody can be uncontrollable and obnoxious brats.'

Jay took in her deeply anxious expression and felt an overwhelming need to attend to it. 'Hey, you're not going to go believing that kind of rubbish, are you?'

'I know he can be a handful. People can't be expected to tolerate it.'

'Bullshit! He's just a kid. He most certainly *isn't* obnoxious, and he's *definitely* controllable.'

'So you see it.'

'What do you mean?'

'I mean, he's a little kid that you see sometimes. One who, for some reason, has latched onto you. You get it good.'

'You mean I only see him when he's bright and cheerful and angelic? When deep down he's a neurotic little beast?'

Sadie glared at him. This was where he got thrown out then. He'd trodden on the live wire again.

But no, he was going to reason with her... 'I mean, come off it, Sadie. Nobody's saying they've got your job, but I've seen Joe good, I've seen him bad, I've seen him hysterical with fright and insecurity, and I've seen him just plain naughty.'

'You don't know anything.'

'I know just about as much as I can figure out for myself. What more is a person supposed to know? And what the hell are you trying to prove?' He paused to regain his point. 'The question was about Joe's behaviour. And I'm telling you, he is a very well-behaved kid. Now get off this guilt. It'll run you into the ground.'

Sadie stared at him. 'Guilt?'

'Oh, you know it...' But her expression demanded more. 'No, I'm not going to get myself thrown out again,' he said, refusing to respond to it. Then he sighed. 'Would you like me to leave?'

Sadie shuffled uncomfortably, before mumbling, 'No...'

And Jay regained his sensitivity a little at that. He knew he had a habit of 'cutting the crap' as he called it, but he also knew that he could hit too hard sometimes.

'Sadie, I understand your worries. You may or may not believe that anybody can come close to understanding what it's really like for you. I don't suppose I ever will. But, just on this point: Joe is a credit to you. You can be proud of him, and of yourself. Whatever has been, *now* you can respect yourself for that... I know I do,' he added pointedly. Sadie was looking straight at him. She had a most penetrating gaze sometimes. 'And that's all I'm going to say on the matter.'

She slowly nodded. 'Thank you.'

'You accepted that?' he joked. 'I'm proud of you!'

A tiny smile broke through her sadness, and right now, he felt close to her. He was getting through. She was a hard nut to crack, but he could see how tremendously vulnerable she could be – the nature to match the face – and this both warmed and alarmed him. For a moment, he couldn't bear the idea of her being hurt by comments like Adam's. By anything, in fact. Since when did he look beyond his own hurt?

Let's face it, there was enough of that...

Sadie sipped her coffee in silence, the small sense of calm she had glimpsed a moment ago spiritedly debating with the right and wrong of accepting Jay's reassurance, and what that might mean for her own strength and independence.

But realising that it was a battle that was becoming equally armoured, she slapped her thighs and changed the subject. 'So, how was your brother's birthday, then?'

'Huh...' Jay shrugged with a humourless smile. 'Eventful.' And, unusually for him, there was no more.

'Oh?' Sadie prompted in what she hoped was a reflection of his own encouragement.

'I'm a rich guy now, you know. So no worrying about expensive toys, OK...? Well, it's only five thousand quid, but it's kinda nice. Won't buy me luxury for the rest of me life, but might just tickle me for a month or two...'

'So...? What happened?' she continued to grease the unusually stubborn lock.

'Inheritance, sort of... You wanna hear all this crap?'

'Yes,' she replied immediately.

'Right,' he laughed with uncharacteristic tension. 'So, when I was 18, my Nan died and left us both four grand. My brother was kind of trustee of both shares. He's quite a bit older than me. At the time, my Nan didn't think much of my ability to look after four thousand quid. She was probably right. So she put in her will that it could only be released "when Jason was responsible." Her very words. Of course it's been at the discretion of my brother, hasn't it? When, or if, he ever regarded me as responsible...'

'And...?'

'Yeah, well, I'm 26 now. I've stuck this thing for a year and a half, stopped shoving things up me nose and getting banged up for smashing stuff. I guess he reckons I can handle it now... He's been a long time realising it. Even now...' he sighed, shaking his head.

'What is it?'

'He's been under a lot of pressure from the solicitors. He doesn't really think I should have it. Think he reckons I've just been on a five-year holiday from being an arsehole, and any day now, this dormant shithead's gonna re-emerge to prey on society.' The tone was mocking, but the hurt pulsed through. 'He's wrong. He's always been wrong. You know...?' And suddenly he was quite animated. 'He said he watched me for the three days I was there, and he doesn't like what he sees. He sees this respectful bloke, not really speaking until spoken to, not getting out of line, and he says to himself – this isn't my brother Jason, he's in some high security prison by now. Or he thinks this is some elaborate con trick to secure enough cash to keep dear brother in acid for a few weeks. He checked my sleeping. He rolled up my sleeves. The bastard even planted five-pound notes around the house!'

Jay glanced over at Joe, realising he had allowed his voice to rise way above a whisper. 'I'm sorry...' He rubbed his face with his hand, and Sadie could feel the vibes of frustration and anger coming from him.

'What *did* you do?' she ventured.

'What, you mean to earn this sparkling reputation?'

'I don't mean to pry, if you don't want to talk about it.'

'Oh, it's not as bad as he'd make out. It's probably not as bad as I'd make out either... Oh,' he sighed. 'Yes, it is. Worse...'

He seemed so distant suddenly. It distressed her. She said nothing, but her quiet, open expression invited him to elaborate.

'Just one or two things that sicken me, even now... But I've left all that behind,' he waved it away with a wholly failed smile. 'I just got involved with this really heavy gang. I'd been, what my parents would say, "going off the rails" for a year or two. But this gang beat it all. They had various initiation rites for a start. Of course, I was completely unsuitable – 18 years old, still a virgin and never been inside. "The Bastard Awards" they called them. Bronze, Silver, Gold and Platinum. I spent six months in prison for my Bronze...' He turned his head away. 'But I only made it to Silver. I guess I bottled after that one. It made me sick. Really regretted it. Couldn't handle it...'

And now he looked really distant, as if the memory burned him. A place he no longer had the stomach to visit. He slapped his thighs and hurried back towards the present. 'I didn't stay long after that. And I've *really* tried to leave it all behind. Just seems my family doesn't want me to. As if I can't punish myself enough on my own... Oh, but—' he screwed up his face. 'No, sorry, I've gone on far too long already.'

'Jay, it's really OK. Please just say it.'

'It's... just... there's so much inside of me, so much spirit, so much life. But they were right about me, in the gang. I never belonged. Oh yeah, of course I went overboard a bit to try to prove that I did. But I got so much else in here,' he tapped the side of his head. 'So much energy. But it keeps colliding with these great masses of hurt and guilt and inhibition. And it just drives me crazy sometimes. I'm just discovering things in me that I can use, and all the time I'm ruining it, slapping myself in the face, or having it done for me, so it's never right.' He stopped and sighed again. 'And if you've sat through that without thinking I'm just fucking bonkers—'

'Oh, stop it. You're as bad as me.' But she didn't really know what came next. 'I'm sorry, Jay,' she eventually plumped for. 'I'm sorry that you've gone through all that.'

'Oh, God!' Suddenly, he was horrified.

'What?'

'I know what you're thinking now. This guy's nuts! What kind of bloke is this to trust with my son? Jesus, I have a big mouth. And that's another thing...'

Sadie looked at him, pulling at his fingers on his lap.

'I'm not like... I'm... Oh, what's the use? You'll think what you choose.'

'Well then, I choose to think no such thing. You're one of the least crazy people I know. You're straight, down to earth and painfully honest. I can see you're in alien territory when you try to complicate yourself.' Sadie's response was unusually immediate and candid, but she pulled back. 'I'm sorry, it's none of my business.'

Jay stared at her. 'Of course it's your business. I've chewed your ear off all evening, haven't I? You're so right. How come you're always so bloody right?'

Sadie snorted. 'I wish that were true.'

Jay looked at his watch. 'Look, it's getting on. I better let you get some rest.' He shuffled to the edge of the mattress. 'I appreciate this evening, I really do. I guess you realised I needed to do some talking.'

'Well, I certainly needed to do some listening...'

22

APPROPRIATE ROLE MODEL

'We just came over to say you don't have to bother babysitting this afternoon,' Sadie said at Janet's door. 'Jay's taking him.'

'Oh,' Janet responded, peculiarly.

'What?'

'Sadie, are you really sure about him?'

'Jay? Yeah. I think so.' It was getting like that. But Janet did not look convinced, and Sadie was getting a little irritated by these looks and guarded comments. 'What is it?'

Janet glanced cautiously down at Joe. 'There's some biscuits on the side, Joe. Why don't you go and have one?'

Joe ambled across her room to generously help himself to several.

'Look, Sadie, while you were away last week, couldn't help notice that Joe was a bit disturbed. Don't know what went on, but I went over to check and he didn't look too good. There was a big bruise on his face and— Well, you must have noticed...'

'Of course I noticed.'

Sadie was more than irritated by now. She was not at all sure if Janet was expressing genuine concern or whether she was just after some story, as usual. She never could be sure with Janet. But now she apparently wanted Sadie to know that Jay had been left alone with Joe for some considerable time and was she quite sure that the two were not related?

'I am absolutely positive, Janet. I really appreciate your concern, but it was actually Jay that prevented anything worse happening. I don't need to give you any details. It's kind of you to be concerned, but Joe is very fond of him, and I'm beginning to think that is not such a bad thing.' Really, these admissions were getting easier.

But they didn't seem to be quite so persuasive to Janet.

'I suppose so, then. If you're sure you know him *quite well enough*,' she said, with her over-the-garden-fence conspiracy face. 'Look, I know what you're like, so I ought to tell you.' She paused to take in the inevitable curtain of concern that immediately drew over Sadie's face.

'Tell me what?'

'Well, when I popped in while you were away, he was swinging Joe round, wearing a party hat and sunglasses and singing into a wooden spoon.'

Sadie stared at her. Her gossipy friend seemed to be inviting some kind of outburst.

'Really?'

Janet nodded earnestly and Sadie could barely contain herself from laughing her way out of the door. She called Joe over instead. He uncurled himself from the curtain and trotted back, spraying biscuit crumbs as he went.

'Joe, do you remember when Janet came round when I was away? When Jay was here?'

'Yes,' he replied.

'What were you doing then? Can you remember?'

Joe's eyebrows knitted. 'We were making tea. I was helping.'

His expression cleared with recollection. 'We were dancing!' He'd forgotten that, but was delighted with the memory. 'Jay was a Blues Brother. I want to be a Blues Brother!'

Sadie turned back to Janet, a grave expression on her face, as if she was playing this game. 'Well then, thank you, Janet. I will have to have very serious words with Jay when I next see him...'

Back in her room, Sadie creased up laughing. Joe, who always picked up on her mood, laughed even louder.

'Is Janet funny, Mummy?'

'Yes, she is very funny, Joe. Very funny indeed...'

They were still sniggering when Jay arrived at the door.

'Hi! Come in.' She stepped aside and burst out laughing again.

'What?' Jay spontaneously joined them. Joe had been at his feet instantly, and he was giggling, too. This was new. What had come over her? She seemed quite transformed by that laugh. Like the odd occasion while they were rehearsing the Christmas show, when she would have a fit of the giggles and just couldn't stop... 'What's the joke?'

'Oh, it's only Janet. I've just heard a funny story, that's all... Hey Joe, show me what you told Janet you wanted to be?'

Joe did not comprehend, but as soon as she nodded to his party hat on the sideboard, he ran over to it. Grabbing her sunglasses, he put them both on and stood in front of the sink. Then, to her surprise, he put a spoon to his mouth and semi-sang, *'Everybody needs somebody to luuuurve...'* And in her present mood, Sadie nearly wet herself laughing.

Jay could do little else but join her. Joe was absolutely delighted, giggling furiously at having such an enthusiastic audience.

'Sorry,' Sadie sniffed. 'It's been a hell of a morning. Janet just set me off, that's all. She has this very odd notion that strange men in party hats and sunglasses, holding wooden spoons, are not appropriate role models for my son.' And then she roared with laughter again as she looked at Joe. 'She has a point...'

'Well, I was only trying to divert Joe from my awful cooking. You probably noticed I ruined your saucepan.'

'Shit, the beans!' Joe exclaimed. Another delightful memory re-ignited.

Jay stopped laughing then, and bit his lip. 'Oh no, sorry...'

But Sadie was too far down this playful road, so she just tutted, wagging her finger in mock reproof. 'You are two very naughty boys.' Still, she turned to Joe and added, 'I don't want to hear that again, Joe.'

'Sorry,' Jay repeated. 'I do try. I will try harder.'

'I know. It's OK.' And then she grinned again. 'I shall expect a full performance sometime. Come on Joe, Elwood's waiting...'

As he walked with Joe back across the campus, Jay reflected on the previous few minutes and Sadie's apparent ease with him. Though he was still very wary of what he could or could not do and say, it did seem to be getting more relaxed. A spontaneous smile crept over his face. She would be a good friend to have. And it would be so much easier to see Joe. In an odd way, he was almost grateful to Adam. The episode seemed to have allowed him into some kind of position of trust.

All he had to do now was get rid of those unexpected images that had been floating around his head alarmingly frequently since Joe's comment about the bed the other day.

Bugger...

.   .   .

'Oh God, you've no idea how tedious two philosophy lectures in a row can be.' Sadie sank down at Jay's table later that afternoon. 'I was so bored I was counting the panels in the floor.'

'Believe me, it's much the same with Plant Sciences.'

'So tell me, what made you choose it?'

'Well, I managed to scrape a biology and chemistry A'level and I spent most of my childhood in the garden,' he laughed.

'Do you enjoy it?'

'Sometimes, I suppose. I can't get very serious about it, you know. I don't live and breathe the stuff, like some people. I don't do enough work and I got finals next year. Tell you the truth, I don't care that much if I get it or not.'

'What do you want to do, then?'

'Oh, I don't know, do I?' Jay replied hotly, but then apologised.

'No, I'm sorry, it's my fault. It's getting like Twenty Questions here.'

'No, really, I am sorry. I just hate that question. It shits me up a bit 'cos I really don't know, and I ought to.'

'You've got plenty of time.'

Jay nodded distantly.

'What is it?'

'Oh, nothing,' he dismissed. But then, as he glanced at her, he suddenly wanted to take the chance. 'I... I'd kind of like to just... well... be a drummer,' he shrugged sheepishly.

'Cool!'

'Is it?'

'Yeah! And why not? You are rather good at it...'

Jay had had this dream for so long. His parents had barely tolerated it, and the bands he'd played in were no more than an amateur diversion. The fact that he could actually make a living out of it, make it his life, had never received the slightest encouragement before. He'd have to think about that. And the fact that she made him feel something, lots of things, that nobody ever had before...

'So, you tell me. Why Humanities, and why here?'

'Because it sounded the best I could do with three average A'levels. And I once had a nice holiday at Bognor Butlins.'

'Oh, such vision,' he laughed.

'You can talk!'

'Did you find you were a bit rusty, taking a break after school? I did. I'd been out for six years and I'd forgotten it all. I'm only just getting it back... Did you?' He added, as there had been no response.

'No, not really.'

'Sorry, I'm treading on the past again, ain't I?'

'Mummy went to evening school,' Joe piped up from his books on the floor. 'While she worked in C&As.'

'Joe...'

Joe looked up, bewildered by the caution.

'Jay doesn't want to hear about all that.'

'Yes, he does,' Jay muttered. Sadie looked straight at him. But not with the indignation of previous occasions; this time she seemed more uncertain. Jay thought he could pick up on it. 'Well, you know half my life story. It's more difficult talking to you when I don't know anything about you... I'd like to,' he added poignantly.

Sadie's expression fixed itself. She got up, picked Joe's hand from the floor and pulled him up. 'Come on Joe, it's teatime.'

'Jay said we could have tea with him!'

'Well, we can't.'

'Hey look...' Jay scrambled to his feet. 'Don't... Forget it. I'm sorry.'

'I don't want to talk about it. We're going home for tea,' she concluded, almost dragging Joe across the floor. His feet were not registering quite the urgency to leave this place as hers.

Jay was at the door immediately. He shut it, leaning on his hand. 'Look, leave by all means. But please, because you've got something planned, or you can't stand the sight of me. Not this.'

Sadie glared at him, but did not reply.

'You're being unreasonable,' he sighed. 'I don't have the slightest intention of wanting to hurt you.'

Still no response, and Sadie looked deeply uncomfortable now, staring at his hand on the closed door. All their previous light-heartedness obliterated.

'I'm not getting through, am I?' Jay pushed himself from the door and flicked it open provocatively.

Sadie swept silently out of it, pulling Joe behind her.

Jay slammed the door and backed up against it in annoyance.

'You don't fucking know anything, Jason, you really don't,' he muttered under his breath, turning away and sinking back onto the mattress.

23

BEAUTIFUL FAMILY

Janet had organised a Thursday night baby-sitting rota, to give
Sadie at least one free evening a week. Karen and David were on
duty tonight. Sadie had not realised, however, that her rare
night out in the bar was actually the Ellis House social commit-
tee. And she was, apparently, joining a ghost-story-themed pub
crawl in London on Saturday. Janet was taking her 'help Sadie
have more fun' responsibilities far too seriously.

She stared out to the room, as if searching the space for
some means of escape. Jay was at the bar with some friends,
although he didn't seem to be participating in what looked like
a lively conversation. He caught her eye and pulled a miserable
face, obviously imitating her. She hesitantly smiled.

'Anybody want another drink?' Sadie interrupted Janet's
continued plotting, took some glasses and went to the bar.

'Surprised to see you in here,' Jay said.

'So am I... Look, I'm sorry about yesterday.'

'Well, I guess you can't help it if I say things you don't like,'
he shrugged. 'Any more than I can help it when you don't say
anything at all.'

'Yes, but there are better ways of dealing with it than just running out on you every time.'

'True,' he agreed. 'Let's just forget it, shall we? It'll never be resolved.'

The disappointed inevitability in both his voice and his conclusion saddened her. But what could she do? The panic every time anyone wandered into her past had become so ingrained as to be a virtual reflex.

'Let me get you another drink.'

'Na, I'm alright, thanks,' he said, lifting his glass. 'Only came in for a quickie, got an essay to write. Just oiling the rusty cogs, you know. Or avoiding the bugger, one or the other.'

'You wouldn't like to do me a massive favour, would you?' She hesitated to ask. There was no reason he should, after yesterday's performance.

'Yes, I would.'

Sadie swallowed a little emotion, and a lot more guilt, at his premature acceptance.

'You wouldn't be free to have Joe on Saturday, would you? All day?'

'Uh, sure, yeah, but—'

'Have you got something planned?'

'Well, yes... no,' he corrected. 'It doesn't matter. Where are you off to then?'

'Haunted London pub crawl. Obviously not suitable for children.'

'It doesn't sound like it holds a million thrills for you, either,' Jay laughed.

'Well, you know how it is. You kind of get railroaded into these things.'

'Don't you want to go?'

'Of course I don't want to go!'

'Well, don't then.'

'I've kind of agreed now.' She still wasn't quite sure how that had happened.

'Well, sorry then, I can't have Joe at my place on Saturday...' Sadie's brow furrowed at this so matter-of-fact change of mind. 'Because I have the drama club minibus this weekend, and I'm going to Chessington World of Adventures.' Jay's eyebrows raised, a childlike smirk playing around his lips. 'So you'll just have to *suddenly remember* that you promised to take your son to Chessington on Saturday, won't you?' The grin belied the twist in his stomach; he was not half so confident in her response as he appeared. So he was mightily relieved by her immediate enthusiasm.

'Yeah? Oh Jay, it's so good of you! Are you sure? Joe'll go potty with excitement.'

'Just as long as his mum promises to enjoy herself as well.' He half expected that to hit another explosive nerve. But it didn't.

'Are you kidding? You just watch me! Back in a minute...'

She took the drinks back to the table and explained to the group what Jay had 'reminded' her. It surprised him that she left her own drink on the bar and returned to stay with him. And as she chattered away, reminiscent of Joe, he was amused, and a little bemused, how her mood just seemed to turn on a sixpence...

'Joe? Guess where we're going today?'

Joe dropped his spoon. He knew that conspiratorial grin, and it always meant something good. 'Where?'

'What's the big place some of your nursery friends have been that you've always wanted to go, too?' she teased.

'Windsor Safari Park!'

'Nope.'

He thought again. 'Chessington!'

Sadie silently raised her eyebrows.

'We going to Chessington?' he screeched.

'Yep. Jay's taking us today in the van.'

'Jay, yeah! Chessington!'

Joe's breakfast was now mostly on the table. And an hour later, Jay was almost knocked off his feet as he charged across the Union car park and jumped on him.

'Hey there, buddy.' Jay plucked him off the ground and swung him round as usual. 'Are we gonna have a good time, or are we gonna have a good time?'

'We're gonna have a good time!'

'He's been such a case this morning,' Sadie trotted to catch him up.

'Oooh me too,' Jay laughed. 'Let's get going then, shall we...?'

Heading north, Jay suddenly swerved off the road into a service station. 'Good job I noticed that – no petrol. Sorry,' he giggled as Sadie and Joe clutched the dashboard.

Sadie reached for her purse. 'Let me pay for the petrol.'

'Get off!'

'No, let me—'

'Put it away.' Jay jumped out of the cabin.

Sadie settled Joe and followed him to the pump. 'I insist.'

'Do as you're told.'

'I will not!' she laughed.

Joe leant out of the window, giggling as she attempted to stuff a ten-pound note into Jay's pocket, both play fighting and pretending not to laugh. Jay hung up the pump and Sadie ran off to the shop, but he chased after her and caught her at the door. They fought with each other to get in first, as the cashier looked on in bemusement.

Sadie pushed ahead and slammed the money on the counter. 'Number Six,' she panted.

Jay snatched the note away before the cashier could touch it, and thrust his Access card into his hand instead, ramming the money back into Sadie's pocket. 'Give up, will ya? You're beaten, OK?'

But she ducked under his arm and made for the counter again. So Jay just grabbed her round the waist, lifted her off the ground and carted her out of the door. He dumped her on the kerb, slammed the door behind him and leant up against it. And although she had to concede defeat now, Jay couldn't stop laughing when he caught sight of her standing outside, pretending to be angry, hands on her hips.

He reclaimed his card and opened the door. 'Thanks,' he said to the cashier. 'And sorry about her, they've only just signed the release papers, you know.'

'Thank you very much!' She punched his arm as they both returned to the van, giggling, neither really caring who paid for the petrol. It was just a game. But a telling one. Sadie hadn't behaved like that for years. And, as Joe eagerly mirrored the laughter, she was happy.

Just so long as she didn't think about the fact that she was...

'We've got plenty of time to see everything, sweetheart.' Joe was pulling on her arm like an untrained dog on a leash. He attempted to contain his enthusiasm.

It lasted about twenty seconds...

After a couple of hours of clambering on and off everything he saw, they found a quiet spot for lunch. Just as they were packing away, an older couple approached. 'Would you mind taking a picture of us with our granddaughter?'

'Sure,' Jay replied, on his feet at once...

Photo taken, he handed the camera back. 'Hey, could you take one of us as well?'

'Of course.'

'Come on, we're having our photo taken. Give it here.' Jay grabbed Sadie's pocket instamatic.

Joe was already posing. 'Me in the middle!' They squatted down on either side of him, Joe draping an arm over each of their knees, unbalancing them slightly. Jay put a steadying around them both.

'You have a beautiful family,' the lady smiled, as he retrieved the camera. Jay looked back at Joe and Sadie, and it stopped him in his tracks. Yes, they were. *Both* of them.

But they weren't his. *Neither* of them...

Sadie sat silent on the ground, her head turned away, biting her lip, and he knew she must have heard the comment.

'I'm sorry,' he sighed. 'Just forget it.' He picked up their bag of litter and took it to the bin. But she was still kneeling on the grass when he returned. 'Come on,' he squatted beside her. 'Please... don't let it upset you. It's nothing. Please,' he gently reasoned, his hand on her arm. 'We're having such a good time.'

Sadie looked up at him, her face full of wounded defiance. But it melted into a resigned acceptance. She nodded and got up.

The silent walk back to the fairgrounds saddened him. They'd come so far today. But he resolved to let her be. And it seemed he was right to do so. He could almost see her deliberately dismantling the tension; her fingers uncurling and shoulders dropping. She smiled at a hapless girl in a rabbit costume; she laughed at the grotesque stuffed toy he won on the hook-a-duck; and lit up in the reflection of Joe's delight on all the remaining rides...

They finished the day on the go-karts. Joe was almost out of his seat with excitement as he sat beside Jay, racing Sadie round the track. She'd just got ahead on the final lap, but much to Joe's delight, Jay took the final corner at break-neck speed and charged over the line by a nose.

'Oh, that is not fair!' she laughed breathlessly as she climbed out of her car.

'True,' Jay grinned. 'I mean you didn't have the bonus of Emerson Fittipaldi here telling you what to do...'

Sadie woke Joe in the university car park. 'We're home,' she whispered, stroking the hair from his drowsy face.

'I been sleep,' he mumbled, as she carried him out of the cabin. 'Thank you for a lovely day,' he drawled over her shoulder.

'Yes, it has been,' Sadie echoed. 'Thank you so much.'

'Well, thank *you* for coming,' Jay smiled. 'I haven't had so much fun in ages!'

And no, he did not want it to end.

'Coffee?' she offered. And his smile just broadened...

'How come you've got the drama club van, then?' Joe in bed, they sat on the mattress, the TV turned down beside them.

Jay paused, then grinned coyly. 'I wanted to go to Chessington...?'

'Oh, smart!' she said, to his relief. 'Nice that you have it at your disposal.'

'Well, they don't know about it, actually. I'm not exactly Mr Wonderful at the moment.'

'Oh? Have you fallen out?'

'Sort of. They picked me to play this guy in a new play. I said no.'

'Why?'

'Didn't like the part,' he shrugged, but he could see she would not be satisfied with that. 'Well, it was a love story. And they were going to cast Anna opposite me again. So I just thought I'd refuse before she had a chance to put her bloody great oar in. I couldn't go through all that again.'

'How do you know she'd make a fuss?' Sadie protested.

'She would,' he sighed. 'I don't need having my nose rubbed in it all over again.'

'Come on, it wasn't your fault what happened at Christmas.'

'Oh, you weren't there. You didn't see all the arguments, the bitching. And a load of other stuff. The woman has a fucking coven following her everywhere... never mind...' Jay had no wish to recall the baying and the condoms. 'Anyway, to save my pride if you like, I quit before she could. Let her get it on with the lovely Jeremy instead.'

'I'm sorry you feel that way.'

'Well,' he shrugged. 'Not very mature, I know. Guess I'm just stupid.'

'Of course you're not...' And now *she* was reassuring *him*. In the most unexpected way. 'She's not entitled to make you feel like that, Jay. You have nothing to feel that way about.'

'Thank you,' he muttered, edged with surprise. 'Anyway!' He slapped his legs. 'That's neither here nor there. I'm not spoiling my day with that nonsense...!'

They decided to watch the late film. Jay was wide-awake still, though Sadie was having trouble keeping her eyes open. She leaned back against the cushion...

The film ended. Jay sighed, looking down at her, sleeping beside him. He got up and took the coffee cups to the sink. She did not stir. Should he wake her? But she looked so peaceful there. Should he go? He flicked the channels on the TV. There was another film starting on BBC2. No, he didn't want to go back and be on his own.

The film was dull. His eyelids were heavy. Just close them for a moment or two... The warm glow from the two-bar fire; the companiable murmur of a background TV; the quiet, peaceful rhythm of a woman and a child's sleeping breath...

Sadie never slept a whole night through. Single-mother antennae, from that first lone night in a bedsit in Watford with a tiny alien creature utterly dependent on her. She squinted at the clock, the unconscious breathing of Jay beside her. Quarter to three. She quietly got up, turned off the TV and the fire, and tip-toed to the cupboard to pull out a spare blanket. She lay it over him and settled herself back against the cushion, wrapping the end of the duvet around her. Let him sleep; was there really any reason to disturb him...?

The sun streaming through the window failed to wake either of them. Joe stood beside them and jogged her with his foot, not in the least bit disturbed to find Jay still there.

'Why have you still got your clothes on?'

'What?' Jay groaned, turning over, his leg slipping beneath Sadie's. He perked up immediately. 'Oh, God...' Sadie was awake now, rubbing her eyes and moving her stiff limbs. He withdrew his immediately. 'Jesus, I'm sorry.' But she just grinned at his barely conscious expression. And looking at her, so sleep tousled and drowsy, a lump came to his throat. Again.

'I want my breakfast!' Joe broke through this alarming train of thought with his usual demands.

'What time is it?' Sadie yawned.

'Half past seven,' Joe replied, always eager to show off that he could read a clock.

'Oh, Joe, you know Mummy sleeps in until nine on Sundays.' Well, she tried to. It never worked. But the protest was worth a go.

'Yes, but Jay's here,' Joe reasoned, nonsensically.

'I'll make it. It's the least I can do.' Jay scrambled to his feet, picking up the blanket with an enquiring look.

'I woke up in the middle of the night.'

'You should have shoved me out!' But as Sadie twitched uncomfortably, he just smiled and said, 'Thanks.'

Joe followed him round in his pyjamas, and soon they were all lined up on the mattress eating cereal.

'Well, I have most definitely outstayed my welcome, so I'll leave you to it now.'

'Where are you going?' Joe demanded, as if he lived there.

'I'm going home,' Jay smiled, tousling the boy's hair. 'I've got stuff to do,' he added as Joe made to protest.

'When are you coming back?'

Jay couldn't fail to notice the anxiety returned to Sadie's eyes, so trying to analyse it, he concluded. 'I'll see you next week sometime, OK mate...?'

Jay did indeed have 'stuff to do', but today it was a pensive task. And he was glad that the props and scenery for the next production seemed to have been left to him to shift today. He needed to be alone. The previous day had filled him with so many emotions. Excitement and calm; warmth and laughter; challenge and delight. And for a moment, he had felt like that family in the photo, so obviously mistaken. Something he'd never had.

He so loved to be with people who could share joy in a situation. Any little thing; as shallow as a play fight in a petrol station, or as deep as a sunset on the South Downs. But it was an entirely different game to be with someone who could share sorrow in the same way. Who drew him from his darker thoughts and accepted and eased them. And it scared him. This was much more than just the occasional pornographic image floating about in his head, so easily dismissed with a thrash around on his drums, or a quick tumble with a pillow.

Double bugger...

This was getting too much. Too out of place. He didn't feel these things. He didn't get these things.

24

THE CRASH

Joe was at her feet at the knock on the door. Just to check that mummy wasn't going anywhere without him. A policeman asked to come in. That was quite interesting. But so was the chocolate Penguin he could have if he went to play with his car park at the other end of the room...

'Joe!' Jay opened the door, dishevelled and sleepy, dressed only in a pair of jogging bottoms. He scanned the corridor, but Joe was alone.

'Mummy says can you look after me today, please?' Joe faithfully repeated Sadie's instructions. 'I've to go straight back if you're not in. You are in. Or if you can't.'

'Well, sure, yes of course I will, but— come in,' he stepped aside. Joe removed his anorak and hung it up, as he always did.

'Sorry about the gear, Joe,' Jay pranced about, his hand through his bed-headed hair. 'So, come here a minute.' He jumped back onto the mattress and Joe flopped down beside him, leaning into his chest.

'Is Mummy going out then?'

'I don't know,' Joe shrugged.

'Did she say why she wanted me to look after you?'

'No.'

Jay paused. 'Is she alright, Joe?'

'No, I don't think so. She was alright at first. And then the policeman came, and when he was gone, she was kind of... funny...' Joe didn't really have an explanation for this one. He hated that.

'What did the policeman say, Joe?'

'I don't know...'

Jay could not guess what had passed that morning. But that Sadie had let Joe come here on his own, so she could deal with something, whatever the police wanted with her, deeply worried him. But whatever it was, his duty was to deal with Joe, and his unusually uncertain manner.

'Right then, little man,' he clapped his hands and looked at his watch. 'Time to get you to nursery. Which means... I better put a shirt on. Or shall I go like this?' he teased, throwing his arms wide.

Joe giggled, hugging his chest. 'You'll be cold!'

'Well, I guess I just might be, so...' He jumped up, slipped on his trainers and a jumper, splashed some water over his face, and returned to lift Joe back into his arms. He clung to him, and Jay was happy for him to do so, sensing he needed that extra bit of stability today.

'Don't be late,' Joe wagged his finger at the nursery door.

Deciding he wouldn't be able to concentrate on his practical today, Jay returned to his room and dived back onto the mattress, chewing his thumb. The only reason he could think of for the events of the morning was something to do with Joe's father. Perhaps all this time Sadie had been looking for him? Maybe suddenly he'd been found? Jay's mind leapt into overdrive. What if he came here? What if he wanted Joe? What if he wanted Sadie back?

What if... what if... what if...?

He slapped himself. This was fruitless speculation, and it was driving him mad. He didn't even know it had anything to do with *him*. He didn't know anything. Because she wouldn't tell him. Leaving him fumbling around in the dark with his own selfish reactions. But what would he do with the sudden appearance of a long-lost father to Joe? He'd lose him, surely. He'd lose Sadie. Obsessively, he searched. What else did he have? A drum kit and a pillow...?

'Oh, what is this?' he muttered irritably to himself. Wouldn't that be what Joe wanted most in the world? And wouldn't he give anything for that little boy?

Disillusioned by his selfishness, his jealousy and resentment, he kicked the wall and buried his head in the duvet...

For today, however, Joe was going nowhere, and spent the afternoon glued to him as usual. Lunch in the café, drums in the basement, Blues Brothers on the hi-fi, Cartoon Time on the TV. And beans for tea that didn't have to be scraped off the bottom of the pan...

With Joe settled in front of Crossroads, which he, inexplicably, seemed to find utterly absorbing, Jay decided it would be OK to leave him for a bit.

There was no answer at Sadie's door, until he heard shuffling and a small voice returned, 'Yes?'

'It's me.'

'Oh, sorry, have you brought Joe back?'

The door remained closed.

'No. He's in my room watching TV. I'll take care of him as long as you like. I just want to talk to you.'

'Oh.' She still had not come to the door. 'Look, I don't—'

'Oh, Sadie, please let me in. I'm so worried about you. Please let me in and tell me what's happened.'

The door opened a fraction; Sadie left it hanging there.

'Thank you for having Joe,' she said, sinking back onto a chair by the table. Jay followed. 'I know it's a liberty. But I just had to be on my own for a bit.'

'I understand. Anytime, you know that. Tell me why, though, please. What's happened?'

'I... I just needed to be on my own. I've been turned inside out today, and I could see it coming. I didn't want Joe to see it... It's my brother and his wife. They were in a car accident yesterday. They're both dead,' she concluded, almost casually.

'Oh... God,' Jay breathed. 'I'm so sorry.'

'It's OK,' she sighed. 'That's the funny thing. I just don't feel... *loss*. But I think that's partly what's upset me the most.'

'You weren't close, then?'

'They brought me up,' she shrugged. 'Dad died when I was eight, and Mum a few months later. But John and Barbara were never parents to me. They gave me nothing. Even with Joe, it was me that gave to them. The surrogate mother. Their surrogate child. They threw me out, but they'd have taken him. He's all they ever wanted. Not me. I hated them...'

Jay put his hand over hers. 'You don't mean all this.'

Sadie sighed, tears in her eyes, and shook her head. 'They're gone now. I never wanted them. But what now? Joe and me, we've got no-one now. No-one with any obligation, any responsibility. I've known it for years. But now it just seems... *so real*. Joe's got nothing but me. And I can't tell you how scared that makes me.' She looked up at him so directly, and in the rarest honesty he'd ever seen from her, or anyone really, she concluded, 'I'm frightened, Jay.'

Those words. He just wanted to gather her up right there and then, and hold her from it all; take it all from her.

But instead he just tried to speak it. 'I don't know what to say to you. There's so much I want to say, but I don't know if it's what you want.'

'I don't care what you say!' And now the tears came. She'd not cried properly all day. Perhaps now, as she spoke the words, was the time.

'Oh, Jesus,' Jay mumbled, feeling so inadequate. 'It's all I can do...' He slipped off his chair, crouched by her, and pulled her to him. Unexpectedly, she responded immediately; clinging to him, moving off her chair so they were both kneeling on the carpet. He could feel the tears on his collar, his arms tight around her, closing his eyes over her shoulder to prevent his own.

'I want to tell you you're not alone,' he whispered, hardly able to contain himself. 'I'll always be here for you and Joe.'

'Oh, shut up, Jay! Shut up! You don't know anything. You don't know!' And if it wasn't for the fact that she still clung to him, he would have been crushed by that.

'I'm sorry,' he muttered.

'John and Barbara, they had no choice. If anything ever happened to me. He was my brother. They were our family. They had no choice. Oh, Jesus!' Her fists clenched and she almost thumped him. 'I hate the bastard. I hate him. I hate him!'

And Jay knew she was not talking about John...

'This will pass,' she sniffed, drawing away from him finally. 'Soon we'll be back to normal. Just me and Joe.' She knelt back and turned her head away. 'I suppose you think I'm terrible, that I don't care for them, that they're dead.'

Jay shook his head. 'One day, maybe, you'll give me credit

for a bit more understanding than you obviously think I can have... I'm sorry,' he added. 'I shouldn't—'

'No,' she whispered, touching his face. 'I'm sorry. I can't think. I don't know what I'm saying...'

The gesture intrigued him. And everything he had said, everything he had ever thought and done, just magnified in its intent.

'Well, that makes two of us,' he joked instead. 'I just don't want you to be scared. I can't stand to see you so scared.'

'I'm not,' she tossed back instantly. 'I'm alright.'

Jay sighed. This is where the drawbridge raised again.

'I better go and get Joe.'

'I'll go,' Jay stood up. 'Just...' he turned at the door. 'You *can* depend on me. Please, let yourself...'

Sadie stood in the middle of the room, a strange numbness in her head. How could she depend on him? Or anyone? He didn't understand. Whatever he had tried to say to the contrary... Yet she felt oddly comforted by his honest words and gestures. There was some kind of trust there. Or was it that? She did not really know what *trust* was. But, at least for the moment, he would take care of Joe. Questions on how long even that could last brought her right back to the crux of her anxiety. Jay had absolutely no obligation to them at all. So maybe her developing trust in him only worsened everything...?

Tying herself in knots, he saved her the trouble of unravelling as he returned with Joe. Sadie tried the best she could to eradicate the traces of her tears, but Joe went to her immediately and hugged her.

'Have you had a nice day?' She tried to smile.

'Yeah,' Joe replied. 'But Jay and me, we's worried about you.'

Jay sat down. He wasn't leaving just yet.

'Joe, I've got some bad news.' She glanced to the table over his shoulder. Jay gave her a faint, encouraging smile. 'It's Uncle John and Aunty Barbara. They were in a nasty accident yesterday, and so I'm afraid that they've been killed. Do you remember what that means? You won't be able to see them again.'

Joe pursed his lips. 'They're dead,' he said, half as a question, half as repetition. Sadie nodded. 'Where will we go at end of term?' There didn't seem to be anything else about the absence of these people that occurred to him.

'I'm sorry, Joe. I don't know. We'll be here or somewhere else, but not with John and Barbara.'

Joe nodded. 'Are you very sad?' He clearly couldn't comprehend enough to really feel himself. But Sadie could not answer that.

'We'll be alright, won't we, Joe?' she said instead.

'Yeah,' he replied.

She hugged him tightly. 'We will, won't we, Joe?'

'Yeah. We will,' he repeated hypnotically.

She pulled away and got up, wiping her eyes with the back of her hand. 'It's about time you were in bed then.'

Joe went to fetch his pyjamas.

'Are you going to be alright?' Jay whispered. 'I can take him back to my place if you like.'

'It's OK,' she replied with renewed steel in her previously exposed, open green eyes. 'I'm alright.'

She was probably right, Jay thought. There was a distance and determination about her now. And it excluded him.

'Well, I'll be off then.'

And Sadie just nodded. She was clearly somewhere else now... But she called him back from the door. 'Jay... you know, thank you.'

Well, that was something.

The next morning, after an entirely sleepless night, there was a letter in her pigeonhole from Barbara's parents. She'd met them only once since John and Barbara's wedding. Although she had not really thought about it, she was so glad there was somebody else to take care of the arrangements; the funeral, and everything. She was the only one on John's side. But the letter upset her. She honestly felt for Barbara's parents' suffering. Then there was the guilt that she just didn't feel the same.

The funeral was to be next Monday in Croxley Green. They offered to put her up for the night. And that was another thing to think about...

'I just came to see if you were alright,' Jay said at her door that evening. Sadie sighed, and Jay sensed the... what? Annoyance?

'Well yes, we're alright, thank you,' she replied tersely. Jay nodded sadly. There was no place for him here, clearly.

'Well, OK then,' he concluded, preparing for a disappointingly premature departure. 'There's nothing you want or anything?'

Sadie sighed again. 'I'm not an invalid, you know.'

Jay looked at her straight. 'Yeah, and I wouldn't push you across the road if you were.' He turned on his heel. He hadn't deserved that.

Sadie tossed her head, grabbed his arm, and pulled him into the room. 'Look,' she hissed, pointing to Joe asleep in his beanbag. 'He's fine. He's asleep. It's way past his bedtime. He's OK.'

'I didn't doubt it,' Jay retorted. Sadie stared back at him, confusion rapidly blunting the sharpness, until she looked nothing but lost.

'Well, he's alright,' was all she could say.

Jay gave a humourless half-laugh. 'Well, what do you expect? He's a five-year-old kid. He won't understand.'

'No,' Sadie agreed.

'What are you talking about, then?'

Sadie's eyebrows knitted, and she did not answer.

'Oh, I get it... Look, I know it's gone nine o'clock. If I came to play with Joe, I'd have come earlier, wouldn't I? I came to see how *you* were. That is what I said.'

'Why?'

Jay's laugh was again entirely without humour. 'Because you've just lost your family, that's why!'

'Oh...'

'Look, I'm sorry, I'm obviously doing this all wrong,' he concluded, hands up. 'This is like having one of Joe's little nursery mates coming round to ask how you're doing, yeah? Well, OK, sorry, if that's how it is, I'll try not to worry about you... But don't put money on it...' His voiced disappeared down the corridor.

'Jay...' she barely whispered after him.

She sank into a chair, chewing her fingernails, until all she could feel was regret and inadequacy. All she wanted, now that she was alone and so confused, was some gentle company, some concern, an ear, maybe even a shoulder to cry on. And there was none. There had always been none. What made this different from all the other times she might have wanted this, she now realised so starkly, was that she had just shown them the door. She couldn't handle them. They weren't real anyway, were they?

Not for her.

25

SHOULDER TO CRY ON

The progressively heavy burden of new emotion put Sadie in the lowest mood she had experienced for some while. The sudden realisation that she and her son were completely alone in the world, with no one who had any kind of obligation towards them, was running headlong up against the growing need she had been experiencing lately for companionship, for sharing, for trust.

And she didn't know how to cope with it.

The long evenings were the worst. With Joe asleep, the quiet and loneliness unnerved her like never before. And all she seemed able to do was sit, miserably, trying to figure it all out...

Janet appeared at the door. Facial expression out of a textbook, she was barely in the chair before a torrent of sympathy and well-meaning psychology poured out of her.

'Janet,' Sadie finally got a word in edgeways. 'Shut up.'

'Oh, that's a fine thing to say to me, isn't it? I'm only trying to help.'

'Well, I appreciate it, but you're not,' Sadie replied, somewhat unreasonably. 'You don't understand.'

Janet rose from her chair. 'People can only take so much, Sadie, and don't forget it.'

'Jan... I'm sorry. Please. Don't go,' she said, and instantly regretted it. She sensed a self-satisfaction in her friend that she did not like and did not want.

'That's what I thought.' Janet resettled herself at the table. 'That you might need someone to talk to.'

Sadie nodded distantly. 'Look, if you really want to help, stay here with Joe for an hour?'

Janet sighed. 'Yeah, alright...'

Raised voices and laughter drifted down the corridor of Jay's block. 'He's in here,' came a voice from the open room next door.

Students lined the walls of the room; one of them whistled.

'Excellent. Just what we need,' he said to the bloke next to him. 'Come in, come in... Looking for Jay?' He threw an empty beer can at the corner behind the door. 'You've got a visitor.'

'It's OK, I don't want to interrupt—'

'Hey, you're not allowed to leave,' the whistler stopped her. 'This is a very public party, you know. And you are most definitely very welcome.' He grabbed her arm. She tripped in and looked nervously around her, until she focussed on Jay.

'Sadie!'

'Ah, Sadie, is it? Right...' The whistler and some of the others were still looking her up and down, clearly well past the merry stage.

'Sorry,' she mumbled. 'I didn't want to disturb. It's OK, uh, I'll see you...' She backed towards the door, strangely unnerved by this 'party'. She felt foolish and inadequate. But that was not all. The Specials were playing on the hi-fi. There was something about the low light, the music, the raised voices, the smell of the beer, and the looks of the men...

'No, hang on.' Jay scrambled to his feet. He did not like the look on her face. He could see her trying to smile, but she was... *frightened*? His response was visceral. Stepping over legs, pizza boxes and empty cans, he grabbed her hand and pulled her from the room.

'Oh, no,' she sighed. 'You stay. I don't want to interrupt. I'll go—'

'I don't think so.'

She was still protesting as he led her next door.

'You want to go home?'

Sadie shuffled, but eventually shook her head.

'Shut up then,' he winked. 'I'm not missing out on anything. Nick has open doors all the bloody time... Sometimes you just don't want to be on your own, I get it. But there are some places that really won't do as an alternative, eh?' He cocked his head towards Nick's room next door.

She stared at him.

'Thought so.' He went to the fridge. 'Do you want a beer now, or shall I put the kettle on?'

'OK,' she replied with a faint smile.

He sat down beside her on the mattress. 'So, it's nice to see you. What's on your mind?'

'I... I just needed... like you said,' she mumbled, taking a steadying gulp from the beer can. 'I've been doing stupid things all day. Knocking stuff over, getting uptight with Joe...'

'Where is Joe, by the way?'

'Oh, he's alright,' she sighed. 'He's asleep. Janet's with him... It was a bad idea coming.'

Jay held her back. 'Come on,' he coaxed. 'I know what it is. I was only asking about Joe to see if we had to go back to him or anything. Come on, I've chewed your ear off enough times. It's not fair, you know, to cut out on me like this all the time. I'm not just one of Joe's mates, you know that. I'm concerned about you.'

Sadie shook her head, and Jay misunderstood this act of confusion.

'I am. Why shouldn't I be? What's so unbelievable about that? You're concerned about me. I know you are. You listen to my shit. Why don't you ever want to talk to me?'

'I do,' Sadie responded instantly, unconsciously. But there was no more.

Jay paused, gently attempting to oil the conversation more subtly. 'I'm never quite sure about her, you know, but Janet's pretty helpful sometimes, isn't she?'

'Yeah. And she wanted to help this evening.'

'Is that what she said?'

'Yeah. Along with a whole lot of other things.'

'Like what?'

'Oh, she gave me a long lecture about not being afraid to talk about my brother and letting all the emotion out. I didn't have the heart to tell her you couldn't fill a sweet wrapper with what there is to say about him... There I go again,' she sighed. 'I don't mean it. I just seem to go the other way. I don't know if you can understand it, but because there is something happening to me because of their death, and it's got nothing to do with losing them as people, I just seem to exaggerate their lack of worth to me. I don't know why. It must sound awful.'

'Not really,' Jay mused. 'If I thought about it, I might just feel the same about my parents. Maybe not. You never know until it happens, I guess.'

'It's just I think I resent them. I resented them when they were alive. But I seem to resent them even more now. For leaving me like this. For leaving Joe. Both of us, on our own.' She screwed up her face. 'But I know that's not fair. It's not

their fault. Any of it. I don't know why I feel this way. I feel...'
She paused, needing to draw the courage to speak her emotions
from a very deep and overgrown well.

'I feel a lot of things that I don't know why. Suddenly it all
just seems to have come to a head. Everything that's happened.
And I just don't know how to deal with it. I've spent so long
setting up these systems of being and thinking, so that I can
cope, I guess. But now, it's like there's this wall in my head,
almost. It feels so dense that I can't even see or think over it.'
She glanced at him, her eyes moist. 'I can't stand not knowing
what I'm doing, or going to do. It's so confusing...'

'What's confusing?' Jay gently coaxed. 'Can you tell me?'

She shrugged. 'I suppose that for years I've wished that
there was nobody about, nobody around me and Joe, that
could say or know or want anything. But recently I've started to
want things for us both. I've wanted people around us. I've not
wanted to be alone. But at the same time, I can't seem to handle
it, so I mess it up anyway. And on top of that conflict in my
head, I'm suddenly confronted in big bold type with the fact
that I *am* very much alone. Whatever I feel about John and
Barbara, they were our only security.' She bit her lip, trying to
stem the potential tears, but it didn't really work and she
thumped her thigh. 'And that's what makes it so awful for me
to hate them so much!'

Silence followed and Jay knew he should try to fill it, for
what it was worth. 'Well, they have gone, whether you hate
them or not. Maybe in a way they've freed you. Perhaps you feel
you can't handle that freedom. Not right now. But they were
your only link with the past. Perhaps if you're beginning to not
want to be alone, to want different things, it's time to shake off
all that?'

'Oh, Jay...' she sighed. Another time, she might have
snapped at the suggestion.

'Come on,' he urged. 'Argue with me. Put me right.'

'I live the past. Joe is it. Don't drag me into it, because I'm just not going there. But I'm never going to be freed of a reminder of all that's happened. All my life, all Joe's life, is enough... And you've no idea, especially now as I'm changing, and now this has happened, the responsibility of that. That'll never go away. You know I love my son, but how I wish he'd never been born.'

Jay tried hard to comprehend this notion, and eventually nodded. 'I wish I could tell you how it all should be.'

'Nobody asked you for a magic wand, Jay. But thank you. I can't see much of a resolution, but I can see a bit of what I think I mean. I'm grateful...' She shuffled to the edge of the mattress. 'Look, I better get back and relieve Janet.'

'I guess so. Tomorrow evening, I'll could come round, if you like? Then you can say it all again. Or a whole new set of things...? I'd like that,' he added in encouragement.

'Thanks,' she smiled faintly.

'I'm glad you came round,' he said at the door.

'Me too,' she agreed, defences unexpectedly off duty.

It was past eight thirty when Jay arrived the next evening. Although he missed Joe every day he didn't see him now, he had to assure Sadie, by this very obvious gesture, that his concern was for her at the moment.

'I got a couple of beers in. I'm beginning to get caffeine highs,' she laughed weakly, offering him one. 'It doesn't help with the current bout of clumsiness.'

'Know what you mean. It's another student disease.'

There was a shoebox on the bed beside them, a few photos lying on top. Jay recognised it from the drawer with the birth certificate.

'How've you been today, then?' he ventured. After her first attempts at light-hearted banter, there was a distant subdued quality about her, replacing the previous evening's edgy confusion. And the silence didn't seem to be improving matters.

Sadie shrugged.

'Been looking at photos?' he persisted.

Still, she just nodded wordlessly.

'Can I see them?'

She handed him a slim pile.

'That's Barbara,' she said as he scanned the first photo. 'And that's John.' There were a couple more of the two of them together. 'I've been thinking about tomorrow and looking at these pictures. I just feel a bit... I don't know... lost, really. I know I didn't mean all those things I said about them.'

'Tomorrow?'

'The funeral.'

'Oh God, yeah, of course. I didn't think.'

'Shit, I am so selfish. I've left it until now. I don't want to take Joe. Could you have him? Until Tuesday evening? I'm sorry, this is hardly much notice. I could take him, if you can't. But I won't leave him with anyone else. Not now. Sorry, that's putting pressure on you—'

'Hang on, hang on,' Jay laughed. 'Stop! I'd love to have Joe, you know that. I'll look forward to it.'

'I forget,' she mumbled. 'Thank you.'

'I've got a job to do driving the minibus in the afternoon, but it's no problem. Joe can come.'

'If you're certain.'

'Absolutely... So, how do you feel about the funeral?'

Sadie bit her lip. 'I'm dreading it,' she admitted. 'It's not that I'm going to get upset or anything. I don't think so anyway. It's just meeting everyone else. And the finality of it all, I suppose... I've got to stay with Barbara's parents on Monday night. I don't relish that very much. They always thought Barbara was marrying down. Despite John being a complete snob himself.'

'Couldn't you come back after it?'

'There are things to do apparently, they said, on Tuesday.'

'Oh, the will, I suppose, and all that?'

'Do you think so?'

'Well, I don't know anything about these things, but maybe.'

'I hadn't thought about that.'

'Have they...? Well, have they got anything?'

'Only the house, really. And that was part paid for by Barbara's parents, so that'll go back to them... Oh, do I have to go? There doesn't seem any point.' As if he would know. But through all of this, she just wanted someone to tell her what to do. Take some of this responsibility from her.

Jay sensed a little of this and attempted to respond to it. 'Well, you are the only one on John's side, didn't you say? So I guess you will. Don't worry, it'll be over before you know it.'

'Yeah,' she sighed. 'I'm lucky, really. I haven't had to do anything. I should be grateful.'

'I guess so...'

In the silence that followed, Jay picked up the rest of the photos. The first was of Barbara, holding a baby. 'Is that...?'

'Joe, yeah.'

The next was an older picture from John and Barbara's wedding. Beside them was a little girl of about six or seven. She looked like Joe, with her big grin, twinkly eyes and blond hair falling over her eyes.

'That's me,' Sadie said.

'Yeah?' Jay smiled.

There were a couple more of Sadie as a child with John and Barbara. Then there was one of an older girl, in dishevelled school uniform, with bright red spiky hair and heavy black eye make-up.

Jay stared at it. 'Who's that?'

'It's me!' Sadie retorted.

'You? Never.'

'It is,' she said, with a hint of foolishness. All that seemed so long ago now...

'Going through a bit of a punk thing, yeah?'

'Guess so. Just to piss off the olds, you know.'

'I went out with a girl from Bushey Meads once.' Jay recognised the uniform. 'Year or two above you, I guess.'

'Did you? God, that was a bit of a trek, wasn't it?'

'Yeah, pain in the arse meeting her from school,' he grinned. 'Still, I did it religiously. Boys liked that kind of thing. Makes us look cool, you know?' he laughed self-mockingly.

'You might have seen me then.'

'I think I'd have remembered with that barnet!'

'Well, I don't remember you either.'

'You wouldn't,' Jay muttered and put the photo to the back.

Next was a picture of Barbara holding a baby Joe again, John and... 'Is that you as well?'

'Yes!' Sadie sighed with a quizzical smile. 'What's the matter with you?'

'Well, it's nothing like that,' he said, putting the two photos together. 'And it's not much like you,' he concluded, holding one on either side of her face. 'You've changed so much.'

'Maybe,' Sadie shrugged. 'Grown up a lot, I guess.'

There were a few more photos of Joe at various stages of development. Nothing of Sadie until a couple with her and Joe at three or four. A step change in her appearance by then, as if she had come into her own. A more relaxed, natural look, free of the rebellious outfits and dark, heavy make-up, to reveal a really quite strikingly appealing face. He glanced up at her. Yeah, that was true... And he lowered his eyes again instantly, replacing the photos.

'Well, what a photographic history,' he smiled instead.

'I suppose it's just helped me think a bit, that's all.'

'I'm glad you let me see them.'

'Why wouldn't—? I didn't think about it,' she muttered edgily. And Jay feared he'd lost her again. Why did he have to go and say that? To remind her of her reasons to hide?

'And I suppose you're just bursting with questions about why there aren't any of Joe's father?'

'No,' he sighed.

'Oh, you've got it all sussed out then, have you?'

'Sadie,' Jay pleaded. 'Stop it, please. I'm not asking. Please. You know me better than that. Don't bring it up like this. Of course I'd like you to be able to tell me, to talk about it. But I'm not making my own conclusions,' he lied, but it wasn't a lie in the sense she thought; he wasn't judging. 'I don't want to upset you. I'm not making an issue.'

Sadie sighed irritably. The tension returned and his gentle reasoning was just making it worse. 'Good. Because it's a closed book! And you can bloody well think what you like. You can all just think whatever you like. I don't care,' she lied. In every sense.

'Sadie... please...' He touched her arm. She turned away. She could feel her eyes moistening and bit down on her lip to suppress the tears. Of course, the subject was the fastest finger on the button of her agitation and, as always, she just wanted it to go away. Her usual means of achieving that was to get rid of the company. But now she found that she just wanted *it* to go away, so that *he* would stay.

'I'm sorry,' she mumbled.

'Let's just forget it, shall we? You've got enough on your mind as it is.'

'Can we talk about something else?'

'Sure...'

But as the pause lengthened, Jay guessed this, too, was his responsibility. So he offered the sidetrack and drew her down other conversational paths.

He was good at it, and she was laughing in the end...

'See you Tuesday then. And all the best,' he touched her arm on the way out.

'Thank you,' she whispered as the door closed behind him, looking down at the empty space on her arm.

And in her heart.

26

COMPLICATIONS

Jay knew he was in trouble as he lay in his bed that night. Sometimes when they stopped talking for a moment and she looked at him. Those soulful green eyes. He was going to kiss her. Something with the strength of a tank pushed him back in his place. And he was so glad it did. What was he thinking? Why had this happened? Why was he looking at her like that now? No more just the odd guilty fantasy when he was alone. Now it was everything. Every time he looked at her...

And maybe it didn't matter before, when he was just Joe's friend, and she was just Joe's mum. And Joe's mum who bawled him out and constantly withdrew from him. But now her behaviour was changing. And there were these barely containable urges to hold her gaze, and just... *kiss her*. And those brief moments when he had touched his lips to hers in the Christmas panto filled his mind now. But not as they were. Acting. A show. And a comedy at that. But his reality now. His fantasy.

His tragedy.

He buried his head in the pillow. God, it was so fragile. He was so stupid. Why did he always want more? He was so happy to have Joe in his life. So happy to be let in this far with Sadie, and he was so genuinely concerned for her. Why did he have to forcefully stop himself from blowing it all away? As he knew he would, if ever he went anywhere near her. It would shatter the delicate trust. If he didn't know that instinctively from, well, pretty much everything about her, the revelation of Adam's motives would be quite enough on its own. He'd lose her altogether. He'd lose Joe. He couldn't bear the thought.

So this had to stop. It was too much. And it was selfish. He might have a good new friend whose company, opinions and kinship he valued highly. He had the love and trust of a little boy he adored. It was more than he'd ever had before. And he would not throw it all away.

This is the way it was, and it was good, and this is the way it would stay.

27

THE FUNERAL

It was one of those days you never want to come, and in some distant part of the brain lies the hope that it may never do so; something would change just in time. But it was here, and Sadie's every move was rooted in reluctance.

Joe was tearful on his way to nursery. Although he was happy enough to be left in Jay's care this time, unspoken memories of her last absence remained deep within him. It did nothing but turn the screw of panic and regret as she walked away from him to the station...

Three hours later, she was knocking at a door she had never visited before.

'Come in, Sarah,' Barbara's mother said, with a painted smile and a twitch of her thin, glossed lips.

'Thank you. And it's Sadie, please.'

'As you wish.'

Barbara's father and two brothers sat in the lounge with a few other relatives, and Sadie instantly felt she didn't belong there. The only one on John's side, they seemed keen to remind her, although doubtless there would be friends and business associates at the church. They all seemed suspicious of her; and she just wanted to run there and then. But she responded politely, the best she could.

She knew she was surprising Barbara's parents. Indeed, her current demeanour must have puzzled them greatly. This troublesome, rebellious child with her dyed hair and ripped clothes who got herself pregnant at sixteen – doubtless sleeping around, you know – was a mature, tidy young woman, studying for a degree at university.

'You didn't bring the boy, then?' Barbara's mother asked, displacing Sadie's cool. For a start, she hated the cold reference. They knew his name.

'I thought it best if Joe stayed with a friend. He's a little too young to understand, and I thought it might upset him.'

'And how does he find university?' The father enquired with barely disguised sarcasm.

'Fine,' Sadie replied, defiantly matching him. 'He's thinking of going on to PhD next year.'

'This is no time to be flippant.'

'I apologise,' she lied.

But they had set the atmosphere for the day. Sadie was bored by the service, felt distanced by the burial, and thoroughly sickened by the 'buffet' that followed. She managed to creep away after an hour or so, on the assumption that she was too upset to stay. In reality, she knew that if she allowed herself just one more glass of wine, she would not be able to stop herself throwing it at one of the pompous idiots who ceaselessly patronised her. So she retreated upstairs, with a book and a couple of vol au vents, and wasn't seen again that day.

The conversation over breakfast was superficially polite. Sadie remained calm and restrained, even though she suspected digs at her and dubious suspicions that would normally send her into a rage. And then they set off for a solicitor's office, though Sadie knew not why. What possible reason was there for her to be here any longer?

John, Sadie knew, was a man of ridiculous fastidiousness. It should have been no surprise to her, therefore, that the will that was read to them was ludicrously long and detailed, and that he had also willed this ceremony. Sadie even had to stifle a giggle on a couple of occasions. Like the box of Eagle Magazines being left to Barbara's younger brother. She just could not see the point of all this. At least of her being there. What the hell would she do if she were landed with some dreadful load of old ornaments or something? Probably just dump them in the bin at the entrance to the tube. But the chances of that were diminishing, as the list went on and on, and she was not mentioned once. The thought of John and Barbara actually sitting down to plot all this did absolutely nothing to improve her thoughts about them. And poor Barbara's family was going to be landed with the lot of it.

It wasn't as if they had anything to speak of, either. There was the car coming up now. That went to Barbara's younger brother, too. Oh well, she couldn't afford to run a car anyway; and as small compensation for the crap comics and Airfix collection, he deserved it. So, it was as she wanted. She had nothing. She supposed Barbara's parents might make a bit on the house, which they were coming to now. Prices had risen ridiculously recently...

'And the property of 42 Byron Avenue, or the value thereof accruing from sale...' the solicitor droned. 'To Joseph Emmett.' Finally, he closed the book in front of him.

Sadie was not the only one to scan the room in shock. Surely they could not mean Joe? He'd never been Joseph. But neither had anybody else.

'Joseph Emmett?' Barbara's father spoke the incredulity first.

'My son, I think. Joe,' Sadie offered quietly.

'That boy?' The elder brother exploded. 'That bastard boy!'

Sadie's jaw dropped. She'd never felt such rage in her life, and she rose so fast her chair clattered to the ground. She strode over and slapped the man so hard he nearly lost his own balance.

'How dare you! How dare you and your sanctimonious family speak about my son like that! I hope I never set eyes on any of you ever again. But if I do, if you ever even *think* like that again...' There was no need to go on. She stormed from the room.

The solicitor stopped her at the main door. As she would be trustee of the inheritance until 'Joseph' was eighteen, he would need her signature. Sadie could barely hold the pen from shaking.

'His name's not Joseph. It's Joe,' she muttered. Did they not know that? Or was this just another of their pompous assumptions? 'That's what's on his birth certificate. Does that matter?'

'Well, I will check,' the solicitor replied. 'But I doubt it. I believe there aren't any other living relatives.'

Except me, Sadie thought. But she didn't count, clearly...

Out on the street, gulping lungs full of air, she headed straight for the tube station. And she cried on the train from Victoria. She couldn't contain it any longer. And on top of everything else, she had to reconcile herself to the fact that her five-year-old son now owned forty-eight thousand pounds' worth of suburban semi-detached house...

. . .

These two days were much more fun for Joe and Jay. He was the only one who could come close to making Joe forget the absence of his mother. After nursery on Monday, Jay took him in the minibus with several other students to a centre for disabled children. Jay explained he was only driving Nick and some other students from the Health and Social Care Department, to take a group of children out for the afternoon. Joe could stay in the cabin with him. But Joe was having none of it. He was curious and enthusiastic.

Nick sat up front with them for the journey. Joe didn't mind, as long as he was nearest Jay and could help him with the gear stick. He delighted in the game, as Jay sped down the road, yelling, 'Now!' whenever he depressed the clutch, and Joe's two little hands pushed the gear knob into place. Once on the dual carriageway, however, more for the sake of the other passengers than anything else, Jay persuaded him that it wasn't necessary anymore.

'So then, Jason,' Nick launched into the moment's peace that followed, wiggling his eyebrows suggestively. 'Who was that lovely bit of stuff you got to go home with on Saturday night? And don't make it up. Alan in particular is champing at the bit to take over from you. He said he was going to have a word with you on Wednesday.'

'Really.' Jay was distinctly unimpressed by that prospect.

'Well? Who is she then? Admire your ambition mate. I wouldn't mind a bit of her either, actually—'

'Nick,' Jay glanced down at Joe, who was driving one of his toy cars over his leg. 'Pack it in. She's Joe's mum, OK?' Joe looked up and between them. 'It's OK Joe. Hey look,' Jay pointed out of the window and swiped the car from his lap.

'What?' Joe peered through the windscreen.

'Oh, missed it,' he shrugged and Joe looked back down to his game. And then around the seat, and onto the floor.

'Jaaaay,' he whined. 'I've lost my Beetle!'

'Surely not. Have you looked behind the seat?' Joe wriggled out of his seatbelt and stood up.

'Has anyone seen my Beetle?' he called to the students behind. Jay held it up and put it on his head. The students solemnly shook their heads, and Joe sank back into his seat. 'It's my favourite,' he moaned, looking beseechingly up at Jay. 'It's on your head!'

'Don't be ridiculous, Joe.'

'It is!' he protested, grabbing it. 'How did it get there?'

Everyone was laughing now, and Jay had successfully diverted Joe from Nick's comments.

Nick was not to be similarly diverted, though. 'Bummer,' he continued where he had left off. 'That rather puts a different complexion on things. Poor Alan will be disappointed.'

'She's got a child, not a second head,' Jay retorted.

'Well, I can see it doesn't put you off,' Nick sniggered.

'Look Nick, just shut up. She's a friend, alright?'

'Not fooled, Jason. You're blushing.'

'I am not!' But Jay sensed that he probably was now. There did seem to be a heat rising from his stomach at the subject of this exchange.

'Well—'

'Nick, no! OK?' Jay interrupted for the last time, nodding towards Joe, and hoping he had put an end to that...

The minibus full of children from the centre, Joe immediately went to sit in the back with them. He gave them sweets, he shared his cars, he talked to them with a candour only a child could manage. And he touched them all. He hugged them and held their hands. And he insisted on going round the petting zoo with them, and would not let Jay stay in the van.

So Jay pushed a wheelchair with all the others, pretty soon turning his child-friendly conversational talents towards his charges. He talked and laughed with them too, lifting them up to see the animals and calming them when they screamed. And he felt a tremendous progression within himself, soon feeling at ease and even enjoying himself with them all.

But still he watched Joe with fascination. The boy seemed to command an affection from the children from the very first moment. Even though, or perhaps because, he was a child himself; smaller than most of them, but clearly more able in every respect. And he was openly enjoying every minute, pointing at the animals and giggling with them all. Just another facet to this adorable boy. How had Sadie achieved this...?

'I love the children,' Joe announced as they set off home. Obviously regarding himself as different, but transcending that.

'And I think they love you, too.'

'Jay, can you bring Joe again sometime?' One of the students called from the back. They had all seen him leave the children with a hug and a kiss, and had heard those that could articulate for the rest ask the same question.

Joe swung round. 'Can we?'

'We'll have to ask your mum.'

'OK,' Joe readily agreed. That didn't seem much of a problem. Not now that she liked his friend Jay...

Joe was pensive after tea. 'Jaaay?'

'Yes, mate?'

'Can we go into town tomorrow?'

'We could, if you want.'

'Can you help me buy a present for Mummy?'

'Well, yes, of course. That's nice of you, Joe.'

'It's her birthday on Friday.'

'Oh...? Is it?'

'Yes. I only remembered, because she said she was getting old,' Joe giggled, knowing it had to have been a joke. 'I asked her when she would be old, and she said when she was 30. I think she was joking. But I said I would give her a special birthday when she was 30. And she hugged me... I miss my mummy.'

'I know you do, petal.' Jay gave him a gentle squeeze. 'But she'll be back soon.'

'I don't mind, though, 'cos I'm with you! And you'll help me choose a present for her, because it was a special birthday last year and she didn't tell anyone. So I'm going to make up for it.'

'She's not 30 yet,' Jay laughed.

'No, but I think Aunty Barbara said it was a special birthday.'

'A special birthday?' Jay mused. '21?'

'Yeah, yeah, that's it. 21,' Joe enthused, although he didn't have a clue why this number should be significant.

But it seemed to make an impression on Jay. '21?' he breathed. *She was 21 years old?* That would have made her barely 16 when... This had even more hidden depths than anyone suspected. Bloody hell! He'd guessed that she was 24 or 25 maybe, and having a child at 19 or 20 was bad enough. Tragic without a father on the scene. And it filled him with a heightened concern, admiration and warmth towards her. Twenty-one, eh? Well, if Joe was right, and she'd missed out before, he'd be damned if she wouldn't have a bloody good time this year...

In town, Joe produced the seven fifty pence pieces he had sneaked out of his piggy bank.

'I know what she wants. She says our room is boring. She wants a big green plant for it.' Just like Christmas, Joe knew his own mind clearly.

'That'll be lovely, Joe. But if Mummy's birthday isn't until Friday, you'll have to leave it in my room, won't you? So she doesn't see it?'

'Yeah. Can I? Yeah...'

Joe knew exactly the one he wanted when he saw it in the garden shop. It was a large glossy cheese plant, and it was £5.50. Jay told him that was what seven fifty pences came to, slipped in two pounds when he wasn't looking and took it to the counter.

Joe beamed all the way home.

Leaving the plant in Jay's room, they returned to Ellis House to wait for Sadie's return. She was asleep, in her coat, on the mattress. Joe scrambled from Jay's arms and raced towards her. 'Careful Joe,' Jay whispered, as he seemed intent on waking her most violently. But her sleep was light, and she was conscious already, hugging him to her. Jay could see the traces of tears as she looked up at him over Joe's shoulder.

At a loss for anything else, he put the kettle on. Joe stopped his chattering mid-sentence to complain that's what adults always do, and he was hungry.

'Shall I make it? Or do you want to be on your own?' Jay was keen to hear every detail and didn't want to leave, but he would give her the option.

'I can do it, but... would you stay?' she ventured. 'Please?'

This was new. And Jay was both touched and concerned by the need in her voice. 'Of course,' he nodded with a gentle smile. 'And let me make it. We bought some stuff in town. Joe decided he wanted sausages.'

'Can my cookware stand it?' She managed a small smile, and made him laugh as she mouthed, 'Shit, the sausages!'

.   .   .

Joe finally at rest a couple of hours later, Sadie cracked open the last of the beers. Despite her head already feeling like a prune, she needed the prop.

Jay immediately launched in. 'Come on then, I've been dying to hear all about it.'

'Oh, it was awful,' she began. 'I could feel it the moment I walked in the door. I felt so out of place. They seemed very suspicious of me. It was a bit weird. I suppose they'd all formed their opinions about what I was going to be like, from what they knew, or heard. Don't know if I lived up to them or not. But they were just so patronising.'

'How did you feel about the funeral itself?'

'Oh... nothing,' she sighed. 'I still don't. All the time I was thinking, what am I doing here? It was like I was encroaching on someone else's ceremony. I felt for them, I think. But I just wanted it over and done with. I don't know if it'll ever really hit me...' She seemed to be struggling to reason this, or to admit it, one or the other. 'I feel so guilty. He was my brother. It doesn't matter what I felt about him.'

'Of course it does.'

'I don't know,' she sighed. 'We went to the solicitors, though. About the will, like you said...'

'Yeah?'

'Oh, it was all so stupid. Read to us like we were some so important landed gentry. As if *they* were so important, with their horrific gilt ornaments and boxes of boys' magazines... It doesn't matter,' she muttered. 'I was grateful I didn't get any of it. And I mean it. I don't think I could have handled it. It's bad enough...'

'They didn't leave you anything? I thought you and Joe were John's only living relatives?'

Her lip quivered slightly. 'They... they left the house... to Joe.' She turned her head away, trying to hold back the tears she felt so close to once again. But, wisely or not, Jay drove her to them by gently putting his arm around her shoulders.

'Why did they do that? Why did they have to do that?' she cried, turning abruptly and burying her face in his chest. 'It makes it so much worse! It was theirs. Barbara's family. They should have had it.'

'Why?' Jay gently reasoned. 'They obviously wanted Joe to.'

'What? My *bastard son*?'

'Who said that?' Jay retorted. It was clear someone must have; she would never come out with such a description herself.

'They were upset, I suppose...'

He pulled her a little closer. But her mood had changed already.

'How dare they?' she breathed. 'He's my son! He held them together.'

Jay recalled her saying something similar before. 'What do you mean?'

'They couldn't have children. For a time, a long time, they looked after Joe while I worked. They wanted to adopt him.'

'They *what*...?' But Jay sensed his bemused indignation would not help. 'Well, doesn't that explain it to you?' he suggested instead. 'Joe must have felt the nearest they had to a child of their own. What more natural thing to do than leave their property to him?'

'I suppose so... Yes, I know,' she sighed. 'They don't – Barbara's family. But he deserves it, doesn't he? It is right, isn't it?'

'It's what they wanted. It's right. It's the way it is,' Jay concluded, attempting to provide the 'permission' she was so obviously seeking. 'Have you thought what you're going to do with it? I suppose it solves one or two problems for you?'

'Yes, it does,' Sadie agreed. 'That's what hurts in a way.

When I feel so bitter towards them. I just don't know what I feel. What do I tell Joe?'

'Nothing,' Jay replied. 'It's not his yet, surely?'

'Held in trust by me until he's 18.'

Jay nodded. 'You'll just have to say that John and Barbara are gone, this is ours now. When he's old enough to understand, then he can know.'

'The trusteeship says I can decide whether to sell it or not.'

'Will you?'

'I don't know.'

'Well, there's no sense in thinking about that now. Let things go for a bit. It could be anytime. You have all the time in the world.'

Sadie took a deep breath and conceded. 'You're right.'

'I know it's a responsibility, but you mustn't worry about it. I know you feel guilty too. But it's all over for them. Try and enjoy the freedom they've given you.'

Sadie looked directly at him. It was close to how much he could actually bear now.

And then she hugged him, and it got ten times worse...

'I'm so glad you're here,' she said spontaneously. Jay was quite overwhelmed. But she pulled away instantly. 'I'm sorry...'

'Oh, don't. It doesn't matter what you say to me. I'm glad to be here. I'm very happy you want to talk to me.'

At last.

'I can't explain,' she said. 'You probably know anyway. Just lately I've seemed to have to talk. I'm not content with what I had before. But it's all a bit foreign to me. I'm not very good at it,' she laughed sheepishly. 'It's very good of you to listen.'

'People do, you know. If you let them.'

'I don't know...'

'Besides, you are very interesting,' he smiled lightly. 'Look, the way I see it is, you just say what you want to, no more, no less.'

'It's not as easy as that.'

'I know,' he sighed. 'I know you're not saying all you want to sometimes. And you seem to say things you don't want to now and again. That's probably my fault. But it's a developing art.'

'Yeah,' she responded abstractly. 'I guess I just want you to know that I'm grateful to you, but I don't want you to feel you have to hear it all the time.'

'Are you kidding? Have you noticed me not speaking? I should say you've got a fair bit of catching up to do!'

'Oh, I don't know...' she smiled faintly. 'Sometimes it's just so much easier when things stay unsaid in your head. Then you only have to deal with your own reactions.'

'You might be right. But me? I've never been any good at that. Big mouth, see. I always want someone to talk to.'

'Well, you know you're always welcome now,' she said, getting up to search for more beer.

'Thank you,' he stuttered, the shock rendering the words almost inaudible.

28

'SPECIAL' BIRTHDAY

Jay invented an excuse to take Joe for the afternoon on Thursday. They had a cheese plant to wrap and hide in the toilets at the end of her corridor.

Jay found Joe very excitable that afternoon and, despite his own natural high energy, he nearly wore him out. He really was getting a glimpse of what having a child about all the time was truly like. But the time alone together did give him an opportunity to explain the plan for Sadie's birthday tomorrow night. Joe was hugely enthusiastic. Sworn to secrecy, he seemed to remember what his part in the proceedings would be.

Joe was also delighted to be in the botany 'greenhouse' again. Jay had left an experiment unfinished, and they returned to clear it away on their way back to Ellis House. Joe was happily comparing his cheese plant to a Heartleaf Philodendron, when the Head of Department walked in.

'Well,' he said, glancing at Jay busy at the other side of the lab, then winking at Joe. 'A small new student, eh?'

'This comes from the rainforests in Brazil,' Joe told him,

and they were deep in conversation by the time Jay noticed and scooted over.

'I didn't know you had a family, Jason. What a lovely little fellow he is.'

'Yes, but—'

'How old is he?'

'Joe's five, but—'

'Five? Well, you must be very proud of him.'

'Yes, I am, but—'

The man turned back to Joe. 'And perhaps you can be just as clever at getting daddy to a few more of his lectures, eh?'

'Joe is not my son,' Jay finally managed to squeeze in. 'And if people would just give me half a chance to say it before jumping to conclusions, well, that would be bloody nice!'

Jay looked down at Joe in his arms as he strode away and knew that, once again, the misunderstanding had unbalanced him. 'Sorry, Joe,' he mumbled, at a loss for anything else.

Joe's eyebrows knitted and his lip quivered. 'Why aren't you my daddy if everyone thinks you are?'

Jay sighed. Short of giving him a potted facts of life, and he was pretty sure Joe wasn't quite ready for any birds or bees outside his nature books, what else could he say?

'Somewhere, Joe, is a man who is your daddy. I wish it was me...' That came out spontaneously. He immediately thought it shouldn't have. 'But like I said, it doesn't matter who people think he is, there is only one and, well, that's just the way it is... But listen, don't you worry about that now. We've got a plant to deliver and a brilliant day to look forward to tomorrow!'

It was the most skilful diverting tactic. Joe's eyes lit up.

'Yeah! Tell me the plan again. I like it...!'

. . .

'Oh,' Jay said, on his way out of their room that evening. 'You know the children Joe visited on Monday? The local paper wants a picture for a story on it. Nick asked if Joe'd be in it. It's tomorrow evening. Would that be OK?'

'Tomorrow?'

'Got nothing on, have you?'

'Oh no, no...' Sadie replied, deciding against mentioning her birthday. It would be much of a non-event anyway.

'I'll have to go too, so I'll drive him. Well, look, why don't you come as well?'

'Oh, alright,' she agreed indifferently.

'Fine, OK... Oh yeah, it's some kind of award or something. They said it's quite formal, so maybe smartish clothes? You might have to be in it too, so you as well, I guess. I don't know, what do you think?'

'Well, I've no idea. But no harm, I suppose, as long as Joe gets to be in it. I'm sure I can dig out something.' She did have one dress as it happens, hadn't seen the light of day for a while. Not much call for a slinky black number when you're carting a five-year-old everywhere.

'Great!' he smiled. 'I'll pick you both up about six, OK?'

'Yes, alright then. Joe won't be kept up too late though, will he?'

'Well... I don't think so...'

Sadie wondered in her bed that night why she hadn't told Jay that tomorrow was her birthday. Just like her 21st, it would go unnoticed again. Her great coming of age. Except that she'd had a bit of a coming of age thrust on her sometime before. The only people that knew her birthday had been John and Barbara, and Joe probably, if he remembered. Well, that was the way she wanted it. Or was it, now? She'd changed. She wanted different things now.

But there you go. It was just the way it was going to have to be...

Joe was up first. He would have been excited anyway, but Jay had injected a proper sense of occasion. And he loved the subterfuge, even if he didn't really understand it. Though he didn't know why really, he knew that today was special, and this evening, in particular, was really important. And he was going to do everything he could to help make it so.

For now, his first job. He got a bag from the wardrobe and crept to her drawer. So unusually quietly he pulled out a handful of things and stuffed them in the bag. Then he did the same with his own drawer before shoving the bag back in the wardrobe. Then he reached up and silently let himself out. He just about struggled back with the clumsily wrapped plant, but the scraping on the floor finally woke Sadie.

'Uh oh,' he said, standing in front of it in the corner. He scuttled to the sink and made a glass of orange squash.

'Happy Birthday, Mummy!' He presented her with the squash, spilling it from her hand as he hugged her.

'Whoa, what a treat!' she grinned, shaking herself from sleep and taking a courtesy gulp. 'Thank you, Joe. What a lovely surprise.'

'I make your breakfast now,' he scrambled from her. Sadie smiled to herself, but knew she'd have to get up now. And it was still only 6.45. She managed to tactfully help the cereal, milk and sugar into the bowls while maintaining the illusion that he was doing it all. 'You eat this in bed,' Joe commanded, carrying her bowl carefully over to the mattress. He was always allowed to have his breakfast in bed with her on his birthdays. Sadie brought his, and soon they were tucked up against the wall eating and chatting nonsense.

Joe scrambled away again to drag his present from the dark corner. He left it in front of her and went to his drawer, where he pulled out a piece of folded card. 'I made it,' he announced, as if it wasn't obvious. 'It's a dog and a tree.'

'I can see that,' she lied, feeling a very real sense she was going to cry any minute. They'd never done her birthday alone together like this before, and his efforts amazed and touched her deeply. She pulled off the clumsily wrapped paper.

'Oh, it's beautiful Joe!'

'I chose it!'

'I can tell, because it's just what I want,' she wiggled his nose between her fingers.

'Where are you going to put it?'

'Well, I thought that corner needs something, don't you?'

'Yeah, that corner needs something,' Joe repeated, amusingly. 'I'll put it there!' He dragged it back across the floor.

'Oh yes, that's much better, isn't it?'

'Yeah!' He crawled back into bed with her and there they stayed until nursery time.

And Sadie felt good tramping across the campus, Joe's hand in hers, chatting incessantly as usual. Back in her room, though, a great sense of anti-climax descended. There was no post in her pigeonhole. There rarely was anyway, but she felt it today. And she thought about John and Barbara. There was no-one else. No-one who had an obligation to acknowledge her on this, or any, day. And she felt that creeping anxiety of being all alone in the world with her child again.

But then she looked at her plant in the corner and the card on the shelf. Yes, but such a child as this...

That afternoon, Joe did his best to make it different. They took a picnic to the park, and he tried to help her prepare it, and the tea. He said he wasn't hungry, so he only wanted a piece of toast and chocolate spread. This was surprising; Joe never refused food. But they'd had loads of picnic and she wasn't either, so she went without altogether. Maybe she'd order a pizza and get a bottle of wine as a treat when he was in bed this evening, after they got back from the children's centre. Maybe Jay would come in and share it with her? But that would mean telling him, and she felt foolish about that now. She knew Joe must have had some help to buy his gift. But if it was Jay, he clearly hadn't remembered when he'd arranged their participation in this curious photo-call...

Joe insisted on getting his best clothes out for the evening. He even insisted on wearing the one tie he had. Barbara had bought it for him for their Christmas dinner party. Adornment for the trophy. Sadie hated it. But with his best grey shorts, white shirt and shiny shoes, it seemed right, and she smiled. He looked lovely. Joe was very proud of it too and joked that if she didn't put on her black dress, she would show him up. So to go along with his mood, she did. She even put on a little make-up.

She stopped a little longer at the mirror than she was used to, not quite sure who was looking back at her. The dress hadn't seen the light of day in ages, but she realised it had been a very good buy...

At 6pm prompt, Jay stepped in, unusually punctual, and even more unusually smart in a dark grey two-piece brush velvet suit and tie. Even if the tie did have a drum kit on it.

'Oh Joe, you look smashing!'

Sadie turned from the mirror. 'Wow, this really is some photo,' she grinned at him.

And Jay was quite dumbstruck for a second. She looked absolutely stunning...

'Yeah, daft, innit?' he shrugged. 'But Nick insisted. All seems a bit stupid to me, but there you go. You gotta air the old things every now and again... You look lovely,' he added, shuffling his feet.

'Well, I'd pass you in the street as well,' she fluffed.

'I hope you get in the picture after all this,' he said, quickly changing the subject.

'Oh, I don't mind, as long as Joe does. He's been very excited about it all.'

Jay winked at Joe, a finger to his lips. He whispered something to him as Sadie turned back to put on some earrings. Joe scuttled to the wardrobe and pulled out the bag he had hidden this morning.

'What you got there?' Sadie smiled as she collected her purse and made for the door.

'Joe said he wanted to give the children some of his old toys,' Jay replied lightly. 'Hope that's OK.'

'Only ones from the Tesco box, Joe,' she said, referring to the box they collected anything he'd outgrown, to take to the next nursery Bring and Buy. Joe nodded fervently, and she left it at that...

The minibus was empty.

'Is everyone else making their own way, then?'

'Oh, they've been there all day. I'll just have to take them home.'

'How come you always have to drive this thing?' she laughed.

'Insurance,' he grinned, 'I'm the only one with more than twenty-five birthdays, aren't I?' Jay momentarily lost his cool then. But she said nothing.

Sadie didn't know if she liked this. She wanted him to know now. She didn't want anything, of course, just a good wish or something. And maybe some company later with the pizza. But it was too late. She couldn't bring it up now, and Joe had long since forgotten it all...

'Hey Joe, do you recognise this road?'

They'd been travelling for half an hour and Sadie had been thinking this was going to be a bit late for Joe to stay up if it was this far away. They did seem to be heading quite deep into the countryside, trundling along a very narrow B-Road.

Joe looked out to the darkening sky. 'No, don't think so.'

As if he would, Sadie smiled to herself at Jay's naivety. He was still learning about what being a five-year-old was all about, obviously. And paying attention to road directions was not part of it.

'Damn.' Jay pulled sharply in to a farm gate. He leant over and opened the glovebox. 'No map in here either,' he sighed, then started up again and followed the road to a junction. 'Eenie, meenie, miny... moe!' He swerved to the left. He didn't seem to be finding the fact they were lost all that troublesome.

Another deserted country road. He pulled off it and up a gravel driveway. 'I'll go and ask in here...'

Sadie peered out to what looked like a castle, but was clearly an extremely posh hotel.

Jay jumped out. 'Won't be a sec...'

'I'm coming. I wanna come!' Joe screamed. Jay smiled to himself. He was doing so well.

'Oh, let's all go then. It's cold out here,' he said casually. Sadie tutted, trying to restrain her wriggling child, and followed with Joe in her arms, merrily poking her necklace down her cleavage.

She looked around the foyer in some awe. This place was something! She'd never been anywhere like it. Jay was speaking to the receptionist.

'We have to go this way,' he said, disappearing through an elaborate oak panelled door.

'Oh, we'll wait here, shall we?'

Joe's brow furrowed. This wasn't in the script.

But he improvised. 'I wanna go. I wanna see in there.'

'Joe, be quiet,' Sadie whispered, his voice cutting through the opulent hush of this grand place.

'I wanna go! I wanna see in there!'

And to save further embarrassment, Sadie briskly followed where Jay had gone.

'Ah, there you are,' he smiled at the door of a low-lit, cosy but stylish restaurant. 'Well, useless people round here don't know where we are either...' He picked her hand from her side, raising his eyebrows provocatively. 'So we'll just have to stay here, won't we?'

Jay led her a few steps to a secluded alcove. Joe scrambled from her arms as she just stood and stared. The private little corner was elaborately decorated, with a table in the middle and three chairs. And in the centre of the table was a cake, with the piped iced words, 'Happy *Special* Birthday, Our Love, Joe and Jay'. Sadie could not believe her eyes. They were blurring with tears anyway.

'Oi mushy, none of that,' Jay laughed. 'Happy Birthday...' He leant over and kissed her briefly on the cheek.

'I... I had no idea,' she gaped.

'Course you didn't. You're dealing with professionals here, eh Joe?'

'Yeah!'

'Sit down, then... Did you like your cheese plant...? Hey! I'm talking to you!'

Sadie was still marvelling at everything around her, biting her lip like an excited child.

'Yes, it was really lovely!'

'What else did you get then?'

'Nothing,' she replied, with no trace of surprise or disappointment. Jay looked bewildered, and she laughed. 'It's OK, no-one knew anyway.'

'You didn't tell anyone?'

Sadie shuffled uneasily, so Jay dropped the incredulity.

'Oh, well then, if you don't want any pressies. I'll keep this.' He swiped a small gift-wrapped box from the table and shoved it in his pocket. Sadie looked at the pocket and then back up at him in shock. 'Oh, it's so nice to give you and Joe things. You're always so... surprised!' he giggled. 'Here you are, then. Hope you like it...' He almost threw it at her. In truth, he was a little worried about it, but really had no idea what to get her. He just knew he wanted it to be special.

'Oh, God...' Sadie lifted a silver chain from the velvet box, with a deep green stone matching her eyes. 'It's lovely! You shouldn't have—'

'Na, na, none of that.'

Sadie dispensed with her own far inferior version and fastened the chain around her neck. 'Thank you.' She got up and returned his kiss on the cheek. 'I can't believe it all. It's all so kind of you.'

'Nothing to do with me,' Jay grinned. 'It was all Joe's idea. All coming out of your piggy bank, innit Joe?'

Joe's eyes widened. 'I haven't got anything in there!' Which sent them both into fits of giggles.

'Right!' Jay clapped his hands together. 'A nice St Emilion, I think. What do you reckon...? Great, there's one. Ooh! That must be good,' he chuckled over the wine list. It was £25.00 a bottle.

'Jay—'

'Shut up,' he sang, not even looking up from the menu.

Alright then, if this was how it's going to be. She would just damn well enjoy it. 'Lovely, yeah...'

The marvellous bottle was indeed gorgeous. Sadie savoured every drop as they tucked into a delicious and very carefully crafted starter. Jay had thought of everything. He'd pre-ordered something simpler for Joe, who munched happily on his egg mayonnaise with fish and chips to follow, even if they were rather elaborately presented, washed down with Cherry Cresta. Those were his favourites, and that was what he was going to have. Sadie marvelled at Jay, and it was obvious in her expression. And he smiled to himself, the tiny remnants of his nerves dissipating. Yes, he had done something right…

Joe dived into his fish and chips, even before they had finished the first course.

'Maybe I should get that put back. He'll be an absolute case when he's finished,' Sadie laughed. 'You will have noticed a bit of an absence of patience, I don't doubt, by now.'

'S'no problem,' Jay winked at Joe. 'He's got the video of ET upstairs, where I believe there is also a very nice lady who is going to sit and help him watch it, before putting him to bed. Isn't that right, Joe?'

'Yeah! Nobody else has seen it, Mum! Wait until I tell George on Thursday!' And the re-ignited prospect only encouraged him into even faster consumption.

Sadie gaped at Jay.

'It's not really a bag of toys,' he giggled. 'Christ knows what's in there, though. Joe packed you an overnight bag. So…' he lifted the almost empty bottle of wine, 'I reckon it's high time for another one of these!'

Jay waved the bottle at the waiter, and when he turned back, she was still staring at him. His smile faltered, knowing he was letting his enthusiasm carry him away, as usual, only heightened by half a bottle of this gorgeous stuff.

'S'OK, innit? Just thought you could really relax if we didn't have to rush off. I've told the nursery he won't be in tomorrow. We're going to Arundel—'

'Jay…' For a second it looked as if she was going to object, but then she shook her head and laughed. 'This is just... amazing...!'

Joe finished his Knickerbocker Glory as the second bottle of wine arrived. He crashed the spoon down. 'Can I go now?'

Sadie looked at Jay, who was already gesturing to the waiter. 'Well, I guess so...'

Joe's chaperone arrived to take him away.

'It's all OK,' Jay reassured. 'You've got a suite with two rooms. She's gonna stay with him, alright? So...' he grinned, lifting the second bottle of wine. 'You can get as pissed as you like!'

Sadie giggled; she was getting there already. And for the next couple of hours, they thoroughly enjoyed the gorgeous meal, wine and increasingly nonsensical conversation. By dessert, they were telling jokes, spinning cutlery and making shapes out of the food. Jay was on top form, feeding off her excitement and happiness. She was looser than he'd ever seen her before, recounting funny stories and displaying a wonderful gift for mimicry he had only glimpsed while they were doing the Christmas show. She was funny. Incredibly funny.

'Stop it!' he finally demanded. 'I'm gonna piss myself in a minute...!'

They, of course, had no room for the lovely cake, which was wrapped to take home. But neither wanting the evening to end, they retired to the lounge over a huge cafetiere of coffee and a couple of brandies, laughing and joking and chatting until the early hours. At several points, having to restrain each other from a level of noise and behaviour most unbefitting such a place as this. Eventually, though, they had to give up, chasing down the corridor to their rooms, with lots of mock ssshing and suppressed laughter.

Jay handed her a key. She was looking at him more soberly now. He wished she would stop...

'Thank you, Jay. Thank you so much.'

God, he could really kiss her now. Standing there so flushed and gorgeous, so witty and warm and giggly. Christ, how he wished he could...

'Thank *you*,' he replied instead. 'I've had the best time.'

'Me too.'

Jay smiled and tore himself away through the door of his room, his head spinning pleasantly.

And his heart full.

'You OK?' Jay laughed. Sadie was dressed for breakfast in the jeans and jumper that Joe had indiscriminately packed the day before, but was fidgeting a little in her seat.

'Sorry,' she grinned, leaning over to whisper, 'I am wearing the most uncomfortable knickers in my repertoire. Joe, bless him, did not make too good a choice.'

Jay joined her laughter, although a part of him had no wish to be contemplating her underwear at that moment.

She made a quick detour into the supermarket for something more comfortable, before they enjoyed a lovely day at Arundel Castle, followed by the Wetland Centre. Joe was absolutely beside himself. Chessington, a castle, nature park and ET...? The man was a god!

It was gone eight o'clock by the time they returned to the university, Joe asleep in his mother's arms. Jay declined to come in. He had his reasons. He'd had a wonderful time, best to quit while he was ahead. Go and calm down and sort himself out, rather than risk his enthusiasm bubbling over into something regrettable and ruining it all...

Sadie didn't stay up long herself. The rarity of her limbs at rest and her mind at peace, she just wanted to lie in her bed and savour it. Revelling in the time they had had. The laughter, the relaxation, the company and generosity – of spirit as much as anything else. She knew perhaps her reactions were exaggerated, child-like even. But, in a sense, the responses of a child were the only ones available to her. For so many years she'd been rationed all these things, the attention and the freedom to enjoy it. And she didn't really know how to deal with them. Sometimes her responses seemed foolish and inadequate to her.

In reality, it would only take Jay to tell her, they were the sincerest and most heart-warming he had ever known.

29

EASTER

'Ta-da!' Jay threw his arms wide towards the gleaming black Ford Capri blocking the entrance to Ellis House. 'What d'you think of that then? Just got it! Blown half my cash. Isn't it gorgeous?' He looked at his watch. 'Time for a quick spin before Joe's bedtime...?'

The Capri clearly suited Jay's style of motoring much better than a minibus. They sped and swerved around the country roads in the early evening light, before heading back to put Joe to bed. 'So,' he concluded, still with that wild light in his eyes. 'I can take you home tomorrow. If you like.'

'Great!' Sadie eagerly agreed. 'Are you sure?'

'Of course. There's only about ten miles between us. No problem.' It wouldn't have mattered if it had been ten thousand. He knew that now. Just a few more hours with them...

And a few *less* hours in Chorleywood. He did not relish the prospect of returning to the parental nest again. It had been tough for him at Christmas. It always was. But he was a little more settled in himself now. He had his car; he had some plans for the future, for the first time ever. He'd bear them; he'd manage. It wouldn't be for long. Maybe by the summer he'd get a place of his own...

Sadie's own worries about what she would find at their new/old house proved needless. Nothing had been moved at Byron Avenue. All the furniture, the kitchen appliances, beds and carpets were as numerous and immaculate as when John and Barbara were there.

'Well,' Jay breathed. 'I think you're gonna be alright then...'

Joe was already running around the house. She made some tea – she didn't even have to unpack her kettle – and they sat at the kitchen table. Neither had much to say.

'Well, I guess I better be on my way...' Jay scribbled a number on a piece of paper. 'Call me sometime, about going back, if you like.'

She nodded, wordlessly.

'Well...' he slapped his thighs, but no more words came to him either.

'Bye, Joe!' he called up the stairs.

There was a heavy bump, followed by Joe tearing down the steps. 'You going now?'

'Yeah,' Jay replied. 'So, I'll see you next term, OK? Be a good boy, and look after your mum.'

'Yeah, I will,' Joe confidently assured him. Jay knelt down to hug him, screwing his eyes shut to hold back the emotion.

'I'll miss you, Jay.'

And that made it ten times worse.

'Oh, and I'll miss you too,' Jay whispered. He'd been here before, at the end of the last term. But the magnet had been charged a hundredfold since then... 'Right, I'm going, before I make a complete berk of meself by bursting into tears.'

Sadie returned his weak smile. 'Take care,' she said, touching his arm. 'And thanks for everything.'

'And you...'

Tearing himself from their light for the last time, he walked out towards the darkness.

It didn't take Sadie long to be comfortable in the house. Joe enjoyed the space and freedom, of course, and it was inevitable that she would, too. Rightly or wrongly, she rarely thought about John and Barbara, slowly beginning to stamp their own personality on the house and décor. She got to know the neighbours a little. Many of them were new since her schooldays, so she could exercise the old make-believe with them. Even so, she felt a little wary in this place, not knowing who she might bump into. Well, she had changed, and if Jay had been right, they wouldn't recognise her anyway.

Stuffed full of chocolate and silliness, Easter was an enjoyable affair. But Sadie found the long days afterwards a little tedious. Joe was happy enough, although he missed the nursery and the unusual university life to which he had become so accustomed. And he clearly missed Jay. He took so much delight in exercising his expressions. 'Ain't', 'innit?', 'petal', 'cool', 'cop that', 'do me a favour, mate...' Sadie guessed it was some kind of comfort to him, keeping him in mind. And so, she realised, did she. She was lonely. Especially in the evenings, with only the TV for company after Joe had gone to bed. Why she felt restless now, she still didn't understand. It had always been this way...

So one morning as they returned from shopping, she dug in her bag for the bit of paper with his number on it, and bundled Joe into a phone box. She felt a little uneasy about doing so, but the need to speak to him was growing by the day. It worried her.

She was beginning to realise just how fond she was of him, and this surely involved her in some kind of dependence...?

She replaced the receiver without dialling.

'What are you doing?' Joe twirled the phone wire around his fingers, clearly much more settled and excited at the prospect of speaking to Jay.

She stood still, biting her lip. Then, with a quick reflex, she grabbed the receiver, dialling hurriedly before she could change her mind again.

A man answered. Sadie assumed Jay's father.

'Hello,' she hesitated. 'Could I speak to Jay, please?'

'He's not here,' came the brusque reply.

'Oh, well, never mind. Will he be in later?'

'I mean, he's not here. He's gone. I wasn't having him in the house a moment longer.'

The tone, as much as the open conclusion, shocked her.

'Right. Well, could you tell me where he is?'

'No idea. Some friend, I think.'

'Do you know which one?'

'I expect my wife could tell you, but she's got her Canasta group at the moment.'

'Could you ask her? Would it be too much trouble?' Sadie politely persisted, her unease growing.

'Oh, really,' the man sighed. 'Bridget...!'

'Jason you want, is it?' A woman's voice returned a moment later.

'If you have a forwarding number or address, I'd be very grateful.'

'Well, there's a number here. That looks like his writing. Try it if you like. It's Redhill 610526.'

'OK, thank you very m—'

She'd hung up.

'Alright, Joe?' Sadie smiled, trying to hide her concern from him. 'One more minute matey, Jay's moved house...' She dialled the new number.

'Where's he gone?'

Sadie gestured that she didn't know, as the phone was answered again. This time by a much more friendly voice. But Benny said he'd left four days ago, might have gone to Nick's place. He gave her another number.

'Look, he might get in touch. I borrowed some books off him. Do you want me to give him a message if he does?'

'Oh, well yeah, you could just say that I rang. My name's Sadie. Well, that's it really. I hope he's OK.'

'*Sadie*, right,' he said, peculiarly. 'OK Sadie, I'll give him the message if I see him. I'm sure he'll be very sad to have missed you. I hope you get in touch with him soon. It'll do everyone a bit of good...'

Not understanding and deeply concerned now, she continued to pull happy faces at Joe as she searched in her purse for more change to ring the next number.

The story this time was that Jay had left this morning and there was no forwarding address. He'd only stayed one night. Nick had a big family with five younger brothers and sisters, and there just wasn't room for him. Nick sounded guilty, although he too seemed very interested that she had called.

'Oh dear, Joe,' Sadie said as lightly as she could. 'Just can't find him.'

'Where is he?' Joe repeated.

'Well, I don't know, Joe. But never mind. We'll see him again soon, at the university.'

Joe pouted and noisily tramped the few yards back to the house, slapping the neighbours' walls with a stick. But he quickly regained his cheer, watching some nesting blue tits in the bird box in the garden. Sadie found it a little more difficult. It didn't sound like a very happy sequence of events.

Where was he indeed...?

Jay arrived back at Benny's house in Redhill in his new Capri and yet another tank of petrol. He'd only come to pick up his books and maybe get a trip to the pub with his mate. He'd had enough of being on his own. Benny was concerned about him; he didn't look all that with it. But he'd already made arrangements for the evening, and Jay assured him he didn't expect to stay; he knew it wasn't convenient. Benny felt uneasy, knowing his family hadn't made him all that welcome. He gave him the phone message anyway. He knew by the way Jay was staring at him, it meant something.

Jay slept in the car that night, as he had done a couple of times in the last few days. The reasons he hadn't gone to her when he was kicked out of the parental home over a week ago had not changed. Yet she had been trying to contact him. Surely that made some difference? It was very important to him, in fact, and right there and then he just wanted to be with her and Joe. But he had wanted that all along. It was all he seemed to want nowadays. But it was three o'clock in the morning, and he would just have to think it out in daylight...

Jay headed north the next morning. He still hadn't made up his mind where to go, but he had to feel as if he was going somewhere. As soon as he decided one way, he would change his mind. Until, on the spur of the moment, he took a sharp turning off the M25 onto the Watford exit. Well, it was done now...

Sadie had just come out of the shower when the doorbell rang. 'Joe, answer the door please,' she called down the stairs.

Joe trotted down the hallway and opened the door a fraction, as he had been taught, but as soon as he saw who it was, he threw it wide. 'Jaaaay!'

Jay picked him up, but there was none of his usual exuberance with the boy. 'I suppose I can come in then...'

'You're all hairy,' Joe giggled, his fingers through Jay's short beard.

'Yeah, it's the Monster from the Black Lagoon,' he tried to joke, pulling a face, which worked on Joe in any case.

'I'm pleased you're here, Jay!' As if it wasn't obvious. 'I got lots to tell you. I'll put the kettle on first,' he said, clambering down from his arms. 'Mummy showed me how...'

'Jay!' Sadie jumped down the stairs two or three at a time. Taking in his unkempt and unshaven appearance, all her worries gathered in her, and she found herself hugging him. 'Where've you been? What's been happening?'

Jay sighed, closing his eyes over her shoulder.

'Can I stay?'

'Of course,' she replied instantly. 'What's happened?'

There was no answer.

'Jay?'

'Oh, the welcome,' he sighed abstractly, sounding so drained and tired.

Sadie studied him for a moment. 'Come on...' She changed tactics and led him to the lounge, where she sat him down and put the fire on. 'You're cold.'

'Thanks,' he mumbled with a faint nod.

'And I bet you're starving as well. I'll get you something to eat. Where's Joe?'

'I'm putting on the kettle!' Joe called from the kitchen.

'Very fetching,' Jay muttered. At any other time it would have been a shared joke, delivered with panache.

'You go and talk to Jay while I make the tea.'

'Yeah!' Joe sprinted back and climbed onto his lap, chatting away, oblivious that Jay was not really listening...

Joe engrossed in Abbott and Costello re-runs, Sadie felt safe to switch to the sofa and gently venture, 'Why the treks round the country, then? It's been like a chain letter trying to get hold of you.'

'Sorry,' he shrugged. 'What did you want?'

Sadie looked at him. He was different. And it wasn't just the dishevelled clothes, unruly hair and the beard. What was it? She wanted to know so much.

'Nothing,' she replied lightly instead. 'I just wanted to talk to you.'

'Anything wrong?' he asked indifferently.

'No.'

'Oh, you just wanted to talk to me. Whatever the bloody hell for?'

'Jay...?' Her eyes narrowed. 'What's happened? What's the matter?'

'Oh, it's nothing,' he sighed. 'Am I being rude? I apologise.' It sounded as insincere as it looked from his indifferent expression.

'We'll talk when Joe's gone to bed, yeah?'

'If you want...'

Face obscured, eyes lowered, there was a detached edginess about him that disturbed her. So unlike him. He was a man of extremes of emotion, she knew that now. Not this cold indifference... But after Joe had gone to bed, with assurance that Jay would still be here in the morning, she didn't want to appear like the Spanish Inquisition, so she returned downstairs to an armchair in front of the TV.

Suddenly, though, she could sense him. She could feel his

eyes on her. She turned back towards him. And yes, he was staring at her. Unusually, disturbingly, he didn't look away. His expression was intense, his eyes part fearful, part angry. And for a second, her breath caught in her throat. There was something about that look... But no, it passed, and she could see him again. Feel his pain. She got up and crossed the room to sit beside him.

'Jay...?' Nothing. 'Speak to me.'

'What do you wanna hear?' he drawled.

'I want to hear what's going on up there,' she replied, tapping the side of his head, and finding herself stroking his face as her hand withdrew. He flinched, and she moved away instantly.

'Why?'

'Jay, stop it. Please. What's happened to you? You're scaring me.'

And with that, his eyes changed, and his expression softened. *Scaring her*...? That was just not in his rulebook.

'I'm sorry,' he said, eyes back to his lap. 'It's nothing. It really is nothing...'

No more came. Sadie tried another approach. 'I phoned your parents yesterday. Why did they kick you out?'

'It don't take much,' he muttered contemptuously. 'Any excuse. I'm in the way. The affairs and the card clubs... Oh, that's not true. It's always been that way. Look, they're fucked off because I got this money and they pretend to be awfully uptight about the fact that I blew it on a car. And the best I can do for a future is think I wanna be a drummer. So, I get the crap about irresponsibility and all the usual fucking rubbish they're always throwing at me. So...' he concluded hotly. 'We all threw me out. And, since you want the whole stupid story. I went down to my mate Benny's, where I'm less than popular with his horsey parents as well and obliged not to hang about too long. And so I went down to Kent to visit Nick, where the house is already bursting at the seams with the Parker millions. In between all of which I've been kipping in the car...'

So there it was, the potted story. All the while, his tone so bitter and sarcastic. Sadie was upset by this as much as the sorry tale. Exaggerated or not, it was all he needed to feel that he was not welcome anywhere he went.

'Why didn't you come here?'

'Oh yes, why didn't I?' he retorted in a tone she did not understand. 'Well I did, didn't I? Here I am.'

'I'm glad you are.'

'Oh yeah?' he fired back. 'What do you want me for, eh?'

Time for yet another approach. 'I don't. You're all I need. Fuck off then. Go on, get out of here!' And it worked, of a fashion. Jay's rigid expression crumbled, until it was really quite pitiful.

'Don't... Please don't. Don't make me go.'

'I had no intention of letting you.' She touched his hand. 'Look, Jay, you're unfortunate. Families have their own routines that don't always accommodate the unexpected. And you've got a couple of shits for parents! You've got to find some room for yourself and where you fit. Jay, you're 26. It's about time you didn't have to rely on them anyway.'

He looked to the ceiling. 'Don't you think I know that? You've gotta understand... It's like... it's like being on probation. Trapped and watched. And then you get to a stage when you can't think of surviving without it.' He looked back to her, so searchingly. 'You gotta understand. Somebody please has got to understand...'

And she nodded, trying so hard to.

'When I'm at the university, I can forget about it all. Mostly. I don't think about it. It just is. I've been away from home. I did bad things. I went back. That's the way it's been. That's the way it is. But... Christ, I hate them!' he concluded with such passion, it all made sense. 'And what's *so* bloody funny is that they just plain hate me too...'

It did Sadie good to see this in him. She'd glimpsed it before; the clouds behind the enthusiasm and open playfulness, which she sensed was his real place in the world. Now she could see the bitterness that had grown within him. She understood that kind of thing only too well. And she felt a tremendous desire to resolve it all for him. But what was she doing? Thinking she could free anyone of these feelings, when she was commanded by a deep root of bitterness within herself every day. What she was seeing, though, was that the past leaves its scars on everyone.

But there was something she could offer.

'You can stay here. I want you to stay here. And Joe would want you to stay here.' She was hammering the point as hard as she could, pulling back the rejection he had suffered over the past couple of weeks. 'You're so capable, Jay. You've got so much going for you. You can leave all that behind. Stand on your own?'

He glanced at her before lowering his eyes to his lap again. 'You don't know what it's like, do you? I know you've got it tough, but you're good at it. You wouldn't understand how frightened I get just at the thought of being alone.'

'It's better than being oppressed,' she replied with a dry smile. 'But believe me, I know all there is to know about being alone. And I know it's frightening.'

Jay screwed up his face. 'I know, I know, I'm sorry. I don't know what I'm saying.'

'It's OK. You've got some thinking to do,' she gently concluded. 'And you can do it here. Just say whatever you want at anytime. But do remember you *are* welcome here.' She knew that would have been impossible for her to say months, even weeks ago.

'I'm so grateful to you.'

'Mutual Appreciation Society,' Sadie smiled, rubbing his knee as she got to her feet. 'I'll make the spare bedroom up...'

He had expected the sofa. What a luxury. There really was room for him here. And he was welcome. She said so. Maybe he could feel secure here. But first, he had to make sure he never said or did anything to threaten it.

30

OUR HOUSE

The switch flicked, there was a dramatic difference in Jay from the very next day. The smile and the laughter returned, playing with Joe in his normal over the top manner. Joe was, at first, extremely excited to have him around the place, but very soon settled down. It became normal. It just was; as it should be. Jay was just a part of his life now. Living with him, in his house. In *their* house.

Jay noticed, however, that Sadie would sometimes look at him and the slightest something would come to her eyes. As if it really was him that was scaring her now. It disturbed him. But he got his answer when he was hunting for some batteries for his razor.

'Thought I might get this off,' he said, fingering his untidy beard. 'Can't make up my mind. What do you reckon?'

'Well, I don't know. It's up to you...' she replied, but she couldn't meet his eye.

'I bloody hate shaving,' he laughed.

'Well, I guess you don't have to...'

'Ah, not a fan, I can tell.'

'It's not that...' she hesitated. 'I quite like it... Just reminds me of someone, that's all,' she mumbled.

Oh, terrific! That was bloody obvious. So he had a beard, did he? Jay wondered how much more she might tell him. He must have been a bit older than her then. Not another 16-year-old carried away in teenage experiment. His mind was already doing the rounds of possibilities. And he almost pursued it there and then. But he stopped himself.

'Well, clearly, that is not a good thing,' he laughed instead. Although she quite liked it? That was a nice thing to hear. Nevertheless, the next time she saw him, it was gone.

And Jay was learning fast now. Or thought he might be.

'I was speaking to your neighbour this morning,' he gently began as they sat in the lounge after Joe's bedtime. 'He asked me about my trip to the Far East?'

Sadie looked up sharply. 'What did you say to him?'

'What was I supposed to say? I just said it was fine, but I was glad to be back, you know—'

'You *what*?'

'Look, just tell me what the story is, so I don't drop you in it.'

'You pretended to be...?' She could hardly get the words out. There was a tight knot in her stomach; bitterness, anger and, yes, embarrassment, which only heightened her pricked defences.

'What did you want me to say? You want them to think you're having an affair or something while hubby's away on business? Or can you afford a live-in gardener nowadays?'

'You've no right!'

'Oh, do try and see sense,' Jay reasoned. 'What's worse, dealing with me or them? Come on, it doesn't matter to me. I'm just trying to save you embarrassment. Don't feel foolish. You've got nothing to hide from me.'

'Oh, haven't I?' she snapped, shades of previous confrontations.

'Alright,' he sighed. 'I'll go round there right now and tell them I'm not Joe's father, I'm just staying for a while.'

'It's the truth!'

'And since when have you been bothered about the truth?'

Sadie was battered into silence, and Jay knew he had gone too far. 'I'm sorry...' But she was already out of the room. Jay was on his feet instantly. 'Sadie! I'm sorry!'

Her bedroom door slammed.

So he'd blown it again. He didn't have her trust. But despite his sharp reaction, she was being unreasonable, wasn't she? Why wouldn't she tell him? Why couldn't she let it all out? *Why* wasn't he allowed to know? God, this hurt. Because... because he cared so much for her. This was all wrong. And suddenly, he was the one who was scared. He didn't want to get caught in this. He didn't want it to go any deeper. He was feeling so hurt already.

Standing alone in the silent empty hallway. Desperate for her just to let him flood his arms around her. Cry his apologies. Make her cry hers. And let him take it all from her.

Because he loved her.

Didn't he...?

Did he...? Was that what all this was about? The talking, the closeness. The gentle open concern for him, despite her own closure. The reaching out to him. The laughter, when it came. Her hysterically funny wit, and that gorgeous girlish giggle. Those penetrating, vulnerable big green eyes. And the touch of her near him lately. So soft, so magnetic... Had he really fallen in love with her? Not just her adorable boy? *Had he...?* He'd never been here before.

And he couldn't handle it...

· · ·

Sadie's heart sank when she heard the engine of the car. And it was worse by half-past-two in the morning and he still hadn't returned. She could not bring herself to go to bed, knowing he had left in the mood that she had driven him to, and not knowing what had happened to him. But just as she was about to get undressed, she heard the car on the kerb and his key in the lock.

She ran down the stairs.

And Jay was the closest he had come to being resolved when she threw her arms around him, crying, 'Don't do that to me!'

He was hers.

Over the next few days, the last before they returned to the university, things got pretty much back to normal. Neither of them mentioned it again. And Jay not showing any hint of the desperate progression he had made in his mind. He would just be there for her. No questions, no demands, no demonstrations. And he would take what he had, for as long as it lasted. It was possible, he assured himself. He was managing. He was with her. He was with Joe. In fact, he didn't want to go back to the university, where although he knew he would be welcome to visit, there would not be the freedom and interdependence they were sharing now...

But back they had to go. Sadie was packing, while Jay kept Joe out of her way, when a letter fell out of one of his nursery books. She immediately came downstairs to where they were playing garages in the lounge.

'Joe...? What's this?' She held up the letter with his nursery book. Joe looked away. 'Why didn't you tell me, lovey?' She sat down on the settee and patted the space beside her. Joe got up and sat in it. She put an arm around him, but there was no response. 'It doesn't give us much time now, does it?'

She passed the letter to Jay, looking quizzically at her, and he too learned that the nursery was putting on a show at the beginning of term. Each child had been asked to prepare something to perform with a parent.

'Never mind,' she reassured her unusually silent boy. 'We'll work something out. What would you like to do?'

Joe shrugged. 'Nothing.'

'What is it, Joe?' Sadie pulled him to her.

Joe shuffled in his seat. 'Mrs Turnbull kept talking about our daddies. All the boys are doing something with their daddies.' His tone was clearly hurting now, although he could barely articulate it. 'George's dad juggles. They're going to do juggling. And Norris is playing goals with his.'

'*Norris?*' Jay mouthed at her, stifling a giggle. But she did not feel inclined to join him at that moment. Joe was crying.

'Oh, Joe,' Sadie whispered, pulling him onto her lap and cradling him. 'Come on, matey, let's go and see the bird house...' And she picked him up and strode out through the French windows, leaving Jay looking sadly after them.

Of course, he'd jump right up and take Joe on that stage. Do whatever he wanted, anything. Give him a daddy to show off for a day, just like George and Norris. But he knew that was a step too far for Sadie. Especially after the other night. So, this wasn't his game. And he must let her play it...

Out in the garden, although it hadn't been her intention, the family of blue tits was clearly in preparation in the bird box, the male flying in and out with bits of foliage for the nest.

'He's back,' Joe almost smiled.

'Oh, yes. He's very busy, isn't he?'

'When will the baby birds come?'

'Soon I think, Joe. Perhaps we'll look tomorrow. Maybe we'll hear them before we go.'

'What will happen then?'

'Well, they'll be very small and they won't be able to fly just yet. So the mummy and daddy birds will bring them food and feed them for a while. And then, very soon, they will grow their feathers and the mummy and daddy birds will leave them to fly away on their own. Then we'll have lots of them in the garden, won't we?' she smiled, her hand to his face.

'Yeah,' Joe half-enthused. 'But don't the mummy and daddy birds stay with the little baby birds...?'

Well, she'd walked right into that one. But, she supposed, it led quite neatly to the conversation she wanted to have.

'No, they don't, Joe. When the baby birds are big enough to look after themselves, they will go.'

'When will I be big enough?' He looked searchingly up at her.

'Oh, not for a very long time yet,' she smiled, hugging him to her.

'And then you'll go?'

'Well, we're a bit different from the birds, Joe. With us, it's you that will go. When you're ready.'

'I won't.'

'One day you will Joe, and it'll be alright.'

'I won't.'

'And I'll always be around. You know that.'

Joe was thoughtful for a moment. 'I wasn't big enough when Daddy left me.'

Sadie sighed. 'No, you weren't.'

'So why did he go?' he pleaded, so pitifully.

He was never there in the fucking first place! Sadie's temperature was rising. But she turned from her own reactions to settle her son.

'He got it wrong, Joe. That's all,' she said as gently as she could. 'Sometimes people don't do the right thing. And he didn't. So, he never knew you. If he had known you, I'm sure he would have loved you, just like I do...'

She knew that was a lie. But she could never tell him. Never tell him how he came to be. What kind of father he really had...

But now it was time for Joe to tell *her*. He'd never mentioned this before.

'Jay said you could choose me another one.'

'Did he?' she replied tersely, but she softened. Clearly, Jay was having to deal with these conversations with Joe. And she knew him now; he would be doing all he could to make them right for him.

'But *you* have to choose him,' Joe continued anyway. 'Not me.'

Sadie nodded, although the notion was about as far from her mind as it could be.

'That's not fair!' Joe protested. There was no real answer to that. And then he came right out with it. '*Why* isn't Jay my daddy?'

Sadie sighed. This was so difficult. 'Because he isn't, Joe,' she said gently but firmly. Joe started to cry again. 'Oh, Joe...' She squeezed him to her. 'I know it's hard. I'd give anything to make it right for you. But Jay's here now. You can play with him... like a daddy.' She almost didn't say that. It was just too distressing.

Yes Joe, and one day he'll bugger off as well and break your little heart.

She couldn't bear it. And she knew then that they had been better off without him. When Joe had never known the love of a man. And such a love as this. Which would eventually be taken away from him. It had to be...

But Joe was elsewhere now.

'Would Jay play with me? In the show?'

And she also knew that she had to let him have this. For as long as it would last. She couldn't be the one to take it away. Not now.

'Well,' she tried a smile. 'Why don't you ask him...?'

When they returned to the house, Joe was unusually hesitant.

'Alright?' Jay looked up with a gentle smile. She nodded, not entirely convincingly. 'Come on, Joe. This one's run out of petrol.' He waved a car in the air. 'We better get it back in the garage.' But Joe still clung to Sadie. And Jay wondered what he had done. Or said. Or what might have passed between them in the last few minutes. He looked at Sadie. At least she didn't seem quite as wary as Joe.

'OK, down you get, poppet. I've got to finish the packing,' she smiled, dropping him to the floor. 'Go on, Joe. What have you got to ask Jay?'

Joe glanced between them. Jay tried to look encouraging. He was still a bit confused. 'Go on, matey,' Sadie gave him a little push. 'I'm going back upstairs.'

Jay was encouraged by the small smile she gave him, as Joe ambled back to his side.

'Alright then, Joe, spill the beans.'

Secured by Jay's arm once more, Joe looked up at him.

'I haven't got a daddy, Jay.'

'I know, petal,' he whispered, kissing the boy's hair.

'Will you be my daddy? Just for the show? Can you play with me in the show?'

Jay leant his cheek on the boy's head and sighed.

'Yes, mate. Of course I will...'

He let the silence be for a moment before checking. 'Did Mummy say that would be OK?' That couldn't be easy for her.

Joe nodded. 'She said I should ask you.'

'Well, that's alright then... Hey!' And now he was grinning. 'Are we gonna show Norris a thing or two? Football? On a stage? I ask you... Right then, Joe-mo, what say we give them some *real* entertainment?'

Joe had little conception of what he was saying, except that it might involve being better than Norris, which pleased him hugely; and that Jay had that wide-eyed enthusiasm again that never ceased to rub off on him.

'How about it then? Joe-mo and Jay-mo, the Blues Brothers!'

'Yey!' Joe shrieked. Even Sadie could hear him from upstairs. And she smiled in relief, albeit with the twist in her stomach remaining.

'OK, you leave it to me. Wednesday, yeah? Loads of time. I'll square it with your mum so you can come round and we'll do some practice before, OK?'

'Yeah. I'll be good. I'll learn it real good!'

'And Joe...' Jay leaned in. 'What say we keep it a big secret? Nice big surprise for your mates, yeah? And your mum...'

Sadie was grateful to him, and said so. And, of course, she agreed to the planned rehearsals. But, he told her, she would just have to wait and see...

31
EVERYBODY NEEDS SOMEBODY

Sadie sat in the university theatre with the other parents and children as the curtain lifted on the first performance of the nursery show. It wasn't a long production. Each piece was short. Thankfully. Most of the parents were lecturers and university staff, quite a bit older than her. And of course these events were a delight for some of them, watching their little darlings in the spotlight, but it was inevitably limited. There was some singing and dancing, some poetry reading. George's dad was quite a hit, evidently pretty skilled in the art of juggling, and George did very well to catch the balls thrown to him. But poor Norris didn't manage to return any of his dad's headers and scored no goals against him between the makeshift posts. Sadie thought that was a little unfair. The man could at least have let the poor boy have a few hopelessly easy shots.

No sign of Joe and Jay. It looked like they were going to be last. And this time, the curtain closed, the shuffling behind intriguing the audience. But then there was music; an insistent blues beat, looped round and round. The curtain opened and a swathe of bright coloured lights bathed Joe and Jay. Standing centre stage with their backs to the audience, wearing tight black suits, one leg cocked to the side, the other tapping the beat; one hand holding black trilby hats to their heads. As the music pounded, they both swung round, holding microphones in one hand and clicking the fingers of the other to the beat. With big black sunglasses almost covering Joe's face, he looked an absolute picture. Sadie could hardly contain her delighted giggles already, and the surprise of the audience was audible.

But Jay was speaking now, striding up and down the front of the stage, his words to the rhythm of the music.

'Well, I was walking down the street just the other day...'

'Just the other day,' Joe echoed.

'And Joe here came up to me and he said, Jay, he said, you know what he said?'

'I said...'

'He said, Jay, you know... *Everybody* needs somebody to love.'

'I said...'

'Yes, he said, everybody... *needs*... somebody to love. Ain't that right, Joe-mo?'

'That is right Jay-mo.'

'All those people out there. They need somebody to love.'

'They do.'

'Even those tiny ones right up there at the back. They need somebody to love.'

'Uh, huh.'

'All the little children down at the front. They need somebody to love.'

'Oh, yes.'

'And all those mums and dads out there. They need somebody to love...' Jay winked at Sadie, encouraged into even further theatricals by her delighted expression.

'Even Mrs Turnbull there. *She* needs somebody to love.'

'By the look of her.'

The audience, enchanted already, roared at this one.

'And Joe here, *he* needs somebody to love.'

'I do!'

'Hey! Even *I* need somebody to love.'

'You got it!' That had been Joe's suggestion.

'And so we say to you. Each and every one of you. Everybody out there, in the whole wide world...'

'1, 2, 3, 4...'

'Everybody...' And Jay was singing now. So well.

'Needs Somebody...' Joe joined in, though not quite as tunefully. And they were dancing too, turning to each other, exchanging phrases.

'Everybody needs somebody to love...'

It was an absolute delight. They looked and sounded fantastic, with the lights and the music and the clothes and the reverb on their microphoned voices. Sadie was astonished, never losing her delighted, wide-eyed grin, as they danced and wiggled and sang, pointing to each other, and at the audience, roaming around the stage in an exaggerated walk, Joe copying everything Jay did.

And as it came to an end and the blues loop pulsed on, they again took centre stage.

'And we need you and you and you,' Jay chanted, pointing round the audience.

'Yeah, we need you and you and you,' Joe repeated.

And then they sang together, the music slowing. 'And we need you...' They held their arms wide to the whole audience, dropping to their knees, side by side.

'And you!' Heads together, throwing an arm out to point directly at Sadie.

'And you.' They turned to each other and pointed.

'Yes, I need you...' They sang in finale, in long drawn out

notes, looking directly at each other.

And there the music finished, with the echo of their voices disappearing into the air. For a moment, they stayed on their knees, failing to suppress the growing grins, resting their foreheads together. At its end...

Jay leapt up and took Joe's hand. The audience was already going wild with applause. They bowed, Joe giggling ferociously, Jay just grinning. And he turned a look to Sadie, cheering and laughing in her seat. He winked again, and she bit her lip and shook her head with that awesome smile. And Jay knew. It was worth it all just for that...

Although it hadn't really been a talent competition, Joe, of course, won the small prize that there was. And he shared it with the tearful Norris. Because that was the kind of boy he was. And on top of everything else, that just sent Sadie to tears.

Joe jumped into her arms as they met out front, giggling even more as she showered him with praise and kisses. Jay followed behind, having packed up the lights and sound system. He threw his arms wide. 'Hey Joe-mo, were we awesome, or were we *awesome*?'

'We were awesome!' Joe shrieked. Although he didn't know what it meant. He'd heard this word from Jay before, and it was clearly a good thing! And left standing there as Joe and Sadie embraced, she spontaneously extended her arm and beckoned him into the group hug. And he wrapped his arms around both of them. The perfect end to the tremendous high.

'You were absolutely terrific!' Sadie laughed so warmly as they made their way out. 'Thank you so much!'

'No problem. I enjoyed it. Had a great time.' And she could see that he had. 'I think I need to be on a stage, you know?' he said, as if it was a revelation.

Jay willingly accepted her invitation back to their room, and picked up a bottle of cheap sparkly from the university shop on the way.

Joe, of course, would not go to bed and was, in fact, quite 'obnoxious and uncontrollable'. Tearing around the room, running up to either of them and pushing them around, and then running away again. Sadie was not inclined to be too harsh with him, but it was getting pretty tiresome.

'I'm sorry,' Jay said, 'I've wound him up terribly, I can see.'

'It's OK. It'll pass,' she smiled, but he could see her weariness. So when she popped out to the toilet, leaving him being thumped by Joe, he caught him in his arms and restrained him.

'Now come on, Joe, you're being very naughty.'

'No, I'm not!' Joe protested, punching him again. Yes, Jay was learning. He could see the boy trying to push the boundaries in his excited state; trying to see just how much he could get away with. So Jay decided to draw them.

'Yes, you are,' he said. 'And I don't like it. And neither does your mum. So I think it's high time you packed it in and went to bed.'

'No,' Joe replied defiantly. But he was still looking for the smile.

'Yes,' Jay persisted, really feeling he wasn't very good at this, but if he was to take the good, he had to deal with the bad.

'I won't!'

'Well, I think you will,' Jay concluded, picking him up under one arm and carting him across the room. Joe screamed and thrashed about in his arms.

'Stop it, Joe. Stop that right now.'

'You're not my daddy. You can't tell me what to do!'

Well, that came from nowhere, and for a moment it battered Jay into silence. He swung him round and set him down on his beanbag.

'Well, that's true. But if I can't tell you what to do, then I can't take care of you. And then I can't play with you, and we can't be Blues Brothers anymore, can we?'

Joe stared tearfully at him.

'Come on, Joe,' Jay softly reasoned. 'What's this all about, eh? Haven't we had the best time?'

Joe's lip quivered, and he nodded. 'Don't go away, Jay.'

And finally, perhaps, that was all it was.

'I won't,' he said, so gently, so securely. 'Come on now, there's no need for that.'

Sadie returned to find Jay hugging a tearful Joe on his bean-bag. 'Everything alright?'

'Yeah,' Jay replied over the boy's shoulder. 'Joe's just agreed to go to bed quietly. Haven't you, Joe?'

And Joe nodded, finally...

Joe settled down to sleep with no further tantrums. But Jay was edgy now. Sadie picked up the bottle he had bought. He sighed. 'Look, I'm sorry, can we have this some other time? I'm a bit shagged, you know. Think I'll just go home.'

Sadie sensed that was not entirely true, but reluctantly let him go. Whatever it was, he had given enough.

32

ALL TOO MUCH

Jay searched his memory. Body-swerving the really terrible bits, he tried to recall if he'd ever felt as happy as he had on that stage yesterday. He drew a blank. It was simply the best time he had ever had. He'd loved every minute of it. Being Joe's dad for that day, amongst all the other boys and their dads. And topping the lot of them, as he knew he had done. Now he knew he could do it. And Joe knew he could do it. And he'd had to say that he would not go away.

But how could he say that? This was the most unusual situation to be put in. His love for a boy who was not his own. Well, that happened, he guessed. But usually to people who took on their partners' children. It wasn't like that for him. He had another life. So how could he say to Joe that he would not go? How could he commit any more of his life to another man's child, especially when he had no real ties to his mother?

But how could he ever leave him?

How could he ever leave her?

And he knew then that his strategy was not working. That's

why he had to get out last night. He had to have some space away from them, to try to sort this out.

He wandered through the next week. He couldn't bring himself to go to his classes. Well, on past performance, he'd probably failed the year anyway. He just didn't care anymore. Right now, he had other needs. But it was so boring and aimless. A part of him, a big part, just wanted to get back to what they had. Take it for what it was. Not worry about the future. And he longed for the Easter holiday that had passed. The warmth he had felt when things were good. The shopping and sightseeing trips they had made, the walks, the painting and playing, the talking. The three of them, together. Every little memory took on an exaggerated quality to him now.

But he would not be knocking on their door every day. He had too much pride for that. And despite his deep need to see Joe, to be with them, he couldn't cope with seeing her anymore. Every time he looked at her now, she moved him so deeply. When he had seen her in that audience, his heart had just skyrocketed.

And the futility of that crucified him.

In his current frame of mind, Jay was even more than usually enthusiastic to be invited to join another band. It was one that had been around for sometime, with easily the best reputation on the local scene. But having lost their drummer, they said it was *he* who had by far the best reputation as a potential replacement. And to hear that so easily spoken lifted him immeasurably. Yes, this was something he could do.

So he threw himself into the endless rehearsals and jamming sessions. And it was working. It was an excellent diversion. No wonder they thought he was good; he put his heart and soul into it.

Because his heart and soul were being entirely lost somewhere else...

'Joe, have you seen Jay this week, at the nursery perhaps?' Sadie knew he can't have. Joe would not have been slow to tell her about it. And the irony that she was the one who was asking was not lost on her.

'No,' Joe replied. Then he was thoughtful. 'He's *very* late this week, isn't he?'

'Late for what?'

'Everything!'

Yes, everything. Joe had, as usual, put his finger on it in his own unique way. Absent without leave. No reason given.

'Well, let's see what he's doing at the weekend, shall we?' The tone was light, but a new stream of anxiety rippled through her...

'Anything up?'

Jay was on his way out as Sadie appeared at his door that evening. Suddenly, she felt foolish and inexplicably out of her depth.

'Would you believe I've come to borrow a cup of sugar?'

'No,' he laughed.

'No, well, I just popped round to see how you are. Haven't seen you in a while?'

'Yeah, I've been busy. Got meself in a new band last couple of weeks.'

'Oh, really?'

Her immediate enthusiasm touched him, and Jay suddenly realised that his 'keep busy policy' was not working at all. Had she only to come back into his vision for all his carefully constructed diversions to crumble...?

'Yeah, Funkination. Know them?'

'Oh yeah, I've heard about them. Apparently they're very good.'

'Well, they're even better now,' he replied with uncharacteristic conceit. 'I'm off for a rehearsal now, as it happens.'

'Oh, OK...'

'Well, why don't you come? You've obviously been relieved duty for a bit.'

Jay turned away to lock the door, his smile falling unseen, kicking himself at this knee jerk offer. But obviously his need to see her, be with her, had bypassed his conscious efforts not to.

'Yeah, Janet's minding Joe. But I'd been in the way, wouldn't I?'

Well, he couldn't back down now. Even if he wanted to. Which, unfortunately, he knew he didn't. 'Rubbish. There's always a few hanging around. Don't worry about it. Come on...'

As she followed him out, Sadie felt a little hurt that he hadn't told her about his new venture. She thought back to that short period when neither of them did very much at all without telling the other, talking it over, sharing it. And she looked at him as they walked silently over the grass, some indefinable distance that had not been there for so long. It saddened her. Perhaps he was bored with her company now? Perhaps he didn't think that she cared about his whereabouts? Perhaps Joe's demands were getting too much for him? And hers? *Perhaps? Perhaps? Perhaps...?* She sighed. It was all getting far too important to her. This had to stop. He was, what you might call, 'a friend of the family'. He had absolutely no obligation to her. And not so long ago, she would not have had it any other way. Why had she changed so much? It was landing her in places she didn't know how to deal with. She was ill-equipped to cope with these feelings. At least she'd had years of practice in loneliness and rejection.

But then again, if that were so, why couldn't she even cope with that anymore...?

Jay noticed her sigh. 'Alright?'

'Yeah,' she brightened, pretending. 'Tell me about Funkination, then. And the obvious elevation in the percussion department!'

And so he did. In great detail.

Christ, he'd missed her. Would he tell her that too...?

Sadie found a seat at the back of the practice room in the Union. There were two other blokes talking, and three girls sitting in different places. Obviously the partners... Or were they? One of them came and sat down beside her.

'You're not Jay's girlfriend, are you? Gary said he didn't have one.'

'Uh...no,' Sadie replied, after she'd got over the temporary shock of her sudden appearance.

'Good.' She shuffled closer. 'My name's Fiona.'

'Sadie.'

'So Sadie, a good friend of Jay's, then?'

'Well, yes, I suppose.'

'But nothing...' Fiona gestured the rest.

'Uh...no.'

'Excellent.'

Sadie twitched. 'Got your eye on him then, have you?' she asked with a conspiratorial smile, although she didn't really know why.

Fiona leaned in. 'I think I'm going to like you. Yeah, he's

cute. What do you reckon? You obviously know him better than me. You can give things a helping hand.'

Like hell she would!

'Well, how're you doing so far?' Sadie asked instead. It fooled Fiona. She'd obviously latched onto Sadie as a means to her goal.

'Well, it's difficult to know, isn't it? Think he's noticed me.'

Has he?!

Sadie's reflex reactions were troubling her.

'What do you reckon about a girl asking a bloke out?'

'Absolutely nothing wrong with it, in principle,' Sadie replied, going off this conversation by the second.

'You don't sound sure. Don't you think Jay's the kind of guy who'd appreciate it?'

Sadie had to avert her eyes to prevent Fiona seeing her distaste with this subject now. She didn't want to be a part of this conversation anymore.

'I don't know, really,' she muttered. 'Perhaps he would.'

Perhaps he would...?

'Hmm,' Fiona concluded and left it at that for the moment.

It was getting difficult to hear anyway, as the indiscriminate noises of the band progressed into a thorough warm-up bash. Sadie watched Jay closely. He seemed to display an extraordinary amount of skill. Again. But her mind was really on other things. *Cute?* That was for teddy bears, surely. God, she was so out of this scene.

But yeah, bloody hell, he was...

It occurred to her that the two of them sitting there, both pairs of eyes fixed on the same area of the room, must surely be noticeable, so she began studying the rest of the band.

The same had obviously not occurred to Fiona.

'Your tongue's getting dirty,' Sadie said during a break in the music.

'Eh?'

'On the floor. It's picking up the dust.'

Fiona thought this was hilarious.

'Tell me,' Sadie pursued, although she still didn't know why. 'You don't just drop in here whenever they're practising, do you?'

'Oh no, how gauche,' Fiona laughed. 'I'm Gary's twin sister. The trombonist.'

'I see.'

'So I came along last week. Gary wanted a second opinion on the band. And I thought, mmm. I've been on the lookout for a while, anyway. And I don't like them too tall. And after about ten minutes, he was doing this hilarious thing with a tambourine – you must have seen it – and I just jumped on the challenge. I like a man who can make me laugh.'

Sadie nearly threw up. But it was not just Fiona's cringe-worthy words that made her stomach turn. And that's what hit her the most.

'Well, he can certainly do that...'

It surprised Sadie that the band actively involved the specta-tors and encouraged their opinions. 'Loooove the rhythm,' was Fiona's contribution, as she openly winked at Jay.

Sadie watched as he grinned back at her, mouthing, 'Thanks.' He caught Sadie's eye and shrugged cheerily. And when they finished and were packing away, Sadie nearly fell off her chair at the speed at which Fiona homed in on him, obvi-ously encouraged by that exchange. Jay looked a little uneasy about it, which strangely comforted Sadie. Although it surprised her – he looked earlier as if he could handle it. But as they finally left, Fiona gave her the thumbs up and linked her arm in his. Sadie forced a smile and followed them out.

'We're going to the bar,' Jay said. 'Apparently.' Again, he shrugged that slightly quizzical expression. 'Coming?'

Sadie hesitated. 'Love to. But I better get back for Janet.'

'Oh, OK...' But he was already being urged away by Fiona.

'Uh, Jay?' Sadie called after him. 'Could you...uh... come and see Joe sometime? He misses you, you know.'

Jay smiled more genuinely then. 'Yeah. Of course.'

He couldn't run away forever. Even if this was another new diversion, for some puzzling reason, as Fiona dragged him away.

33

FIONA

Over the next week, Jay was a bit stunned by the onslaught he received from this girl, who he had barely noticed before. Fiona clearly had a plan of attack and she was pursuing it relentlessly. It all went completely over the top of his head. As if it were happening to someone else. But on the evenings they sat in each other's room or in the bar, she laughed at his jokes and 'listened' avidly to anything he had to say. Although he suspected he might as well have been talking to the wall for all the real notice she was taking.

He decided to test it one evening and slipped in a 'why don't you just fuck off?' in the middle of a sentence, and she didn't bat an eyelid. So, he wondered what she was doing here. She demanded him to speak, but wasn't really listening. There was a tremendous pressure for him to 'perform' though. He didn't understand it. But if he amused her, it flattered him. So he let it continue.

She was getting persistent now, though. More and more available. But when she kissed him, he thought only of Sadie in his response. Clearly, he could have more by now, anything he wanted. And certainly, he wanted. It'd been a long time. But Sadie was in his head and in his heart, and even if he did have the talent of an actor, he couldn't pretend with this one.

Perversely, this made him angry. She even stopped him from this! And his ambivalence was clearly puzzling Fiona.

He was even more annoyed one Thursday when he had been planning to go and see Joe. With Sadie's Thursday evening babysitting rota, he had thought that would be a good day. He could play with Joe and then maybe they could go to the bar for a bit themselves in the evening. Although her request had prompted him to see Joe a couple of times since that band practice, he had been planning to take advantage of a Thursday evening for two weeks now, but had to forget it. This time because Fiona would not leave his room, despite some pretty heavy removal remarks. She had had barely anything on when she arrived that afternoon, and had been getting progressively more suggestive as the evening wore on. He looked at her. She was attractive enough. And he tried to keep looking at her. But no... he couldn't.

'Let's go to the bar,' he said as her hand slipped beneath his trouser belt. Fiona sighed, but agreed. And because it was early, he was frustrated and bored, he got thoroughly hammered.

By 9.30, both of them were rather the worse for wear, and Jay was finally allowing his ego, and a few other places, to be massaged. He resented the fact he was always thinking about Sadie and, in his current inebriation, he finally allowed Fiona to give him some of the attention that he so longed for. He was of course flattered by her attention, and her intentions, and since at that moment he would probably have cartwheeled across the floor to get some, he settled for letting her give it to him.

It was positively cruel that if Sadie did nothing else on her Thursday night off, she'd go down to the bar with some of her friends. Jay saw her first. And it spoiled it all. It was enough to sober him up completely.

Fiona was sitting on his lap, facing him, one mini-skirted leg on either side of him. Sadie looked away immediately.

But Janet, at least, had noticed her expression, and followed where her eyes had left.

'Hey,' she grinned. 'Who's that with Jay?'

'Her name's Fiona,' Sadie replied in monotone.

'And you don't like it evidently,' she laughed.

'It's none of my business!'

Janet sighed. Sadie had been in good spirits this evening, but she was sick of these sudden changes in mood.

'Well, why don't you just bloody well stop arsing around and make it your business!'

'What do you mean?' Sadie demanded.

'Look, I came in here for a quiet drink, so I'm not getting into a slanging match with you, however much you drive me to it sometimes. All I'm saying is that if looks could kill, she'd be six feet under already.'

Sadie glared at her.

'Oh, calm down Sadie, for God's sake. It's not that big a deal. Like I say, if you fancy him, go for him.'

'I... don't,' Sadie retorted, much more hesitantly.

'Really?' Janet looked to the heavens. 'Oh, come on, Sadie. I'm not getting into this either. But you're on your own, I know that. I know you haven't really got any ties...' Janet was on dangerous ground here and she knew it. Any hint of Sadie's subterfuge being rumbled would obviously send her into a rage. So she added as a diversion, 'You're an irritatingly attractive girl, Sadie. And you're really not all that bad, once you get to know you...' Sadie almost lost her glare and smiled at that, which both relieved and encouraged Janet. Probably more than it should have. She turned to the others. 'Hey, come on guys, back me up here. Who reckons it's about time Sadie got back out into the field?'

'Absolutely!' Bradley agreed first. 'I'd be happy to show you the ropes.'

'I think Sadie has someone else in mind, Brad,' Janet quickly interceded, nodding across the room to the bar.

'Jay?' Gail giggled. She had been in the Christmas show, of course. *Oh, God...* 'Hey, I had no idea you were after Jay.'

'I... I...'

'Well, he does rather look like he's got his hands full already,' Bradley protested.

'No contest for our Sadie, I don't think,' Hilary chimed in.

'Yeah, she's a sponge cake to Sadie's gateau, I'd say—'

'Janet!' Sadie eventually called a halt to this. Apart from anything else, she was aware that Jay had noticed them looking at him and giggling. 'You don't know what you're talking about. You don't understand.'

'Yeah, yeah,' Janet lost her smile finally. 'So you keep telling me. On and on and on,' she exaggerated. 'And he's the only one who does, isn't he? Precious Jason. And you just can't stand it, can you? Well, it's tough on you then, isn't it? Because if he's got any sense, he'll steer well clear!'

Sadie stared at her friend, slammed down her glass, and stormed out of the bar. Yes, Janet had been a friend. She was often outspoken, and very often stupid and wrong, but she stuck with her. Did she really deserve all that? Did Janet really think that?

And could it be true...?

Jay had watched all this, though he could hear nothing, and he looked on Sadie's dramatic exit with bewilderment. And suddenly, he was bored with all this nonsense with Fiona. It lost any attraction it may have had. He pushed her off him. 'I'm going now.' And he walked straight out.

He contemplated heading for Ellis House, but as he could barely walk straight, he decided against it. The booze, the frustration, the longing, might just unleash his mouth into something regrettable...

Sadie collected Joe from Karen and David. Although he was asleep and she was reluctant to disturb him, she wanted him. She wanted his presence. To be reminded of her proper place in the world. The one she knew and understood.

But lying in her bed that night, she could only hear Janet's parting words. *If he had any sense, he would steer well clear of her...*

It was true. It was coming true. That was *obviously* the reason for the new infrequency of his visits. She was an unapproachable, self-centred, and undoubtedly tedious companion. The more she thought about it, the more real it became to her.

And she buried her face in the pillow, not knowing who she had become...

Jay called a couple of times over the next week. Sadie was both disappointed and encouraged to find his visits uncomfortable. He was mostly concerned with Joe, anyway. Well, that was how it was, wasn't it...? And he seemed happy as he chatted about his band and other things. Sadie didn't like the resentment she felt at that. God, she was a selfish bitch, she thought.

Add it to the list...

'Oh bollocks,' Jay muttered, spotting Sadie sitting down with her group from the block at the other side of the bar. He'd forgotten it was another Thursday.

'What's the matter, babe?' Fiona asked.

'You are, you old cow. Get off me, will you?' He snatched Fiona's hand from his crotch and shoved it back on her lap.

'Jacey!'

'Don't call me that!'

'Oh, what's the matter with you? You've been in a rotten mood for days. I thought you were coming out of it tonight.'

'Well, that's your psychology degree out of the window, isn't it?'

'Oh Jay, you know I study French!'

'In Christ's name, why are you so dense?'

'Oh, really! Just what is the matter with you?'

'You wanna know?'

'Yes.'

'You *really* wanna know?'

'Yes!'

'You sure?' He leaned towards her, an uncharacteristically menacing look on his face.

'I said so, didn't I?' Fiona sighed irritably.

'Well, I'll tell you then... her.'

Fiona followed his pointed finger. 'What's Sadie got to do with anything?'

'Oh, on first-name terms, are we?' Jay mocked, although he was a little surprised.

'For heaven's sake, stop it!' Fiona retorted. Probably the only sensible thing she had said all evening. But she had to ruin it by pursuing. 'So? What has she got to do with it?'

Jay leaned towards her again so that their noses were almost touching. 'I... want... *her*,' he breathed spitefully.

'What do you mean?' Fiona shrilled, pulling away immediately.

'D'you want me to draw a diagram, or what?'

'You bastard!' Fiona shrieked, accurately at that moment.

She sprung off the bar stool. This is where he got his payback. 'Who do you think you are? Just what have you got to be so bloody self-assured about, anyway?'

'Oh yes, I always knew you knew me inside out Fiona,' he called after her. 'That's so right. That's me all over...'

All this had gone unnoticed by Sadie until Fiona swanned past her. 'Bitch!' she cried.

Sadie stared after her.

'What was that for?' David laughed, similarly bemused.

'I don't know, really...'

Sadie looked over to Jay at the bar. He caught her eye, slammed his glass down, and walked out after Fiona. And that really upset her. It was all a little bewildering, and a bit too much for her already heightened senses. She fidgeted for a while, half a dozen beer mats shredded on the table, then excused herself and went home herself.

In that light, she was very surprised to see Jay at her door the next evening. It was nearly ten o'clock, but he was in the door before she could even say 'hello' anyway.

'Can I come in?'

'You are in.' He was already sitting down on the mattress. Sadie was not best pleased. She was fed up with this whirlwind he was creating all around her. She wanted her stability back.

Unfortunately, she realised, he had provided that too...

She sat down beside him, but there was a heavy silence as they sat looking out to the room.

'Are you pissed off with me as well?' Jay eventually muttered.

Sadie didn't like this at all. 'Should I be?'

'Oh, don't you start talking in riddles too.'

'Too? As well? Am I suddenly being included in some

cosmic partnership here? Have I been chosen for one of your biology experiments to see if two brains can think the same way at once?'

Jay frowned at her. 'Are we going to have a row? If so, I'm going.'

'Be my guest.'

But he didn't budge. And he looked a little worn now. So, in the silence that followed, Sadie became a little more conciliatory. 'Come on then, spit it out. What's on your mind?'

Jay fidgeted uncomfortably. He didn't really know what he was doing here, anyway. It was way passed Joe's bedtime. But he'd had a bad day with his tutors. He'd had to apologise to Fiona, who made him grovel and then promptly jumped on him as if nothing amiss had passed between them. He had just wanted some peaceful companionship and understanding. He'd just wanted to be with her. Not this antagonism. Or in fact, now it was here, this potentially dangerous concern.

He shook his head, picking at his fingers.

'Alright then,' Sadie offered provocatively. 'Tell me why your new girlfriend called me a bitch last night?'

'My new *what*?'

'Oh, come off it, Jay,' Sadie laughed at him. 'Fiona,' she corrected as he continued to glare at her.

'Don't avoid the issue,' Jay huffed. 'Don't call her that. Don't even think it...'

Oh God, they were going to have to go through some great relationship trauma now. Sadie couldn't stand it. She needed something else. 'OK then, what say we crack open that bottle of sparkly and you can spill your heart out.'

'I'm hardly in the mood for champagne.'

'Oh, give over. And it's hardly champagne, is it? Shut up and do as you're told. It's burning a hole in my fridge.'

Jay looked at her, bemused, as she jumped up. This was a

somewhat strange mood. He watched as she took the bottle outside and opened it down the corridor.

'Joe,' she whispered in explanation, pouring a generous helping into a mug.

'Whoa! Are you trying to get me pissed?'

'Well, why not?' she grinned. 'It might loosen your tongue.'

This was indeed strange. He frowned at her again.

'Oh, come on, Jay,' she coaxed with a playful nudge. She'd already downed half a mug herself. 'So, what about this girl-friend of yours, then?'

Jay sighed, still peeved by this line of enquiry. 'I told you, stop calling her that.'

'Why not? What else would you call her? You seem to be getting on so famously, and she does think you're awfully funny and a tremendous challenge.' Sadie gulped the rest of her drink and refilled immediately.

'And since when did you start talking about me with her?'

'Oh, don't get so heated. It was only at that practice.'

'Hadn't you better slow down?'

'Ah,' she giggled, brandishing another empty mug in the air. 'Not to mention cute!'

'Cute?' Jay retorted. 'For God's sake, stop laughing... I'm not cute. Am I cute?'

Sadie grinned, grabbing his chin and squeezing his cheeks. The wine was obviously making her take leave of her senses.

'Oh yes, you are...'

Jay's jaw dropped. But before he could pursue that, even if he was able to, she was off again.

'I wasn't much help to her, anyway.'

'What do you mean?'

'She was trying to enlist my assistance in pulling you!'

'Are you enjoying this or something?'

Sadie sighed. He was quite serious. Perhaps she had better

stop. 'Alright, I'm sorry,' she conceded, her giggly smile dwindling. 'Has she really upset you?'

This was much more difficult. Of course she was concerned. But it was much easier to be flippant and bury herself in that bottle, than have him really pouring his heart out about some girl. But if it was what he needed...

'Oh...no,' Jay sighed. 'She just gets up my arse, that's all.'

'Yep, it certainly looked like that kind of thing!'

She couldn't help it. Any excuse to lighten this potentially difficult conversation and divert him from anything too serious.

Jay crossed his eyes. 'You asked... This is not like you. I don't understand. I thought better of you.'

That hit Sadie hard. She bit her lip, sobering by the second.

'I'm sorry Jay, really... It's just...' Should she tell him this was difficult for her? Well, sort of. 'It's just that I really don't want to talk about her.'

'Why not?'

'I... I just don't like her. Sorry.' Well, it was the truth. Just not all of it.

'Neither do I!'

'It doesn't look that way, Jay.'

'I know,' he sighed.

'Well, what is it then?' she prompted. 'No, sorry... sorry, it's none of my business.'

'Oh, how can I possibly talk to you about this?' But he could tell by the look on her face that he couldn't get away with that. 'It's just, I suppose, I'm flattered by the attention. She does rather ladle it on. But I don't really like her. I don't really want anything to do with her.'

'Oh Jay, that's awful. You mean you're tagging her along just because you want a bit of attention? I thought better of you,' she deliberately echoed his words.

'I know, I know...'

'You probably like her more than you think anyway,' she fished.

Jay sighed. 'Oh, I can't stand this conversation anymore. I'm going... Thanks for the drink.'

'You bought it,' Sadie muttered. But he was gone.

And she felt very inadequate now. She could not ease his way, like he had told her she had so many times before. She hadn't even tried. And she knew she'd behaved badly.

And, for Christ's sake, did she just tell him he was *cute*? Thank God he had gone. It might have prevented her from saying anything else so daft...

It chewed at her all the next day. And so, after she'd given Joe his tea, she took his hand. 'Let's go and see Jay, shall we?'

'Yeah!' Joe's face lit up in a way that it had not done for a couple of days. He had been listless since the weekend. Not exactly ill, just not his normal bouncy self. She suspected he might be coming down with some bug, although he complained of no tummy upset or headache, and there was no temperature...

Jay opened the door, looking a little dishevelled. Sadie could see Fiona lying on the bed behind, fingering her blouse.

'Hi,' he said, nonetheless. 'Hey, Joe!' He picked him up and turned into the room. 'Hey Fiona, this is Joe. The light of my life.' He winked at Joe; this was, of course, more addressed to him than her. But Fiona responded anyway.

'You should be saying that about me, not him.' She flashed a sneery smile at Sadie, which unnerved her again.

'Look, I just came over to apologise.' Sadie drew him away from the door. 'I won't disturb you. I can see you're... *busy*. So, I'm sorry, I wasn't at my best last night. I didn't mean to upset

you. Anytime you want to talk, you know. I promise to try and
do better.'

Jay didn't really know how to respond to this. Of course it
would be completely inappropriate just to slam the door and
follow them down the corridor as he so wanted to.

'OK, we'll be off now. Let you get on.' She almost added
'with it,' but stopped herself.

'Hey Sadie, don't...' But what was he going to do now?
She'd come to him. And he just wanted to be with her, not go
through any more of this charade with Fiona, who had clearly
taken his apology as a cue to continue exactly where she'd left
off. 'Look, can we do something at the weekend? Go out somewhere, the three of us?'

'Yey!' Joe had already agreed.

Sadie smiled. 'Yeah, OK. I'd like that...'

And she left them to get on. *With it*.

But not according to Jay. She had crossed his vision again and
blinded him to anything else in the entire world.

He turned back to Fiona. 'Alright you, enough. I've got
work to do. Time you were going.'

'Oh, but—'

'Really, I must finish this essay. I'll see you later, OK...?'

He closed the door after her and stood with his back to it,
kicking himself.

What a fucking coward...

34

REALISATION

'Hey, this is just like old times!'

It was a pleasantly balmy May day on the South Downs.

'Yes, it is,' Sadie agreed. And how she'd missed it.

She watched Jay chase Joe around with his kite, and they talked as they strolled through the countryside. She must have this, she concluded. Even if he was being diverted elsewhere, maybe he did still have room for them. Maybe she could settle for that. As she well knew, she didn't know how to do anything else anyway...

But that churning deep in her stomach when she had left them in his room that night? She had felt so upset; she had shown none of that. So... jealous? So inadequate...

Joe was clearly wilting by the time they returned that evening. And, as usual, trumped any of her other concerns.

'I'll put him to bed,' Jay offered. But as Joe stood up, he stumbled and fell to the floor.

Sadie rushed to him. 'Joe?' He didn't seem to be hurt. 'What's wrong? You OK?'

Joe nodded, but started to cry. 'I felt dizzy,' he sniffed. Sadie put her hand on his forehead. He didn't feel hot.

'Well,' she tried to be encouraging. 'What a day you've had. You must be very tired. Let's get you to bed, eh...?'

'Want a drink?' she offered once Joe was asleep. He went off like a light. It was always so lately. She'd even had to wake him herself for the last couple of mornings. Most unusual...

'Yeah. Got any of that bubbly left? Or did you polish off the whole bottle the other night?' The laughter worked, a little, and she raised a smile.

'Sorry, it did go to my head a bit. I am sorry if I said anything... *inappropriate*.'

'Oh, bollocks to that,' he dismissed, though he wondered if she was thinking the same thing as him. He would dearly love to pursue that... But she looked a little worn and anxious now, so keeping it light seemed the best antidote.

'There's a bit left. And David gave me this.' She held up a bottle of Smirnoff. 'Duty Free. He was in Brussels last week.'

She brought over both bottles, with two mugs and a bit of Joe's lemonade to water down the vodka. They shared the half a mug of remaining sparkling wine. But he could feel her anxiety.

'You're worried about Joe?'

'He's not been himself for a while. But there's no temperature or pains or anything. I just don't know...'

'I'm sure he'll be fine.' Jay tried to be reassuring.

'I'll take him to the medical centre next week, just to make sure.'

'Yeah, good idea...'

But she was still somewhere else. In that maternal anxiety vortex. He so wanted to relieve her. She looked so lost and vulnerable all of a sudden. This is what it was like. This parenthood. With no-one really to share it with.

Well, that was what he was here for, wasn't it?

'Hey,' he whispered. 'It'll be OK.'

She nodded, but it was unconvincing.

Jay sighed. He could do no other. 'Can I give you a cuddle?'

Sadie bit her lip as she faintly nodded again.

'Come here, then...'

Her eyes pricked with tears as she nestled into his shoulder, but she breathed them away, finding herself so at home there.

'It'll be alright,' he whispered, resting his head on hers. 'Everything'll be alright...' He so wanted it to be...

'Want some of this Belgian import, then?' He lifted the vodka bottle.

'OK.'

'This is getting a bit of a habit,' he laughed, refilling the mugs. 'What happened to Sadie the caffeine addict?'

'Yeah,' she smiled wryly. 'I'm turning into a lush. Guess I'm rediscovering my youth.' She had drawn away a little as he poured the drinks. She really wanted not to, but could not move back herself. So the constriction in her chest eased as he returned his arm around her.

'Yeah, I remember the photos. One of the crowd down the park with a bottle of the cheapest cider, eh?'

'Yep, that was me,' she laughed distantly. 'Then, well... when Joe was conceived, I didn't touch a drop.'

'Giving the poor bugger a break during gestation, eh? Nine months and no booze? You champion, you!'

'No, it was about four years.'

'Really? Why?'

Suddenly, she was edgy.

But then there was a voice deep within her, screaming to tell him now.

'Let's just say that I went off it. An experiment gone wrong if you like...'

Yes, tell him. Tell him now!

'I have to say that Joe might not have been conceived without it. And I rather kicked against it for a while...'

'Oh?' Jay prompted. This was a rare revelation indeed.

Could she go on? He was the only one she'd ever come close to doing so. The only one she'd ever come close to *wanting* to.

But no. It would never happen. She would never speak of it.

'And that's all I'm going to say on the matter.'

Jay could feel her tense beneath his arm. That was not what he wanted. 'OK,' he whispered. 'That's fine...'

They drifted into silence, only the quiet hum of the TV the barest distraction. As time went on...

'Hey, this is good, this is,' Jay whispered as the late film came on. No response. 'Sadie?'

She was asleep.

Jay closed his eyes, allowing his head to rest upon hers. God, how this moved him. And he let his other arm encircle her, turning to gently pull her to him. He could feel her so completely now. The gentle rise and fall of her breathing against him. The warm fragrance of her coconut soap... And he kissed her hair.

'Oh, Sadie...' He let himself drink it in. He was holding her now. In that place he longed to be...

The credits were rolling on the film by the time Sadie awoke. She unconsciously brushed his chest with her hand. His head back against the wall, he was not sure he could take any more of this.

'What time is it?'

He looked at his watch. 'Quarter to one. Time I was going...' This evening had been very telling for him. He had no wish to let his present state become visible to her. He would have to get himself out of it, to think and resettle himself...

But as he lay in his bed that night, there was no more doubt for Jay now. No more running away. She held him completely. And he knew. He loved her desperately. He couldn't run anymore. And he held his pillow, as he longed to hold her, whispering her name into the darkness...

As the morning arrived, he had not a clue what to do. He could not go back. As if he ever could from that moment so long ago when he looked at her and first felt that so powerful pull. But he knew one thing. One thing he must do...

Fiona knew he had a rehearsal that night, but insisted he come round to her room afterwards. He finally had to do it. This was nothing. It wasn't even a diversion anymore. It was just a bloody nuisance.

She opened the door, wearing absolutely nothing. They ended up on the floor within seconds. So much for his courage. But he had so much in him. So much longing. So much frustration...

The signs were encouraging for Fiona as she discarded his shirt. What had taken him so long, anyway? She wasn't used to this reticence. And she was fed up with his moods and his barely disguised ambivalence towards her. She'd get her fuck, show him what he was missing, and then he was out the door.

Until, just as she was about to coax his trousers off him, which were visibly a nuisance to him anyway, he leapt away from her. He'd encouraged her into this. For his own ego, his own selfish needs. But he couldn't do this. He couldn't see her. He saw only Sadie. He felt only Sadie. He breathed only Sadie. And grabbing his shirt, he ran choking from the room.

35

FOR THE LAST TIME

Jay stood round the corner of Ellis House as Sadie led Joe to nursery. And he watched them go, so deeply moved by her.

For the last time...

There was a note under the door when they returned at lunchtime.

> *Sadie, I've been a bloody fool. Nothing's happened. I'm not in any trouble or anything. I know you'd worry if I didn't tell you that. And I appreciate that. I appreciate all the care and concern you've ever given me. You'll never know how much. My mind's a mess. I'm no use like this and I do crazy things. So, I'm going away. Please don't waste your concern. I don't deserve it. Hope everything's OK with Joe at the doctors. All my love, Jay.*

Sadie read it over and over. How could she *not* be

concerned? What did he mean he was going away? It sounded so final. She had to see him...

Joe requested an afternoon nap. This was getting a bad habit. She would be glad of their doctor's appointment in the morning. But for now, she lay him down on the mattress, then slipped out, knowing he would not stir for some time.

As she feared, there was no answer at Jay's door. She knocked at the next room.

'Hello, Sadie!'

For a moment, Sadie could not understand Nick's exuberance. Hadn't the world just changed...?

'Hi,' she tried to form something with her mouth that mirrored his smile. 'Sorry to bother you, but do you know where Jay is?'

'No, sorry. Saw him a couple of hours ago in the car park on my way in. He had a bag. Looked like he was going somewhere.'

'Oh...' Whatever acrobatics she had managed with her mouth disintegrated. 'Could you lend me a pen and paper...?'

What to write? So much to say. So inadequate a medium. But she slipped the note under Jay's door, hoping he had not gone. Not just yet.

Not ever...?

> *Jay, I don't know when you'll get to read this. Soon I hope. If you've not left yet, please don't go. Please come and tell me about it. And stop telling me not to worry about you. How can I not do? I won't say anymore, because I'll say it to your face. Come back. Love, Sadie.*

Outside the Union, his car was not in its usual place. She stopped and stared at the empty space. Now that he was gone, she couldn't begin to face the need she felt for him not to be.

But there was a poster in the foyer. A gig and disco, Friday night. *Funkination*. Surely, he would not neglect that? It gave her some hope...

Joe was still sleeping when she got back. And the next morning, she promptly took him to the clinic. The doctor reassured her he could find nothing obviously wrong with Joe. He thought he might be a touch anaemic and offered to run some tests. But Joe cried like a baby when he took the blood. So unlike him. But he said it hurt too much. Like his hand was being 'killed'. She left with a prescription for some mixed vitamins and an appointment for a week's time. The doctor encouraged her he would perk up by then, anyway...

Sadie called at Jay's door the next day, and the next, just on the off chance. But there was still no sign of him. And tonight was the big gig. Joe had been looking forward to the nursery sleepover that weekend, and seemed well enough, a little improved that morning, to go. So she dropped him off at lunchtime and went into town. On the way back, she popped into the Union and up to the hall where the gig was to take place. At least she could see if the band knew they didn't have a drummer tonight. Or glean some information from them, if they had any. So she was very surprised and mightily relieved to see Jay at the back of the stage, lifting boxes of drums. For a moment, she was pinned to the door. Her heart had jumped a little at the sight of him, and she needed to steady herself.

He didn't notice her until she was right beside him.

'Jay...' She hardly had the voice. His eyes raised instantly, and for a moment, they just looked at each other.

'Well, there you go,' he shrugged with an unconvincing smile. 'So much for my disappearing act. I forgot about this.'

'Well, thank God there's something that'll keep you here.'

'The things that keep me here are the things I've got to get away from...'

He was called from the sound desk.

'You're busy,' she said. 'I didn't expect you to be here. I'm not getting on your back. Just remember, if I can help...'

Jay wanted her to go and wanted to detain her both at once. 'How's Joe?' he called.

She turned back. 'Seems a bit better today. Gone on the nursery trip.'

'Oh... yeah, really?' There was something uneasy between them. A friction, he couldn't read. 'Come tonight? It'll be good.'

Sadie nodded. 'I'd like that...'

36

LITTLE GIRL

No babysitter required, the whole group from the block went down to the Union that night. There was a relaxed camaraderie between them, and Sadie was enjoying not having to think about Joe for a change. Music piped through the room as people stood drinking and chatting and waiting.

Backstage, Jay was being powered around by adrenaline. He would not sit still with the others. They laughed at him, but were not irritated. The restlessness of excited nerves always brought out his humour and high spirits. And so he was providing a sideshow for them all, cracking jokes, battering his tambourine, and playing silly games. So far from what he really felt tonight...

'So...' Janet grinned around the table. 'I hear good things about this band.' She turned her focus on Sadie. 'Drummer's supposed to be pretty hot.'

As Sadie met her eye, she felt a little hot herself. And Janet could see it.

'I think you know him, Sadie, don't you?'

'You know I do,' she laughed. 'We all do.'

But there was something between them now, that both of them recognised.

'Time to get to know him a little better then, is it?'

Sadie could have, as she normally did, bitten her head off right then. But she didn't. 'I... I...' Clearly, she was struggling for something. What it was, even Janet did not know, despite her relaxed teasing. Perhaps neither did Sadie herself. But suddenly she *wanted* to know. To see this reflected in someone else's eyes. To help her.

'Jan, could I have a word with you...?'

They went to the bar. Janet was now more than usually sensitive, as she watched her friend squirm.

'What is it, Sadie?'

Sadie could not form a response. What on earth was she doing here?

But the impulse, the need...

'Jan, I... I am a bit lost,' she finally confessed. 'Can I tell you this?' But she didn't wait for an answer. 'I don't really know what to do. I don't really know how things are... with... men and things...'

'Sadie? For Christ's sake, you have a child! And never mind that, just look at you. Don't try to tell me you have a problem with men. Just don't!' Janet was laughing, but this was a rare exchange, and she knew it. Of course, on their nights out, they had done the usual girlie chat, but Sadie had never applied it to anything anywhere near herself, ever.

'I... I don't know,' Sadie stuttered. 'I don't know any of it. I don't know what to look for. I don't know how it's supposed to feel.'

'You are not serious. Surely you've had—'

'Jan... there has been no-one since...' Sadie almost ran back to the table right then. 'Since Joe.'

And that hardly counted, did it?

'My God,' Janet breathed. 'Well, you must have left a path of disappointed hopefuls then.'

'Jan, you keep saying these things. I... I don't know...'

And it was true, she didn't. Not since those lapping spotty adolescents, and they hardly counted either. And she was different now. Apart from the fact that the only person who had ever come close to her had apparently done so out of some kind of hateful violence, not anything approaching love. It could not even be described as lust. That kind of thing didn't happen like that, even she knew that at 16. But she had a child now. She was a package. It was a whole different ball game.

Janet could not know any of this, of course. All that she saw, and perhaps that was enough, was that Sadie had not been truthful about her life. She wasn't awaiting the return of some loving husband. As if she didn't know that already. She was just a 15-year-old little girl who didn't know how to chat up men, seeking guidance from an older, more worldly-wise sister. And it astounded her. All that she saw in Sadie... But that didn't matter for the moment. She would attempt to deal with this in the only way she knew how.

'So, what you're saying is that, finally, you are ready to get out there. And you are not quite sure how it goes.'

'I... I don't know...'

'Well Sadie, we all just make it up as we go along, you know?'

'I guess so.'

'I don't think you'll have any trouble. You just need to relax a bit. Just try and say, not necessarily in words, "well, here I am" and see what bites.'

Sadie winced.

'Bradley would, you know? And I know a few others... Get with it Sadie,' Janet laughed, as she just stared at her. 'I like

Brad, you know that. And I think I can work it round. If you'd just get out of the way...'

The lights were dimming, there was activity on stage. The band was assembling. Both women turned to look, along with the rest of the crowd. And Sadie was staring. To the very back of the stage.

'You're not interested in Brad, are you...?'

The lights swivelled to the drums, the reverb from the sound desk sending Jay's thumping spinning around them. The sound was so enclosing, like a vortex powering around their heads.

'It is Jay, isn't it...?'

The other eight pieces of the band kicked in with a mighty roar.

'Sadie...?'

The crowd were on their feet to the deafening beat, the relentless parp of the horn section and the swirling keyboards and guitars. Sadie put her hand to her ear, and retreated to their table, shaking her head in resignation that their conversation could not compete.

Or something else...

And Janet had to concede, for the moment, but to add at the table, 'Just watch me, if it helps...'

The band had a break half way. Jay had already spotted Sadie in the crowd and in his present lifted mood, he jumped straight off the stage and made a beeline for her group. By the look on his face as he hurried through the hall, she could see his mood had changed. Just how much she didn't know, until he rushed up and plucked her off the ground.

'Hello group,' he said, swinging an arm around her shoulders and turning her away from them. 'Do you like it?'

'Yeah, it's great!' she smiled, picking up his mood and determined to reflect it back.

'Yeah,' he laughed. 'It's going so well!'

'Glad you came back for it, then?'

'Yeah, yeah,' he dismissed any reminder of that notion for the moment. 'Oooh, I feel so good. I want you to like it!'

Sadie laughed too. She had to be carried along with this enthusiasm, or she might have been a little put out by the force of it. Besides, he really was amusing. He could hardly get his words out properly, and the things he did say were a little rash and slightly uncoordinated.

'I do like it. Very much,' she responded to his obvious need to be told again.

'You gotta share this with me! I knew it was gonna be good as soon as it started. This is the best thing that's happened to me for ages!'

Sadie tried hard to understand his excitement, but obviously communicated some kind of appropriate response to his continued gabbling, as he seemed to be extremely pleased with her.

'I'm really glad you came!' he concluded, ten minutes later. 'And I fully intend to be right back when it's all over...'

The band's second set rocked the crowd even more. But Jay thought in his quieter moments on stage about the way he had just behaved. A little more soberly, he concluded it hadn't been quite right. He hadn't given her a breath to get a word in edgeways...

Two encores later, Sadie sensed a distinct change of mood as Jay came off stage. Far less manic, she assumed he had not been as pleased with the second set.

'Well, I thought that was even better!' she said.

'Yeah!' he beamed, his self-imposed restraint immediately busted. Evidently, he was incapable of containing himself.

'Oh, you think so too?'

'Certainly...' Then he proceeded to explain exactly why.

Until Janet cut in. Pretty well-oiled by now, she put her arms around his neck. 'Thanks, Jay.'

He stopped mid-sentence, and they both looked at her.

'Well, he's got you out of the way and Brad and I are getting on very well, thank you! Have you been watching, Sadie?' she winked and sprinted away.

'What was all that about?' Jay laughed.

'Oh, nothing,' Sadie fluffed. 'We've just been having this joke, that's all. Janet insists the only reason Bradley hasn't asked her out is because he's after me.'

'Is he?' Jay shot a look at the tall modish blond rejoining Janet at their table a few feet away.

'Oh, I don't know. That's just what they all say. And Janet keeps up this mock-duelling. It's a laugh, really.'

'Well, I wish her luck.' Too true, he did. 'Don't fancy him then?'

'Oh, I don't want him,' Sadie snorted.

'Don't you want anybody?'

The instant reply surprised them both. Sadie lost her smile then, and Jay kicked himself for it. *Fucking stupid thing to say...* And what for? He didn't even want to hear that answer. So, swiftly making the question rhetorical, he said, 'I'll get us another drink as well then, eh?'

When he returned from the bar, Sadie appeared to have let him off the hook. Laughing and joking, barely another serious word was exchanged between them. They built castles out of empty glasses, flicked beer mats and gossiped about all the people around them, including Janet and Bradley. And it wasn't long before they were on the dance floor. Jay displaying his natural rhythm, and Sadie evidently hers too, now she was feeling rather looser than normal. It intrigued and excited him.

They never seemed to tire, despite the number of times either or both of them nearly ended up on the floor. Every time, they'd steady each other and collapse in giggles. And for the first time in ages, Sadie was enjoying herself completely, with careless abandon to the appearances and consequences. Least of all the appearances and consequences to Jay. He was just lovely, and she didn't care. Right now, she refused to get bogged down with what she should and should not be doing or saying. He seemed to be enjoying her company, and that was just fine by her. Especially after her recent fears for his disappearance...

The evening went too quickly, and they were soon into the slow dances. In their present mood, they just wanted to carry on running around the room. But Jay's smile steadied suddenly, looking deeper into her eyes. And as the next soulful ballad began, he lifted her chin and said, 'Come here.' And he enclosed his arms around her. Unthinkingly, she responded, her arms slipping around him. And they just breathed together, treading water to the gentle music.

Just where Jay so wanted, *needed*, to be.

And Sadie suddenly felt so comfortably warm and safe and connected. His breath over her shoulder, his hands moving slowly over her back. And maybe... *maybe*... Did she have to ask these embarrassing questions? Did she have to watch Janet?

But with this unexpected surge of emotion and arousal, the fear returned in an instant. From wanting to be with him, to wanting to know how to see it, to ask, she was just wanting to hold him now. Here in this place. Just like the other night. That immediate surge of warmth and longing, when he had asked if he could give her a cuddle. And sitting there beneath his arms that night, the warmth of his body pressed to hers, the enclosure of his arms, the faint aroma of his aftershave...

Just like now...

And suddenly it overwhelmed her. She pushed herself from him and walked away.

Jay sighed, his hand through his hair. He'd gone too far. Everything he had promised not to put himself through. The dominoes were falling before his eyes, one after another. Her inevitable rejection of him – of anyone – to her inevitable withdrawal, all the way to the inevitable loss of Joe. His adorable boy.

Except, of course, he was just *her* adorable boy.

Why did he keep putting himself here? That was why he had left, so that he could not do it anymore. And, right now, he wished he had never come back. No gig, however blinding, was enough to compensate for this torture.

'What's the matter with you?' Janet stood right in front of him. 'Where's Sadie?'

'Gone to the loo. I think I've upset her,' he sighed, although why he was admitting this to her, he did not know.

'Well, don't,' Janet retorted. 'She's a pig to live with in a mood, and I want her out the way until I get Bradley out of here.'

'Oh, she's not interested in him,' Jay replied irritably.

'Well, he's interested in her, OK? Do you get what I'm saying?'

Her pointed tone irritated him even more. 'No Janet, I do not.'

'Oh, for heaven's sake, Jay!' Clearly, the alcohol was dulling her diplomacy. If she ever had any. 'She's really a great girl underneath all that angst. You know that. And let's face it, she's no gorgon. Are you blind?'

'*What*? Of course I'm not.'

'Well, for God's sake, stop upsetting her and get on with it then!' Janet turned on her heel.

'Janet, wait! Are you saying...?' He didn't know quite how

to put this. 'Are you saying that I might have... you know... a chance?'

Janet sighed as she retraced her steps. 'I should say so, yes,' she replied, somewhat painfully. 'But I warn you, if you stuff up, I'll be after you.'

'*What...?*'

'You seem to me, Jason, to be a bit of an attention grabber, if you don't mind me saying—'

'Yes, I do mind you saying, as a matter of fact!'

'Well, I'm saying it anyway. She's not some arm candy, OK? She's got too many issues. You're good with Joe, clearly, and she trusts you. That is not an easy thing for her, as you will know if you've got half a brain. So, not the type for a quick fuck, right—?'

'Well neither am I, actually!'

'Good. So now we understand each other.'

'I wish I did,' Jay muttered, but Sadie's return prevented any further illumination.

Sadie glanced between them. 'What's going on here, then?'

'Nothing,' Jay replied instantly.

But Janet was having none of it. 'I was just putting Jay straight on a couple of things.'

'Oh, were you? Really?' Sadie swallowed her alarm. 'Well, I'm sure he knows, Janet, that you mostly talk bollocks, so with any luck he won't take a blind bit of notice.'

'Bugger, that's the end of it,' Janet sighed as the music died and the lights went up. 'Where is that man...?'

'You OK?' Jay said, as Janet disappeared in search of Bradley.

Sadie nodded, not meeting his eye.

'All over now anyway,' he concluded sadly. Despite Janet's implications, Sadie's words and demeanour showed she thought quite differently.

'Have you got to put your stuff away?'

Jay thought quickly. He didn't *have* to. Maybe he could leave it until the morning. He had hoped they could go and have coffee, or some more vodka import, just not to end the evening quite yet. But she was probably searching for an excuse to get rid of him now.

'Well, yeah, I suppose.'

'Oh,' Sadie replied. 'Shall I help you?'

Jay's smile was immediate and broad. 'Yeah, that'd be good...!'

Under strict instructions, she helped him unscrew his kit on the stage. 'Sorry,' he laughed. 'I'm a bit of a tyrant when it comes to this thing, I know.'

'And so you should be. You're bloody good, you know that, don't you? I shall definitely want to see those business cards as soon as you finish with this diversion into academia. Jason Barratt, Professional Drummer!'

'Do you really think so?' Suddenly, he was serious again.

'Well, what do I know? But why not, Jay? Go for it. And Joe'll be your first pro roadie, I'm sure!'

Jay stared at her. She was talking about the future. A future with Joe in it. Perhaps the dominoes were not falling...

'You are...' he shook his head. 'Just amazing, you know that? Thank you. Thank you for everything you ever do or say...'

But unfortunately for both of them, Fiona was buzzing around backstage. Her pride very worn, she had every intention of taking it out on him.

'Had a good evening, have you?'

'Yeah, great thanks,' Sadie replied as Jay did not.

'Yes, it looked like it. Well, Jason, perhaps you always get what you want. Let's hope,' she turned to Sadie. 'That he's not as *disappointing* as he was with me.' And with that, she flounced off.

Jay busied himself with his drums. 'Sorry about that,' he mumbled.

'Silly cow,' Sadie merely grinned...

By the time they had finished with the drums, they were chatting and mucking around again and, much to Fiona's distaste, they tangoed out the door into the fresh air.

'Well,' Jay breathed through this continuing rollercoaster. 'Now we can have that drink?'

'Which is *that* drink?' Sadie laughed.

'The one in the bottle on the second shelf of your cupboard,' he replied boldly, her joking giving him confidence.

'Oh, *that* one,' she nodded. 'Right...'

Sadie went to the kitchen, while Jay put on a tape. He didn't seem all that put out that there was nothing in her collection post-dating 1981.

'Wonder what Joe's up to now?' he giggled. 'Wild toddler party, heavy on the cherryade?'

'I hope he has the energy. Still, he did seem a bit better today, certainly well enough to go.'

'I'm glad he has,' Jay replied rashly. It was, of course, rather different to be sitting here at this late hour, talking at a normal volume, with music on beside them. 'I feel like staying up all night,' he continued, couching a very real need in light words. No, he did not want to go, but then again, if he stayed much longer, he'd end up saying so.

So he retraced a little. 'I'm sorry about Fiona, I really am.'

'Oh, don't worry about it. Like I said, silly cow. I guess you've split up, then?'

'Split up?' he laughed. 'It was hardly the romance of the century.'

'Didn't get what she wanted, evidently,' Sadie teased.

'No,' he agreed with a sheepish laugh. 'And boy, was she persistent.'

'Well, why not then?'

There she was, doing it again. *Why*? There was no part of her that remotely wished to have any discussion about his relationship with Fiona. Especially after tonight.

Jay was looking straight at her. She didn't quite know what that expression meant...

But he did. Bloody hell, he couldn't maintain this a minute longer. What did it matter now, anyway? It couldn't get any worse than this, surely. He'd known it that moment on the A27 last week when the fleeting notion had passed before his eyes. One tiny jerk of the steering wheel... Just conclude the whole damn thing.

And now, suddenly, half a mug of vodka later, he just did not care anymore. Whatever happened, this was driving him absolutely crazy, and he was going to explode any minute. And he didn't have an escape now, as he had that day on the A27 – swerving onto the grass verge, slamming the car door behind him and sinking down on the roadside in tears...

'Other things on my mind,' he finally replied, still looking straight at her. It unnerved Sadie a little. 'Other people on my mind,' he added. 'Some other *person* on my mind... Oh, fuck it Sadie, I can't do this anymore! I just wished it was you! Christ, how I wished it was you!' He grabbed her arm. The change was so abrupt it was dizzying. 'Sadie, I wanna be with you. I can't get you out of my head. I really can't. I need to be with you. I have to—'

And there it all stopped, as suddenly as it had started.

Because he knew now, he had been wrong. Yes, it could get worse. There was a look of sheer terror in her beautiful eyes.

'Oh, fuck...' What the hell had he just done? Realising the manner in which this had all come tumbling out of him. Of course, she was frightened. And all of a sudden, a spot of dodgy steering seemed attractive again. Now he was frightened, too. As he had been then. By his own thoughts. His own desperation.

'I'm sorry, I—'

'Don't,' she whispered, but could not go on.

'I know,' he breathed, his eyes lowering.

'Jay...' Sadie was at a complete loss now as he mournfully pulled at his fingers in his lap. So drawn to him. But this was confusing. This outburst. Her own feelings.

And yes, she was frightened.

'Jay, don't say things to me that you might not mean.'

'I haven't—'

'Look, we've had a good evening. Perhaps that makes you think things—'

'Oh, Christ no! I'm not thinking anything about your feelings for me. Just because we've... No, I was just saying what I felt. It doesn't matter now.' His eyes lowered to the carpet again. 'Look, it's said. There's no point in telling you to forget it. I've told you the truth. That's all I can do. I'm sorry. I am really sorry. I shouldn't have said it like that. I shouldn't have said it all.'

Jay knew he should go now. He should just run. Run until he had no breath left. But still, he remained rooted to the floor... Could he rescue this? Attempt some reason...?

'You said I was cute,' he ventured. 'Janet said... well, she implied, I might have a chance...'

She was still here, looking back at him; that look that seared him. She wasn't running. And he was right, he couldn't contain it. He couldn't stop this...

As soon as his lips touched hers, Sadie backed away. And it all came crashing down on Jay. All that he had tried, but *kept* failing, to save himself from. He screwed his eyes shut and rubbed his face, muttering desperate apologies.

'Oh, stop it! Just stop apologising, will you?'

'I have to. I don't know what else to do! I know I've ruined it all now—'

'Stop it! Ruined what, for God's sake? See? You don't know what you're talking about!'

'I don't know because I don't know what to say! But please stop telling me I don't know what I mean. I know what I mean. And I mean to apologise... Look,' he held his hands up. 'I've made a mess of things. I'll go.'

'No, don't!' she grabbed his raised hand. 'Don't go... Please, stay.'

Time had stopped. And so had his ability to move. To do anything at all now, except stare right back at her. How long was this going to go on? He felt like he was losing himself in those eyes.

He watched as she inhaled deeply, her hand reaching to the back of his neck.

'Please don't go, Jay...'

And she touched her lips to his.

The shock was electric. It made him jump. She drew away, retreating once again, not able to look at him.

'Oh... please...' And then he moved. His hand to the back of her neck, pulling her back to him. His mouth on hers, open and searching, kissing her deeply, warmly, so needily, moving his arms around her, engulfing her. Feeling her arms slowly creep around him. Pressed to him completely now. Her open mouth feeding him, filling him...

She dropped her forehead to his.

'Oh, Sadie. Did you just do that?'

'Jay, I...' she could barely meet his eye. 'I want to be with you. I do... like this,' she concluded clumsily, the clueless little girl again.

'Oh...' Jay couldn't quite connect. What kind of twisted reality was this? It wasn't his. *Was it?*

'Do you mean that? Do you really mean it?'

As she looked up at him, the confusion remained in her eyes, but... there was something else, too... Something far more dangerous.

'Sadie? You're shaking.' He pulled her to him. 'Oh, please Sadie, what is it?'

'I...I'm frightened...' The honesty speared them both. If he needed any further reminder of her independence and fear of trust and truth, he was seeing it all too clearly now.

'Oh Sadie, please. Please don't be scared of me.'

And the honesty had begun now, so she nodded weakly.

'I'll try. Jay? Please know. I'll try.'

'Oh God, Sadie...' This was beyond his dreams, her response. Had that really just happened? But despite his arms enclosing her in a desperate attempt to contain it, the tremor remained. 'My gorgeous Sadie, please... I don't understand any of this. But please, *please* don't be frightened. I won't hurt you. Is that what you're scared of? I would never hurt you. I wouldn't hurt... anybody.' His voice trailed away. He, too, had his memories. A shame he would carry to his grave, with no compassion or forgiveness. But it was never who he really was; and it was far away from this moment, here with her...

But she couldn't look at him, remaining silent and hidden away.

'Please Sadie, just be honest with me. If you mean this, if you want this, we'll work it out. I don't understand it. I can't quite believe it! But if you say it's what you want, I *will* be here.' Still, she did not move or speak. 'But if you *don't* mean it. Please, Sadie, I have to know that too. Promise me. Don't do that to me.'

Finally, she raised her head, venturing tentatively out of hiding. She had to have the courage. 'I do mean it. Whatever I say. Whatever I do, because I don't know... I *do* know this...' And it was more than the fear and uncertainty at that moment, this longing to hold him close, to see him, to touch him...

She pressed her mouth to his.

Again, it was like he had been plugged into the mains. The touch of her against him, her mouth responding to his so deeply, so warmly. The shaking subsiding, the loving response subsuming everything.

'Oh, God...' Jay was breathless between her kisses, reconnecting heatedly, unstoppably every time. His mind spinning and his body electrified. He lowered her back onto the mattress. Feeling completely displaced; as if in another world. And a world where he would never be able to take his mouth from hers ever again.

Until she did. Her head dropped to his shoulder. Despite the spontaneity of her response, and the free passion of the last moments, there was no getting away from the fear that remained...

There was nothing in the world Jay would have liked more than to allow their increasingly free embraces to take their natural progression. Except the possibility of hurting or losing her. When they had crossed this line. When he had touched her lips. When he had held her this close. He knew there was no going back for him. Everything he knew in his heart was true. She and Joe were his life. And he would do anything to keep it. And so he held her head to his shoulder. He would do anything now. Anything.

He levered himself up on his elbow. 'It's OK...' Pulling the duvet from beneath them, he gently lay it over them both, and pulled her back into his arms. 'I'll just lie here with you...'

Sadie was so overwhelmingly drawn to him then. And she felt so inadequate. But there was no way she could cope with any more honesty right now, and she would have to delve deep into that to go any further. But she felt closer to him than she could ever imagine as he concluded, 'We'll sleep, yeah? I don't know, maybe you're getting carried away by me. This is hard for you, I can see. And we do it your way, OK? Nothing you don't want. Ever. Nothing...'

It was sheer incredulity in Jay now. But it felt like strength to her. *Nothing she didn't want?* How different could this be? How different could *he* be...? And as he kissed her hair so lightly, softly stroking her arm, she felt tears prick her eyes.

She closed them and nodded, her head to his chest.

37

IN HIS ARMS

A knock on the door woke Sadie the next morning. It took her a moment to orientate herself, looking up at Jay, asleep, holding her still. The second knock, louder, more insistent, woke him. They stared at each other.

'Christ, the time,' she broke the spell. 'Joe!'

Inevitably, it was Joe at the door, with Mrs Turnbull. Sadie had neglected to be at the nursery to pick him up at eleven o'clock.

'Oh, hello,' she stuttered, smoothing down her dishevelled shirt, her fingers through her hair. 'I'm so sorry. Slept in.'

Mrs Turnbull was visibly trying to convey that she had not noticed Jay in the bed. Hadn't she always said her husband was working abroad long-term...?

'Thanks ever so much.' Sadie lifted Joe into her arms. 'Hey there matey, had a good time?'

'Yeah!'

'He's not himself, Mrs Emmett.'

God, she hated being called that. Whoever gave them that

title, anyway? It was a damned assumption! And then she always remembered. It was her.

'I know, he hasn't been well. But he seemed so much better yesterday. He's going back to the doctor on Wednesday.'

'Good.'

'Well, thanks again for all your work.' Sadie encouraged her out...

'How do you feel, Joe?' She kissed him in her arms.

'OK. Hello, Jay!'

'Joe, answer me. You've no pains?'

'No. But I'm tired. Can I go to sleep for a bit?'

Sadie sighed anxiously. 'Yes, alright. Have you had something to eat this morning?'

'Yes, lots! But can I have a drink, please?' And that was another thing. He was always thirsty nowadays. Sadie put him down and went to the sink. He ambled over to the mattress.

'Hiya, Joe.' Jay propped himself up. 'How's my favourite boy, then?'

'Tired,' Joe yawned, flopping down beside him.

'You been up all night?'

'No,' Joe giggled. 'I just tired.'

'You had a good time, though?'

'Oh, yeah! It was a big place. In the woods. We all had sleeping bags, and we had games and a party!'

'Well, no wonder you're tired then,' Jay laughed, trying to lighten both their concerns about the boy.

'You look funny. Have you just woken up?'

'I have.'

'And both of you have still got your clothes on! Were you cold? I told you Mummy gets cold. Is that why you slept in there too?'

'More or less,' Jay grinned.

'I'm glad you did. It's nice.'

'Yes, it certainly is,' Jay replied, his eyes turning to Sadie and locking there.

'I wanna go sleep.' Joe wasn't allowing this, either. 'Can I get in with Jay?'

Her head still swimming with the newness of all this, Sadie did not know how to answer. But Jay saved her the trouble.

'You can if you like, but I've got to go soon.'

'Oh, why?' Joe whined. Surely if he was sleeping here, he'd moved in now?

'I've got lots to do,' Jay lied. But he knew he must go. Leave her for a while. And come back. See how it was in the cold light of day. But always come back. Please God, she'd let him.

'Anyway, give us a cuddle first.'

'I'll get my pyjamas on...'

Joe tumbled back under the duvet with Jay, as Sadie busied herself in the kitchen. Her mind so full. Of questions, of emotions, of needs.

But Joe was back now...

Joe was asleep within seconds. Jay raised his eyes over his shoulder. She smiled, so slightly, so hesitantly. He beckoned her with his head, and she put down her tea towel and went to him. He shifted as she sat down, clearly some unease between them. At the same time, a kind of electricity that neither of them seemed to know how to read. But Jay lifted his free arm and pulled her down to him, and suddenly it was just like a jigsaw being fitted back together.

Sadie's chest heaved a little. The two of them in his arms. For a second, the image quite overcame her.

Jay could feel her emotion. 'What is it?'

She looked up at him. 'I don't say it enough, but... thank you for loving my son.'

And Jay sighed. Well, here he was.

'He's not the only one...'

38

HONESTY

Joe was alert enough to go to the park that afternoon. It was a warm, sunny day, and the two of them splashed about in the paddling pool in shorts and T-shirts. It took Sadie's mind off the turmoil within her a little. What the bloody hell was she doing? With all this emotion, all these new things? Take her back to this simple life...

But when they got back to Ellis House, Jay was standing leaning on the wall by the door, and it all flooded back, instantly.

'Sorry,' he smiled. 'Couldn't keep away.'

'Been waiting long? We've been to the park.'

'Na, only a few min—' Joe had grabbed his hand and dragged him inside.

'Guess it's OK if I come in then.'

'Guess so...'

Just as they were slipping back into that hypnotic gaze, Joe wrenched them apart again, insisting that Jay play Lego with him. And so they sat on the floor, building a drum kit, while Sadie made tea.

Joe was tired again though, and went to bed straight afterwards. And despite his warm longing all day, and the insistent pull between them that neither of them could really reason, Jay was anxious now. What would it be like in the light of a new day? Especially as Sadie didn't seem to have a lot to say to him.

'So, you, uh... you OK?' He tried to begin this. Sadie nodded, but did not speak. There was a distance about her and the merest hint of that fright again. 'You... uh... regret it?' he persisted. 'All that was said last night?'

'Do you?'

'I'm here, ain't I?' He tried to smile, but the silence pulsed on. 'Could you... could you say it, do you think? Yes or no?' Still nothing. 'Please?'

'Yes... and... no,' she mumbled.

'Oh. And do you think you could tell me what that means?'

'I don't know...' The response, such as it was, was virtually inaudible.

Jay sighed. 'Look, Sadie, I am trying to understand. But I'm really, *really* not over-brimming with confidence at the moment. I'm trying to know what to say. Maybe I shouldn't have told you how I feel. But I did. And I'd kinda like to know about you now.'

Sadie nodded, but remained silent.

'Alright,' he sighed. 'I'll ask the questions, one finger for yes, two for no. This one for fuck off. OK?'

'Oh, Jay...'

'It talks!'

'I'm sorry.'

'S'alright,' he said gently. 'I really just wanna talk with you.'

Again she nodded but did not speak.

'OK then,' he breathed deeply, deciding to lay it out simply. 'Well, here it goes... So, do we split, are we friends, or more?'

Sadie looked as if she was going to evade the question again, and suddenly, he was compelled towards truth.

'Which?'

Still, she was silent.

'Sadie, come on. Which? Answer me, please!'

A small sound escaped her lips. 'More...'

And Jay's tightly held breath fell. He closed his eyes. He could run screaming out into the night right now. She had said something. She had chosen. And she had chosen... *him*.

But still, she held herself away. The two did not correspond somehow. He did not know quite what to do with it. But she needed to hear something, and he needed to say it.

'Great! That really makes me very happy, you know?'

'What's so great about it?'

Jay winced. Oh God, this was torture! Giving with one hand, taking away with the other. But he decided to just try to answer the question. 'It's great because—'

Because I absolutely fucking love you, Sadie! Can't you see that? Can't you see what this is doing to me? The voice inside him screamed. But he couldn't. His sleeve was full already. And he was getting nothing back.

'Well, because it's what I want,' he eventually settled for.

'Is it?'

Jay shook his head. 'Sadie, please... tell me. What is it you're feeling? Look, do you not believe me or something?'

Although he was laughing now, Sadie became quite defiant.

'No,' she snapped. 'Not a lot, no.'

'Sadie!' The smile wiped from his face. 'How much clearer can I make it?'

No answer.

'I think,' he ventured bravely. 'That perhaps *you* are the one who doesn't know how they feel.'

She looked away.

'Yeah,' he sighed. This was the truth he perceived still.

But he could not leave it there. He had come this far.

'Sadie, please try. For me. Please try to tell me. Do you really not know how you feel?'

'I think I do... But I don't know what it means; where it's going to lead me. And I can't really cope with it.'

In the best of worlds, this was not the conclusion Jay would have liked. But in this one, his one, it was perhaps the best he could hope for.

'Well, that's a start. Sadie...? Isn't it? And maybe you could tell me how you feel, and we can work out where it's going to lead together?'

It was a reasonable conclusion, but still she said nothing.

'Come on, have a go. Look, I'm cute,' he grinned at her.

The tiniest smile touched her lips at that. But it was soon gone.

'Come on, Sadie.' He really could not stand this a moment longer. 'Please, for God's sake, say something!'

'Alright!' She finally broke, neither of them succeeding in keeping below a level that would normally wake Joe. 'I want you here with me! I can't see ahead without you! I need you! And I hate it!'

So, Jay had his confessions. He'd broken in. She wanted him. Christ, she wanted him! But her conclusion confused and hurt him.

'So, tell me. You were going to suss it all out for me; tell me where it's all going to lead now?'

'Sadie, please,' Jay winced again. 'Please let up. How am I supposed to accept what I think, what I hope, you're saying to me when you're so openly antagonistic towards me? Look, I was wrong. I haven't got all the answers. But, please, you must know what this is doing to me. Couldn't you just let me be a tiny bit elated that you want some kind of relationship with me...? Don't you?'

'I've said...' she sighed irritably.

'Well, say it again. As if you mean it. Say, "I want to be with you Jay, and I trust you" this time, and mean it. Or don't say anything at all and I'll just get out of here right now. I really can't cope with this anymore.'

'Oh no, don't do that,' she replied instantly, and then she crumbled. 'Don't go. I will. Please say I can. Oh, please God, make me!'

And Jay was so overwhelmed by love for her at that, desperately hanging onto the implication. He pulled her to him and held her tight. 'You can do that. It's easy. I'm a complete pushover, you know.' He attempted a smile. 'You *can* depend on me. Try to feel that, Sadie, please... I need you. I trust you with that. I depend on you. Does that make it any easier...? What do you reckon? Jay and Sadie, Mutual Dependence Society?'

With every minute he held her, it was like an enclosure to the fear, sucking her resistance, and breathing warmth and love into her. 'It's the truth,' she said, finally. The honesty nearly killed her. 'I'll join that...'

'How about a kiss for the initiation rights, then?'

The question was clearly rhetorical as he pressed his lips to hers. And she responded, again, with more warmth than he expected her to be capable of. And when he broke from her, she looked at him, so directly. Nobody had ever come close to looking at him like that.

'Oh, Jay...'

And now, so suddenly, she was lifting one leg over to sit on him, her open mouth on his, her arms round him, her hands in his hair, over his back... It shocked him at first. But oh, how he loved it. And within milliseconds, he was responding wholeheartedly; within seconds more pushing her back over the mattress.

It was like a floodgate opening. Laid across her now, kissing her deeply with all the pent up longing in his head and his heart. And she was responding.

'God, I want you.' A rush of heat from his feet to his head, his hand moving unstoppably up inside her shirt...

She gasped. 'Jay, no... Joe.'

He broke away, eyes lowered, pressing his face into her shoulder, looking out into the room towards the sleeping boy. And he breathed the heat down as best he could.

'Yeah,' he sighed. 'OK...' He gathered her up and pulled her over him, holding her head to his chest. He could do this. He *would* do this. 'Bedtime...'

39

I CAN GET EVEN CUTER

Joe was delighted to find Jay had slept the night again, and was still here in mummy's bed the next morning. He tumbled in with them both.

And yes, Jay thought, he was here now. He wasn't going anywhere today. But so was Joe, and a change of gear was required, or else he'd never survive.

'Right then,' he clapped his hands together. 'As it looks like another fantastic day, what say we head off down to the beach?'

'Yey!'

It was the most animated Sadie had seen Joe in days...

'Hey, look,' Jay said as they reached the car. 'I got a child seat!' They giggled together as he deposited Joe in it. 'Now is that commitment, or is that commitment?'

Sadie nodded slowly. It seemed so important somehow, it momentarily numbed her into silence.

'Hey,' he touched her arm, kissing her lightly. 'Now we can do this properly, can't we...?'

And from the moment they arrived in Bognor, it seemed that is exactly what he was determined they would do; holding both their hands on their slow, child-restrained amble towards the beach.

'Christ, it is hot,' he laughed as they laid out the towels. 'OK, last one in the sea's a big wuss!' And he ripped off his T-shirt and hared off down the beach. Joe, at least, had responded to the challenge, fervently relinquishing his clothes and jumping up and down, demanding his trunks.

'Come on Joe, it's not gonna be you or me!' Jay returned to sweep the boy off his feet, carting him, giggling furiously, under one arm towards the sea.

'Your mum's a big wuss!' He called back to her from the shallows. For a moment, it looked as though she had no intention of engaging with this game. But then she grinned, ripped off her T-shirt, jumped out of her shorts and tore after them in her bikini.

'You wanna bet?' She hared past them and threw herself into the sea. 'Fu—' she leapt out of the freezing water. Then took a few deep breaths and made herself sit down again. 'Come on then, you big sissies!'

'Oi!' he called back, still negotiating the shallows with Joe. 'I'm hampered by a spot of parenthood here, OK?'

And as always, it warmed her heart that he was taking this role so readily...

'Phew!' Jay sank back onto the beach mat afterwards. 'That was cool. Bit cold now though.' Sadie had already engulfed Joe in a towel and threw one at him. 'Ta.'

Joe plonked down on the sand, eager to get on with the business of sand castle making.

'Always last, eh?' Jay pulled out the remaining towel and enclosed her in it, rubbing her wet and cold limbs. Well, he was here now, and he would share this. Completely. If she'd let him.

'Christ, I really like this development,' he grinned, drawing her to him and kissing her.

'Jay...' She pulled away. 'Joe...'

Hearing his name, Joe looked up. 'What you doing? You wrestling? Can I play too?' And he flopped down on top of them both.

And yes, Jay sighed to himself, he could do this too...

It did seem, after this day, that it was more than a gear that had been changed. Jay held her hand all the way back to the car, and spent the entire journey home neglecting the road to look at her. As if suddenly he had been transported to a place of calm. A place of safety. Although she had not said much, she had said enough. She had said one word. 'More.' She was going to follow this.

And he would do everything from now on to show her that he was 'more'. And today, it had looked as if she was going to let him, which just lit the most powerful torch to his natural ebullience. He could not stop grinning all the way home.

Then there was Joe. He watched him too in the rear-view mirror, asleep in his new child seat. He had him as well. And today it had felt like that 'family' in the snapshot. So mistaken. Yet so right.

But then there *was* Joe. The focus of her life...

Sadie gently woke Joe to dunk him under the shower, but he was virtually asleep again by the time she got him back and into bed.

'Think I better have one myself,' she said, picking sand from between her toes.

'Ooh, can I come?'

Her smile was faint. 'Joe.' She cocked her head towards the sleeping boy.

Jay nodded. Of course. Joe...

'OK, think I better do the same,' he said on her return.

'Shall I go home? Or can I stay again?'

'If you like.'

'Of course I like,' he grinned, stroking her cheek and kissing her forehead. 'Lend us some stuff, then...?'

He seemed so light now, Sadie reflected. So open and playful and affectionate. And she wanted that; she knew that now. But she also knew that she couldn't always respond the same. Sometimes it was unconscious; her instinctive warm and wholehearted response. But sometimes something else gripped her. And she knew she had to continue to fight with this...

He came back with a pack of beer. 'It's been a great day, thanks,' he said, going straight to the fridge, as if he lived there now. 'Want one?'

'Yeah,' she smiled.

'Thought you might.'

Sadie finished putting out her rinsed beachwear and joined him on the mattress.

'I like that bikini,' he grinned. 'I like what's underneath it even better.' His pulled her to him, his hand at once up her shirt. 'Can't keep my hands off you,' he muttered in between fervent kisses... 'Oh,' he whispered, as he touched the soft underside of her breasts, uncontained by a bra. 'That was a surprise.' She drew breath, but he was restraining her with his open mouth now. And whatever his resolution, his natural playful warmth and affection for them both; his delight at being in this family... 'Oh Sadie, I wish he wasn't here.'

He was looking deep into her eyes now, and she felt it again. Every time she looked into those eyes... But hers lowered. Despite her deep, visceral response, her mind rebelled and her body froze at the implication of those words.

'Hey, hey,' he could see the fear returning. 'Don't leave me again. Say it.'

But how could she? The very touch of him. She wanted

him so much. But she could never begin to speak her fears. Nobody had ever known...

'I'm crazy about you, Sadie,' he whispered. 'I never thought I'd be here. All that we've been through. And every time I look at you now. And you taste so good, and you feel so good...' He stroked her cheek, still not letting her eyes go free. 'But I know,' he sighed. 'I know it's different for you. There's Joe. And, well, it's just different for you.'

'Is it?'

'Look, I'm just a bit overwhelmed, I guess. Can't hold it in, you know. I'm sorry, I'm bulldozing you. I can wait. I know you don't feel the same.' And then he injected himself with a little humour again. 'Yet,' he grinned. 'I'm working on it. Gimme some time, yeah? I can get even cuter...'

It worked; there was a flicker of a smile.

'Come on,' he concluded. 'Let's knock this on the head and have an early night. I'm not in love, you know,' he sang the words of the famous song. 'So don't forget it.' And he lifted her over him and reclined on the bed, gathering her up and reaching over to switch off the bedside lamp. 'This is enough.'

And despite her continuing silence, it was. He felt so relieved that she was allowing him this close. So privileged that they had even started something now. And he found he did have control, as he breathed the arousal away. Yet again. And as the minutes passed, he relaxed into a contented doze.

'Jay?' She almost woke him with her gentle whisper. He turned his head. 'You don't have to work on it.'

And again, something just moved him so deeply. He could have picked her up that moment and run screaming out into the night again. Chanting from the rooftops. She wanted him! Christ, she wanted him!

But instead, he was gentle in his response.

'And you know I lied. I'm hopelessly in love with you...'

40

ANOTHER THURSDAY NIGHT

They both took Joe to nursery the next morning, although he had to be woken again. Another night together, so close, so overwhelming still. And sitting in his lecture theatre, Jay knew, right then, he couldn't spend another minute away from her. He couldn't wait until this evening. He had to see her *now*. Maybe they could just go for a walk. Just be together. Remind him that she was with him now.

He shuffled out of the room, ran across the campus to the Humanities building and plonked himself down in the small room adjoining the two lecture halls.

Soon, both doors opened and a flood of students emerged. Sadie was talking with two other girls, one of whom he recognised.

'Hiya,' he said at the door.

'Hi!'

'That's you finished for the morning, innit? Come for a walk with me? Just until Joe's pick up time?'

'Oh, I always go to the Union for coffee with Heather and Julie on a Thursday.'

Jay faltered. 'Can I... Can I come?'

'Of course!'

He hadn't dreamt it! He didn't have to work on it. The instant enthusiasm of her response flooded him. Just that little thing. Any little thing.

And yes, he was *hopelessly* in love...

'Hello, Jason.' He turned towards an old face. Such a different face. Such a different tone. But all of a sudden, he couldn't give a flying fuck.

'Hi Julie, how's tricks?'

'All the better for you not being around anymore,' she said, only half jokingly. 'I saw you on Friday night, with your Funkination. I'll give them another couple of weeks before they realise what you're really like and kick you out as well.'

'I don't think they're gonna do that actually, Jules,' he laughed. 'So thank you very much for detesting me so much to get me thrown out of Danger Zone.'

'Good God, he's actually got something right!' Julie turned to Sadie. 'What is your association with this person? You do know he's perfectly awful, don't you?'

Sadie just laughed. 'Yeah, I hate him.' And with what seemed to Jay to be one of the greatest acts of courage he had ever seen, given everything that she was and felt, she kissed him and took his hand right before them. And he couldn't help the broadest smile bathing his face in satisfaction.

'Sadie?' Heather was looking closely at Jay. 'This isn't... Joe?' She, like all her friends, knew not to mention that subject lightly.

'No!' Sadie retorted, dropping his hand.

'I'm sorry, sorry, it's just he looks... sorry...'

'Really Heather,' Julie mocked. 'Anything he fathered would be long and slimey and wriggle a lot, not a gorgeous little thing like Joe.' She never was any good at reading signals.

'Oh, fuck off the both of you!' Sadie turned and strode away across the grass.

And Jay was instantly reminded how fragile this was still...

Joe announced that David was going to teach him to play Yahtzee that evening. Sadie knew this already; he'd told her umpteen times.

'Yeah, what are we gonna do on your night off?' Jay said, finishing the washing up and preparing to leave them for afternoon tutorials. 'Somewhere along the line, it must be my turn to have the pleasure of a Thursday evening. Can I come round? We'll talk about it then...'

Jay, however, had one plan already. He retraced his steps to David and Karen's door.

Jay... Joe.

Thursday evening.

No Joe...

Jay's tutors did not notice, or chose to ignore, the relentless fidgeting of his hyperactive legs. His second tutorial went on for an hour and a half and he was halfway out the door with the concluding remarks. Until he was called back to see his personal tutor, to 'discuss' the course, and most notably, his apparent lack of interest in it. For another hour! Jay was like a greyhound out of a trap...

Inevitably, David called for Joe before he'd got back.

'Got all his stuff, then?'

'Oh, is he staying over with you tonight?' Sadie replied at the door.

'Yeah, that is what you wanted, isn't it?'

'Well, I didn't say, but maybe it would be best.' She was thinking fast now.

'No, Karen said Jay told her.'

'Oh. Really? Did he?'

'Entertaining, eh?' David winked.

Sadie felt a flush to her head and stomach. 'Well, don't know about that,' she fluffed. 'Thanks anyway.'

'We'll take him to nursery in the morning as well, OK?' David offered. 'Just in case...'

Jay was standing at the door when she returned from the shower block. 'Hey,' she smiled. 'Sorry, left you loitering about the corridors again.'

'Yeah, I'll get a reputation... Ooh, that's nice,' he said, unstoppably kissing her, his head into her neck, drinking in the warm coconut of her soap.

He'd have to calm this. Slow down. Just be with her. Give her time. That was what he had resolved. Time. Together. That was what this evening was about.

Because tomorrow he wouldn't be here...

'Sorry I'm a bit late. Bloody man.'

'What's up?'

'I've just had a fucking hour with my personal tutor. We're all very concerned about your waning interest, Jason,' he imitated. 'Like bloody hell they are.'

'That bad then, is it?'

'Obviously,' he replied with a weary sigh. 'Oh, I'll snap out of it. I just got bored with it, that's all. And too many other things on me mind... I might get a bit more settled now,' he grinned, pulling her to him again. 'I've promised to buck up a bit. Didn't tell them I was gonna run away into the sunset with the woman of my dreams and her fantastic son and become a professional drummer.'

'Sounds good.' She barely had time to return before his

mouth was on hers again.

'Oooh, that *is* nice...'

His resolution wasn't working. *Jay, slow down...*

'Joe gone then?'

'Thanks to you, I hear.'

'Yeah, sorry, I meant to be here earlier to put it to you properly, you know. Only I'm off on another bloody field trip tomorrow for a couple of days, so I wanted some time to ourselves. What d'you think?' He didn't need to ask. He could see immediately what she was thinking. 'Na, it's OK. I just meant be together. Talk, you know.' Then he giggled. 'Well, there might be some kissing involved, obviously... We could go out somewhere if you want. Proper date, like. Or get a video and a bottle of wine. I could bring my machine over—'

Jay, slow down!

'Do you always talk this much?' Sadie laughed. He really was amusing sometimes, even without the jokes.

'Oh, you know it,' he grinned back. 'I'll tell you what. Why don't we do both?' He was off again. 'Go on, get dressed and we'll go down the pub. A proper one. Go on. I'll watch.'

But despite his light-heartedness, there was something serious in her eyes now.

'I'm sorry, Sadie,' he sighed. 'Can't help meself, you know. I meant what I said. Everything at your call, OK?' If she could just cope with his verbal artillery. And his constant need to touch her lips...

But what was that? She was looking at him like *that* again.

'I don't want to go out.'

'Don't you?' he squeaked.

She slowly shook her head, looking deep into his eyes. Then she kissed him, her hands through his hair.

And now it *was* her call. As far as she could take it...

And she took him to the bed.

Jay practically fell on it, pulling her down on top of him. The control he thought he had, instantly slipping away.

'I want to touch you,' she breathed, her hands beneath his shirt.

'Oh, you can...'

She pulled the shirt over his head, and he just lay there against the wall, head back, so powerfully ignited as she traced her hand through the hairs on his chest. He watched her. As if she was exploring, discovering. And it was almost too much for him. She looked up again, as if needing direction. He pulled her to him, mouths re-engaging, his hands over her back beneath her shirt. And then drawing forwards. Tracing across her stomach as they kissed, the lightest of touches against the underside of her breasts, tracing around them, it held her breath once again. And now he held her...

But it wasn't just this sensation, the tremor taking hold of her. And he had to stop. 'Sadie, no,' he whispered. 'You're shaking.' Withdrawing his hand, he touched it to her face. 'What is it? Are you sure you want this?' he said so directly. 'Like I said, I can wait.' Neither of them were sure that he could. But whatever his own needs, it broke his heart that she still seemed so frightened. 'Sadie, please tell me. Tell me what you're thinking.'

But how could she? She wanted him. That was no pretence. But she was sick with anxiety. And she could not bring herself to speak its name. How could she begin to make him understand, without recounting it all? And that had never been. She was a young woman of 22, but a frightened and naïve child. Lost in her feelings for this man, but unable to shake the images of what had gone before. If only he knew. If only he could understand without her having to speak of it. And then he could make it alright. Because he *could* make it alright. He made everything alright. He could make it all happen without her memories and hurt taking over.

But this was just fantasy. An impossibility. She either had to make him understand, or banish it from this place. And what must he think of this shy and frightened youngster? So scared and inhibited to the point of running away.

'Please Sadie, talk to me.' He held her head to his chest, his heart breaking that the tremor was still there. That she could not speak. That she had no words for his collection now.

'I'm sorry...'

'Hey now, it's OK.'

'I know it's not fair on you. I don't want to lose you.'

Now he had some more words. And they were ones that enclosed him once again. Because they were ridiculous!

'Well, you ain't gonna do that!'

'I wish you could understand.'

'So make me.'

'I can't...'

Jay had seen this so many times before. Something she would not talk about. And it was all for the same reason.

'Joe's father.'

He had to have this now. Now he knew: It was not Joe who was standing in the way... It was Joe's father.

'This has to be about him.' Jay knew this was brave. He could feel her tense beneath his arms, her temperature rising. She tried to pull away, but he would not let her. 'No, Sadie. Not this time. Don't push me away. I can't begin to understand when I don't know anything about him. I don't know anything about you and him.'

'I don't want to talk about him!'

'Christ, he must have really hurt you bad.'

'Stop it!'

'Did he hurt you, Sadie? Is that it?'

'Shut up!' Her hands were up now, as if to cover her ears.

'No, Sadie. Come on, you've got to tell me now.'

'I... I can't... I won't.'

'Then how can I begin to get close to you when this so obviously stands in our way?'

'It doesn't,' she lied, ineffectively.

'Oh, of course it does.' He was trying so hard to remain gentle. But it hurt him deeply that she had felt something – something so dangerous – and he was not allowed to know.

But he would surrender it for now. 'Come on,' he sighed in submission, pulling her back to him. 'I'll just lie here with you, yeah?' He touched her face. 'Sadie, look at me.' She raised her eyes. 'I love you... I love you with all my heart. I will do anything for you. Or nothing at all...' And he folded his arms around her once again.

And she felt it then. The love. Yes, he loved her. Could it not be more obvious? Could it not be more... *different*?

And she couldn't fight with this anymore. Surely, there was nothing so strong as this? If she didn't have him now, if she couldn't touch him now, she thought she would physically scream. And it was no longer the memories, but the fear of not allowing herself to take what she wanted that made her look up at him again, so directly.

'Jay... there is nothing... *nothing* that stands in our way.' And she would not let him go this time; not allow his eyes to stray from her. 'I want you very much.' It was working. Just admitting it, saying it out loud, was chasing away the demons.

'Oh, you got me...' Jay could not reason anymore. But she was kissing him again and he, too, was scared. Scared of the passion she invoked in him, that she would not, *could not* let free. Despite his words, he did not know if he could go down this road again, only to be pushed away.

But there was something new in her eyes now.

'Sadie...?' He could not look away, his temperature climbing. As if she was stimulating him with just that look. Control slipping away. He made to speak, but her fingers touched his lips and she shook her head. Turning, so that she was sitting on his lap, one leg on either side of him, she raised her arms and slowly pulled her shirt over her head.

'I want you very much...' Because now, it was not something she had to overcome, but something she so desperately needed to allow. Her whole body tingling, her breathing uneasy, she lowered herself to him, and kissed him. Taking his hand and returning it to her breast.

Just that gentle movement drove into her. And suddenly she was all over him. Jay felt quite displaced, as if transported to another world. And as her mouth followed her hands down his chest, he was not even sure he could take any more.

Her hand traced the top of his jeans, and then pressed firmly against him. His breath drew sharply.

'Just show me, Jay...'

Sadie did not know whether to laugh or cry, so deeply emotional at his last breath, and the scream of her name, collapsing on her. Taking his whole weight, but it was so comfortable. His open mouth over her shoulder, head into her neck, she felt the silent tears on her skin. She'd never seen him cry before.

'Jay? Are you OK? Was that... OK?'

'Oh, God, Sadie... you... are... incredible. *That* was... incredible.'

It was true. He'd never felt anything quite like that before. The most incredible and urgent release. He could hardly bear its intensity. Perhaps that was inevitable; he had held this in so long. And it left him so powerfully emotional. So unstoppably moved. 'Oh, Sadie,' he finally lifted his head, a cloud of drowsiness over his face. 'I love you...'

And what was that? A slight, gentle smile of... *what*? It almost looked like wonder. Had he put that there?

'Jay, I—' but she stopped. How would she know? This was all so alien to her. 'Thank you.'

And again, he couldn't quite believe this. The incredulity washed over his face, and the love flowed through his body. Energised once more, by the sound of her words, the smell and taste of her, the feel of her, all of her, pressed so closely against him.

'Thank me...? Come here...' His hand to the back of her neck, he pulled her mouth back to his. 'Now you just stay right there...'

Sadie had never felt anything like this before. This depth of sensation. This urgent need, and complete submission. But in absolute safety. Nothing more she could do.

Nowhere she needed to run...

'No going back now.' Jay drew himself up beside her, noses touching. 'You'll never get rid of me now.'

And the thought of that just seemed to excite him to the most incredible light and energy again. 'So!' He threw off the heap of duvet. 'Since I have at least another fifty years, I am absolutely fucking starving!'

Sadie couldn't help but laugh at his familiar animation. Hopping around the room, pulling on his trousers.

'Don't you dare go away! In fact, you can just stay right there. Give me something really special to come home to.'

Come home to? It was so right. Because he was home now...

It felt like he was on an elevator as he sprinted out into the night. His legs were moving, but he didn't know how. And he screamed into the cold night air. Oblivious to the passing students. Oblivious to the world.

And what was he doing out in it? For God's sake...

Now he knew his legs were moving. Haring back in the door some twenty minutes later. Twenty minutes that had felt like a lifetime.

The very sight of her again as he came in the door, having done exactly as he had told her. 'Well, that can wait.' He slung the pizza box and two bottles of wine on the table and dived back onto the bed beside her.

And there they spent the evening, eating pizza, sharing wine, pouring it over each other and licking it off. And the more excitable he was, as he always was, the more relaxed and open she became, until she was initiating as much as he and gleefully throwing herself into all these games.

They wore each other out by midnight, as she was merrily trying to wring the last of the wine out of his hair with her mouth.

'Christ, woman, give a bloke a break...'

'Never,' she whispered, accepting the warm solace of his chest. And it touched his heart so deeply. That this woman who he loved so intensely could share his passion and excitability, responding to him so wholeheartedly. And, apparently, with a vision that this was going to go on.

And on...

When he woke the next morning, Jay couldn't quite connect for a moment. The touch of every part of her against him, the smell of wine and coconut and loving. And he just lay there drinking it in.

Until he turned his head to the clock. 'Sadie,' he whispered. 'It's nearly nine. We gotta go and get Joe for nursery.'

She smiled sleepily and shook her head. 'David's taking him. He thought I might be... *entertaining*.'

'Result!' Jay's eyes lit up, kissing her again. 'And you are entertaining. Extremely entertaining...'

It was a physical wrench to pull himself away from her two hours later. Two hours of such passion, such connection, warmth and affection. But he had to go. The minibus went at midday, and he hadn't even packed.

'What am I going to do without you for two days?' she moaned.

'Oh, I daresay you'll manage,' he said with his usual self-effacing smile. Whether *he* would or not, he really did not know...

At ten to twelve, there was a knock on his door. Sadie had spent the last half an hour just lying on her bed. Still a slight mist of confusion over her, but the emotions and sensations flooding her body and mind. So strong. So powerful.

And he didn't know...

'Hey,' he grinned. 'Did I leave a sock?'

She looked a little breathless, as if she had been running.

'Hey Sadie, what is it? What's wrong?'

'Just... just...' Her hesitation concerned him even more.

'Come on, it's OK,' he whispered, his arms around her. 'Tell me.'

'Jay, I...' He could feel her deep inhalation. 'Couldn't you go without... I love you, Jay.'

And his eyes screwed tight shut, head back as he pulled her as close as he could. 'Oh...' he breathed. And they just stood there for a moment. A moment too long. 'I will carry that with me every minute of the next two days. Every minute of my life...'

41

REALITY

Sadie soon had the most primitive of diversions. Picking Joe up from nursery, he really was the most deathly pale.

'How're you feeling?' she asked, yet again.

'OK,' came the usual, lethargic response.

'Tired?' she suggested.

'Yes. I'm alright now, but I had to go to bed early because I was dizzy. I cried. I didn't like it.'

And what was she doing? While her son cried in anguish? Seeing to her own needs. But she tried to dismiss these thoughts. If Jay had meant half of what he said last night and this morning, she had secured him to the both of them. And that, she had no doubt, was seeing to both their needs. For as long as she could make it.

'OK,' she tried to reassure them both. 'I think you better have a rest. See what the nice doctor says tomorrow...'

Joe awoke after a couple of hours. Although he looked as if every movement was made through treacle, he insisted he wanted to get up. He played with his cars. Quietly. So unlike him to be so slow and quiet.

And then from the sink she heard his voice. 'Mummy...' And she turned to see him collapse on the floor. Dropping the plate from her hands, she ran to him.

'Joe!' No response. His eyes were closed. He was still and lifeless. She desperately pulled him into her arms. 'Joe!' Nothing. She panicked, picking him up and running from the room.

She banged on David's door, the only one of her friends with a car. No answer. She ran out and across the grass to the Union car park. 'Somebody, please! Take me to the hospital!'

Blank expressions returned from students and staff, until one ran over. 'This way...' Sadie hastily followed him to his car. 'What happened?'

'My son. He just collapsed.'

'Don't worry. We'll soon be there. I'm sure he'll be OK...'

That journey seemed like hours, although it was barely twenty minutes.

'Thank you so much...' She should get his name. Follow up this kindness. But the curtain of purpose had drawn, and she fled, carrying her unconscious son into A&E.

It all happened so quickly, at first.

But then, the waiting...

'He's a strong boy,' the doctor said. 'His breathing is strong. We just have to wait.'

The tears rolled silently down Sadie's cheeks. 'But what's the matter with him?'

'It's impossible to say,' he repeated. She'd asked a million times. 'I'm sorry. It could be a number of things. We can only wait for the test results. Try not to worry...'

Fat chance. The sight of him there in that clinical bed. Her boy. Lying so lifeless, a drip in his arm, monitors whirring and pulsing.

'Talk to him. It sometimes helps. There'll be a nurse nearby...'

For some time, Sadie could not even open her mouth. But when she did, the floodgates opened. And somehow it calmed her too... Jay was here now. He was with them. And he would stay with them. They would all be together soon. All the things they would do. If her lovely, beautiful boy would just come home. 'Please come home matey, please wake up Joe...' As if he was still here, and not in some distant dark place that she could not reach him...

She refused every encouragement to go home as the hours ticked by. Until she could not keep her eyelids open any longer, and sank her face into the side of the bed, still muttering words to him. Kicking herself as the morning sun streamed through the window and she was told that he had stirred in the night. She could be encouraged by that, they said. She so wanted to be. But now, again, not a flicker.

Still, she talked to him through the morning.

It came about midday. His eyelids twitched.

'Joe?' Sadie's breath caught, hardly daring to hope. 'Joe, can you hear me? Please God, please hear me.' Another flicker. 'Joe? Wake up, please wake up. Can you hear me, Joe?'

'Mummy...'

Sadie burst into tears of joy and relief, urgently jabbing the bell beside the bed. She rubbed his hand between hers. 'I'm here, Joe. Can you hear me? Can you see me? You'll be alright now, Joe. You'll be alright.'

'I feel funny,' he drawled. 'I wanna sleep.'

'No Joe, don't sleep. Not just yet. Stay awake for a minute. Just for a little while. Do you hear me?'

He nodded faintly. 'I try...'

A nurse bustled in. 'He's awake...'

She fetched the doctor immediately.

'I think that's good,' he concluded, examining Joe and

taking some readings. 'Perhaps the worst is over. If we can diagnose it.'

'You've no ideas?'

'Not really. There are markers in the blood tests that don't fall into the usual suspects, I'm afraid. But we're still waiting on one of the test results, and the senior consultant will be in shortly. But it doesn't seem as if little Joe's in pain. I think it's safe for him to sleep. We'll monitor him carefully to try to prevent him becoming comatose again...'

Sadie did not really take in the long name that Mr Gregory, the consultant, gave her, only the information that devastated her. It was a blood disorder. Hereditary. Inevitably, he asked if she was a carrier. Of course she was not. He nodded. 'It's usually passed through the male line, anyway. It is an extremely rare condition. I've personally not come across a case.' The consultant seemed fascinated by it all. 'Joe's father, can I see him, please?'

Sadie slowly shook her head. He understood. Or rather, he didn't, as Sadie's rage engulfed her shock and anxiety. As if it wasn't bad enough, that bastard had to be one of the extreme rarities!

'It is treatable, I'm told. We've called in a specialist to advise, but I understand that if it's treated in time, it can lie dormant.'

'Please,' Sadie begged. 'Do everything you can.'

Really, she could not take much more of this.

42

HIM AND HIM

Sadie fell into Jay's arms as soon as he appeared at her door that evening. He instantly lost his broad greeting smile, dropping the flowers he had bought for her.

'What is it? Where's Joe?' Of course he made the immediate connection. The room was lit; it was way past his bedtime… and he wasn't here. Jay sat her down at the table and knelt by her side. She was shaking.

'He's in hospital. He collapsed.'

His body jolted. All the needs and compulsive longing bearing down on him in these past two days, instantly forgotten.

Sadie tried to remain calm as she recounted the story, but when she came to the diagnosis, it seemed all the anger and bitterness had just gathered in her for this moment. This moment when he was here, back with her.

'It's a hereditary condition,' she repeated. 'A fucking hereditary condition! Do you realise? It's not me. That bastard's given him this!'

Jay sighed in anguish. This just had to come out now. 'You

must tell me now,' he said, as gently as he could. 'Are you in contact with him? Can you reach him? He must know. He might be able to help.'

'No.'

'Sadie, come on. Think of Joe. You must.'

'I can't.'

'Where is he?' he persisted.

'I don't know!' she lashed back. 'I don't know...'

'We'll find him.' Jay was resolute now. 'A name, anything. I'll do it. I'll find him...'

Sadie was in such a state that she couldn't stop herself firing back, 'I don't know! I don't know who he is!' And, unsurprisingly, as it was the first time that had ever passed her lips, she burst into floods of tears.

Jay sat back on his knees, a long slow breath blown from his open mouth. A space on a birth certificate didn't really mean 'unknown', he knew that. It just meant 'fucked off'. And that was bad enough. But apparently, in this case, it meant exactly that. And he didn't even need to be told now. He didn't even need to imagine. It was clear enough from the way she was at this moment that whatever it was... it was deeply wrong.

'Oh, Sadie... I... I'm so sorry.'

But her bitterness was still lashing out. 'Now, what do you think? So many possibilities I just couldn't make up my mind which it was?'

'Oh Sadie, please—'

'Well, you're wrong. Very wrong.'

Jay sighed, pushing his hand through his hair. 'Tell me what happened, Sadie,' he begged. 'Please...'

And for once, he felt she might. It was only tragic that it had to be because of this. He kept hold of her, clasping her hands and entreating her with his expressions. He knew what a breakthrough this was and the impact of the disclosure was clear enough for anyone to see. But they would get through it. He would make it better. If it took every breath in his body...

Sadie stumbled through the story, the words forced out of her. Just turned 16, she told of her state of mind; the rebellion, the drink, the party... and *him*. Jay listened to every word. Increasingly, it chewed at him. He'd been through a time when her experiences were very real to him. All part of his sickening gang games...

And now, suddenly, it *was* taking every breath in his body.

Because she was stepping slowly through this... That night, that party, that group... *that man*...

There was a whirlwind in his stomach now. A sucker punch to his chest. He felt sick.

Because the more she said...

The more he knew.

'So,' Sadie spat, as Jay's stomach heaved and his hands began to shake. 'Rape, I think you call it, don't you? That's when you scream and kick and struggle and cry "no" over and over again, isn't it? And you're held down and silenced and forced...'

Jay could barely breathe. Could not draw enough air. Could not even feel any air around him. His lungs imploding. His stomach churning. His body shaking. Suffocating in her despair. And his own memories...

'And so, I've no fucking idea who he is. I've got nothing. No name. Nothing. Just a stupid little picture which might just be his back! I wouldn't know.'

She reached for the drawer. And the lockbox at the bottom. Well, he'd had the whole story now...

Then the old photograph was in Jay's hands. As if he had been taking tiny steps towards a cliff edge that, although he held the blindfold tightly across his eyes, he knew was coming; he looked down at the picture, and fell. To the very bottom of the chasm below.

Sadie stopped. His face contorted; he made some sound, some indistinguishable sound. And the picture was crushed in his hand...

For a moment there was the most disturbing and violent of silences. Until all he could force out of him to say was, 'Phenylkaionaemia...'

Sadie stared at him. 'That's the name of it, I think...'

'No!'

And then he ran.

Jay collapsed in the bushes outside Ellis House and threw up. He hauled himself to his feet and tore towards the car. Crying bitterly, totally uncoordinated. All his thoughts entirely without structure or compassion. He arrived at the hospital within minutes, lucky to have escaped with his own life after the manner of his getting there. And inside, he screamed and cried at enough people to be carted off to a quiet room. He was joined by a white-coated man whose name was on the desk plate in front of him. 'Mr R Gregory.'

'Joe...' he stuttered before the consultant had a chance to speak. 'He's got Phenylkaionaemia?'

'Joe Emmett? Yes,' Mr Gregory nodded.

'Oh, God!' Jay collapsed over the desk. 'What are you doing for him?'

'We're waiting for the specialist, but—'

'Don't wait! It's late already. He's already comatosed once!'

'Sir, we have to wait for the specialist to advise on proper treatment—'

'Don't wait! There's no time! You've got to operate. Transfuse him.'

'But—'

'I know!' he cried, the tears rolling down his cheeks. He could not feel them. 'I know!'

'You know the disease?'

Jay drew breath, his chest rising and falling urgently. He could hear his heart beating so fiercely. Finally, locating enough air to speak, he explained, as coolly as he could, his story. How he had been rushed to hospital at the age of seven, where he had a complete blood transfusion. He went on to tell all he knew about the condition. And how that, with treatment, all the enemy cells in his own blood were permanently outnumbered, he should be in remission for life.

The consultant was fascinated. Now that this frenzied man had found some vestige of reason. He decided to trust him. 'I'll get onto the specialist. Perhaps we'll be able to do it right away.'

'Please,' Jay begged, desperately trying to keep a hold on himself.

The consultant paused, his hand over the phone receiver.

'You're his father, aren't you?'

Jay stared ahead of him, at some tortured place in the middle distance.

'Yes...'

Nick called him down the corridor. Jay walked straight past. Didn't even register. There was nothing. Nothing he could do. Nothing he could say. Nothing he could think. He slammed the door to his room and turned the key, wanting to lock himself away forever. Where he could be no further harm to anyone. To let the shock seep through and to endure, alone, the excruciating pain of full realisation.

The pain he deserved, and would carry with him for the rest of his life.

43

UNKNOWN?

Sadie was summoned to the hospital in the early hours of the next morning. She had gone to Jay's room after he had left her so suddenly last night. To reassure him, as best she could in the circumstances of her own despair. Clearly, his was matching her own. And if that were so, she could have no further doubt of his love for her and her boy. But she was confused, and she also wanted him to make sense of this. He knew its name. The condition. She was sure she had not mentioned it. She wasn't even sure she had remembered how to say it properly.

But he had not been in his room. She could not reassure him, and he could not reassure her. She was alone again. And she had returned, dizzy with it all, to her bed.

And she was still alone this morning; a volunteer driver delivering her back to the hospital... To consent to a complete blood transfusion for Joe. Sign here, quickly... The pen jagged across the page, her signature barely legible. So many questions; she could not form any of them. A nurse gave her a cup of tea. Write them down, Mr Gregory told her; he'd answer her questions afterwards...

. . .

'But... so soon...?' Sadie stammered, refusing yet another cup of tea, as Mr Gregory ushered her into his office. But it was alright, Joe was through.

'What was it? What made you... How did you know...?' She had not written them down; the battalions of questions still skirmished, untrained, in her head.

'Well, thanks to his father mostly—'

'Wait a minute!' Sadie was not having that. On this, at least, she had certainty. 'What do you mean, his father? Joe hasn't got a father.'

'Now you and I both know that is a biological impossibility,' the consultant replied, slightly less than kindly.

'You know what I mean.'

'Well, if you really weren't sure, I can tell you, you know now.'

'Stop!' Sadie cut this dead. 'Look, what I mean to say is...' *Oh God, not again...* 'Joe's father is unknown. I... I don't know who he is.'

'Well, he certainly knows who *you* are, and his son. So might I suggest that you do...? Jason...' He checked his notes. 'Barratt?'

'Jay? No...' A small humourless smile touched her lips. 'He's just— He's been here? He told you that?' Of course, he might have had to, to get in to see Joe. 'But—?

'Look, there really is no doubt about it, having examined them both. Now I suggest you just go and talk it over with him. He should be able to give you some confidence that Joe will be alright and can lead a perfectly normal life.' He stopped there as Sadie's expression was quite unnerving. They were a somewhat strange pair, these parents. Not quite with it. Such desperation and bewilderment, verging on the hysterical. Well, at least she was a bit calmer than he had been. Still, she looked as if she was about to keel over any minute.

'I'm afraid, though, as Joe is not quite out of the woods, you won't be able to see him until later. Come back this afternoon.' Still, she stared wordlessly at him. 'Look, why don't you just go home, sit quietly and think about it all.'

Well, full bloody marks for the fucking obvious! But she obediently left the room, and the hospital, a heavy fog of confusion around her. This had no sense at all. She could not begin to work out what was happening...

Her door was open. It had been forced. As Jay's silent shock and devastation had transformed again into hysteria, after a tortured sleepless night, he had broken in.

Sadie scanned the room. It was a mess. Her drawer turned inside out, the shoebox emptied on the floor, the lockbox smashed open. Jay was sitting huddled by the wall, drawing himself inwards, holding two photographs in his hands, crying bitterly. It moved her completely, but it was also shockingly disturbing.

'Jay?' she pleaded. 'What's happening?'

'It's all too wrong. Too unfair!' he sobbed, thrusting one of the photos towards her. 'Tell me! Tell me, please, that isn't him. Please, please, please...' One last desperate attempt at reprieve from this sentence. That he knew could never come...

Drowning in confusion and shock, Sadie did not even know if she could move that small distance. But slowly she took the photo and looked down at it in her hand. A clear front view of a laughing, long-haired, heavily bearded, leather-clad youth, of about 19, 20 years old. Outside the gates of Wormwood Scrubs prison.

And Jay watched, dying inside, as her gaze broadened, her mouth open...

And she screamed.

Jay was up and at the sink, his stomach churning, desperately retching what little was left in his food and sleep starved body. Then he fled the room. Unable to bear her response a moment longer.

Sadie stood motionless in the middle of the room. Forcing herself to look again at the picture. She searched every inch of that face. It almost killed her with the memory. But staring at every concealed feature now. And that just about finished her. More than the memory. So much more...

No. She wouldn't let herself... it couldn't... it wasn't... She slowly turned the photo in her hands. Scrawled across the back was a caption.

Happy Moments.
Jason on his way to The Scrubs
Ricky Randoms Bronze Award
14 August 1980

Sadie was too overwhelmed to move, too shocked to cry, almost too disbelieving to even breathe. Until her head spun, her legs gave way, and she collapsed on the floor. All the diverse threads rushing together in her mind, until she could only scream in pain and despair, great heaving sobs racking her body. Every little thing he had ever said about his past now fitting so neatly and cruelly into her own.

And she had hated him all this time...

44

SILVER AWARD

Sadie did not know where the strength came from, but she had to get up and return to the hospital that afternoon. Just as well that Joe, though assured to be stable with a good prognosis, was barely awake enough to communicate, because she could hardly formulate speech anyway. She could barely feel her own senses.

When she finally left him that evening, Jay was sitting in the foyer, head in his hands over his knees, staring out over them. She ran straight past him and out of the door.

'Sadie!' He was up and after her immediately. 'Sadie, please! You have to speak to me. Please, I need to tell you... Stop, Sadie, please!'

He dived into the car park, darting between the cars and into his own, screeching out of the gate into the road. She was still running, so he kerb crawled her all the way down the road, oblivious to everything else around him, pleading through the open window across the passenger seat.

Sadie ignored him, silent tears rolling down her cheeks.

But she had to stop. Her lungs were burning. Jay pulled up to the kerb and got out of the car. She ran again. She was fast.

He returned to the car and pursued her, desperately pleading with her to get in. She couldn't get away from him.

She stopped, breathless and shaking. 'Go away, Jay! Leave me alone!'

'I can't! I can't, I can't...'

'Get out of here, Jay! Don't come anywhere near me!'

'I can't! Please, just get in. I have to talk to you!'

Horns were blaring, cars swerving, pedestrians staring. She thought her legs were going to give way. And as one pedestrian approached her in alarm, she pulled open the car door and got in, slamming the door behind her.

Jay instantly pulled into a layby.

'Drive this car!'

'We've got to talk—'

'Just drive!'

'No, I—' She scrambled for the door handle. 'Alright, alright, I'll drive...'

Jay pulled out into the path of a lorry. Yet another horn shook the air. 'Sadie, please, I've got to... you've got to let me—'

'Don't speak to me, Jay. Don't even speak to me.'

'Sadie, please—'

'Not now, Jay!' she screamed at him. 'Not now. I can't think, I can't speak. Please. Not yet.'

Not ever?

But he couldn't. 'You've got to forgive me. I have to have your forgiveness—'

'Don't!' she cut him dead again. 'Stop it. Just don't!'

And this was too much for Jay, his desperation removing all reason. 'I'll pull you out of this car and drive it straight into a tree!' Those thoughts were back again. There he was on the A27.

'Don't you bloody dare!'

'I will. I shall. And don't think I won't! If you don't just say it. No, no, I'll go back, tell Joe, and then drive it into a tree!'

'And I'll hate you until the day I die!'

'No! No!' Jay was just screaming now. In reality, he'd almost crashed the car several times already. But they were pulling off the road into the campus.

The moment he stopped, she was out of there. He slammed the car door and ran after her. They fought with each other all the way to the door of her room. Verbal reasoning failing, she thumped him hard on the chest as he pushed his way in. And she just broke down now. This was not reasonable.

'Please! Please, just leave me alone. I have to think,' she begged, as he began recounting how it had all happened. His Silver Award. It had to be 16, or younger, virgin, and no name, within the space of an hour of meeting. Not a complete stranger, no dark alleyways at knifepoint, he had to engage, but the object's will was irrelevant; in fact, the lack of it highly commended.

'I didn't want to do it! But they... they made me. And I just... let them...? Oh God, I'm so sorry...'

Sadie could not take any more. 'Please. Stop...' And at last Jay realised what he was doing to her. Unable to witness her devastation a moment longer, he backed out of the door, but turning the knife as he did so. 'I'm scared Sadie... So scared. I love my son, you know that. But more than that... I love you both. So, so much.'

She would not look at him.

'I can't force you to feel for me. But I swear I'll kill myself if you don't forgive me...'

And with that last cruel threat, he was gone. Leaving her broken and tortured, with not a scrap of sense or reason left in her world.

45

DADDY

Joe was clearly perking up by the next day. And Sadie was calmer as she returned to the hospital. Had to be. She couldn't have been less calm than the day before. And although she hadn't slept a wink all night, she had some determination about her now. Marking the huge progression she had made in the last few hours, in a quiet moment, she spoke.

'Joe, I've got something to tell you. Something very important.'

Despite this decision, her mouth was dry, her throat barbed. She swallowed hard and persevered. 'Joe, I know you've always wanted a daddy. And I've always said that you have one, but you might never see him. Well—' She stopped, blinking back the tears that pressed mercilessly at her eyes. Despite everything in her life, this was by far the most difficult thing she had ever done.

'You have a daddy, Joe. And he's here.'

Joe's eyes popped. 'My real daddy?'

'Yes Joe, your real daddy.'

'I thought you might choose me one if I never saw him, but this is my *real* daddy?' This was clearly unbalancing Joe. But in the most enthusiastic of ways.

And it broke her heart.

'Yes Joe, not one I've chosen for you.'

Christ, no! She never had any bloody choice in the matter, did she?

'But where has he been?'

Sadie sighed. How could she even begin to tell him this? She could barely tell it to herself. Apart from the fact that it hammered at her minute after minute until she thought her head and her heart would explode.

'There's such a lot for you to understand, Joe. But he loves you. It's just that he didn't know he was your daddy until... recently. Until you were ill.'

'Did *you* know?' Joe was clearly fascinated by this notion.

Sadie was forced to shake her head.

'How do you know now?'

Joe's questions. The soundtrack to her life.

And now they were her life.

'Joe, it's the truth... it's—' She could barely go on with this even if the nurse had not interrupted her. There was someone outside to see her.

'Well, that might just be him. So I'll go out and see, shall I?' She attempted a smile at Joe, who was eagerly pushing himself up on his pillows in anticipation. And it tore her in two...

She was not surprised that it was Jay. Sitting in much the same desperate position as yesterday. He got up immediately. Sadie could not even look at him. Whoever he was.

'Please, I haven't come to bother you. Please, I just want to see Joe. I need to—' But he stopped, obviously having progressed to a little more calm, as she had, at least externally. 'Obviously, I respect your decision if you say no.'

Sadie sat down. She had to suddenly. Her legs as heavy as her heart. She knew he loved Joe. That was never in any doubt. But did she want that for her son anymore? From *him*. This other person? But whatever her feelings, or indeed his, as she had realised through the night, the bottom line was that Joe loved him. And being without a father was bad enough, but knowing and loving and losing one? She could never do that to him.

So she took the small remnants of her courage and concluded, 'Go and see him. Tell him. You tell him.'

'But—'

'I've begun it. I was telling him he can see his daddy now... Christ,' she muttered with utter distaste at the word. 'So,' she breathed deeply. 'You tell him. Tell him it's *you*.'

'I'm not sure that's fair on you.' Perhaps the first considerate thing he had managed to say since this whole business began.

But Sadie lost it a bit then. 'Just tell him!'

As soon as he saw him, *his son*, Jay's legs gave way. Joe, however, was oblivious. He wriggled up in bed and threw his arms wide for a hug. 'Jaaaay!'

'Are you alright?' Jay whispered over his shoulder, forcing back the tears.

'Yeah! I'm getting better now, I think.'

Jay nodded. 'I know. I know, Joe. I had the same as you when I was a boy.'

This only seemed to excite Joe even more. 'Oh, I'm getting better. I'm going to be out soon!'

Jay had to turn his head away.

'I wasn't expecting you,' Joe continued innocently. 'But that's OK. Do you know what? Mummy says I'm going to see my daddy!' And Jay broke again at that. Into tiny little pieces. 'A *real* one,' Joe added, twisting the knife.

'Joe...' He drew in as much air as his battered lungs could manage. 'Be a good boy and listen to me for a minute. I have something to tell you. It's a lot for you to understand, and you shouldn't have to, but please try.'

Joe nodded solemnly.

'Try to imagine your daddy becoming your daddy even before you were born. But then he didn't know he was... Can you grasp that at all?' Jay felt the inadequacy of this explanation pulsing through him, but Joe nodded again. Although it was highly unlikely and he looked quite bewildered. 'And then he only found out he was your daddy now. Could you forgive him for not being around?' He knew the question was stupid, and the intensity of his imploring would be enough to unbalance anyone. But both the intensity and the stupidity were lost on Joe.

'He didn't know?' he replied thoughtfully, but not giving Jay a moment to answer. 'I forgive him! As long as he wants me now that he knows... And he loves my mummy,' he added poignantly.

Oh yes, he does, Jay despaired. More than life itself...

'Joe...' he had to clear his throat from the suffocation. 'Your mummy knew me six years ago. But because it was such a long time, when she met me here at the university, she didn't know who I was.'

'No,' Joe agreed stoically. 'It is a long time. I'm five years and I'm big!'

At any other time, Jay would surely have laughed at this. But right now, he just wanted to helplessly cry.

'Joe...' he choked. 'Joe... I am... your dad.'

Joe stared at him. 'You are?!'

'Can you understand all that I've said to you? Please Joe, I didn't know, I—'

'You're my *real* daddy? Not just a chosen one?' Joe was not in the least bit interested in the explanation anymore.

'I'm so sorry, Joe. I love you—'

'You're my daddy! You're my daddy!' Joe shrieked, and despite the early stages of his recovery, he threw himself at Jay. 'Oh, I'm happy! I'm happy!'

Jay tried desperately to calm him down, after all, he was only two days out of surgery.

It wasn't working. 'I've always wanted you to be my daddy!'

And suddenly, it was all too much for Jay. He burst into tears. Sending the chair to the floor, he fled from the ward...

Sadie had watched it all through the ward door, silent tears falling. He pushed straight past her. Her instinctive reaction was to call out to him, seeing the distress, and fearing he would do something stupid. She glanced back to the ward. A nurse was with Joe, continuing the calming that was so evidently needed. And as her fears intensified, she ran after him.

Jay ran straight out across the grass verge and into the road, right into the path of the oncoming traffic. Sadie dived forward and pulled him clear, and they tumbled back onto the pavement.

'Jay!' She shook him. He was staring disturbingly ahead of him, crying, unreachable, his body shaking. He looked at her, as if the lights had been turned off and his mind had descended into dark, silent chaos.

'I'm so sorry...'

And he ran.

. . .

Sadie could do nothing else for him right now. Her place was with her son. She returned to the ward. Sitting with Joe while he enthused about the identity of his beloved daddy. Her head and her heart in two.

46

FAMILY SNAPSHOT

It was late by the time Jay returned to his room. Aimlessly, mindlessly, wandering the empty lanes outside Chichester. And he had nothing left in him now. Only the compulsive, insistent demands for the removal of all this.

The removal of everything...

It changed too late. As he sat with that photo in his hands; the one taken at Chessington. His family. His family snapshot. A snapshot of his life, when it was good.

'No... Joe...' He could barely speak now. What was he doing to that boy with this? He crawled away from the empty bottles and packets scattered around him. He couldn't even see anymore. It felt like he was crawling through syrup. He banged on the wall. He thought he was banging on the wall. 'Nick,' he pleaded. 'Nick...' But nobody came. He crawled to the door, practically on his stomach. One last desperate attempt at movement, grasping desperately for the door handle. He flicked it open, but collapsed on the floor. There was nothing left for him now...

Somehow, he made it back to the mattress. The darkness

was coming, and he would have to let it take him. Reaching for that photo again, he held it in his hands.

All that he had ever loved.

Sadie's confusion pulled her one way and then the other when she returned to the university that night. She had stayed with Joe until midnight, then walked the entire way back to campus in the early hours. She took a few steps towards Sutherland House and then turned back to her own room, only to retrace her steps seconds later. There was something about the look on his face when she had pulled him out of the road...

But why should she care? She couldn't deal with him right now. If ever she would.

And yet...

His door was ajar, the dim light creeping around it, but a deathly quiet from within. She pushed it open, and froze. Jay was slumped against the wall, the evidence of what he had done all round him. She ran inside, sinking to her knees on the mattress. 'Jay...' She grabbed his shoulders and shook him. No response. 'Jay!' Nothing. 'Oh God, Jay, no!'

As she pulled him to her, she could feel the faintest of breaths, although she couldn't find a pulse, grabbing wildly at his wrists in an attempt to locate some sign. A photo dropped from his hand.

She tried to think, laying him down in what she could remember of the recovery position, then ran from the room, down the corridor to the phone...

Nick emerged from his room, awoken by the commotion.

'Christ, what happened?'

'He's taken something... all this...'

'Oh, Jesus. Have you called an ambulance?'

She nodded.

'Is he breathing?'

'Just.' They could hear the sirens now.

'I'll go and show them the way...'

And she could do no more. Clasping his hand between hers, the rest of him hanging lifeless before her, she wept.

'No Jay, please don't... please, Jay...'

'What's he taken?' The ambulance crew pulled her away.

'Vodka, paracetamol, codeine... these,' Sadie stuttered, pointing at the empty bottles and packets around him.

They knelt down beside him, taking his wrist. 'Faint,' one said to the other. 'Come on, Jason,' they lifted his head. 'Jason, can you hear me?' Still nothing. 'OK,' the paramedic concluded, and they had him on a stretcher within seconds. 'Room in the ambulance for one.'

Nick nodded. 'You go.'

Fucking hell, back to that place. What the hell was going on with her life...?

Sadie spent another night at the hospital. It all happened so quickly, of course. Jay was spirited out of the ambulance. And she was alone again. Only able to watch Joe through the ward door. She was exhausted. And now this. How could he do this? 'Critical,' they said. Not even 'critical but stable.' *Stable*? That was a joke! The bastard. So he'd done it. Joe knew. And Joe loved. And Joe was going to lose.

But what had she felt when she rocked him in her arms so instinctively?

'God Jay, please no. Please don't leave...'

'... Please don't leave *me*...'

47

YOU FUCKING BASTARD

A night of drips and pumps. And she with nothing left to give, lying out in the waiting room, the place beginning to spin with the unreality of mental and physical exhaustion. But she pulled herself up to spend the morning with Joe, playing with the hospital toys across his bed.

'Is Jay coming today?' It was the first question, of course. 'Is *daddy* coming today?' he corrected with glee. 'I can call him daddy now, can't I?'

But she couldn't.

'Not today, Joe...' Sadie tried so hard to remain calm. Something else to tell him now. 'Joe... Jay's not very well.'

'When will he be better? I've got so much to tell him.'

And it broke her heart.

'I hope it will be soon, Joe. But... we have to wait and see.'

She couldn't tell him. She couldn't tell him that his beloved daddy had seen fit to try to remove himself from his life altogether. Now. Now that he knew. She would keep her son happy in ignorance for as long as she could. At least he was through. Perhaps they could begin to make a life again.

But what kind of a life? Without a man she loved and hated. *With* a man she loved and hated...?

A nurse bent down to her ear. He was alive. And chances were he was going to stay that way. 'He's barely conscious, but you can see him if you like.'

Sadie shook her head. She couldn't deal with anymore right now. Let him manage...

'He's asking for you,' another nurse told her that evening. Joe was asleep, and she was considering going home. She needed some rest and a bath. And she was out on the road before she turned back.

She nearly fled again at the sight of him through the private room door. Apparently, it hadn't been pleasant and not the spectacle for a public ward. And it looked it still. Jay was deathly pale, a shadow of himself, drips and monitors hanging off him. Eyelids twitching restlessly.

But he turned his head as she pushed open the door.

'Sadie...' The voice another casualty; a desperate, breathless croak, his throat ripped and burning.

It took all her strength to fight back the tears as she reluctantly sat by his bedside.

'I'm sorry,' he mouthed, a silent tear falling down his cheek.

'How could you?' She had no comfort for him now, despite his pathetic appearance and distress.

'I know...' He closed his eyes briefly. 'I... I didn't mean it...' Every word had to be forced out, but he was determined. 'As soon as... I tried to stop it... Joe... I saw Joe and...' Perhaps he could bear her hatred, eventually, but the boy's loss? None of this was his doing. 'But it was too late... You saved my life. Thirty more minutes, they said.'

'Jesus, Jay. I don't know you at all, do I?'

'Yes, you do... *You* do. Nobody else...'

'Mr Barratt, you really shouldn't be talking. You know that.'

Sadie hadn't even noticed the nurse come in.

'It's OK,' she said, getting to her feet. 'I'm going now...'

Another day in that bloody place. Although Sadie had managed a few hours' fitful rest, the appeal of that hospital had not improved. She had a wave of panic every time she pushed open the door. Every time she even thought about it.

Joe was getting restless. He felt fine, he said, and he didn't know why he had to be here still. Sadie attempted to divert him with games and stories. But no, daddy wasn't well enough to come and see him today...

Joe asleep again that evening, she wandered out of the ward at last. Maybe she would just look through the door? Just see that...? There was nothing she could do to prevent this. This so powerful connection. What they had done, what they had found together. Where was that person now...?

Evidently, he was still there. The tiniest hint of that familiar smile touched his lips as she pushed open the door. His face still so heavily clouded, but with an intimation of colour... and life.

'Thank you,' he whispered, his eyes closing briefly in acceptance.

'It must be pretty lonely in here,' Sadie replied, although with no observable compassion.

He nodded. 'I wish I could speak...' Clearly it was slightly easier, but still a tremendous effort. 'I have so much I have to say.'

'What makes you think I want to hear it?'

Again, he nodded. '*I* want to hear it. I want to hear you say everything.'

'Oh, I don't think you do,' she retorted. 'At least not here.'

'Yes, here,' he sighed. 'While you are here. Is Joe alright?'

'Oh yes, he's fine. And just brimming with excitement about all he has to say to his new daddy.' This was so hard to keep up while he looked at her so pitifully in his current state. But damn it, this was how it was, and he wanted to hear it. 'So I told him. I told him his beloved daddy is a fucking bastard, who not only abused me and abandoned him in the cruellest way possible, but has now seen fit to try and kill himself!'

Jay's eyes widened. 'You didn't...'

'No, of course I didn't! What do you take me for?'

And now she was crying.

'Oh, Sadie...' His own tears fell. 'Tell me. Keep saying it.'

'What am I supposed to fucking say?' she cried. 'What am I supposed to do now? How am I supposed to reconcile all this? This vile person that I didn't know, who I've hated for so long... and... *you*?'

Jay nodded silently. He meant it. He wanted to hear it. Everything he deserved.

'I always thought,' she breathed through gritted teeth. 'That if I ever met him, I'd just stick a knife in him. There and then. And that would be it.' Her voice was steady now, the steel returned to her eyes. But it was quickly lost. 'You made me love you! You made my son love you! And what do you do? To help us? To help me understand? You go and try and top yourself! You fucking bastard!' She almost hit him. She probably would have if he hadn't been so desperately ill and weak.

But she was crying again. It broke his heart. So much more than the words.

'Oh, please,' she begged. 'I can't take anymore.'

And she fled.

48

FATHER AND SON

Sadie pulled herself up to face yet another day at the hospital. Back to Joe.

Today he was tearful. Why was he still here? He wanted to go home. He wanted to see his daddy. Would he ever stop rubbing salt into these open wounds?

But finally, she knew... and she took his hand.

'Come on, Joe. Let's go and see your daddy.'

'Are you taking me home?' Joe beamed as she led him out of the ward in his hospital gown.

'No Joe, you know that. Not for another day or two. I told you Ja— daddy wasn't very well? Well, he's here in the hospital, too.'

'He's here?'

'Yes. And you mustn't worry if he looks a bit funny. He will be alright. And I'm sure you will make him feel better.'

'Will I?' Joe's eyes shone. 'Oh, good.'

'So just be a bit quiet with him, OK? No jumping on the bed...'

Jay vaguely heard this as she pushed open the door. He was

sitting up now, and the broadest smile he had yet managed lit his face, as Joe ignored all his mother's instructions and bounded over.

'Daddy!' Clearly, Joe had no hesitance about the title as he clambered onto the bed. 'Why are you in here? What's the matter with you?'

'I just had a bit of an accident, Joe,' Jay replied, speech a little easier by the day. 'But I'll be alright now.'

'And I'm going to make you better!'

'Yes, I'm sure you will...'

Sadie sat down, away from them, her stomach churning as she watched them, together again. Joe giggling and chatting as usual. Jay trying to respond the best he could, but so openly torn apart, as she was, by his words. Joe gleefully babbling about his future with two parents, with no conception of what had passed to get them to this point. Talking about *now*. About his daddy loving his mummy, *now*. Asking if his mummy loved his daddy, *now*. And overwhelmingly saying that he loved them both. *Now*. It twisted the knife within them, tearing at them both.

But it was *now*.

And perhaps Joe knew. Perhaps he had always known. In some strange, unfathomable way. That this man wasn't just another person he'd happened to run into that day on campus. He was connected to him in some way. A way that nobody could have known.

And all those looks, those misunderstandings. She studied them both now. And she could see it. How could she ever not have? That wide open face, that cheeky grin, those deepest blue eyes that twinkled with the laughter...

They were like two peas in a pod.

· · ·

As she led Joe away to sleep some two hours later, Jay called her back. 'Sadie? They're letting me out tomorrow.'

She looked back at him. For a moment, not able to look away, still seeing her son reflected there.

'Where are your car keys?'

'I'll get a taxi,' he protested feebly.

'Just give me your car keys.'

He pulled open his bedside drawer and dropped them into her hand. She was gone before he could say another word.

Sadie spent the next morning with Joe, until she was told Jay was ready to leave. She led him to the car. He was still quite weak and had to be helped out at the other end, and to walk the short distance to his room.

He tried so hard to be independent of her. Slightly over-whelmed already that she was taking this role. But she tired of his protestations, and lifted his arm around her shoulders for support.

'You shouldn't have to do this.'

'And what should I do, Jay? Tell me that.'

She settled him on his mattress and made some coffee.

'I'm sorry, Sadie. About Joe. I know it must do your head in. He doesn't have to call me daddy. You can tell him not to.'

'Can I?' she snapped back. 'Can I really? He loves you, Jay! Have you any conception of that?'

'Of course I have.'

'Then *why*? How could you think of taking that away from him?'

Jay screwed up his face. 'I couldn't think. I... I thought you'd do that anyway. I didn't think I could live... without you.' He pressed his hand to his eyes. 'I love you, Sadie. God, how I love you. And for that one moment, I didn't think I could live with it. Because you hate me. And you have every reason to. And loving you now should never be enough, however much I want it to be... But it's not the answer. I know that now. I knew it then. I can never take away what I did. I wish that you could say, one day, that you know it wasn't me. Not me now. Not me ever, really. And that one day you'll be able to say that no-one could have loved you the way that I do. But I can't change that either. I will just do whatever you want me to. Even if that means going as far away from you and Joe as possible. If that's what you want, then I will do it. He is young and he will forget. He has you, and he is lucky.'

'None of us are lucky, Jay,' she sighed, calmer now, although she did not know from where it came.

'I am,' Jay whispered unexpectedly. 'I have a beautiful son who I adore. And I was allowed to know him for a while. I was allowed to love you. For a little while. I will carry that with me for all time. Whatever I do. Wherever I end up. I don't care about anything else anymore.'

'Evidently...' Still, she had no comfort for him. 'And perhaps you don't really care about us either.'

'How can you say that?'

'Because you can leave! You were prepared to leave us. So very finally.'

'Because I thought that was the only way. I was wrong. Any way is nigh on impossible. But I will go, if that is what you want. Whatever you want from now on...' And he was crying now. 'If ever I thought I could take you with me. Please God, my life would be worth something. But I pay my price. And whatever I thought that might be, this is far, far worse. Because I will never stop loving you. Ever.'

'Don't...' Sadie's tears joined his.

'Sadie, I—'

'No more, please,' she begged, and ran from him again.

49

EPIPHANY

Sadie sank onto her mattress in the cold and dark. Too numb to move, even to sleep, but shaking with the emotion. And she didn't stir from that spot for hours. So many things flooding her mind. Old things. New things. And it was past three o'clock in the morning when she jumped up and ran. Out of the door, into the night, across the silent campus.

She banged on his door.

'Jay? Let me in. Please let me in!'

Jay was up out of his bed immediately. Of course he let her in.

'It's not fair!' she cried. 'I don't want to do this... I *do* want to do this...'

'Sit down,' he said, trying to ignore the excruciating nerves in his stomach.

She sank against the wall. 'Oh God, I've got so much I have to say.'

'Say it all.'

'I don't want to be here, saying this, in a way... But I have to. I have no choice.' She barely glanced at him, but it was enough to assure her she was right. 'Oh God, please be a father to Joe! I think I've only just really come to believing it. Can you see that?'

Jay was too shocked to respond.

'I just felt, just now in my room, and I still can't reconcile it, but it was a real... *elation*...?' Her eyes widened, as if she was still trying to reason this. 'I think it came from all those years of needing to share the responsibility of Joe with someone. And now, just now, realising that the only person I have ever felt safe enough to do so... *is* his father. You can't back out now. You have to do it.'

'I *will* do it,' Jay replied instantly. This was an amazing revelation, and he would grasp it as surely as he could. 'But... you...?'

'Me? I am frightened, Jay. I have known this for a long time. But I need you for me, not Joe. God, I want you for both for us... How could you do that?' And now she hit him. 'How *could* you? I was so scared!'

She could have been talking about either of two things. Or both. But it was becoming clearer which was on her mind the most at this moment.

'I held you in my arms and pleaded for your life, Jay. For me, God help me! For *me*!'

Jay couldn't stop himself; he took her fists from him and, containing them, pulled her into his arms.

'And you can do whatever you want,' she continued. 'Kill yourself if you bloody well want to! And what do I do? Not knowing who you were for six years is bad enough. But knowing, and loving, and losing you? I couldn't cope... I...' She finally broke. 'I can't hate you anymore. I've loved you for so long.'

Jay's mouth dropped open, but he was too overwhelmed to make it speak.

Until a surge of energy and enlightenment flooded through him. 'Oh... my... God,' he grabbed at her, enclosing her completely. 'Sadie! What are you saying? Fuck, if you want me... Oh please, do you really want me?' Apparently, this was rhetorical as the words tumbled from him. 'Oh God, Sadie, if that's true, I'll never leave you. I love you *so much*. I've told you so many times. If it's anything near what you want, please, please take it. Take me! Anywhere. Anywhere you wanna go...'

'Don't you ever, *ever* do anything like that again. Do you hear me?'

He pressed his cheek to her head.

'No. Never. I promise. Never...'

50

MAN, WOMAN, CHILD

It was appropriate that Joe was the one who really sealed it the next day. Sitting, dressed and waiting for the all clear, holding both their hands over the hospital bed, chattering about how happy he was. And Jay took Sadie's hand too then, needing so much to echo it.

'I love you, Joe,' he said. 'I love your mum. And we have some serious making up to do. And believe me, we are going to do it...'

'Can I stay?'

Joe had settled to sleep back in his old beanbag, and silence had fallen at last. Sadie put down her tea towel and took Jay's hand. The day that they had had. Up on the South Downs, their place. Joining Joe's laughter, the life and colour returning to Jay's face a little. That beautiful face. That beautiful smile. A mirror of her son. A reflection of their future...

'Maybe,' she whispered. 'Maybe you can never leave.'

'I am chained,' he said, unable to take his eyes from hers. 'For as long as you will have me.'

'Then let's make it...' she dropped her forehead to his.

'A life sentence.'

PLEASE LEAVE A REVIEW

If you have enjoyed Family Snapshot, it would be tremendously helpful if you were able to leave a review.

The publishing industry is tough for authors right now and reviews really do help bring my books to the attention of others who might enjoy them.

Review on Amazon via your dashboard, or at:
https://www.amazon.co.uk/review/create-review?asin=173840370X

THANK YOU VERY MUCH!

ABOUT THE AUTHOR

Jessie Harker is an author of stories set in the 1980s.
Things were different then!

Jessie's novels are rooted in her formative years in the early/mid
'80s London suburbs, when the streets were dark, but the
music and hope shone bright. And that duality is reflected in
her writing. Characters may be disadvantaged, in various ways,
but there is always the potential to get to a better place.

Her novels are inevitably peppered with cultural references, but
the deep wounds that the past inflicts are common to any era.
Jessie understands that, so often, we mess up because we were
messed up. Yet she is a firm believer in the potential for
redemption of the human spirit; that even the darkest scars that
bind us can be healed by honesty and love.

Jessie lives in Somerset with a guitarist, a dog and six chickens.
And she still collects Police memorabilia (the band, not the law
enforcers).

**Join Jessie's VIP Club for free content and to be the first
to know about new books and publications, and for an
exclusive sneak preview of her next book, join in at:**

www.jessieharker.com/signup

SAVING GRAYSON
COMING NOVEMBER 2024

An emotionally hard-hitting, but ultimately uplifting tale about the challenge of public judgment and the transformative power of love.

From the back streets of West London, stripped of his self esteem, Billy Grayson is imprisoned not only by an injustice done to him by his so-called friends, but by the deeper chain of society's work ethic, in the unemployment crisis of the early 1980s. Unable to achieve its demands, and therefore a 'lesser' man.

From the leafy privilege of Surrey, expelled from three public schools, a childhood of misunderstanding and an over tendency to hit the emotion button, Sasha Morton has found her place with interchangeable front door keys with her mates, unlimited supplies of peanut butter and digging about in canals.
Saving jam jars. Saving the planet.
Saving Grayson?

Via a rabbit hole in Warwick, a campsite in Llandudno, and a customised hackney cab in Brighton; with a little help from an insightful old lady, a plague of frogs, and Richard Branson.
Neither of them ends up quite where they started...

Get an exclusive sneak peak at:
www.jessieharker.com

Printed in Great Britain
by Amazon